TITANIC

The Untold Story

W. Mae Kent
March, 2008

Copyright © 2008 W. Mae Kent
All rights reserved.

Photograph of the Laroche Family Courtesy of the Titanic Historical
Society, Indian Orchard, Mass.

ISBN: 1-4196-9573-8
ISBN-13: 9781419695735

Library of Congress Control Number: 2008907306

Visit www.booksurge.com to order additional copies.

Death cancels everything but truth.
— Proverb quote

Dedication

This book is dedicated to my husband, Lee A. Kent, whose unwavering support made this book possible.

Prologue

New Orleans
August 1896

Ten year old Nathan Badeau peeked through a rot splintered crack in the wall of the old woodshop. His mother and Xavier Larroquette stood in the light of a full moon, talking. The stovepipe skinny undertaker served Orleans Parish's white gentry and Nathan's Mama occasionally did laundry for him. Through the rickety walls Nathan overheard his Mama begging the old widower to help her get him out of New Orleans.

He saw the old skunk try to kiss her but she turned her head away. Then, he patted her hand and said in that nasally Cajun drawl of his: "Now Annie, you know what I want. I can get your boy out of New Orleans. All you've got to do is cooperate."

Nathan had never liked Larroquette. He'd always been too fond of his Mama for his liking. And now, he hated him even more, for trying to take advantage of her. He couldn't hear his mother's soft reply, and heartsick, he turned away from the crack. He'd seen and heard enough anyway. The thought of Larroquette's blue-veined, knobby fingers all over his Mama rekindled the embers of an impotent rage simmering inside him. He plopped down on the dirt floor thinking, *what's the use? I tried to protect her before and look at what happened? I ruined everything. Seems like someone's always going to be trying to take advantage of her, or put their hands on her, one way or another. It's not safe for a woman as beautiful as Mama in Orleans Parish; probably nowhere else.*

When his Mama came back inside, she had a blanket and made a pallet for them on the dirt floor. He lay down next to her and tried to sleep, but as soon as he dozed off, Larroquette's Negro carpenter, Elijah, showed up. It was the wee hours of the morning, still dark out and Elijah set to sawing and banging like it was the middle of the day.

The scent of fresh pine mingled with the smell of dirt hung in the humid air as Nathan tossed and turned, unable to sleep. Hard as he tried, he couldn't avoid the awful truth: he was witnessing the making of his own casket.

Somehow he must have dozed off because the next thing he knew his Mama was shaking him. "Wake up, Nathan. We have to be ready when Mr. Larroquette comes."

Nathan rubbed his bleary eyes as Elijah called out to his Mama, "told you I'd have 'dis done fo'daybreak. 'Um jess finishin' up." He smiled a gap toothed smile, took a red bandana from the back pocket of his overalls and mopped sweat from his cast iron black bald head and face.

"Thank you, Elijah," his Mama answered.

Nathan's shirt was glued to his back and standing, he guessed it must have been a hundred degrees in the rickety old woodshop. As his Mama and Elijah talked, his eye's latched onto the new wooden casket across the room. Suddenly, his Mama's and Elijah's voices sounded strange, far away, and he could hear his own heart beating in his ears. He started to tremble and a voice in his head screamed, *I can't get in there. I'll die. I just know I'll die in there.* While he stood there dreading and thinking, his Mama's and Elijah's voices became one long, hollow groan.

The rusty creak of the door brought Nathan out of his miserable fugue. Larroquette walked in, his tall black-clad frame silhouetted by a reddish-orange morning sky.

"Bonjour, bonjour," he called cheerfully. He walked over to Nathan's mother and handed her a brown paper sack. "Had my gal fix the boy something to eat. Fried chicken and corn bread. Oughtta hold him over."

"Thank you kindly," she replied taking the sack. "Thank you for everything."

Thank you? Nathan thought bitterly, looking from his Mama to the undertaker. *For what? For the chance to have his old nasty hands all over you? For letting us sleep on the ground in his raggedy old woodshop like animals?* Right then and there, he promised himself that if he lived through this, he would never be put in this position again, unable to protect his womenfolk.

"We got to be down at the dock 'fore seven if we're gonna' get that boy on the ship in time," Larroquette said. "Ya'll get your goodbyes said while me and Elijah load these up." He pointed to the four pine caskets lined up against the wall.

"We'll be cuttin' outta here soon as we're loaded. Come on, Elijah." He waved for the big man to follow him.

"Mama, please don't make me go," Nathan said, looking up at her. "I'm sorry for what I did. Really, I am. I didn't mean to cause trouble."

"I know you didn't." His Mama's eyes were misty with sadness. "But those men are coming back. Next time they'll kill you for sure. They won't let it go, son. I know they won't."

"But Mama, I don't know anybody in France," he said.

"Yes, you do. You know your Pappy."

"My Pappy?!" He was shocked. "How can that be? My Pappy's dead."

Shame faced, his Mama replied, "No, he's not. Nathan, I…,I'm sorry, but I have to tell you the truth. I was going to tell you when you got older, but now this happened, and,… and I don't know what else to do. William Badeau wasn't your Pappy. He didn't die of the yellow fever before you were born. I made that up. Your Pappy is Marcel Legarde. That's why I'm sending you to France, so you can stay with him and those men can't get to you." She reached into the pocket of her dark blue linen skirt, fished out a white envelope and handed it to him. "I wrote this last night while you were catnapping. When you get to France, I want you to give it to Marcel. And I don't want you reading it."

Nathan shook his head, yes, still reeling from the news that Marcel was his Pappy. He felt like he was in some kind of crazy dream, where things got more and more unreal by the moment, where everything he believed was wrong, where everything he thought was true, wasn't.

Glimpses and fragments of Monsieur Marcel flashed in Nathan's mind: tall, rugged, thick gray streaked hair, weather-beaten face, gravelly voice. But try as he might, he couldn't come up with a complete picture of him. But one thing he did know. Marcel was a lot older than his Mama.

"I don't want to live with Mr. Marcel, Ma-"

"Shoosh, boy...," his Mama cut him off, the sternness of her voice a sharp contrast to her delicate ebony features. "Marcel's a good man, and don't you forget it. Who do you think pays for your violin lessons, for that fine Normal School you go to. Marcel don't take no stuff, but if you do right by him, he'll do right by you."

A barrage of questions crowded Nathan's young mind: *If Monsieur Legarde cared so much about me, why didn't he tell me I was his son? If he's so generous, why are you still working, washing other folks clothes, getting pushed around and...* Suddenly he remembered a rumor he'd heard circulating among the grown folks and a chilling question sprang to his lips: "Mama, didn't Mr. Marcel kill a man once?"

His Mama drew him to her and smoothed his thick black curls. "Oh, Nathan, you don't have to be afraid of Marcel. You're his son. He wouldn't hurt you. Believe me, if he killed someone, they had to have it coming. He wouldn't hurt anybody who was innocent. I told you, he's a good man."

Maybe, Nathan thought, but he still didn't want to live with him.

Just then, Elijah rushed into the woodshop carrying two old, beaten up metal canteens. He sat them in the bottom of the only pine casket they'd left in the woodshop; the one he'd just made. It was sitting on two wooden saw horses. "Brang me dat cover," he called over to them.

Nathan's Mama picked the blanket up from the floor, shook it out and took it to him. He folded it and put it and the sack of food into the casket. "Okay, Lil Man…," he said lifting one of the canteens in his hand, "dis heah one wit' the black lid on it got water in it. You take it easy on it too." Then he picked up the other canteen. "Dis heah one wit da brown lid is fa you ta relieves yaself in. And one mo' thang…," He reached in his pocket and took out a small brown ampule and handed it to him. "Dis heah is a old Apalachee engine remedy. Dey calls it bella somethin' n'other. It'll heps ya sleep. But you be raaaal careful wit' it nah. Don't take mo'n a lil' swig in the evenin.' If ya dranks too much o' it, you won't wake up a' tall."

Nathan's whole body was shaking. With trembling hands, he took the ampule and put it in his pocket, a new wave of terror filling his mind. Suddenly, his resolve snapped and he started to sob. "Mama please don't make me get in there." He backed away from the coffin. "I'm sorry for what I did. Really I am. I'll never do it again. I promise. Please don't make me go. Don't make me get in there. Please, Mama. Please." He ran to her, grabbed her around the waist and held on with all his might.

After he'd cried for a couple of minutes, his Mama pried his arms loose and knelt on the ground. She was crying too. "Son, none of this is your fault," she said, drying his face with the hem of her skirt. "You were only trying to protect me. I know you didn't mean to hurt anybody. If anything I blame myself for what happened."

"What, what do you me…mean?" he asked, sniffling uncontrollably.

She shook her head. "Son, I was always too proud of you. So proud, I let you down. Filling your head with that stuff about character and self-respect, getting an education. When I should have been teaching you to stay in your place, how to survive. I should have known it would lead to nothing but trouble. But you were always so smart, and talented, and handsome, I let myself believe things could be different for you, that you'd be given a chance to rise up in the world. Now I'm afraid I'll never see you again."

Nathan's chest was so tight it felt like it was going to explode. He felt sorry for himself and for his Mama. He could tell his Mama was hurting just as much as he was, and he felt sorry for her as much as he did for himself. So he told himself that he had to be strong, for her.

"All right, Mama, I'll go," he said, tearing himself away from her. "But what about you? They might try to hurt you."

She shook her head. "Don't you worry, I'll be all right. Mr. Larroquette's taking me to Jackson as soon as we get you on that ship. I'm going to stay with his sister until things cool off around here."

"Ya'll better be ready in there," Larroquette's insistent drawl drifted into the woodshop. "We got to go."

His Mama held him at arms length and they looked at each other for a long moment. He drank in every beautiful detail of her; the shiny black hair, high cheekbones, full hips, tiny waist, committing them all to memory.

She reached around her neck and took off the necklace she always wore and put it around his neck. "Marcel gave this to me to pray with when you were born. He said it's a St. Jude medal. I'm not Catholic like him but it still seems to work. So if you get scared, or ever get in trouble, you hold onto it and pray real hard, and everything will be all right." She gave him one last hug.

When she released him, Nathan steeled himself for what lay ahead. He took a deep breath and said, "Okay Mama, I'm ready."

"Dat's the spirit, Lil' Man," Elijah said, came around to the front of the casket where Nathan and his Mama were standing.

"Good bye son," she said and walked away. At the door, she stopped and called, "Nathan,

I don't want you to be humble. I just want you to live." Then she walked out the door.

With one smooth motion Elijah picked him up and sat him in the middle of the pine box. "You gots ta lay down nah, so's I can put dis heah lid on."

Nathan did as he was told. He watched in silence as the lid came down putting him in complete darkness. "Don't you worry nah, I put plenty holes in this box so's you kin breath easy," Elijah's comforting bass voice came from outside the coffin. "An' it ain't gone be locked. But jess da same, you's got ta stay in it."

"I will," Nathan called back. Then he heard Elijah talking to Larroquette and felt the pine box being lifted. He jostled around inside as the two men loaded the coffin onto the wagon. A moment later he felt the wagon jerk and begin to move. He swayed gently inside the coffin straining to hear his mother's voice. But all he could hear was the rattle of the wagon and the steady clop clop clop of the horse's hooves.

Nathan's eyes got heavier and heavier. As they slowly closed, he made himself another promise. *When I grow up, I'm coming back to my Mama. You just wait and see…I'm coming back.*

Lulled by exhaustion, and the steady rocking of the wagon, he was fast asleep before they reached the dock.

Chapter One

Paris, France
March, 1912

From the privacy of their box at the palatial Theatre du Chatelet, Nathan Badeau Legarde and his wife, Nicolette, sat in the dark watching Igor Stravensky's Petroshka. To his surprise, he understood the little puppet, Petroshka, felt a pang of sadness for him. For, he too had tasted the bitterness of other people's ignorance. As a young child he'd learned that his life held value only to a few. But mercifully, like Petroshka, he'd escaped into a new, "real" life. Through the darkness, he cast a rueful smile at his wife, thinking, *Sometimes, it feels like Orleans Parish Louisiana was just a dream.*

He turned his attention back to the final act playing out on the stage. Just as the Old Wizard character caught sight of Petroshka's ghost, Nathan felt a tap on his shoulder. He turned to find a theatre attendant standing behind him.

"I'm sorry to disturb you, Monsieur," the attendant whispered, "but someone asked me to give this to you." He handed Nathan a folded piece of paper. "They said it's urgent."

"Merci." Nathan took the note.

"What is it, cherie?" his wife, whispered, leaning toward him.

Keeping his voice low, he whispered back, "I don't know." He lifted the note up before his eyes but couldn't make the writing out. "It's too dark in here. Let's go down to the lobby where there's better light. The play is almost over anyway." He stood up and placed his top hat on his head, then helped Nicolette with her wrap. They walked down the stairs to the frescoed, art-deco lobby.

Nathan blinked his eyes adjusting to the light. He scanned the note written in their housekeeper's precise script. *"Urgent! Come at once! Monsieur Marcel is ill."*

"Oh, no, it's Papa." Nathan was instantly alarmed. He looked at Nicolette. "Something has happened to him. We must hurry." He grabbed her hand and they half-ran, half-walked across the almost empty lobby, their heels clacking loudly on the marble floor.

Over the noise, Nicolette remarked, "I'm afraid it might be serious, Nathan. Papa Marcel hasn't been himself lately. He hasn't been eating well and he rarely comes out of his room anymore. It worries me."

"I know," Nathan replied. "I'm worried too."

Marcel had been telling them he was alright, but they both knew something was wrong. He had slowed down considerably in the last year. His steps were not as sure, he didn't get up before dawn any more, and he rarely played with his grandchildren, something that used to give him so much pleasure.

And he hadn't made a trip to America and it was already February. For as long as Nathan had been living with him, his father had always gone to America by the end of January.

Suddenly, Nicolette stopped. The pearl encrusted comb she'd used to pin up her hair had fallen out. Nathan turned around as she picked it up from the floor. Quickly, she handed it to him. He stuffed it in his pocket and they raced out the door into the frosty night air. All around them was a picturesque convergence of time. Gas lights illuminated the magnificent boulevard lined with gleaming automobiles next to fine, horse-draw carriages in every direction. They rushed down the cobble-stoned sidewalk in front of the theatre, their heels clacking loudly. Finally, they reached Nathan's new Panhard Levassor automobile. He opened the door for Nicolette and raced around and got the automobile's crank out of the trunk. With one quick turn of the crank, the engine sputtered to life. He threw the crank in the back, hopped into the driver's seat and took off. Beset with anxiety, he sped around the sphinx adorned fountain at the center of the boulevard and down Place du Chatelet toward home.

Twenty minutes later he pulled to the curb in front of their house at 46 Rue Montessuey. He jumped out of the automobile and ran up the steps, Nicolette fast on his heels.

Madame Bonet, their housekeeper, swung the door to the foyer open. Clutching her apron, she tried to explain in one breath what had happened. "Monsieur Marcel…, I don't know why…, he came downstairs. He went back…halfway up, he collapsed. Sabine, helped me get him back to bed. I sent the note by one of Madame Jacquet's boys." She dabbed at her eyes with the corner of her apron. "Doctor Chenault is with him now."

"Merci, Madame Bonet." Nathan headed up the stairs. He was afraid something like this was coming. Just last week, without his father knowing, he'd had his doctor friend, Etienne Chenault stop by on the pretext of a 'casual' visit. Marcel got very upset with both of them when Etienne suggested a physical exam. He gruffly told him, "The last time I saw a doctor was to have a bullet removed from my ass, and since I haven't been shot, and I'm not dying, I have no use for your services." He got up and shuffled out of the room in a huff embarrassing Nathan and bewildering Doctor Chenault.

The next day, his father gave Nathan a colorful piece of his mind and warned him not to insult him like that again.

"If only he weren't so darned stubborn… so set in his ways," Nathan thought, reaching the top of the stairs.

Nicolette came up behind him as he knocked softly on Marcel's boudoir door. Dr. Chenault opened it and slipped out into the hallway to speak with them, his expression grave. "Marcel is very sick. He's very weak." His tone was hushed.

"Why? What's wrong?" Nathan asked, impatiently, even more worried by the concern etched on the doctor's round face.

"He's had a stroke. He's paralyzed on his the left side, his speech is slurred and -"

"Is he going to be alright?" Nathan couldn't contain his fear.

"That I can't tell you." The doctor shook his head. "In addition to the stroke, your father's lungs are filled with fluid suggesting congestive heart failure. He could have a heart attack or another stroke at any time. I can't predict the course. In some cases, I've seen these things reverse and the patient recover almost completely. In others, things get worse or become fatal."

Nathan swallowed hard on the lump in his throat. "Can we see him?"

"Sure." The doctor placed a hand on Nathan's shoulder. "But he needs his strength, so please don't wear him out." Then he looked at Nicolette and added, "I think it best if you go in one at a time. I don't want him to get overtaxed."

Nicolette shook her head affirmatively. "I'll be in with the children." She kissed Nathan on the cheek and went up the hall toward the nursery.

Nathan went in and quietly crossed the room to Marcel's bedside. He appeared to be sleeping, his thinning, white mane lying in damp strings about his leathery face. The left side of his face was drooping, his mouth twisted awkwardly. The sight of him caught Nathan off guard, filled him with pity. It hurt to to see him like this; the hearty, fearless man who'd made himself a legend reduced to this. He was seventy-two years old, but still, Nathan wasn't ready to lose him.

At seventeen, Marcel had survived a shipwreck in the Atlantic that took his parents and all six of his sisters. He'd saved his own life by downing a fifth of Scotch and clinging to a growler for two days before being rescued by a passing ship. At thirty, he'd fought and killed a black bear in Louisiana, and lived to tell the story. The bear's head still hung in the drawing room downstairs. Marcel had carved out his destiny in life with raw nerve, boundless energy, and a 'take no prisoners' attitude. He'd used his gifts as a businessman to purchase a profitable plantation and a partnership in a ferryboat company in New Orleans, Louisiana, and to trade cotton and tobacco in Europe. And Nathan admired and respected him for his success.

He pulled up a chair and sat down next to the bed. For several minutes he watched his father's chest rise and fall, thinking, *You can't die, Papa. We were supposed to have more time together, go on walks, have a chance to really talk to each other. It's too soon. You can't leave me now. Not yet.*

He loved his father, yet he felt he barely knew him. He'd heard many stories about his father from people who knew him, but he scarcely knew the everyday, intimate things about him - like his favorite color, how he got involved with his mother, what his relationship was like with his own father, and so much more.

Since Nathan had come to France to live with him, Marcel had seldom been home. He spent most of his time traveling throughout Europe, or seeing to his interests in America. He insisted that Nathan stay at home, focus on getting a good education and learn to be a gentleman, something he had no temperament for but admired greatly.

Nathan unbuttoned the stiff dress collar around his neck and took it off, opened the top button of his shirt and closed his hand around the St. Jude's medal his mother had given to him when he was a boy. He pressed it to his lips and silently recited the Lord's Prayer. When he opened his eyes, Marcel was looking up at him. "Mon fils...," he croaked, a faint smile on his face.

"Don't...don't try to talk, Papa," Nathan leaned closer. "Etienne says you need your strength."

As sick as he was, Marcel rolled his eyes and waved his right hand as if to say 'to hell with, Etienne.'

"Please, Papa...," Nathan said, "...you have to..."

"Ecou...ecouter," Marcel demanded, a thin line of drool trickling from the side of his mouth.

"Papa, you shouldn't try to talk," Nathan replied, his tone firm.

"I must," his father paused, "I am dying."

Nathan tried to close his mind to his father's words. "No, Papa. You're a fighter. You've got some good years left. You'll pull through this."

Marcel shook his head, his eyes welling with water. "No, Nathan…," he said breathlessly, "…you must accept this. You must do as I say."

"No, I won't accept such talk, Papa. Remember, you said yourself that I can be every bit as stubborn as you. It runs in the Legarde blood, remember?"

A faint smile crossed Marcel's face. He raised his right hand slightly from the bed. "Look in the drawer…," he said, "…in the nightstand…an envelope."

Nathan obeyed. He opened the drawer to the heavy oak nightstand next to the bed and saw a plain white envelope. He took it out and showed it to Marcel. "Is this it, Papa?"

Marcel nodded. "Open it."

Nathan tore one end off the envelope and shook out the contents, five First Class tickets for the *R.M.S. Titanic.* Before he could ask what they were for, Marcel began to talk, haltingly, his speech slurred, "You…you must go…to America. Don't…don't…let those…bastards…take…what I worked for."

His father's valiant effort to talk tore at Nathan's heart. "Papa, don't. Don't try to talk," he replied. "We can talk about this later, when you feel better."

Marcel shook his head. "No, I should…I should have prepared you. But I…" His father coughed several times and Nathan could hear the phlegm bubbling in his chest. Yet Marcel still insisted on speaking.

"Promise me, Nathan" he said between spasms of coughing, "…promise me… you'll go to America…" He reached for Nathan's hand. "Claim your…inheritance. Promise me."

Nathan took Marcel's hand. It was rough, clammy, and lacked the strength that he'd always felt in his grip.

"I promise, Papa."

Relief flooded Marcel's face and he sank back into his pillow. "See Robert Toussaint. He has papers," he said, then closed his eyes.

Dr. Chenault appeared at Nathan's side. "He really

must rest, Nathan. I recommend we move him to the hospital as soon as possible. He can get better care there."

"No, no hospital," Marcel said breathlessly, opening his eyes.

Nathan looked at Dr. Chenault then back at his father. "Alright, Papa. No hospital." He touched his hand, reassuring him.

"Overruled again…," Dr. Chenault said, then added, "but he really does need to rest, Nathan. Perhaps you can come back later."

"Okay," Nathan answered, still reluctant to leave. He didn't want to admit it, not even to himself, but his father's weakness and the dimness of his eyes told him death was near. It was as if he could feel him slipping away and the child inside him didn't want him to go. He wanted to be close to him, tell him that he loved him, tell him how grateful he was for the home he'd given him, the opportunities he'd made possible for him. He wanted to empty out his heart, reveal everything he felt inside. But he couldn't. His father didn't believe in such sentimentality for a man. He'd think it a sign of weakness, a character flaw. So he kept his feelings to himself.

"I'll be back later," he said, touching his father's shoulder, and told Etienne to call him immediately if there was the slightest change. Then he quietly left the room.

An hour later, Marcel had a massive heart attack. By the time Nathan reached his boudoir, he had already taken his last breath. He lay there, his eyes blank, his body lifeless. Nathan's hopes that one day he and Marcel would be closer as men than they'd been as father and son was lost.

Deep inside, Nathan felt that life had cheated him again, just as it did when he was ten years old and cruelly separated from his mother. Now death had separated him from his father. And once again, there was nothing he could do to change it.

Grief, bitter as quinine girded Nathan's heart and burned inside his chest. Nicolette came to his side and put her arms around him. He sank into the comfort of her embrace while in his mind he heard Marcel's gravelly voice say, "Be *strong, garcon. Be strong.*"

Unable to hold back the weight of his sorrow, Nathan collapsed into shameful sobs.

"In the name of the Father, the Son and the Holy Spirit, Amen."

Monseignor Uzel made the sign of the cross and the mourners gathered around Marcel's grave began to walk away. Nathan turned up the collar of his black wool coat against the wind and took Nicolette's gloved hand. It was a cold March day, with a beautiful blue sky with billowing cottony clouds overhead.

Nathan stepped away from the grave, glad the services were over. His father's death had taken a toll on his entire household. The house was as quiet as a monastery except for the occasional squeals or laughter of the children. Their housekeeper, Madame Bonet, and au pair, Sabine Fontaine, looked sad all the time. The easy banter and joking that was their custom as they went about their daily tasks was gone. And he was worried about Nicolette. She was eight weeks pregnant with their third child and he feared the strain of grief would cause the anemia she'd had with the last pregnancy to resurface.

And though he tried not to show it, he wasn't faring much better himself. The loss of his father filled him with a melancholy so deep he couldn't escape it, not even when at rest. At night he tossed and turned, his sleep disturbed by a recurring nightmare he'd started having as a child. In it, he was always running from a yellow wall of fire. The next morning he would awaken aggravated, with no clue to the dream's meaning.

Nathan glanced over at the granite headstone next to his father's grave. It belonged to his late wife, Catherine Alfort Legarde. She'd died just seven months before Nathan arrived in Paris. His father never talked about her, but Nathan learned about her from the servants.

Apparently, Catherine was penniless, but of aristocratic lineage, something she never let anyone forget. Her family had lost their money, titles, and many heads during the Revolution, leaving Catherine with nothing but a respectable family name. A haughty, calculating woman, her marriage to Marcel was entirely a business arrangement. But it worked or both of them. As a young man Marcel was ambitious and hardworking, but completely void of gentility or social standing. He needed someone who could open the doors of commerce for him that his lack of breeding and privilege prevented. Catherine was the key to those doors and her name made it possible for him to make lucrative business contacts all over Europe. He used those contacts well, to market the crops and wares produced on his plantation in New Orleans all over the world. For her contribution, Catherine was rewarded with the opulent lifestyle she craved. And due to her husband's extensive traveling, very few demands were put on her time. The situation suited her perfectly since she cringed at Marcel's ignorance of the social graces and detested his vile, frontiersman persona.

Learning about Catherine made it easy for Nathan to understand why his father had been attracted to his mother. She and Catherine were complete opposites. His mother was attractive, warm and giving, while, according to the servants, Catherine was physically unattractive, self-centered, and cold.

Walking to their automobile, Nathan looked around at the people who'd shown their last respects to his father. Most of them were Marcel's age, or older. They hailed from a variety of backgrounds and professions: city officials, merchants, local shopkeepers, laborers. He was surprised at how many of them there were, especially since his father hadn't been particularly sociable. He'd never minced words, rarely attended social gatherings or sat around discussing politics or the news of the day the way Nathan and his friends did. No, his father had been all business. Yet everyone respected him.

Nathan smiled to himself recalling the many times he had ventured into establishments in Paris, Beuvais or Villejuef and found the people there knew his father. They usually couldn't hide their shock when he told them he was Marcel's son. He was sure it was his café au lait skin and curly black hair they found so alarming, features he certainly wouldn't have had were he the offspring of the alabaster complexioned Catherine.

At twenty-six, he was five feet ten, the same height his father was before old age took inches from his stature. He had a naturally strong, powerful build, but unlike Marcel, he was more chiseled with a smaller waistline. He had penny brown eyes, a personality that bordered on cockiness and his father's need to win at whatever he set his mind to. But that's where the similarities ended. He was far more refined in his tastes and activities than his father had ever been. He loved to read, enjoyed lively conversation and debating with his friends, most of whom were professionals or intellectuals. And he had a tender, romantic side that he had to consciously suppress.

Getting into his automobile, he saw Robert Toussaint, his father's lawyer, climbing into his carriage and it jogged his memory. *Papa told me to see him, I'll have to go by his office tomorrow.*

He expected the meeting would go smoothly. After all, as far as he knew, he was his father's only heir.

Nathan arrived at Toussaint's office shortly after noon the next day. The elderly gentleman greeted him heartily and introduced him to his pudgy assistant, Anton Mendes. Out of courtesy, Nathan shook Mendes' hand. He wished he hadn't. It was wet, and an offensive, musty odor emanated from the wrinkled brown suit he was wearing.

Nathan took a handkerchief from the breast pocket of his suit and wiped his hand thinking, "I'm glad *he's* not Papa's lawyer." He couldn't abide slovenliness. As far as he was concerned, the way a man presented himself spoke volumes about his character. He was fastidious in his own personal hygiene and made it a point to dress well at all times.

"So, Nathan, will you be staying in America?" Toussaint asked as Nathan settled into one of the comfortable arm chairs in front of his desk. He poured Nathan a cup of tea from the pot on his desk and handed it to him, his knobby, arthritic hands shaking slightly.

Nathan chuckled. "Certainly you're kidding, Robert. I'd rather live in the deepest part of the Congo than in America. The people there are probably a lot more civilized. The only thing I want in America is what my father left me, and to see my mother, of course. It's been sixteen years since I saw her."

Toussaint sat down in the chair behind his desk. "I'm sure she'll be delighted," he said, picking up a binder from the corner of his desk and taking out a stack of papers. "Everything is in order. Here is the deed to the chatalet in Paris, the deed to Belle Lafourche plantation in New Orleans, and the Bill of Sale for Marcel's share in Delta Ferryboats." He handed them all over to Nathan.

Nathan took the papers and quickly looked them over. From the corner of his eye he noticed that Toussaint's assistant seemed to be paying more attention to them than to the stack of papers he was supposed to be working on. But he couldn't be sure, since he turned his attention back to the papers whenever Nathan looked directly at him. After scanning each document Nathan looked up at Toussaint. "Everything seems correct, Robert, except one thing." He leaned forward, pointing at the Bill of Sale for Delta Ferryboats. "It says here that Louisiana Steamers owns a forty percent share of Delta Ferryboats. But there are no principals listed. Wouldn't you say that's irregular?"

Toussaint shook his head. "I thought the same thing. But I'm not sure what it means. Perhaps they handle such documents differently in America. I would have asked Marcel about it, but I didn't get the chance. The day he dropped them off, he said he wasn't feeling well, so we really didn't get a chance to talk that much. Unfortunately, that was the last time I saw him."

"So who owns Louisiana Steamers?" Nathan wondered aloud. He recalled his father saying that someone named Cholley ran "the line" while he ran Belle Lafourche. But he had no idea who Cholley was. *Was he a foreman, partner, or what?*

"Robert, do you recall Papa mentioning someone by the name of Cholley?" Nathan asked, hoping he might remember the name from one of their conversations.

The old man frowned and scratched his nearly bald head. "No, I don't."

Nathan pushed further. "I remember Papa saying someone called Cholley ran the line. Are you sure he never talked to you about him?"

Again Toussaint replied, "No, I'm afraid he didn't," and leaned back in his chair. "But I was wondering, if you're not planning on staying in America, how are you going to manage things over there? I imagine traveling back and forth like Marcel did would be pretty difficult with a family and your job at the Metro."

Nathan thought about his father and how much he'd wished they'd spent more time together when he was a boy. "Oh, no. I don't plan on walking in my father's footsteps," he replied. "I want to be around to see my children grow up. As a matter of fact, we're expecting our third child."

"Is that so?" Toussaint beamed. "Then this calls for a *real* celebration." He winked at Nathan and opened the right bottom drawer in his desk, pulled out a bottle of Courvossier, and called to his assistant across the room.

"Anton, get us a couple of glasses."

The young man heaved himself up and shuffled from the room. A moment later he returned with two brandy glasses. He sat them on Toussaint's desk and resumed his post across the room.

Toussaint poured them both a drink. On legs bowed from rheumatism, he walked over and handed Nathan a glass. Watching the old man retrace his steps, Nathan couldn't help but think about his father. He and Toussaint were about the same age, but Toussaint appeared physically older than Marcel had. Yet here he was, still living and working. *How unpredictable life is,* he mused, *that someone who's strong and robust and we expect to live forever, doesn't. While others who are frail and weak sometimes live much longer.* It was one of those mysteries of life that no one really had the answer to.

Toussaint raised his glass in a toast: "Here's to a bright future, a blessed family, and to Marcel. God rest his soul."

"Salute." Nathan raised his glass, then took a sip. As the liquor burned a smooth path down his throat, he noticed Mendes watching them again. Irritated, he said to Toussaint, "Might we have some privacy."

"Oh, surement." Toussaint called to his assistant while nodding at the clock across the room. "Anton, it's past lunchtime, go on and take your break."

"Oui, Monsieur." Mendes lifted his heavy bulk from the chair and shuffled to the door, his head sunk between his shoulders. As soon as the door closed behind him, Toussaint remarked, "So, tell me about your plans."

"Well, beyond taking care of the legalities, I'm not really sure what I want to do. My mother is running Belle Lafourche now, so I'll probably let her continue. As for Delta Ferryboats...," he let out a sigh, "well, I'll have to find a way to manage somehow. The railroads are becoming strong competitors nowadays, but I guess that's a battle I may have to face. At any rate, it was Papa's wish that I claim what he spent his life building, so that's what I intend to do. Plus, I'm really looking forward to seeing my mother again".

His Mama was fifty years old now. When she sent him away to France, he'd been angry with her for a long time. But he'd long since gotten over that. In fact, he'd come to realize that it was the best thing she could have done for him. France had been really good to him. He'd gotten an excellent education and earned a bachelor's degree in civil engineering, something he doubted he would have had the chance to do in America.

Suddenly, Toussaint sat up straight in his chair, his wrinkled face brightening with memory. "Oh, I almost forgot." He sat his brandy glass down on his desk and opened the center drawer in front of him. He rummaged around a minute, then held up a key in his hand. "Voila!"

Curious, Nathan watched him walk across the room and open a bulky black trunk that was sitting on the floor. Toussaint reached inside, took out a tapestry carpetbag and brought it back across the room. He sat it on his desk and said to Nathan, "I almost forgot this. Marcel asked me to give this to you the last time he was here."

"Is that so?" Nathan was surprised that his father would go to all the trouble of bringing something to Robert that he could have easily given him at home. Baffled, he asked, "What is it?"

"I don't know, he didn't tell me," Toussaint replied. "All he said was to give it to you when he died, and that he trusted me not to open it. And that was that. So, whatever is in there is between you and him"

Nathan sat his drink on the side table next to his chair and walked over to Toussaint's desk. "May I?"

Toussaint shrugged. "It's yours."

Nathan opened the carpet bag and found a rough hewn oak case sitting on top of a pile of American currency. Lifting the case out, he guessed there was probably several thousand dollars in it. The money didn't surprise him; his father had always been generous with him. But the case he couldn't figure out. It was a little larger than a cigar box, the lid carved with a woodland scene of a buck and fawn drinking from a stream. Mystified, he opened it. Inside was an ivory handled .38 Smith & Wesson revolver and an ivory handled sailor's knife. His blood ran cold as his father's words came reeling back to him: "*Don't let those son-of-a-bitches take what I worked for…*"

"Nathan's instincts told him his father expected him to have trouble in America. *Why else would he leave these things? But trouble from whom?*

He picked up the knife from the black velvet lined box, gripped it in his hand and inspected it. It appeared to have been custom made and, from the looks of it, never used. The ivory on the knife handle matched that on the handle of the gun. The gold inlay and nickel vining scrollwork on both weapons also matched. He touched a finger lightly to the knife's blade; it was razor sharp. He put it back in the box, picked up the gun and examined it too. He'd seen the model before, known as a "lemon squeezer," nicknamed for its distinct shape and safety features designed to prevent children from using it. To fire it, you had to depress a lever on the back while simultaneously pulling the trigger.

Nathan put the gun back in the case, closed it, and placed it back in the carpetbag. Worried, he said to Toussaint, "This gives me a bad feeling, Robert. I remember the night Papa died, he said something quite strange. He told me not to let those bastards take what he worked for. But he didn't tell me who he meant." Hoping the old man could offer him some clue he added, "Who was he referring to, Robert? What might he have been thinking? Can't you tell me something? Anything?"

Toussaint looked worried too. He ran a knobby hand over the sparse strands of hair on his mottled head. "I wish there was something I could tell you Nathan, but I don't know any more than you do. Everything I know about your father's affairs is in the papers you have in your pocket. But it does look like he was expecting some sort of trouble. And you know as well as I do what Marcel's motto was."

"Yes." Nathan nodded, and he and Toussant said simultaneously, "'Always be prepared.'"

They both fell silent for a long moment, pondering the mystery.

Finally, Toussaint touched Nathan's arm. "If you're really concerned, perhaps you shouldn't go to America." He pointed to the carpetbag. "You have a nice sum of money there. You have a good job, a nice home. Why take a risk, when you don't have to."

Nathan reflected for a moment. In a way, Toussaint was right. His life was pretty comfortable. He didn't have to go to America. With the assets his father left him in France alone, he could live well for quite some time. But it was more than money or financial assets that motivated him. It was a matter of pride, self-respect, and above all, principle. It was *his* inheritance. He had a right to claim it. He'd promised his father he would, and he was honor bound to keep his word. And no matter what the risk, he would not forfeit what his father had left him, not after the way he had left America.

An intense sadness washed over him as he recalled the awful decision that had been forced upon him as a child: leave everything he knew and loved, his home, his mother, his country, or be killed. He recalled the nightmare of crossing the ocean to France, shut up in a coffin for nine whole days and eight nights. All he could do was listen to the sounds of the waves as he yearned for the occasional snatch of conversation, or escape inside his own mind to sooth his restlessness and hunger for human contact. And every night, when the holes in the coffin filled with darkness, he trembled with fear until he couldn't stand it anymore. Then, he would take a swig of the potion Elijah, the cabinet maker had given him and fall asleep. Once, when something was placed on top of the coffin, he'd had such fear that he would never get out, his bladder failed. It took every ounce of his courage to keep from screaming for help. Then, a couple of days later, he got diarrhea. By the time he reached France, and his father came and took possession of the coffin, he was a stinking, humiliated mess. He was so traumatized by the ordeal, he was unable to speak for almost a year. Only with the help of a tutor did he finally find his tongue again. *No child should ever have to endure such a thing,* Nathan thought silently. *Not ever.*

Finally, he said to Toussaint, "You don't understand, Robert. I have to go. I promised Papa. And I promised myself a long time ago that I will stand up for what is right, even if it kills me. It's *my* inheritance over there, and I'm going to claim it, come hell or high water."

He picked up the carpetbag, placed it under his arm and shook the old man's hand.

"Thank you for everything," he said, and Toussaint walked him to the door.

"Bonne chance, Nathan," Toussaint called after him as he walked down the steps. "I hope you're doing the right thing."

So do I, Nathan thought, taking out the crank for his automobile. *So do I.*

Chapter 2

Nicolette Legarde could hardly believe her eyes. In her hands were five first class tickets for *the R.M.S Titanic.* Five! Enough for the entire family *and* the children's au pair. Stunned, she dropped down on the side of the bed.

"Why didn't Nathan tell me about them?" she wondered. *"Is it supposed to be a surprise? He could have mentioned them two days ago, when he told me he was going to go America."*

She'd found them by accident while searching for her pearl comb. After looking in her jewelry box and dressing table drawers she recalled that she'd worn it in her hair the night Marcel died. She remembered it had fallen out of her hair when they were coming out of the theatre and she'd handed it to Nathan. So she checked the pockets of his suit and found it in his breast pocket along with a white envelope. She would never have dreamed she'd find tickets for the *Titanic* in the envelope.

After the initial shock wore off, she started to turn things over in her mind. Something wasn't right. She Nathan was still grieving the loss of his father, but he hadn't been himself lately at all. He was usually warm and attentive, but lately he was withdrawn and always seemed to be preoccupied, like his mind was somewhere else. She'd noticed it when their neighbor, Madame Jacquet and her boys

41

came over to offer their sympathies. He thanked them, but made no attempt to converse with them. He'd never done that before. And just this morning at breakfast, she had to ask him to pass the butter three times before he heard her. Yet, when she asked how he was faring, he swore he was fine.

She stared at the tickets in her hand. *Could he have actually bought them, then forgot about them? Or, was he hiding them?* She thought they shared everything, but lately she wasn't so sure. Especially since he'd said nothing to her about Marcel's estate until he told her he was going to America. And even then, they didn't discuss it. He simply told her he had to take care of it. When she asked if she and the children could go with him he told her he didn't think it would be a good idea because he'd heard there was an outbreak of yellow fever in New Orleans. He also told her the snakes were especially active in the Spring and he didn't want to risk her or one of the children being bitten. And when he told her about the snakes, she was only too glad to let him make the trip alone. Snakes made her skin crawl.

But she had no idea he'd be traveling on the *Titanic*. They'd talked about the ship numerous times. More than once she'd told him how much she'd love to be on it for its maiden voyage. Yet, he never said a word. And she couldn't help but wonder why he didn't.

Like everyone else they'd read about the *Titanic* in the newspapers. Vivid, exciting stories that were nearly impossible to get away from. Posters of the ship were displayed all over Paris. They touted it as an historic marvel of modern technology, a virtual floating city, 'the unsinkable ship of dreams.'

Everyday there was a new story extolling the ship's elegance, it's first of a kind amenities: Turkish baths, automatic lifts, wireless office, libraries, restaurants, gymnasium, and on and on. European aristocrats and wealthy Americans announced their plans to sail the maiden voyage in the press. It was the thing to do, the place to go to see and be seen. And she wanted so badly to be a part of it. Not to be seen, but to see with her own eyes, the most glamorous women in the world, wearing the most glamorous fashions in the world. The *Titanic's* maiden voyage was going to be the very zenith of couture, and couture was her passion. Being on that ship would be a dream come true, like stepping into the pages of Harper's Bazaar.

Since the age of four, when she was abandoned by her mother and left with the Bonschears, she had been around dressmaking. Olivie, the no-nonsense disciplinarian was a seamstress and gentle Henri, a tailor. The elderly couple taught her how to sew, how to make lace, and how to make patterns. Before long, she discovered she could dream up unique fashions in her head and set them down on paper. At twelve, she designed and made her first ensemble from the scraps laying around the tiny shop. And over the years her skills grew so that by the time she was sixteen she was one of the best dressed girls in the city, despite her humble background.

Finally, Nicolette put the tickets back in the envelope and dropped them in her skirt pocket. Feeling a rush of excitement she thought, "I can't wait for Nathan to get back. There has to be an explanation. He wouldn't have bought tickets for us if he hadn't changed his mind about our going with him."

From down the hall, she heard her one year old, Cecile, start to cry and she headed for the nursery.

When she got there, their au pair, Sabine, was holding Cecile on her lap. The child was sucking her bottle so hard it squealed as a cascade of air bubbles replaced the milk in it. Their three year old, Trista, was sitting cross-legged on the floor in the middle of the room, her springy, sandy brown hair fanned out about her face. She was turning the pages of a picture book, pretending to read.

"Bonjour, Sabine" Nicolette said to the au pair and sat on the floor next to Trista. "Bonjour ma petite jeune fille," she said to Trista.

"Bonjour, Mama." Trista got up, sat on Nicolette's lap and promptly started reading to her.

Nicolette spent a half hour with the children then went to her sewing room. She took out her sketchpad and tried to concentrate. But it was no use. Her mind kept wandering. All she could think about was the glamorous *Titanic*, and how badly she wanted to be on it.

Nathan pulled the automobile away from the curb, his mind on his wife. He'd told her a couple of days ago that he had to go to America to settle his father's estate. But what he didn't tell her was that he'd be traveling on the *Titanic.* Nor did he mention the tickets his father had given him. Instead, he made up some lies to keep her from wanting to go with him. He was ashamed of what he'd done, but his pride, and his sense of himself as a man, wouldn't let him tell her the truth: he was afraid. Not so much for himself, but for her. If there was trouble, he didn't want her involved. They would be especially vulnerable in America, particularly in the American South. A racially mixed couple like themselves was sure to be a target for every hate-filled racist around.

Things were a lot different for them in Paris than they would be in America. In France, the Legarde name afforded them a certain amount of acceptance, respectability, and protection. He and Nicolette had their own circle of friends, and their union was tolerated somewhat in French society. He doubted that would be the case *anywhere* in America. He'd read in the paper the other day that there were over a hundred lynchings of Negroes in the America last year, so he knew things hadn't changed much since he left.

Turning the automobile onto the Champs Elysee, Nathan told himself he was doing the right thing by lying since he was doing it to protect his family.

He had one last chore to do and headed for the Compagnie du Chemin de fer Metropolitan de Paris.

A few minutes later he parked the automobile in front of the Compagnie du Chemin offices and went inside.

Jacques Dupont, the office clerk greeted him. "Bonsoir, Nathan," he called across the room. "I was sorry to hear about your father."

"Thank you," Nathan said. "I'm here to see Echel. Is he in?"

"He should be back in ten minutes or so. You're welcome to wait for him if you want."

"I will." Nathan took a seat on the bench next to the door of Echel Padgett's private office. He leaned on the brass handle of a dark cherry walking stick, one of his favorites from his personally handcrafted collection. He took great pride in his walking sticks and always carried one whenever he went out socially, or on business. He knew it was vanity, but he felt they gave him a certain savoir fare. He'd learned in his study of French history that during the reign of King Louis the XVI, walking sticks were exclusive to the French Court. No one else was allowed to have them. That little tidbit elevated the stature of the walking stick in his eyes and he was determined to have the finest in Paris.

After waiting for the longest time Nathan started to debate with himself whether or not he should come back tomorrow. He pushed a button on the filigreed collar of his walking stick and it popped open revealing a precision timepiece. He checked the time and found he'd been sitting for almost an hour. He was about to leave when the door to the Chemin office opened with a bang. Echel Padgett, his supervisor stepped inside and slammed the door behind him so hard the glass panes rattled.

Padgett was a big, Nordic-looking man with saffron hair, and a stump of a neck. Nathan noticed his lips and meaty cheeks were uncharacteristically chapped from the cold and his boots were caked with dried red dirt.

Dupont jumped to his feet, clearly startled by Padgett's entrance. "Bon…bonsoir, Monsieur Padgett," he gushed, and accidentally knocked over a half full glass of water on his desk. He grabbed a handkerchief from his pocket and mopped up the water, casting furtive glances at Padgett. His jitteriness suggested he was expecting one of Padgett's expert brow-beatings.

Nathan felt sorry for Dupont. He was a kind soul and didn't deserve Padgett's abuse. Nathan gave him credit for working in such close proximity to Padgett all day. He certainly doubted that he'd be able to do it. The man's stupidity would drive him batty. And to make matters worse, he actually believed he was intelligent.

Padgett stomped across the room to the coat rack. He pointedly ignored Nathan, and mercifully, ignored Dupont too. He shimmied out of his coat, and using his right hand, flung it onto a peg in the rack.

Padgett's left arm was missing, the result of a construction accident several years ago that took the lives of three of their workers and injured four more. At the time, he was the site foreman working on the Number Five Line of the Paris Metro. Rumor had it the accident was Padgett's fault. Workers later testified in a hearing that they'd warned him repeatedly about a retaining wall in the tunnel they were working in. They told him the wall was weakening, beginning to buckle, but he refused to listen to them. When the wall gave way, Padgett was trapped for twelve hours and his left arm crushed by a massive boulder. It had to be amputated and he was lucky to be alive.

But in spite of the hearing that followed and the fact that he was responsible for the tragedy, Padgett came out of it looking like a saint. The Paris newspapers focused on the loss of his arm. They touted him as a brave, self-sacrificing hero and shamed City officials into feeling sorry for him. As a result, he was *rewarded* for his incompetence and promoted to assistant supervising engineer for the entire Metro project. The debacle proved to Nathan that not only was justice blind, it could also be downright stupid.

In his opinion, Padgett had learned nothing from the loss of his arm. He still made poor judgments, failed to adequately think things through, was impatient, short-sighted and lacked the ability to envision anything that wasn't spelled out in a book. But what irked Nathan even more was his pettiness. If Nathan or one of his men suggested a different way of doing something, Padgett closed his mind to it and pulled rank. It made Nathan's job as construction site engineer harder than it had to be.

He had little respect for him, yet somehow they'd managed to work out an unspoken agreement: Padgett tolerated his presence while he tactfully compensated for Padgett's incompetence.

But they still had their conflicts. About a year ago the men complained about head injuries from falling rocks. Padgett dismissed their complaints as irresolvable and reminded them that falling rocks was a hazard of the job they'd agreed to live with as terms of employment.

Nathan understood their concern, so he decided to help. He designed protective helmets for them, loosely based on the head armor of the French cuirassier. He fashioned the helmets out of hard leather, glue and shellac. The men were enormously grateful and someone reported it to the press. But instead of congratulating him, or showing some gratitude for helping to keep their workers safe on the job, Padgett accused him of coddling the men and overstepping his authority.

He believed Padgett was still harboring a grudge over the incident and hoped he wouldn't have to deal with his nonsense today. All he wanted to talk about was the time off he needed from work, to do what he had to do. Period.

Finally, Padgett walked over and scoffed, "Okay, Legarde, what do you want? I know you're not here to work, not in that fancy get-up." His steely blue eyes raked over him, taking in his dark brown morning coat, pin-striped trousers and vest, dark brown top hat on his lap, and the walking stick in his hand.

The jibe was classic Padgett. The only thing that would satisfy him was if he dressed like many of the Metro laborers, in the same dirty work clothes every day.

Nathan ignored the jibe. His voice firm, he said, "I need a word with you, Echel."

"Make it quick." Padgett jerked his head indicating Nathan should follow him, so he tucked his walking stick under his arm and followed him into his office.

The wall behind Padgett's desk was plastered with framed commendations and certificates. The large one at the center of the grouping was from the Ecole Polytechnique, their mutual alma mater. According to the professional grapevine,

Padgett barely made it through Polytechnique, and his commendations were gotten through family connections rather than actual achievements.

Padgett sat down in his chair. "Okay, Nathan, what kind of problem do you have this time?" he asked in an exasperated tone.

Nathan felt his jaw tighten. *"How dare you act like I'm always asking you for something,"* he thought, *"when you know damned well that's not true."*

Until his father died, he'd never missed a day from work, and when he asked for something, it was for the men who worked under him on Line Seven.

"I need some time off," Nathan replied.

Padgett glared up at him. "What do you mean, you need time off? You haven't worked for the last three days, and now you want more time off?!"

"That's right." Nathan held his temper in check. He could tell from the moment he walked in the door that Padgett was itching for a fight - probably because he'd had to work for a change, instead of sitting on his lard ass in his cozy office, while he did his thinking for him, the crew did all the work, and he took all the credit. Judging from his mood, things must not have been going well, so he wanted to take it out on someone. That's what he usually did, especially when he couldn't figure something out: take it out on the first poor sap to cross his path.

"Well, you're not getting any more time off." Padgett barked. "You've had all you're going to get."

Nathan tried to appeal to his heart. "Listen, Echel, where's your compassion? My father died. I had to bury him. What else could -"

"Don't talk to me about compassion, Legarde," Padgett interrupted. "Where's yours, is what I want to know? I've been busting my ass every day down there at the Line, doing your job, then running back here and working half the night to do mine. Don't you talk to me about compassion."

Nathan didn't buy it. He knew Padgett well enough to know that maybe half of what he claimed was true. Yes, he had to cover for Nathan at the job site, but as far as his own work, Dupont did most of that. In fact, he seriously doubted that Padgett could read a blueprint.

Nathan loosened the tie around his neck, and said, "Look, "I'm sorry things have been rough for you, but I have to have more time off. I have business to take care of in America. I wouldn't ask if it wasn't important."

"America?!" Padgett sat straight up in his chair. "So I'm supposed to continue busting my ass for you, so you can go on holiday. And just how long do you expect me to do that, Nathan?"

Nathan wanted to wipe the sarcastic smirk off his face. "I'm not sure how long I'll be gone... two months, maybe three. It depends on how long it takes me to handle things over there."

Padgett continued to probe. "And just what kind of business do you have over there?"

"Personal business. My ship leaves April tenth. That'll give me a little over a month to get things caught up here and get the work plans ready to cover the time I'll be gone."

Padgett continued to regard him with a look of sarcasm that made Nathan angrier by the second. If he wanted to grant him the time off, he could easily do it. Apparently, he wanted him to grovel.

"What kind of *personal* business would you have in America?" Padgett asked again.

Nathan's temper ignited. "I told you it's personal." He looked him square in the eye. "I don't ask you about your personal affairs, and you'd don't have the right to question me about mine."

Padgett slammed his fist on his desk. "Like hell I don't, when you come swaggering in here in your Sunday best asking me for time off. You know full well we have to have Line Seven done by June. We're stretched to the limit as it is."

That was the last straw! "Hold it right there, Echel," Nathan shouted. "We're stretched to the limit because you *made* it that way. So don't try to lay the blame on my doorstep. The men down there have been begging for help for months, and you turned me down every time I put in a requisition for you to hire somebody,…out of spite, nothing but pure, unmitigated spite, because *I* was the one making the request. That's stupid,

Echel. Stupid and short sighted, like most of your decisions. By turning me down you're hurting the men on the Line, and ultimately yourself, and you're too damned blind to see it."

"That's a lie," Padgett boomed, banging his desk again.

Nathan refused to be intimidated and came right back at him. "No, you're the one who's lying. You want to know how I know? A very reliable member of City Council told me there's more than enough money in the budget for labor, when you told me there wasn't. As a matter of fact, he said we've underutilized the funds allotted to us for Line Seven. Now tell me why *he* would want to lie. He had no reason to. You keep forgetting, Echel, I have connections in this city too."

"Well, whoever he is, he's lying," Padgett huffed, "I don't know why, but he is…or *you* are."

"I don't have to lie." And he knew David Lefeuvre wasn't lying either.

Lefeuvre was a friend of Marcel's who'd dropped by after Marcel died and quite innocently congratulated Nathan on the Number Seven Line staying under budget in its labor costs. Nathan didn't let on that it was news to him, but mentally filed the information away.

"Listen, I don't have to explain anything to you," Padgett bellowed. "I'm your boss, remember? If it wasn't for me you wouldn't *have* a job in this company."

"Hah! You're deluding yourself," Nathan shot back. "I got this job in *spite* of you. I came here with the best grades in my class, the backing of every professor I had at Polytechnique, and a recommendation from City Council,…who by the way, was desperate for some brains around here after making the mistake of putting you in charge. So don't think I don't know the score. You *had* to hire me."

Padgett jumped up from his chair. "Why you pompous, arrogant Nig…"

In a flash, every muscle in Nathan's body was galvanized with adrenaline. "Call me a nigger, Padgett," he shouted, raising his walking stick in the air. "Say it…and I promise you, I will pound your big ass to a lump of whale fat. I've had about enough of your shit."

For a moment, they locked eyes, chests heaving. One wrong move, one wrong word, and blood was sure to spill.

Perhaps it was the fury reflected on Nathan's face that warned Padgett he'd gone too far, because he gradually sat back down in his chair. "Now get a hold of yourself, Legarde," he said, in a conciliatory tone. "Perhaps you can go later, after we finish Line Seven. You can make another request come Summer."

Frustrated, Nathan answered, "You haven't heard a thing I've said, have you? Let me try this one last time. I need time off starting April tenth. I already have the tickets. That's the day I have to leave."

"The answer is still, no," Padgett said, eyeing him warily.

"Well, I guess that's it," Nathan sighed. "This conversation is over. I'm going to America, and I'll be damned if I'm going to beg you for permission." He headed for the door.

"Then don't bother coming back, Legarde," Padgett flung at his back as he reached the threshold, "If you're leaving in April, don't come in tomorrow…or the next day. Or the day after that!"

Nathan spun around and spat, "Go to hell, Echel," and slammed the door behind him. He tipped his hat at Dupont on his way out and walked to his automobile.

Padgett's horse-drawn carriage was sitting behind his mustard yellow Panhard Levassor parked at the curb. The horse snorted noisily as Nathan took out the automobile's crank and started the engine. He hopped inside and pulled away from the curb thinking, *That ignorant buffoon. I can't believe he just fired me. If he had any sense he'd have waited and gotten the work plans drawn up before I left.* He signed heavily. *Well, it's his problem now.*

The thought wasn't much comfort though. He was hurt and angrier than hell, partly because he hadn't seen it coming. He and Padgett had had rows before, but he thought he at least had enough sense to keep the people around him who made him look good.

And dammit, I'm one of those people! Some reward. I give my loyalty, my sweat, my skill, and this is what I get."

He'd taken so much pride in being an educated man, a professional. His career was an integral part of who he was, and now, in a few short minutes, he'd lost it.

He felt the rug had been snatched out from under him yet again, as though he was losing the most important things in his life. But he refused to wallow in self-pity. He had to go on, but how much more was he supposed to take?

Nicolette was standing in the doorway of the foyer waiting for him when he got home. A broad smile lit up her face as he got out of his automobile. But it quickly faded and he surmised that she'd somehow read his emotions. He certainly felt terrible, like he'd been hit in the gut with a medicine ball.

Concern reflected in Nicolette's emerald eyes as he walked up the steps. "What's the matter?" she asked, her tone edged with worry.

He kissed her on the cheek. "Echel fired me." He took off his hat, walked to the coat closet and hung up it up along with his coat and walking stick. "After all the times I bailed his ass out." He shook his head. "So much for loyalty."

"But why would he fire you?" Nicolette asked, following him into the parlor. "Did you two have another one of your 'disagreements?'"

"You could say that." He sat in one of the plush armchairs in front of the fireplace and Nicolette sat across from him. "He fired me because I refused to tell him why I need to go to America.

"I don't understand," she said, her brow furrowing. "He is your supervisor. Why wouldn't you tell him? That's what most people would do."

"Well, I'm not most people." Nathan's tone was more curt than he intended. "It's none of his business. I told him everything he needs to know, not a bit more." He reached in his pocket, took out his fingernail file and ran it under his index finger.

"Now Nathan, be reasonable." Nicolette chided, "Perhaps you shouldn't have drawn such a hard line."

Nathan chafed at the suggestion. How could she say he wasn't being reasonable? Yet, deep down he wasn't too surprised that she didn't understand. He loved her dearly, and they had many things in common, but they saw the world through different eyes and frequently interpreted things differently.

Frustrated, Nathan threw up his hands exclaiming, "I'm drawing a hard line? I'm not being reasonable? Just because he's my supervisor doesn't mean I don't have a right to some privacy. Remember, this is the same bigoted log head that goes around telling darky and Italian jokes whenever I'm within earshot. So just imagine me telling him that I have to go to America to settle my father's estate. He would either have said I was lying about it or laughed in my face. It was bad enough as it was. Had I told him everything, I would probably have ended up in jail."

"I see," Nicolette said quietly. She picked up a handful of lace and her darning needle from the sewing basket sitting next to her chair. "So what are you going to do now?"

"Well, on the way home I got to thinking. I'm not so sure I want to work for the Metro anymore. Or for anyone else. I certainly don't want to work under another idiot like Echel Padgett. As a matter of fact, I kind of thought it might be interesting to start my own engineering firm."

"Really?" Nicolette looked surpised. "I can understand you not wanting to work for Padgett, but your own engineering firm? Are you sure you want to take on something like that?"

He knew what she was insinuating. She didn't have to spell it out for him. Though he'd been insulated from most of it because of his father's name and reputation, he was well of aware of the racial prejudice and discrimination inherent in French society. Yet, as bad as it was, it was an improvement over the racism in America and the choke hold of colonialism in England.

And he was willing to take the risk, for a chance to build something of his own, something he could perhaps hand down to his own son one day. It was at least worth trying. Besides, with his credentials, his experience, and his late father's connections, he might just be able to make a go of it. Finally, Nathan replied, "Yes, I think I'm up to the task. But it wouldn't make sense to start anything until I get back from America."

Nicolette put her needlework aside. "Speaking of America…," she said, a grin spreading across her face, "…I was looking for my comb today and I found these." She reached in her skirt pocket, took out a white envelope and held it up.

"Oh, shit," Nathan thought, "she found the tickets. Why didn't I remember to move them?" He tried to think of a quick explanation.

"Why didn't you tell me you'd bought them?" Nicilette asked, excitement dancing in her eyes. "You made such a fuss about me and the children not going, I'm surprised you changed your mind. But I'm so glad you did. I can hardly wait to start packing."

"Whoa," Nathan exclaimed. "I didn't change my mind. You and the children aren't going."

Nicolette looked at him as if he'd sprouted another head. "What?"

"I didn't buy the tickets. Papa did. Don't ask me why, but he gave them to me the night he died, when he told me he wanted me to go to America."

"All right, then why didn't you tell me about the tickets before? Obviously, Papa Marcel wanted me and the children to go."

"Perhaps he did. But that doesn't change a thing."

Nicolette's gasped, a sudden epiphany shining in her eyes. "That stuff you told me about why you didn't want us to go with you to New Orleans, they were lies, weren't they? There is no yellow fever epidemic in New Orleans, is there? And I bet the snakes aren't any worse in the Spring than any other time." Her eyes were batting furiously, her voice rising to a shriek. "You lied to me Nathan, to keep me from wanting to go. Didn't you?"

"That's not true," he said defensively. "Well it is, and it isn't. But my mind *is* made up. You and the children are staying home. Period."

For a moment, Nicolette sat there staring at him with a mixture of surprise and hurt on her face.

The thought went through his mind that he should just tell her the truth, that their mixed marriage could make them a target over there and he didn't want her and the children in danger. But again, his pride wouldn't let him.

"How can you be so selfish and insensitive, Nathan?" Nicolette cried, "You know how much I want to go, how much it would mean to me." Her bottom lip started to quiver. "You expect me to be an understanding wife and support you in whatever you do, but when it comes to something I want, something that would make me happy, it doesn't matter to you one whit."

"That's not true, Nicolette. You're making far too much of this," Nathan replied, hoping she wasn't gearing up for one of her week long grudges. "This is primarily a business trip. I expect I'll be busy most of the time taking care of things over there. Perhaps we can all go next year, when I can take the time to show you around. Then, we can all enjoy it. I'm sure the *Titanic* will still be around."

"That's not the same thing and you know it." Nicolette sprang from her seat and flung the envelope with the tickets in it onto his lap. "Here! Keep your tickets. And don't ever tell me again how much you want your mother to meet me and the children, because I won't believe you." She burst into tears and ran out of the parlor.

"Nicolette! Wait! Nathan stood up, took a couple of steps after her and changed his mind. What could he say to her anyway? He wasn't going to change his mind. "Best to let this blow over…", he thought, "…give her a chance to calm down."

But as he sat back down in his chair, he just *knew* she was gathering steam for one of her nasty storms.

Chapter 3

Nicolette avoided Nathan for the rest of the evening. She retreated to her sewing room, the one room in the chatalet that was all her own. It was her sanctuary, a place where she could immerse herself in creativity and beauty and escape life's pressures. Nathan called it a rubbish heap, because it was crowded with stuff; fabric and lace, ribbon and pins, buttons and bows, the tools of her hobby. But it was heaven on earth to her. It reminded her of the pleasant part of her childhood, of the little shop she practically grew up in. And in spite of how it looked, she could always find what she needed, when she needed it.

She spent the evening cutting out a dress pattern and attaching the lining of a coat. But hard as she tried to avoid it, she couldn't keep her husband's stubbornness out of her mind. It made her so angry. He had no concern for what she wanted at all.

At around two o'clock in the morning fatigue finally caught up with her and she decided to go to bed. When she got to their boudoir, she undressed in the dark, put on her peignoir and crawled in bed beside her husband. He turned his back to her, but she could tell by his breathing that he wasn't asleep. For the longest time she lay there, staring into the darkness, tired, but unable to sleep, her mind racing, trying to figure out the change in his behavior. They'd always discussed things before. He'd always been a little stubborn and opinionated at times, but not like this. He'd never tried to dictate to her. He'd always said he respected her opinions, valued her ability to think for herself and make up her own mind. So what was going on? Where was the man who'd said he didn't want a wife who was a servant, but a companion? Something had to be wrong for him to change so drastically. It seemed that overnight he'd become authoritarian, and moody, which wasn't like him at all. She wondered if he was having an affair. Was that why he didn't want her and the children to go with him? Or, perhaps he was suddenly afraid his mother wouldn't like her. All kinds of things went through her mind.

Finally, she turned and touched his shoulder. "Nathan, what's wrong? And please don't lie to me. Are you taking someone else with you to America? If there is someone else, I need to know."

"There *is* no one else," Nathan replied, sounding annoyed.

"Then why won't you let us go with you? We've been talking about the *Titanic's* maiden voyage for months. You know how much I want to go. I've told you often enough. I would have thought you'd be thrilled to take us with you."

Nathan whirled onto his back. "For the last time, you're not going, understand? So stop hounding me about it." He jerked the covers up to his neck and turned his back on her again.

His tone of voice, his refusal to even discuss it hurt her deeply. She started to cry and wiped a tear from the side of her face. After a few moments she decided she wasn't going to try to reason with him anymore. It obviously wasn't working anyway. If he was going to be stubborn and unreasonable, then she would do the same.

"All right, Nathan, have it your way," she said, and turned her back to him. "If you're going to leave me and the children behind, fine. But don't expect us to be here when you get back."

It was an underhanded tactic and she knew it. Nathan adored his children. But she couldn't help it. After the way he'd been treating her, he deserved it. If the prospect of losing her and the children didn't get him to change his mind, nothing would.

She waited for him to say something, but he was silent for the longest time. She was finally nodding off to sleep when his voice came through the darkness. "You wouldn't really leave me, would you?"

She kept her back to him. "Yes, I would. It's obvious you don't care about me or my happiness anymore. If you did, you would want me with you. Demanding that I stay behind tells me you don't really love me, and I see no point in staying married to someone who doesn't love me." She fluffed her pillow angrily and lay back down. "Bonsoir."

She closed her eyes and tried to go to sleep, but a few minutes later, Nathan called, "Nicolette?"

"Nicolette?"

She wouldn't answer.

He called her again. "Nicolette."

Again, she said nothing. A few minutes later she fell asleep.

When she awoke the next morning, Nathan was already up. She threw the duvet cover back and was sitting up when he appeared in the bedroom doorway carrying a breakfast tray covered with a white linen napkin. It was laden with café au lait, a croissant, a small jar of apricot preserves, and a vase of pink lilacs.

"Bonjoir, ma cherie," he said, sitting the tray on her lap, his expression contrite. He sat at the foot of the bed, looked at her and said, "I owe you an apology. I thought about it for a long time last night and I realize I've been stubborn, unfair, and acting like a fool. Will you forgive me?"

"Forgive you?" Nicolette shrieked, still angry with him.

"Yes, forgive me. But before you say anything else, look under the napkin on the tray."

Carefully, she lifted the edge of the napkin and pulled out a folded sheet of white paper. On it was written, 'I love you more than life.' She unfolded it and the tickets for the *Titanic* dropped out.

"Do you mean it? We can go?" she said, almost afraid to believe it.

"Yes, you can go." He planted a kiss on her forehead and took her hand. "I thought about it long and hard last night and I realized that you and the children are the most important reason for me to even go to America. It's you and my girls that give my life meaning. Without you, nothing I do and nothing I have matters. I'll do whatever I have to do, face whatever I have to face to make you happy. So…," he paused, "do you forgive me?"

"Yes." Feeling a whisp of guilt, she threw her arms around him and covered his face with kisses.

She was so excited she could hardly eat her breakfast, her mind taking a mental inventory of her wardrobe. She had to look her absolute best. After all, she was going to be among the crème de la crème of the fashion world.

When she finished eating, she and Nathan went back to bed. They made love in the golden glow of the sun shining through the closed draperies. As always, it was beautiful, long, tender and satisfying.

After a nap in his arms, she spent the rest of the day blissfully making plans for the trip while Nathan read the paper, polished his automobile, and played with the girls. It was a wonderful day, until they went back to bed that night. She was fast asleep when Nathan woke her up. He was having a nightmare, thrashing about and moaning, like he was trying to speak.

She nudged him and he flinched, then settled down and went back to sleep.

Then, she couldn't sleep. The nightmare worried her, made her believe that there was still something on his mind he wasn't telling her. *Perhaps it has something to do with his run-in with Echel,* she thought, tossing restlessly. *The last time he had a bad dream was when he and Echel weren't getting along.* But of course, she knew Nathan wouldn't talk to her about his dream. He'd had a couple of nightmares since they'd been married and all she had been able to learn about them was that he called them the 'yellow terror.'

Yet, her instincts told her the nightmare was not a coincidence. She stared into the darkness thinking, "What is he worried about? And why is he keeping it from me?"

Chapter 4

London, England
March, 1912

Helen Ryerson sat in a pew at London Presbyterian church between her 'peculiar' sister, Dodie, her shrewish aunt, Agatha Boyle, and her empty-headed cousin, Eliza. Her niece, Annabelle was getting married and the Reverend Paul Stalworth was praying over the couple kneeling in front of the alter.

But Helen couldn't keep her eyes on the bride and groom. Her attention kept drifting to the tall, attractive man sitting across the aisle, two pews up. He bore an amazing resemblance to Gerard Wilson Hale, the man she'd almost married twenty years ago. He appeared to be about forty-five, was a little heavier than Gerard, but his hair was combed the way Gerard used to wear his, and the shape of his head was identical. And that profile. It was so much like his, which was etched in her memory, sweet and painful, sharpened by years of bitter longing.

Oh, dear, what if it is he? she thought. *I couldn't face him. I just couldn't.*

She opened her purse, took out a lavender scented lace handkerchief and blotted the veil of sweat covering her face. Her armpits felt soggy beneath the white heavily laced shirtwaist she was wearing, and her underskirts were damp, sticking to her skin.

Helen's pulse raced erratically, as she pulled her eyes back to the front of the church. But her mind wouldn't cooperate. It was still on the man across the aisle.

I'm imagining things. What would Gerard be doing at Annabelle's wedding?

Then she remembered something. In one of the letters her brother, George had written her, he said he'd have a surprise for her if she agreed to give up her role as a dedicated recluse and came to his daughter's wedding. She'd completely forgotten about it.

Is this it? Gerard Hale? she wondered, then tried to talk herself out of the notion. *No, it can't be. As far as I know, he and Gerard met only once, during the summer Dodie…*

Oh, stop it, she admonished herself inwardly, *you're letting your imagination get the best of you.*

Still, she wished she hadn't let George talk her into coming to London. She opened her purse and was putting her handkerchief inside it when Dodie called out, "Helen, I want some candy. Did you bring some candy? Huh? I want some candy…Helen?" Her voice carried through the church frightening a flock of pigeons nesting in the building's eaves. The pigeons cooed, hooted and took flight, rattling the metal troughs. A spattering of hushed murmurs followed the racket. Several people turned around and looked at them. To

Helen, it felt like every eye in the congregation was upon them.

"Be quiet," Helen whispered, thoroughly annoyed. She searched in her purse for some candy, found a peppermint and handed it to Dodie. "Now promise me you'll be quiet."

"I promise." Dodie's voice was happy and child-like. Smiling, she popped the peppermint in her mouth and sucked on it, her cheeks going in and out like a blowfish.

Helen hated being in public with Dodie. Somehow, she always managed to draw attention to them. She was thirty-eight years old, big-boned, buxom, and a woman in every way, except her mind.

When Dodie was ten years old, the same year their father died, the doctors told them she had the intelligence of a four year old child and would probably remain that way for the rest of her life.

When she was little, she couldn't say her name: Dorothy. It always came out, Dodie, and somehow it stuck. Before long, everyone was calling her Dodie.

Their father, and Helen's step-mother, Beulah had argued bitterly about putting Dodie in a sanitarium. In the end, Beulah prevailed and she was kept at home. To this day Helen believed that keeping her sister at home was her step-mother's way of torturing their father.

Helen sneaked another glance at the man across the aisle wondering if he'd heard Dodie's outburst. Mercifully, he was looking straight ahead, so she refocused her attention on the bride and groom. Reverend Stalworth was leading the couple in their vows: "Do you, Anabelle Ryerson, take thee Edgar Van Billiard, to be your lawfully wedded husband?"

Suddenly, Helen felt a sharp poke in her side. "Isn't that your old beau over there? Gerard Hale?" her Aunt Agatha, whispered, her voice a decibel too loud.

"Where?" Helen whispered, pretending she hadn't noticed.

"There. Across the aisle." Her Aunt Agatha nodded in the direction of the look-alike. "Don't pretend you hadn't noticed. I saw you looking."

Helen glanced nonchalantly across the aisle then whispered, "I don't know what you're talking about." Then, an angry, "Sssshhhh!," came from behind them.

Helen turned slightly and met the annoyed glare of a bald man with bushy white eyebrows. "If you don't mind, some of us would like to *hear* what's being said," he said in a hushed, but irritated voice.

Duly chastised, Helen turned back around. She was actually somewhat grateful for the man's reprimand. Left to her own devices, her aunt Agatha would keep trying to *make* her admit that she'd seen the man, if for no other reason than the pleasure of seeing her squirm. Though her aunt Agatha and Helen's late step-mother, Beulah Cass

Ryerson were physical opposites, they had the same spiteful nature.

Helen got misty-eyed as she watched her niece and betrothed exchange vows. She couldn't help but remember the excitement of planning her own wedding, how she'd looked forward to pledging her love to Gerard. But the wedding never took place and she'd spent the last twenty years regretting it.

Helen glanced across the aisle again. She could have sworn the Gerard look-alike had been looking at her because he jerked his head around as soon as she looked at him. The furtive exchange increased her anxiety and she scanned the church for a quick means of escape. Going through the receiving line was out of the question. She was sure to get delayed there. And if that was Gerard… Oh, she couldn't bear to think of it. Her eyes skipped over the pews of finely dressed people, searched around the high-ceilinged church for a speedy exit. She noticed two large oak doors set in intricately carved casings on each side of the church, and decided she'd have to get to one of them as fast as she could, as soon as the service was over.

She sat there, looking straight ahead, yet seeing nothing, nervously tying a knot in the cord of her blue velvet purse. Finally, Reverend Stalworth pronounced the couple man and wife and the church's gigantic pipe organ blared to life with Mendelssohn's *Wedding March*.

Everyone stood and the happy couple proceeded down the aisle. That's when Helen realized her plan was flawed. She was sandwiched in the middle of the pew, blocked in on both sides. She could only go in one direction, toward the center aisle with the flow of traffic. If she tried to go toward the door at the side of the church, she was bound to cause disruption and draw unwanted attention to herself. As soon as the bride and groom passed their pew, Helen grabbed Dodie's hand, urging her to her feet and toward the center aisle. She peered again in the direction of the 'look-alike' and saw he was also standing. And this time, he looked directly at her. His face flooded with recognition and he waved at her, smiling.

It *was* Gerard Hale! There was no doubt about it now.

"God help me. I have to get out of here," she thought, pretending she didn't see him. She followed the crowd inching toward the center aisle, scared to death that he would reach her before she could get out of the church. Her legs were wobbly and sweat trickled down between her breasts. It seemed like an eternity before they finally reached the end of the pew.

As soon as she stepped into the aisle, someone tapped her on the shoulder. She jerked around, terrified that it was Gerard.

But it wasn't. It was the Hennypecker twins, Mildred and Mathilda, affectionately known to everyone as Millie and Tillie. Helen nearly sighed with relief as the two gnomish little women smiled up at her. They were round as butterballs with wrinkled faces and thin, white hair. Though they were in their eighties, they acted like they were in their twenties and, as usual, they were outlandishly attired. They were wearing silk Indian saris fashioned of the most vivid blues, greens and yellows Helen had ever seen.

"Little Helen Ryerson, how good to see you," one of the Hennypeckers chirped. They both took turns hugging her.

"It's good to see you too." Helen smiled nervously, addressing them as one. She'd long since given up trying to tell them apart. They walked alike, talked alike, were deaf as door knobs and as eccentric as loons. They twittered back and forth as Helen nervously scanned the crowd pulling Dodie along with her in the crush moving toward the vestibule.

"How's your stepmother, dear?" one of them asked, laying a tiny hand on Helen's arm.

"Oh…ah, she passed…two years ago, in April…remember? You came to the funeral."

"In September? Oh, that's too bad." They looked at each other as if it was the first time they'd heard about it, making Helen believe they were losing their memories too.

She'd known the Hennypeckers all her life. They were friends of her late grandmother's on her natural mother's side and Helen was very fond of them. They were enthusiastic world travelers and wherever they went they always sent her a postcard. Once a year, they faithfully dropped in to visit her, and continued the practice after Helen's mother had died and her father remarried. When Beulah was living, she always gave them a chilly reception, but her obvious disdain for the two old ladies didn't deter them.

The Hennypeckers chattered away as Helen pulled her sister along in the slow moving crowd headed for the vestibule. Her nerves were doing a tap dance and she was beginning to feel lightheaded.

Looking for Gerard Hale, she surveyed the mass of people ahead of them in the aisle, but didn't see him. *Perhaps he's already left,* she thought, turning around to make sure he wasn't in the crowd behind them. No Gerard. But when she turned around again, he was standing directly in front of her.

Helen gasped, as she heard him say, "Hello, Helen." Then everything got confused. His lips were moving, he was saying something to her, but she couldn't hear him. His face came near hers, then it was far away. Everything got hazy, the voices around her sounded muffled and far away. Her head started to buzz with a snowy white static. Then everything went completely white, then black.

When Helen opened her eyes, she was looking straight up into the face of Gerard Hale.

She was lying on one of the pews, her head cradled in his lap. Dodie, was peering at them over the back of the pew in front of them, and a small crowd was assembled in the aisle.

Helen's first instinct was to flee. She tried to sit up, but Gerard wouldn't hear of it. "Not so fast my lady," he said, "…we wouldn't want you to swoon away again."

My lady. That's what he used to call me, Helen thought, feeling terribly embarrassed. "Please, let me sit up. I'm perfectly all right. I got too warm, that's all."

She sat up and a few of the onlookers gathered around them walked away. One of the Hennypeckers had a glass of water and handed it to Gerard. He held it to her lips and she drank half the glass.

"Feeling better?" Gerard asked.

"Much better. Thank you." She gave him back the glass.

"Thank heavens he caught you," one of the Hennypeckers said as Gerard handed the glass back to her. "You could have been seriously injured." Then she gave her sister a conspiratorial wink and added, "We can see you're in good hands dear, so Sister and I will see you at the Reception, all right?"

Helen nodded and they left, the rest of the onlookers trailing behind them.

She stood up and Gerard escorted her and Dodie outside. As soon as they were on the sidewalk, her brother, George, rushed up to them. "Are you all right? Someone said you had a spill."

"I'm quite all right," Helen replied as Gerard opened the door to George's automobile for them. Dodie got in and Helen followed.

"It wasn't a spill, George…," Gerard explained, "She fainted. Helen's always been the delicate type, you know. I think seeing me was a bit of a shock for her."

"I see," George replied, his eyes asking her if she truly was okay.

Helen reassured him. "I'm fine, George, so please don't make a fuss."

"If you say so," he replied, and discreetly walked away.

"Will I see you at the Reception?" Gerard asked, standing with the automobile door handle in his hand. His steel gray eyes held a hopeful plea that touched her heart. But all she could utter was, "Perhaps."

Disappointment showed on his face as he closed the door to the automobile. She watched him walk away, an emotional tug of war starting inside her.

All the way to the Reception she debated with herself about going. Part of her wanted to ask George to take her back to the house so she could avoid seeing Gerard again. She was petrified at the thought of being with him, afraid he'd ask her about the past, afraid he'd be able to tell she was still attracted to him.

Yet, another part of her wanted to be with him, longed to know what his life was like. *Was he married? Did he have children? Was he happy? What kind of career had he chosen?* She was paralyzed by indecision.

Twenty minutes later she found herself at the Ritz Hotel where Annabelle's reception was being held due to her sister-in-law's endless renovations on their home.

It was dusk when she stepped out of the automobile and ushered Dodie through the hotel lobby and on to the Palm Court Ballroom. She saw Gerard Hale stand up as soon as she walked through the double doors of the Ballroom. He was standing amidst a sea of white linen covered tables, waving to her to get her attention. Then he started walking toward her, quickly weaving his way through the tables.

"Come, sit with me, Helen," he said when he reached her. "I'd love the pleasure of your company." He took her hand and kissed it. Looking into her eyes, he added, "I promise to be on my best behavior."

"Well, I-I-" she stuttered like an unsophisticated schoolgirl, the woodsy smell of his cologne wrecking havoc with her senses. She turned around to check with her brother and sister-in-law, Eleanor, who'd been right behind her. But now they'd disappeared.

Finding her tongue Helen replied, "For a little while, until George and Eleanor get here."

Gerard led her and Dodie to a table. Walking behind him Helen noticed how nervous she was and inwardly chastised herself: *You old fool, get a hold of yourself. He's not interested in you. He's only being polite. What we had ended ages ago. He probably has a wife and children, even grandchildren."*

As soon as they reached Gerard's table, Helen got confirmation that her brother, George, *had* orchestrated the meeting between them. Sitting on the table, etched in gold Olde English script were white seating cards with her name, Dodie's and Gerard's. It couldn't have been a coincidence.

Gerard pulled a chair out for Dodie, then helped Helen with her chair. When he sat down he flashed her a winsome smile that made Helen's pulse catch. She looked away and saw her aunt, Agatha, her cousin, Eliza, and the Hennypeckers coming toward them. "Oh, yes, this is it," her aunt called out when they reached their table. "Nice seating cards, but the lettering's too small if you ask me."

Just like you to find something to criticize, Helen thought, as the group settled in and everyone exchanged greetings. *And just my luck to be seated with a bunch of busybodies and chatterboxes.*

Avoiding eye contact with Gerard, Helen watched as a stout young man walked over and stood in front of the band. Then the band leader raised his baton, and the musicians started to play, and the young man's beautiful tenor voice filled the room. As he sang *Breathe Soft Ye Winds,* the wedding party discreetly entered the ballroom and took their places at the head table.

Suddenly, Dodie announced loudly, "I've got to pee, Helen. I've got to go now." She squirmed in her chair like a toddler.

Helen felt herself flush. She looked around the Ballroom to see if they were once again the object of everyone's attention. But, luckily, everyone was focused on the tenor and didn't seem to notice them at all. Still, she begrudged the intrusion just as she resented always being at Dodie's beck and call.

"Excuse us," she said, standing, and scuttled Dodie off to the Powder Room. When Dodie finished using the toilet, she made her wash her hands, (otherwise she'd forget), and they walked back to the Ballroom. Coming into the room, she really took notice of its ambiance for the first time since they'd arrived. The bride and groom's table was all dressed up in crisp white linen with a large centerpiece of miniature peach roses, white Alencon lace swags and satin bows. The round guest tables echoed the theme with smaller centerpieces and individual nosegays. Black and white clad waiters stood at attention around the walls, waiting to mobilize at the snap of a finger. Overhead, three enormous crystal and gold chandeliers sparkled like jewels casting brilliant diamond-like facets on the room, giving it a magical, romantic aura.

Approaching their table, Helen overheard her aunt Agatha ask Gerard if he was married.

Much as she hated her prying ways, she was glad she'd asked the question. She was dying to know the answer and slowed her steps, listening.

"I'm a widower, Mrs. Boyle," Gerard answered. "My wife died three years ago."

"Oh, that's too bad," her aunt Agatha replied. She looked up, saw Helen and gave her a victorious wink as she and Dodie took their seats. "Mr. Hale's a widower…," she remarked in that haughty manner that always irked Helen, "Been one for three years now." Triumph spread across her thin, hawkish face, indicating she felt superior because *she'd* gotten information she knew Helen was dying to know.

"I'm sorry for your loss," Helen said to Gerard, unable to meet his eyes. Settling in her chair, she felt like a hypocrite. Deep inside she wasn't really sorry at all. She was glad to know he was free.

"Thank you," Gerard replied, and asked her how she was feeling.

"Fine, really. I'm just not accustomed to the weather over here. I didn't know it got this warm during the day this time of year.

"It's quite odd really, it usually doesn't." He smiled at her setting aflight a rabble of butterflies in her stomach.

Just then, Millie, or was it Tillie? Hennypecker said, "Helen dear, we simply must tell you about the Masai witchdoctor we met in Africa. He completely cured our rheumatism. I tell you, it's a miracle. We'll be eighty-seven our next birthday, you know."

The other Hennypecker broke in. "No, Millie, we'll be eighty-nine."

"Is that so? Well, who cares." Millie waved her hand dismissively, and chuckled. "We're older than sin and richer than shit, I'd say that's a blessing, wouldn't you?"

The other Hennypecker twin laughed raucously and Helen snickered. But her aunt Agatha drew herself up straight in her chair and huffed, "Well!"

Gerard laughed too. He obviously found the two old ladies amusing.

Pointedly ignoring the Hennypeckers, Helen's aunt Agatha set into Gerard with a litany of questions. Helen listened in on their conversation while pretending to pay attention to the Hennypeckers babble on about their trip to Africa. In less than fifteen minutes she'd learned that Gerard had inherited an architect firm from his father-in-law, had two sons who were also architects, was partly retired, and planned to leave the family business to his sons.

Helen said little during the entire eight course meal and ate almost nothing. She was far too nervous. She found her aunt's watchful eye especially nerve wracking, and she was petrified that the past would come up.

However, Dodie gorged on everything. She cleaned her plate, had seconds of everything, and downed three glasses of champagne.

After dessert was served, her aunt Agatha and cousin Eliza left to 'pick the grapevine,' their shorthand for collecting and spreading gossip, their favorite pastime.

The Hennypeckers abandoned them too, saying they were going to look for some lively young men to dance with.

As soon as they all left, Gerard asked, "Is my presence upsetting you? You've barely said a word all evening."

"No," she lied, "not all all. But I am curious about something. How did you happen to be here, in London, at my niece's wedding?" She hadn't heard a word from him since November of 1890. She had no idea what happened to him and even feared he might have been dead.

"Oh, that." Tiny laugh lines creased the corners of Gerard's eyes. "The groom. He's my nephew, my sister's son. He introduced me, or should I say re-introduced me, to George at his and Annabelle's engagement dinner."

"So, was it you who put George up to twisting my arm to get me over here?" She felt it was a presumptuous question, more daring than anything she'd said or done in years. Self-conscious, she dropped her eyes to the tablecloth.

Gerard reached over and took her hand. "I'm guilty as charged. So please don't be angry with him. I was desperate to see you again. I hounded the poor fellow night and day until he told me you'd agreed to come to the wedding. I'd have written you myself had I thought you would have answered me."

"Of course I'd have answered," Helen said. "Why wouldn't I?"

"Well, I guess because you didn't respond to the other letters I wrote you.

"You wrote me letters?"

"Yes, for at least two years after you stopped seeing me."

"I never got them," she replied, her instincts telling her what must have happened to them.

Gerard's steel gray eyes reflected sadness. "That's a shame, for both of us. It may have changed everything."

"Hmmmm," was all Helen could say, guilt and sadness washing over her. She wasn't at all sure he was right.

Just then Dodie patted her arm saying, "Helen, I don't feel so good. I'm sick."

Before she could reply, Dodie pushed herself back from the table, bent over in her chair, and started to vomit. Puke pelted Helen's legs, her skirt and part of her shirtwaist. A collective, "Uuuughh!" spread through the ballroom and couple of waiters rushed over to their table, their noses turned up in disgust.

After she finished vomiting, Dodie slumped back in her chair whining, "Helen, I'm sick. My stomach hurts." Over and over she repeated, "My stomach hurts. Helen, I don't feel good."

Helen was mortified. Tears stung her eyes as she tried to push some of the lumpy, pink slime off her skirt with her handkerchief. It got on her hands and the awful smell made her own stomach queasy.

Gerard sprang into action. He grabbed a linen napkin from the table and wiped the vomit off Helen's skirt. "It's going to be all right, dearest," he assured her. "It was just an accident. The waiters will clean it up."

For several minutes, they were surrounded by activity as waiters moved chairs, mopped the mess up and changed the table linens. One of them brought some warm towels and lemon for her and Dodie to freshen up with. Wiping her hands, Helen wished again that she hadn't come to London. *"I must have been out of my mind to think I could go anywhere with Dodie, especially without help. She manages to ruin everything that might give me a little bit of happiness."*

A few minutes later, George, showed up. He told them Eleanor had a headache and they were going home.

"All right," Helen said, and reached for her purse.

But before she could stand, Gerard leaped to his feet. "Please, George, don't take her away. I've just now managed to get her to talk to me. We've got years of catching up to do. Why not take

Dodie with you so she can rest. I'll bring Helen home later."

"That's all right, George." Helen stood up to leave. "I smell terrible. I'd better go."

Again, Gerard intervened. "I wouldn't care if you smelled like a skunk. I'd still rather spend the evening with you than anyone else. Please stay, won't you?" Helen looked to George for help, but he hunched his shoulders, indicating it was her decision.

An awkward few seconds passed.

Unable to stand the tension, she finally said, "Okay, okay, I'll stay."

After George left with Dodie and they were alone, Helen was amazed at how quickly her fear subsided. She actually started to relax. It could have been the Champagne, but then, Gerard just naturally seemed to know what to say, what questions to ask, and what to avoid. She even found herself laughing as she admitted to him that she still enjoyed reading mystery stories and the poetry of Emily Dickenson and Ella Wheeler Alcott. However, her self-consciousness returned momentarily when she confessed that she'd never married and had spent the last twenty years caring for her step-mother and Dodie.

Some time later, Gerard looked at his pocket watch and exclaimed, "By Jove, I think my watch has speeded up. We've been talking for well over an hour."

Helen laughed. "That long? And I still smell like a garbage dump."

"Oh, go on with you," Gerard said. "But if you're still concerned about it, you can come up to my suite and freshen up. I'm staying here at the Hotel."

The mere suggestion made Helen feel like a Jezebel. "No, I...I couldn't," she stammered. "How would it look? Me, a middle-aged woman, leaving my niece's wedding reception to go to a man's room."

Gerard covered her hand with his. "I hope I'm not just any man, Helen. I don't know what went wrong between us, but I do hope you can find it in your heart to forgive me, for whatever it was I did wrong."

Something about the way he looked at her, that mixture of hurt and longing, touched Helen so deeply she changed her mind. "All right, I'll come up. But you go up first. I'll come up in a few minutes." The last thing she wanted was to be seen going into a hotel room with him. Why, if her aunt got wind of it, it would be trans-Atlantic gossip within hours.

Gerard gave her the room number. "I'll get us some drinks ready," he said, and left. She watched him navigate the tables of the Ballroom and marveled at how little he'd changed. He was still kind, gentle and as handsome as ever, while she had changed so much.

She wasn't the cute little brunette anymore, but a plump, graying spinster. The unfairness of life had scarred her, stole her innocence along with her faith, and turned her into an unhappy, bitter woman.

Yet, as she slipped out of the Ballroom and climbed the stairs to Gerard's room, a glimmer of hope flickered inside her. Maybe, just maybe, the future would be brighter than the past.

"I can't believe I'm doing this," Helen said to Gerard who was washing her skirt and shirtwaist in the lavatory of his hotel room. "I feel absolutely shameless."

She was wearing one of Gerard's white cotton dress shirts, curled up in an armchair in front of the fireplace sipping a glass of champagne.

"Why do you say that? Gerard asked, stepping into the room with his sleeves rolled up, and water dripping from the wet garment in his hand. "You've done nothing to be ashamed of, and besides, you are of age."

"Quite of age, if nothing else," she laughed sarcastically, thinking to herself, *a graying middle-aged woman, the embodiment of withering virtue.*

Then it came to her. *Is that why I came up here? To give myself to him?* The thought filled her with shame, but she had to admit she was curious. Most women her age had experienced intimacy many times, had come to terms with their sexuality. But beyond the passionate kisses she and Gerard had exchanged when they were young and innocent, she knew nothing of love making. And what little she knew about it was gleaned from the romantic prose of Emily Dickenson.

Gerard draped her shirtwaist over the back of a chair saying, "I don't think the skirt came out very well. It's clean, but it's going to take an awfully long time to dry." He darted into the lavatory and came back with a huge, dark lump in his hands. It was dripping all over the carpet. "Gee, this is heavier than I thought," he announced, opening out her skirt and holding it in front of him. "It really looks different wet."

"Oh, no…," Helen exclaimed, realizing it had shrunk. "I should have told you to use cold water. What was I thinking?"

"I'm sorry. I'll replace it," Gerard said. He couldn't have looked more sheepish had he ruined a Monet. "Just tell me where to find another one."

"I wouldn't know where to tell you to go over here. You wouldn't be able to find one tonight anyway. Let's just hope I'll be able to get into it when it dries."

Gerard pulled another chair over to the fireplace and draped her skirt over it remarking, "This thing must weigh ten pounds."

Helen took a sip of her champagne and quipped, "Count yourself lucky. You don't have to wear it."

Gerard came over and knelt beside her chair. Peering up at her he said, "I'm a lucky man. I thought I'd never see you again, and now you're here, close enough to kiss." He leaned over and kissed her gently on the lips.

From deep in her subconscious, a scathing voice condemned her: *You lousy slut. That's why you came up here, to bed down with him like a common whore. Don't fool yourself, Missy. You may still be in love with him, but that doesn't mean he loves you. His wife's dead. He just wants to satisfy his carnal lust.*

Helen pushed the voice away as Gerard cupped her face in his hands, still kissing her.

I'm only human, she silently countered the voice. *What about my needs? Don't I have a right to happiness, to pleasure, just like everyone else?"*

She let herself sink deeper into his kisses. Slowly, a whole new world of sensation spread through her body, growing stronger and stronger.

"Oh, sweet, gentle, Helen," Gerard moaned, his breath hot on her face, "I want you so badly. Please say it's all right."

"Yes," she whispered, desire coursing through her.

He picked her up, carried her into the bedroom and laid her on the bed. With great tenderness he made love to her, giving her the most exquisite pleasure she'd ever felt.

Afterwards, she laid with her head on his chest, listening to his heart beat, loud and fast, it's tempo gradually slowing to a normal, steady rhythm. She smiled to herself in the darkness, amazed at the beauty of what they'd shared. Then her mind turned to his late wife and a wave of sadness washed over her. *It should have been me,* she thought. *It was supposed to be me."* A silent tear rolled down the side of her face.

Gerard caressed her face and noticed she was crying. "Why are you crying? he asked, "Did I hurt you?" His voice held concern. He smoothed the tear away, then kissed her forehead.

"No, I'm fine," she said. "Really. I'm just a little overwhelmed with everything that's happened today. I would never have dreamed that we'd meet again after all these years and make love, all in the same day."

"It is amazing, isn't it?" He kissed her forehead again. "And I want it to last forever."

Forever?! The word broke the magic that she had so willingly given herself to. She sat up and pulled the sheet up to her chin. "Let's not make promises we can't keep," she said. "You have a life here in London and I'm still…well, I'm in New York. Let's just be glad for what we had."

Gerard sat up beside her. "How can you be so cavalier about this? Can't you see I'm still in love with you? I know that may sound absurd, having been married, but I swear it's true. I never *stopped* loving you."

"Then why *did* you marry, if you were still in love with me?" She felt ashamed for asking, but was unable to stop herself.

"Classic rebound stupidity, I guess." Gerard wove his fingers through hers. "It's a pretty long story."

"I'm listening."

"Well, after graduating from Adelphi I had a really bad streak of luck. For a whole year I couldn't keep a job. I'd work a few weeks and the next thing I knww, I'd be laid off."

"Laid off? Why?"

"I don't know. Perhaps it was youth or inexperience, I mean, I've always done my best at whatever I did, but it

never seemed to work out. Every time I was politely told my services were no longer needed. And since you wouldn't see me or answer my letters, I thought I'd give England a try. So I came over here and my uncle helped me get a job with an architectural firm. That's where I met Millicent, the boss's daughter. Her father liked me, and since he didn't have any male heirs, he encouraged the relationship. A year later we got married and six months after that he made me vice-president of the company."

Jealousy eating at her, Helen said, "how fortunate. A generous father-in-law, a loving wife, children - life has really been kind to you."

"Yes and no," Gerard sighed. "My marriage, well, let's just say Millicent and I were ill suited for each other. Nothing I ever did seemed to please her. But at least her father adored me." He laughed, a short, sarcastic laugh. "Millicent used to say I should have married her father."

"Did you love her?" Helen steeled herself for the answer.

"Oh, I guess. I think I loved her because I'd made a commitment to her and she was the mother of my sons. But it was never the kind of love I felt for you. And I think she knew it. From the very beginning we started to drift apart, until...," he paused, "...I know this sounds cruel, but when she died, I realized we'd never been close, never really knew each other at all."

He fell silent and Helen assumed he was reflecting on the past. Knowing that the intervening years hadn't been all goodness and light for him either only increased her sadness. They both had missed so much.

Gerard wrapped his arms around her and smoothed her hair. He kissed her and slowly their passion re-ignited. They made love again and afterwards he held her in his arms and asked her if she would stay in London a while longer.

"That wouldn't be wise. Besides, we're already booked for the *Titanic*."

"Then let me come to New York with you." She could hear the excitement in his voice.

"No," she answered sharply. "That wouldn't be a good idea either." She hoped he wouldn't press the issue, but he did.

"And why not?"

"Well because spending too much time together can only lead to disappointment. We'll both be better off if we just leave things the way they are."

"I can't believe that," Gerard replied. "I don't understand why you won't give us a chance."

"Because we missed our chance. We just have to accept that."

"I can't," he whispered, hugging her. "I lost you once.

I couldn't bear losing you again."

Though it broke her heart, Helen forced the words out of her mouth, "I'm sorry, Gerard, but it's for the best. Let's just keep the memory of tonight in our hearts."

"Believe me, I will till the day I die." Gerard kissed her forhead then fell silent as she nestled close to him.

He was such a good man and she still loved him. So much so she *had* to discourage him. There was no room in her life for him. She was tied to her sister, Dodie, her awful, constant burden; a burden that only death would release her from and she didn't want him a party to that.

Listening to the steady rhythm of his heart, Helen fell asleep.

At the ripe old age of forty-two, she had lost her virginity and spent the night in Gerard's bed, two things she'd completely lost hope would ever happen.

Chapter 5

New Orleans, Louisiana
February, 1912

Jimmy Ray Tuttle handed the telegram to his Pa and fiddled with the brim of his Stetson trying to be patient while he read it. When his Pa finished he looked up at him and scoffed, "This is old news, boy. What the hell are you bothering me with this for? I've got work to do." Scowling, he flung the telegram at him, dismissing him.

Disappointed, Jimmy Ray stood abruptly, alarming old Colonel, his Pa's hound who was lying by his desk. With a wary eye on Jimmy Ray, the dog got up and slinked out of the office with his tail between his legs.

"Don't you see what this means? Jimmy Ray exclaimed. "This is exactly the chance I've been waiting for. That bastard is finally going to pay for what he did to me."

"Is that a fact?" his Pa snickered. "And now just how do you propose to do that?"

Jimmy Ray felt himself getting riled up inside. But he put on a poker face for his Pa. He was twenty-four years old now, and he'd lived with his demeaning since he was four years old, when he and his Ma left Mississippi and moved to New Orleans so she could marry him. Focusing his mind on his goal, Jimmy Ray answered. "I'm gonna to make that bastard suffer the way he made me suffer. Then, I'm going to kill him."

In his mind he'd murdered the object of his hatred a thousand times over, each time in a way more terrible and gruesome than the last.

"Wait a minute, wait a minute." His Pa raised his hand in a halting gesture. "I didn't ask you *what* you want to do. I asked you *how* you plan to do it?"

Jimmy Ray took a deep, tense breath. He should have known that was coming. Now he wished he'd waited until later in the day, after three o'clock. By then his Pa was sure to be drunk and would ask fewer questions.

"Well…uh…it's pretty simple," he stammered. "Me and…, and Earl Lee will take the train up to New York. Then we'll take a ship over to Ireland. You can be sure of one thing, that bastard will never set foot on American soil."

"Simple as that, huh?" his Pa scoffed, leaning back in his chair. "You and that washed up prize fighter are just going to show up and take care of him."

Jimmy Ray bridled at the comment. *"Nothing ever changes around here, does it?"* he thought bitterly. His Pa never missed a chance to badmouth his best and only friend, Earl Lee Earl Lee either. He didn't like him because Earl Lee was a free spirit, the exact reason Jimmy Ray *did* like him. Earl Lee did what he liked and didn't have to answer to nobody. He lived with an old German woman twice his age who raised livestock and gave him money, didn't care about him patronizing the local whorehouse, and didn't make a fuss no matter how long he stayed gone. Sure, Earl Lee wasn't the shiniest spoke in the wheel, but he damned sure knew how to live.

Jimmy Ray's Pa eyed him doubtfully. "Boy, let me tell you somethin'. You're talkin' about goin' after an educated man with city smarts, not one of these country bumpkins around here. This guy is nobody's fool. Maybe you ought to reconsider. I can hire somebody to- "

"No, this is my fight," Jimmy Ray retorted angrily. "I have to handle this myself, in my own way."

His Pa laughed and took a cigar from his inside jacket pocket. He lit it and leaned back in his chair again. "Yeah, you'll take care of it alright." He put a boot clad foot on his desk. "Like the time you got that fool notion to build a tree house, and fell and split your fool head open. Or the time you robbed that old lady and we had to git you out of jail, again. Or, the time you sodomized that ten year old white trash over in Jackson and we had to pay the boy's family to keep 'em from pressing charges. Yeah, Jimmy Ray, I just bet you can handle it."

Jimmy Ray felt his blood begin to boil, a burning mixture of shame and anger. *That shit's in the past,* he thought, *"why do you have to keep throwin' it in my face?"*

He focused his eyes on the bottom of his Pa's boot. "All right, all right. So I've made some mistakes. But this time it'll be different. No mistakes. I promise."

A cloud of gray smoke encircled his Pa's head. "Look, I've got a stake in this too, boy. The last thing I want is him showing up around here. As long as he makes no waves, I keep everything, by default. The whole kit and caboodle. But if you botch it and tip him off, it could cost me plenty."

"I'm not goin' to botch it up, Pa," Jimmy Ray said, confident in the power of the rage bottled up inside him. "You gotta trust me on this. I know what I'm talkin' about."

"I see." His pa nodded then put his other foot up on his desk. "And you say you've got everything figured out." He was pensive for a moment, eyeing Jimmy Ray thoughtfully, then continued. "Okay, so how do you plan to finance your mission? Travelin' is expensive. I doubt Earl Lee can lend you any money. From the looks of it, that old broken down kraut of his is barely able to feed her animals."

"Well, I was gonna git to that. I… I'm gonna need a loan." He hated asking him for money. But the pittance he earned as a clerk in his Pa's business barely paid for clothes and weekly visit to Lillie Belle's whorehouse.

A little too quickly his Pa answered, "Okay, Jimmy Ray, I'll lend you the money."

It caught him off guard. He'd never agreed to lend him money that fast. His Pa's loans usually came after a good deal of groveling and a thousand questions.

Then his Pa took his feet off his desk and added, "On one condition." He stood up and looked down at Jimmy Ray.

"What condition?"

"That you'll accept my proposition."

I should have known, Jimmy Ray groaned inwardly, observing the smug look on his Pa's wrinkled face. *He always has somethin' up his sleeve.*

"What's your proposition?"

"Namely this: if you accomplish your mission, and kill the bastard, I'll give you full partnership in the business with a salary equal to mine. And mind you, I want proof he's dead, not just your word. Now..." he paused and sat on the edge of his desk, "...if you fail, I don't want to see you, or hear from you as long as you live. Is that understood? I want you to disappear, like you'd never been born. (He snapped his fingers for emphasis). And I don't want you contactin' your Ma either. You've given that poor woman nothin' but heartache and misery your whole life. You understand what I'm sayin'?"

Jimmy Ray considered the proposition. His Ma was the dearest thing to his heart, the only one who loved him no matter what he did or how he looked. He hated his Pa for forcing him to choose between her and the satisfaction of revenge he'd waited for so long. But he knew he was testing him to see if he had the guts to carry it out. And sure as rain, if he backed down now, he would call him a coward for the rest of his life.

"Yes...," Jimmy Ray looked his Pa in the eye, "I understand. And I accept your proposition." *Once and for all I'm gonna prove to you that I'm better and smarter than that worthless piece of cow shit.*

A hint of amusement danced in his Pa's eyes as they shook hands, sealing the deal. Then he walked across the room, toward the large portrait of Thomas Jefferson that concealed his safe in the wall. Watching him, Jimmy Ray thought bitterly, *Just like him, no matter how things turn out, he's goin' to make sure he benefits.*

His Pa took the portrait off the wall and called to Jimmy Ray's over his shoulder, "Boy, I sure hope you know what you're doin.' I sure do."

Chapter 6

The big day had finally arrived. The Legardes rose at dawn to start their journey, but started off on an unsettling note. Just before they left the house, Nathan was giving last minute instructions to their housekeeper, Madame Bonet, when she burst into tears. She became hysterical and begged them not to go. She kept saying she was never going to see them again and Nathan had the worst time getting her to calm down. He had to reassure her repeatedly that the *Titanic* was the safest ship in the world and they'd be home safe and sound in a few short months. It upset everyone and when they finally piled into the automobile, they were all teary-eyed and more than a little rattled.

Jules, one of Madame Jacquet's boys from next door chauffeured them to the train station in Nathan's automobile. The ride was somber and Nathan kept thinking about Madame Bonet. She was a good woman, stern but kind, and not usually taken to such bouts of emotion.

Nathan's father had hired her to take care of him soon after he came to Paris. In many ways, she'd become a surrogate mother to him, teaching him the French language and customs, chastising him when he misbehaved, and encouraging him in whatever he did as he grew into manhood.

By the time they got to the train station, passengers were already boarding, so they quickly got on and settled into a carriage for the long trip to Cherbourg. As the train chugged along, the bright orange morning sky outside their window burned away to reveal a clear, beautiful day.

Another couple, Monsieur Adam and Madame Antoinette Renard and their three year old son, Auguste, shared the carriage with them. They, too, were taking the *Titanic* to America. Trista, the Legarde's outgoing three year old, broke the ice by offering Auguste a piece of her chocolate. Before long, they were all talking like old friends.

At four o'clock, the train screeched and puffed into the maritime terminal at Cherbourg. Nathan and his family disembarked and sat on the bustling jetty. They watched the crowds in the warm afternoon sun while their luggage was taken from the train and put on the *Nomadic*, the quay that would take them out into the harbor to meet the *Titanic*. They were told by a dock worker that the *Titanic* couldn't drop anchor at the dock like other ships because it was too big. A band assembled nearby and played a string of rousing marches. Everywhere, the mood was expectant and joyful as people milled about, anxious to get a look at the famous ship. Photographers waited with their cameras at the ready. Newspaper reporters interviewed excited travelers, frantically scribbling comments on their pads. Friends and family members laughed and cried, kissed and hugged, awaiting the final farewell.

At five thirty the Legardes were hustled aboard the *Nomadic* and into a carpeted reception room, only to have to wait again. They saw the Renards and decided to sit with them. By then, everyone was tired except the children who were still full of energy, in spite of missing their afternoon nap. All Nathan wanted to do was get his family settled on the *Titanic* so he could relax.

After an hour of waiting, Nathan got up to stretch, and he and Monsieur Renard decided to go outside on the deck for some air. They leaned against the rail and looked out into the harbor. The temperature had dropped drastically in the last hour and Nathan couldn't help but notice it. It had been at least sixty five degrees during the day and now it felt like it was no more than thirty degrees.

Ripples of gray water lapped and splashed against the side of the *Nomadic*. Behind them, two expensively dressed men, obviously aristocrats approached. "I heard she's late because of trouble in Southhampton," one of them remarked, "a dock hand told me there was an accident."

"An accident?..." the other man replied, "That doesn't bode well for a maiden voyage."

"Indeed," Nathan said to Monsieur Renard, "I don't like the sound of that at all." Again, he remembered Madame Bonet's hysteria. The uneasy feeling it had given him earlier, returned.

"I don't like it either," Monsieur Renard replied, and made a dismissive gesture with his hand, "but it's probably just a rumor, something more to tantalize the public with. You know the newspapers these days."

"You're probably right," Nathan nodded in agreement, only too happy to dismiss what they'd overheard as gossip. "Why don't we agree not to mention this to the women. No sense upsetting them needlessly."

"Good idea." Monsieur Renard pointed over his shoulder with his thumb. "I just hope the gossip isn't circulating in there."

"Mmmm," Nathan barely responded. He stared down into the water, absorbed in his own thoughts, wondering if he'd done the right thing by caving in to Nicolette and letting her and the children come with him.

Perhaps *I should have stuck to my decision,* he mused. *I shouldn't have let her manipulate me. God, if anything happens to her or my girls...* Quickly he pushed the thought away. He couldn't bear to think about it.

Suddenly, Monsieur Renard pointed toward the harbor. "Hey, I think she's coming."

Nathan looked up as loud cheers went up behind them. People spilled out onto the *Nomadic's* deck to get a better look. In the distance, he saw a constellation of light pouring from the *Titanic's* portholes and sidelights. Slowly, the ship entered the harbor off Grande Rade and dropped anchor near Passe de l'Quest.

Thoroughly chilled by the evening air, Nathan and Monsieur Renard rejoined their wives in the reception room. A few minutes later, the *Nomadic's* engine sputtered to life. With a slight jerk, they pulled away from the dock and headed out to rendezvous with the *Titanic*. The band on the jetty played La Marseillaise as people cheered, waved the French flag and threw kisses at their departing loved ones.

A short time later, the *Nomadic* moored alongside the *Titanic*. Nathan was struck with how small the tender looked beside her. *Like a fly next to an elephant.* He and his family waited for their turn to board, then took the automatic conveyor from the *Nomadic* to the *Titanic*. Once on board, they had to wait yet again. Nicolette complained that her feet hurt and, Sabine, the children's aupair, looked wilted. The children were finally tired and whining, and Nathan was so hungry he felt like he could eat a horse.

Finally, a steward came to take them to their accommodations on B deck. With a look of disgust he took their Boarding Passes, told them their luggage would be brought later, and instructed them to follow him. He guided them through a maze of carpeted corridors with cream colored walls. When they finally reached B14, the steward stopped and handed Nathan two keys, one for their stateroom and one for the adjoining room where Sabine and the children would sleep.

He halfheartedly explained the safety precautions, told them where to find their lifebelts, and where the emergency routes were.

As Nathan and his family stood in the hallway listening to the steward, two tall, skinny women wearing large hats adorned with bird's nests and ostrich feathers approached them. The older woman appeared to be about sixty with dark, beady eyes, a long pointy face and hawk beak nose. The younger woman had the same build, same thin lips and pointy face. They were both quite unattractive. Nathan surmised they were related. As they passed, the older woman remarked loud enough for them to hear, "...disgraceful, what's the world coming to?"

Nathan ignored the remark and the women entered the room next to theirs. When the steward finished, Nathan opened the door to their suite and followed Nicolette and the girls into their elegantly appointed, Louis XVI styled rooms.

Grateful that the hustle and bustle was finally over, he let out a great sigh of relief. Standing in the middle of the parlor he spread his arms wide and announced, "Well, ladies, this is it. We're finally headed to America on the great *Titanic*."

Chapter 7

Nathan was famished. To take his mind off of his stomach, he played hide and seek with the children while waiting for their luggage to arrive. It wasn't long before there was a knock on their stateroom door. He went to answer it, his daughters on his heels. When he opened the door a young, freckle-faced steward was standing there, but he didn't have any luggage.

"Can I help you?" Nathan asked.

"Ah, yes…," the steward paused awkwardly before adding,… "Sir. It see see see see seems we're having a pra- pra-problem…," he stuttered, "and uh, you have to moo-moo moo-move to another roo-roo-roo-roo-room." He fidgeted with his necktie and glanced sheepishly at the door next to theirs.

Nathan was immediately suspicious. "What kind of problem?"

The young man attempted to hold Nathan's gaze and the stuttering got even worse. "Well, uh, suh-suh-suh-suh-some of the ah, some of the uh-uh-uh-uh-other pa pa pa pa pa pa…"

"Oh, spit it out man," Nathan said impatiently, his stomach rumbling with hunger.

The steward tried again. "Yes sir, uh, some of the pah-pah passengers are un ha-ha, don't like the roo-roo- roo…" His face was tomato red and Nathan was afraid that if he didn't get out what he needed to say soon, he was going to strangle himself.

The poor man tried again and finally got out a whole sentence. "Some pee-people don't like the roo-room assignments."

"What's that got to do with me?" Nathan asked, his tone curt. He was in no mood to wait a half hour for an answer, but he had to ask.

"We nee-nee-need you to moo-moo-moo move," the steward replied. Then, as if agreeing with himself he nodded, "Yes, to-to the end of the hu-hu-hall."

From the corner of his eye, Nathan saw the stateroom door next to theirs crack open. He caught a glimpse of the buzzard-faced woman they'd seen when they arrived.

Oh, so that's it, he thought. *She put him up to this.*

"Listen, young man," Nathan said loud enough for the woman to hear him, "Our tickets say B14 and B16." He took the ticket stubs out of his pocket and showed them to him. "So if someone has a problem with that, *they* can move."

The cracked door swung open and the eavesdropper stepped into the corridor. She fixed Nathan with a glare as black as her dress and huffed, "I was hoping you'd see reason and move to where you're better suited."

"Better suited?" Nathan was indignant. "Let me tell you something, lady. We have just as much right to be here as you do."

The woman's beady eyes flashed hatred. "Not in my book, you don't. You should be down in the hull with the rest of the steerage. I did not pay top dollar to have to lodge next door to a Nigger."

The poor steward stood there quaking, his eyes darting back and forth between them.

Nathan felt his jaw tighten. He ignored her attempt to belittle him and shot back, "Look, if you don't want to be next door to us, that's fine by me. You can move! We're not going anywhere."

"We'll see about that," she crossed her bony arms in front of her. "I've got a good mind to have you and that half breed litter of yours dumped in the middle of the ocean like the garbage you are."

Before Nathan could respond she darted to the safety of her room. Standing in the open doorway, she pointed a skeletal finger at him. "Mark my word, you'll rue the day you crossed me." Then she slammed the door.

Nathan ground his fist into the palm of his hand. He felt like breaking every bone in her skinny body. He had never hit a woman in his life, but as far as he was concerned, she had crossed the line. How dare she attack his family. They were every bit as good as she was. In his eyes, better.

Inching backwards, the steward said, "I gu-gu guess you're not moo-moo-moving, huh?"

"Hell no!" Nathan shouted and the steward jumped and took off down the corridor.

When he turned around, Nicolette was standing in the doorway of their suite with the children. "What was that all about," she asked.

He walked inside and closed the door behind him. "That old battle ax next door. She wants us moved."

A knowing look passed between them. But before Nicolette could say another word, little Trista yanked on the leg of his trousers. She peered up at him, her face sweet as an angel and asked, "Papa, what's a nigger?"

It caught Nathan off guard. He wasn't expecting a question like that for at least a few more years. He reached down and picked her up. "Well, a nigger is…"

Nicolette flashed him a disapproving look and shook her head, so he decided to put the explanation off. "I'll tell you when you have a few more birthdays."

"Why can't I know now?" Trista complained.

He rubbed his nose to hers like an Eskimo, and made her giggle. "Because right now your Papa has a very hungry tummy and we need to have dinner so you and your sister can go to sleep in your brand new bed. And if you show your best behavior at dinner, we'll let you have some ice cream for dessert. How's that?"

"Yummm," she said, then jumped down and ran into the adjoining room yelling, "Sabine, Papa said we're going to have ice cream."

The luggage finally arrived a few minutes later, then Nathan and his family went to dinner. They were sitting in the Jacobean styled dining salon and had just placed their orders when Nicolette remarked, "You know, Nathan, we could have moved to another stateroom. The luggage hadn't come yet, so it really wasn't worth alienating that woman over it. Really, I don't know what's gotten into you lately."

"What's gotten into me?" Nathan said defensively. "I didn't alienate anyone. She alienated me."

"Perhaps, but the whole ugly scene could have been avoided."

"I can't believe you actually said that," he retorted. "You know why she wanted us to move, yet you're agreeing with her."

"No, I'm not agreeing with her. But it wouldn't hurt you to try and be a little more cooperative."

"Cooperative? With a bigot?" He had to struggle to keep his voice down.

"All I'm saying is you don't always have to draw such a hard line."

Frustrated with her inability to see that he was right, that he was only defending his family, he shot back at her, "Well if that's the case, then we all might as well just cooperate with the old crow and go jump in the ocean right now."

Nicolette narrowed her eyes at him, letting him know she didn't care for his sarcasm. But she didn't say another word.

Dinner arrived and was served with a Continental flourish. Nathan's steak was sizzling hot and seasoned to perfection. But the tension that hung over their table rendered his excellent meal less than satisfying.

So be it, Nathan thought, chewing his steak. *All I did was stand up for my family, for what's right. If she can't understand that, well, that's just too bad.*

Chapter 8

"Oh, they're cute as buttons, aren't they, Edith?"

"They look like little Japanese dolls," her companion replied.

Nathan and his family had just left breakfast and were strolling on the First Class Promenade. Little Trista was pushing her baby sister, Cecile, who was sitting up in her pram. Occasionally, Nathan or Nicolette helped her steer so she wouldn't run over anyone's feet.

When they were directly in front of the two women lounging in their deck chairs, they exchanged congenial smiles. One of them remarked, "We couldn't help admiring your girls. Such beautiful children. Are you folks American?"

"I'm American," Nathan replied. "My wife is French."

"You don't say. Edith's ancestors are French," the woman remarked and nodded toward her companion. "She's returning from a visit with relatives in Paris. I'm Emma Bucknell, and this is my friend, Edith Evans."

"How do you do?" Nathan replied and introduced his wife. They chatted with them about the beauty of the ship and the crispness of the weather until Cecile started to fret. Then they bid the women a bon voyage and went on to their stateroom.

They'd just gotten in and Nathan was getting Trista settled with her toys when someone knocked on the door. He went to answer it and called over his shoulder to Nicolette who was changing Cecile's nappy, "I hope this isn't more nonsense from that old biddy next door." As far as he was concerned, she'd caused enough strife between him and Nicolette already. To end the impasse last night and restore the peace, they'd finally had to agree to disagree and just let the issue drop.

When Nathan opened the door, a smartly uniformed messenger tipped his hat and said in a rich Irish brogue, "I've a wireless for a Monsieur Legarde." He leaned sideways and looked past Nathan into their stateroom. Then he looked back at him, his brow knit tentatively, "Are you Monsieur Legarde?"

"Yes. Do you need proof?" Nathan snapped.

"I guess that won't be necessary," he handed Nathan a clipboard with a receipt attached. "You have to sign for it." He gave Nathan a pen and pointed to where he should sign.

Nathan signed his name on the receipt and the messenger ripped out a carbon copy and gave it to him. Then he reached in his breast pocket, took out a slip of paper, handed it to Nathan and walked away without another word.

"Who would be sending you a message here?" Nicolette asked, positioning the baby on her hip.

"Echel," Nathan chortled, looking at the wireless message. "Listen to this. 'Urgent. Stop. Encountered solid wall. Stop. What should we do? Stop. Please respond. Stop.'" He waved the message in his hand. "Can you believe it? I told you the man is an idiot. I don't work for the Metro anymore. Did he forget he fired me? He has some nerve contacting me here."

"Well, are you going to answer it?" Nicolette asked, her expression conveying that she already knew the answer.

Nathan felt torn. Shoving the message in his pocket, he said, "I don't know. We were supposed to take a tour of the ship, remember? Why should I spend my time sending him a telegram after the way he treated me?"

Nicolette gave him a knowing smile. "Because that's the way you are."

Deep inside, Nathan knew she was right. He *had* to respond. Not for Echel, but for the Metro workers. They were good, family men. He respected them, and they respected him. If he didn't help Echel, he was bound to do something stupid and the men would be the ones to pay for it. Knowing him, he'd put them in danger by trying to blast through the wall, or work them to exhaustion trying to chisel through it, when the best solution would be to go around it. What if someone got hurt? Or worse, killed? Could he live with himself if he didn't reply?

"Looks like we're going to have to postpone our tour of the ship," Nathan groaned, casting an apologetic look at Nicolette. "Don't worry about it. We can go another time," Nicolette replied. "While you're out, I'll go to the Reading Room and write a couple of letters."

Nathan went to their bedroom, grabbed one of his walking sticks from the armoire, kissed Nicolette on the cheek, and left. He took the automatic lift up to A deck and hailed a passing officer to ask for directions to the Wireless office.

The name on the officer's lapel pin read 'Hitchens.' He pointed skyward and said, "It's up on the Boat deck, off the forward Grand Staircase on the starboard side. Go to the purser's suite and look for the inquiry office. That's where you have to give them your message."

Nathan thanked the officer and headed for the metal stairs leading up to the boat deck. Overhead, seagulls called, and he watched them soar in the clear blue sky above the the ship's massive smoke stacks, spires and telegraph lines.

Once inside the purser's suite, he passed several open front offices where passengers stood in lines to deposit or retrieve valuables, purchase tickets for the Turkish baths, rent deck chairs or obtain passes for the swimming pool. When he finally reached the inquiry office, there was yet another line where passengers waited to send their messages. He got at the end of the line to await his turn.

At the front of the line he saw, a heavily jeweled grand dame with a chinchilla draped carelessly about her shoulders. Nathan overheard her exhort breathlessly, "Oh, just say, 'Having a ball, wish you were here, love, Zette.'" Then she changed her mind and started all over again, holding up the line.

Suddenly, Nathan felt a poke between his shoulder blades. "Get out of the way," a gravelly voice commanded, "I've got business to take care of."

Nathan turned around. An old, nearly bald man was scowling up at him from a wheelchair. He had a brown tartan lap blanket covering his knees and clutched a black walking stick in his knotty hands. A dour-faced manservant stood behind the man's wheelchair.

"I'm in line to send a wireless," Nathan replied as pleasantly as he could, and turned back around.

"I don't care what you're in line for," the old man bellowed. "My business is important. Now get out of the way."

"You tell him, grandpa," a blonde man wearing a grey Stetson yelled from across the room. Then he snickered and whispered something to his companion.

Nathan had seen the two men station themselves against the wall shortly after he'd come in. The one who'd spoken was tall, thin, and pale with a blade nose and piercing, cobalt blue eyes.

His mouth was a wet, red slit beneath a nicotine-stained moustache, and his hair hung in greasy strings from beneath his hat. The fellow with him was dark-haired and burly with a pock-marked face. A bulbous nose sat off-center on his face and a scar ran from the corner of his mouth to his left ear. They were seedy-looking characters, not at all the sort Nathan would've expected to find in First Class on the *Titanic*.

Nathan gave the two men a pointed look and turned his back on the old man, ignoring him. But a few seconds later, the old man poked him in the back again, this time even harder.

"You must be hard of hearing," the old man growled. "Or else you don't know who I am. I'm Horace P. Clinch, one of the wealthiest men on this ship. Why, my company supplied most of the steel for this rig."

The men against the wall burst into laughter. Between guffaws, the thin one called to Nathan, "Better watch out there, grandpa could have you locked up."

"Yeah, or beat the hell out of him with that hobble stick," the other one quipped. "Now wouldn't that be a sight?" They leaned their heads back and laughed hysterically.

Nathan turned around and said to the old man, "Mister, I don't care who you are. I've got business to take care of too." He was angry and upset with the old man and the ignoramuses heckling him. But he was determined not to give them the satisfaction of seeing him upset.

While the old man was well dressed and probably well educated, Nathan could tell he was cut from the same cloth as the hecklers. They were the type who got their kicks from debasing other people.

"What kind of business would someone like you have anyhow?" The old man sneered at him. "Did your master send you up here?"

"I'm no one's servant," Nathan said, proudly. "I'm an engineer."

Shock skittered across the man's withered face. "An engineer?" Then he started to laugh along with the hecklers. "Hah, hah, hah, hah. An engineer... hah, hah, hah, hah. Now I've heard everything. Hah, hah, hah..."

Like an invisible disease, their laughter spread to the people in the line, until everyone was laughing. Nathan felt like the fat lady at a circus freak show.

Suddenly, a wireless operator burst into the room shouting, "Pipe down out here! We can hardly hear ourselves think back here. What's going on out here anyway?"

The old man pointed his cane at Nathan. "Here's your culprit. Forcing his way in line ahead of decent folks."

"Hey, you!" the Wireless Operator gave a sharp whistle and pointed at Nathan. "To the back of the line."

Nathan shot the old man a murderous look and said to the Operator, "You were misinformed. I didn't cut in front of him. I was here first."

"If you plan on sending a wireless you'll do as I say," the Operator shot back, ignoring him. Then he gave Clinch a nod and a wink, as if to say "that ought to fix it," and headed back to his office shouting, "now, keep it down out here. We have to be able to hear if you want us to get your messages right."

Nathan stepped out of the line. "To hell with it," he thought, "I don't have to put up with this shit." But just

as he reached the door, he remembered the men working underground on Line Seven and his conscience started to eat at him. *They're the reason you came up here in the first place. Are you going to let a bunch of morons cause you to put them in danger?*

He turned around, and with his head held high, retraced his steps and got back in line. Standing there he thought to himself, "Be a man, Nathan. Don't let these fools control you with their ignorance."

A few minutes later the hecklers walked past him on their way out. The skinny one flashed him a mocking, rotten-toothed grin and tipped his Stetson while his companion snickered.

Good riddance, Nathan said inwardly.

Then the old man left too. On his way out he was so busy verbally flogging his manservant, he didn't even look Nathan's way.

The line moved quickly with Clinch's departure. When it was his turn, Nathan walked up to the inquiry officer's desk and gave him the instructions for Echel. The Officer typed the message out on a typewriter, then announced, "That'll be twelve shillings and sixpence."

Nathan paid him and the officer put the message in a round metal container and inserted it into a pneumatic tube. With a loud *whoosh* it was sent back to the wireless office. Handing him his receipt, the inquiry officer said, "You're that Negro who claims he's an engineer, aren't you?"

"I *am* an engineer," Nathan replied.

A sneer spread across the Officer's face. "Well, I'd sure like to know what college you went to. Maybe they'd let my dog, Rusty in." Then he threw his head back and howled with laughter.

Anger shot up inside Nathan like a flame and he balled his hands so tight he could feel his fingernails dig into the flesh of his palms. But he forced himself to stay calm and waited for the Officer to stop laughing. When he finally did, Nathan pointed his walking stick at his chest and said, "I'd suggest you remember something. Since you work for the White Star Line, and I'm a paying passenger on this ship, *you* work for *me*."

The officer's mouth dropped open and he went red to the tip of his ears.

Nathan tucked his walking stick under his arm and strode away. Several people waiting in the line flashed him nasty looks, but he didn't care. He'd put up with enough. He wasn't one of those Negroes who laughed it off when insulted, or simply took it. And the sooner the people on this ship learned he was not going to put up with their bigotry, the better things would be for everybody.

Chapter 9

You should see this monster. It scares me when I think about how huge it is. I doubt I'll ever see anything like it again. The babies are well and keep us all busy. Nathan sends his love and so do I. Love always…

Nicolette signed off on her letter to her step-parents. They were in their ninetines now and age had dimmed their sight, so she hoped they'd find someone to read the letter for them. She loved them dearly and it made her sad to think that they might not be around much longer.

She folded the letter written on White Star stationary and inserted it in an envelope. Then she dropped it and the one she'd written to their housekeeper, in her pocket.

Looking around at the incredible opulence of the Georgian styled Reading Room nearly took her breath away. Its ambiance was completely feminine, expressed in its rose colored carpet, pink draperies and sumptuous armchairs. It made her feel pretty just being there. She was about to get up from the writing desk when a strong, female voice came from behind her. "Excuse moi, Madame."

Nicolette turned to find a buxom woman with auburn hair, and a pleasant, oval face smiling at her. "I apologize for intruding, but I just had to speak to you."

"Oui?" Nicolette replied. She remembered the woman's face from Cherbourg. She'd seen her on the *Nomadic* with a lively group of aristocrats.

"The name's Margaret Brown. My friends call me, Molly." She offered Nicolette a lace gloved hand. "I know just about everyone on this ship worth knowing, from bow to stern. Figured there was no harm in making your acquaintance too."

"That's very nice of you. I'm Nicolette Legarde." She shook the woman's hand taking an instant liking to her. She was brassy, dressed a little sassy, and not so full of herself that she couldn't approach a stranger. From what Nicolette had observed so far, almost everyone in First Class associated only with their families or people they already knew.

"Nice to meet you, Nicolette." Mrs. Brown pulled a chair over from a nearby table and sat next to her. In a conspiratorial tone she said, "I have to confess. I had an ulterior motive for wanting to meet you. I'm dying to know who your dressmaker is. Me, and several of my lady friends noticed the brown velvet number you had on yesterday. Never seen anything like it." She looked admiringly at the ensemble Nicolette was wearing. "Boy, they should see this one." It was an emerald green taffata skirt topped with a gold trimmed bolero jacket over a ruffled, cream-colored shirtwaist.

"That's very kind of you," Nicolette replied.

Mrs. Brown leaned close and said in a hushed tone, "Please don't think me rude, but I really do want the name of your dressmaker."

"Actually, I'm the dressmaker," Nicolette replied proudly. "It's sort of a hobby of mine."

Mrs. Brown's smile urged her to continue and Nicolette warmed to her subject. "Sometimes, I get ideas, sketch them out and make them. Other times, I re-work ordinary patterns, you know, experiment. Sometimes it works. But I've had a few disasters." She laughed, recalling a few that were unwearable.

"Disasters?" Mrs. Brown shrieked. "Honey, you've got talent. My friend, Lady Gordon, would defang a lion for a dressmaker with your gifts."

"Lady Gordon?!" Nicolette's heart skipped a beat. "*The* Lady Gordon? The couturier?"

"One and the same. "You folks in Paris call her Madame Lucile. I just call her Lady Gordon. You know, give her the proper respect."

Nicolette could hardly believe it. She was actually talking to a friend of the famous designer, the grand dame of haute couture. Wealthy women the world over flocked to Madame Lucile's salons in Paris and America for their trousseaus. She'd even heard it rumored that Madame designed naughty unmentionables for the women of the British Royal family.

"How wonderful to have such a friend." Nicolette was awestruck.

"Listen, would you like to meet her?" Mrs. Brown replied. "She really is quite a gal, don't let the title fool you. But she and Sir Cosmo are traveling under an assumed name. For privacy, you know. So please don't spread it around that she's on board. Poor gal, the press would be all over her."

"Oh, I understand," Nicolette said. "But it is all right if I tell my husband, isn't it? I assure you he won't breathe a word to anyone."

"Sure." Then Mrs. Brown's brow crinkled. "Uh, speaking of husbands. I hope you won't be offended by my asking, but is your husband the brown skinned man I saw you with on the *Nomadic*?"

Nicolette's excitement started to fade as she scanned Mrs. Brown's face, attempting to read how she was going to react to her answer. Not that she would lie. But people's attitude toward her often changed when they learned she was married to a Negro. More than once, she'd been verbally attacked and called ugly names because of it.

"Yes, that was my husband," she answered softly.

"I see." Mrs. Brown leaned toward her. In a conspiratorial tone she remarked, "Well, between you, me and the doorpost, honey, if he's half as nice as he is handsome, I'd say you're a lucky gal."

Nicolette almost sighed with relief. But she still had a concern. "What about Madame? "Would she be willing to meet me if she knew about my husband?"

"Well," Mrs. Brown paused as two stylishly dressed women who could have been patrons of

Madame passed by, their voices hushed murmurs, "Lady Gordon isn't as open-minded as I am, but she's not a racist. The way I see it, it's irrelevant, anyway."

Nicolette was only too glad to take her word for it. "When do you think I can meet her?" she asked.

Mrs. Brown loosened the drawstrings of her black crocheted purse, took out a calling card and handed it to her. "I'm in cabin B1. Stop by around one o'clock this afternoon. Lady Gordon and I are having lunch together. Afterwards, I'll see if I can get her to swing by my room for a few minutes so I can introduce you. How's that sound?"

"Fantastique! Merci, Madame Brown. Merci."

"Think nothing of it. And call me Molly. I'd like to think I made a friend." She stood and shook Nicolette's hand. "Just try not to be late. I have an appointment at that fancy hair dressing shop at two o'clock."

"I'll be there," Nicolette replied. She watched her sashay away, then grabbed her purse and dashed out of the Reading Room. She couldn't wait to tell Nathan the news.

When Nicolette reached their stateroom, she rushed in and found Nathan reclining on the sofa in the parlor with a copy of the *Atlantic Daily Bulletin* spread across his chest.

"Nathan, you won't believe this. I just met the most incredible…"

Struck by the strained look on his face, she stopped. "What's wrong?"

He closed the newspaper and sat up. "The *Titanic*, that's what's wrong. The people on this ship are a bunch of ignorant buffoons." His voice vacillated between hurt and anger as he told her about the incident at the inquiry office. Throwing the newspaper to the floor he shouted, "Dammit, I've a good mind to report it to the Captain, let him know just how I feel about it."

Nicolette sat down beside him and caressed his shoulder. She wished she knew what to say, but she didn't. Her instincts told her the best way to handle this, was to let him work through it on his own. He was amazingly resilient. He'd get angry and argue and rant, but he'd be back to his old cocky self in a few hours. So she put her arms around him and they sat quietly for a while. Slowly, she felt the tension ease from his body.

After a few minutes Nathan remarked, "When you came in, you said you'd met someone. Who?"

"Oh, it was incredible," Nicolette exclaimed, sitting up straight. "Her name is Margaret Brown. She told me to call her Molly. We met in the Reading Room. She's going to introduce me to a friend of hers. And guess who her friend is?"

Nathan shrugged.

"Le Madame Lucile!" Never in my wildest dreams would I have imagined I'd get the chance to meet the most famous couturier in the world." She still hadn't gotten over it.

"That's not a good idea." Nathan's tone was flat. "I don't want you getting all excited and thinking about working again. Your job is to take care of our home and the children. You have enough to do."

"Who said anything about working? I'm only going to meet her." Nicolette got up from the sofa and poured herself some water from the pitcher on the parlor table.

Nathan rolled his eyes at her. "I know you, ma cherie. I can see how excited you are. Before long you'll be all keyed up again, thinking you can be a mother and a career woman."

"Hmmph!" She took a drink from her glass and sat it on the table. "In case you haven't noticed, lots of women work these days."

"See what I mean? Already you're regressing. We already decided the children and our home come first."

She glared at him, frustration brewing deep inside her. "No, you decided. I didn't agree to any such thing."

"I don't see why you're making such a fuss over this," Nathan complained. "Aren't you happy with the life we have? Don't I provide well enough for you and the children? What else do you want?"

She stood up, crossed her arms, and looked down at him. "For starters, how about respecting that I have a mind and talent, and I want to use them. Or understand that my having a career would not be a threat to you or our family."

"That's absurd. How do you think you working would look to our friends? And what about the children? Don't they deserve to have a mother?"

She threw up her hands. "That's ridiculous! They'll always have a mother."

Nathan wasn't fooling her. She knew exactly what he was leading up to. Every time they had this discussion, he threw it in her face that none of their friend's wives worked and it would look like he couldn't adequately keep her and his children if she did. And then he'd make her feel guilty, accuse her of wanting to put her 'fanciful notions' ahead of her duty to their family.

Aggravated, she groaned, "All I want is to meet Madame Lucile. I don't know how or why we're even talking about anything else."

"I'll tell you why. Because you're bound to start up again with talk about having a career. It's temptation and it'll only lead to discontent."

"So what are you saying? She huffed. "Are you forbidding me to meet her?"

He got up from the sofa and headed for the bedchamber, "Take it any way you want."

Suddenly, Nicolette's frustration turned to anger. Following him, she shouted, "You're a hypocrite. You're always talking about fairness and equality, but in your book, that only applies to men. Women don't count."

He whirled around to face her, his eyes snapping. "I'm not even going to justify that with an argument. I told you how I feel. It's up to you to make the right choice." He went into the bedchamber and closed the door.

Nicolette stood there, glaring angrily at the door. *Why can't he understand? Why?* Her wanting a career had nothing to do with him. She needed the satisfaction of conceiving things in her own mind, seeing them take shape and form and become beautiful works of wearable art from her own hands. She felt proud when other women admired her creations, the same way he felt pride in his profession.

Angry, she plopped down on the sofa, mumbling to herself, "You are not going to dictate to me. I'm going to meet Madame Lucile, whether you like it or not."

Chapter 10

Helen searched for a sunny spot to rest on the enclosed Promenade on B deck. She'd had a hectic morning. First, she and Dodie joined her aunt Agatha and cousin Eliza for breakfast. Then they all went to the hair salon to get their hair dressed. After that she had to go up to the inquiry office to send a message home to notify her driver of their expected arrival time in New York. After she sent her message she rented some deck chairs and had almost reached the Promenade when Dodie started to whine because she wanted her dog, Houlie. So she had to go all the way back up to the Boat deck to get him from the kennel. With Dodie and her dog in tow, she wearily walked the teak-floored Promenade from one end to the other, searching for a spot for their deck chairs. But she couldn't find room anywhere. She was about to give up when she saw a young couple toward the middle of the Promenade get up, fold their chairs and leave. Holding a deck chair in one hand and Houlie's leash in the other, she rushed to claim the spot before someone took it. As soon as they sat down and got settled, Houlie started sniffing at Dodie's coat pocket. Then he tried to get into it with his snout.

"Houlie, stop it," Helen ordered, and yanked on his leash. Then she asked Dodie, "What's in your pocket this time?"

"Nothing," Dodie answered. But Helen knew she was lying.

She sat up in her deck chair, then reached over and stuck her hand in the pocket of Dodie's coat. She felt something warm and slippery and pulled her hand out. Her fingers were smeared with chocolate. *Business as usual*, she thought bitterly. She was always hoarding something; hunks of meat in her purse, baked sweet potatoes in her pillowcase. One morning she had put her foot in her shoe and found that Dodie had lined it with bread.

Helen flashed Dodie a look of disgust, then reached in her pocket for her handkerchief and wiped the chocolate from her hand.

The sun was warm, so she took off her coat and made Dodie do the same. To keep Houlie away from Dodie's pocket, she balled her coat up and stuck it under her deck chair. Finally, she was able to lean back and rest. But she couldn't relax. More and more over the years, Dodie's presence galled her. She was sick of taking care of her. This trip, her first public venture in years, seemed to intensify the feeling that she was permanently yoked to her, trapped forever. She imagined that raising a house full of children couldn't be more trying. At least they'd grow up one day, get married and become self-sufficient. But Dodie never would. She would never be free of her.

Loud talking drifted from downwind and Houlie started barking, rousing Helen from her private thoughts. She craned forward, peering in the direction of the noise and saw the Hennypecker twins. The two old ladies were sporting khaki safari outfits complete with boots and white safari hats. They were arguing with a young, not so innocent, or nice, movie actress Helen recognized from the *Saturday Evening Post.* One of the Hennypeckers was holding onto a deck chair and the actress was trying to wrest it away from her.

"I don't care how old you are," the actress shouted, "I paid for this chair and I'm keeping it. You ought to be inside with the rest of the old folks anyway." Helen could tell the Hennypeckers were arguing back, but their age- softened voices didn't carry as well as the actress's.

Over the ruckus, from somewhere on the deck, came the faint strains of *Let Me Call You Sweetheart,* being played by a violin. Helen felt her pulse catch. The song had been her and Gerard's favorite, years ago when they were courting. It was getting closer and closer.

She looked away from the argument, in the opposite direction and her heart nearly stopped. Gerard Hale was walking toward her followed by two violinists. A red, long-stemmed rose was in his hand and he wore a smile so handsome and adoring she instantly felt like crying. *Oh, no, he followed me,* she thought, suddenly feeling trapped. *Why didn't he listen to me? I don't think I can turn him away again. I don't think I have the strength.*

She'd refused to see him again after that night in London. She thought she'd made it clear, that that was all there would ever be. *Why couldn't he simply accept it?*

Every eye on the Promenade went to Gerard as he walked up to her and dropped to his knees. Speechless, Helen sat there feeling awkward and self-conscious.

Gerard handed her the rose and gallantly placed his hand over his heart. "Dear lady," he said, "I love you with all my soul. The depth of the ocean can't measure what I feel for you. My remaining days on this earth would be blessed with joy and peace if you would be my wife." He reached in his pocket, took out a small, powder blue velvet case and opened it. Inside was the very same ring he'd given her twenty years ago. Time had done nothing to dim its beauty. It sparkled in the sunlight, beckoning to her.

He looked deep into her eyes. "Dear, sweet Helen, will you marry me?"

A part of her wanted more than anything to say, yes, to wrap her arms around him and declare her undying devotion. But she couldn't. Dodie, her albatross stood in the way. She was chained to her and only death would release her.

She sat there, her mouth agape, not knowing what to say. In her heart she knew Gerard truly had to love her to propose to her again, especially after the awful way things ended between them.

Everyone on the Promenade gathered around them and even Houlie stopped barking. The crowd watched in silent expectation and she felt like they were holding their breath, waiting for her answer. Finally, she whispered demurely, "Gerard, please, I thought you understood. I can't."

"But why?" he pleaded. "Helen, I know you care for me. You can't convince me otherwise."

"Yes…,but…but I'm not free," she said, keeping her voice low. "I want to marry you, but I can't.

"Then tell me *why* you can't," he insisted. "You're still single. I don't understand. Please, don't cut me off again, not without telling me why. I deserve that much, don't I?"

She anxiously scanned the Promenade, embarrassment burning her face. People were leaning awkwardly, standing on tiptoes, trying to catch every word of their conversation. She'd always hated being the center of attention and she was certainly the object of everyone's attention now. Two middle aged women walked past the gaping crowd and she could tell by their furtive glances that they were embarrassed for her. The whole spectacle was too uncomfortable for words. Somehow, she had to put an end to it.

"Okay, Gerard, I'll tell you," she said. "But not here, please. I can't discuss something so personal in public."

A murmur of disappointment coursed through the onlookers and they started to drift away.

"All right, then how about dinner tonight, say around eight o'clock?"

She nodded her head, yes, and said, "We're in B69."

Gerard kissed her hand and stood. "Adieu sweet Helen, I'll see you at eight." He bowed slightly at the waist, tipped his hat at Dodie and left. The violinists followed him down the Promenade, still playing their song.

Chapter 11

"Maybe something's wrong with her, Madame. I can usually get her to stop." Sabine, the Legarde's au pair bounced the baby in her arms, but she continued to cry inconsolably.

It was already one forty five in the afternoon and Nicolette was getting ready to leave for her meeting with Molly Brown and Madame Lucile. She had only a few minutes to get there. If she didn't leave now, she was sure to be late.

For a moment, she hesitated, torn between her crying child and her desire to make her meeting. She wanted so badly to leave and let the au pair take care of the child. After all, that's what she was there for. *And besides, it's was probably nothing more than colic any way.*

But Cecile was *her* baby, and her responsibility. How could she leave with her crying like that? And what if she really was sick? She'd feel terrible and Nathan would never let her hear the end of it.

Nicolette dropped her sketch pad and handbag on the parlor table. She took off her white lace gloves, tossed them onto the handbag and went over and checked the baby's nappy. It was dry. She felt her forehead and stomach to see if she had a fever. She was warm, but she wasn't hot. Then she went into the adjoining room, found her bottle, came back and tried to put it in her mouth. Still wailing, the baby pushed it away.

Nicolette couldn't understand why she was crying so. She took her from Sabine, laid her over her shoulder, and walked the floor with her.

"Shhh, Shhhh, ma pauvre bebe," she cooed, gently caressing her back. But it was to no avail. She wouldn't stop crying.

The moments ticked by, and with it her golden opportunity. She'd wanted so badly to show Madame Lucile her sketches, to find out from her if she thought she had any real talent. But that wouldn't happen now.

Finally, she sat on the sofa and rocked the baby back and forth thinking, *Nathan would have to be out when I need him. Any other time, he'd be under foot, like one of the children.*

The more she thought about how easily he came and went, how he had a profession and children and no one questioned his adequacy as a father, the more her resentment grew.

She looked over at the clock on the wall. It was one fifty-five, too late to make it to her meeting, even if Cecile suddenly stopped crying. She stared at the clock through a watery blur and worried about what Madame Lucile and Molly Brown thought of her for not showing up. *They probably think I'm ill-mannered and irresponsible, and who could blame them?* Tears rolled down her face as she continued to rock the baby.

Ten minutes later, when Nathan waltzed in with a newspaper under his arm, the baby was still crying. Nicolette lit into him. "Well, you couldn't have planned that better."

"What are you talking about?" Nathan gave her a quizzical look.

"Thanks to you, I missed my meeting with Mrs. Brown and Madame Lucile. Not that *that* would disappoint you. The baby has been crying for almost an hour and neither Sabine or I can get her to stop."

"I don't see how that's my fault." Nathan said, dropping his newspaper on the parlor table next to Nicolette's purse. He walked over and reached for the baby. "Here, let me have her."

Nicolette gave him the baby and watched him repeat everything she had done: check her nappy, check for a temperature, try to give her the bottle. Nothing worked. Then he sat down with her, and laid her on her stomach across his knees. Rocking softly, he rubbed her back, and gradually, she stopped crying. In a couple of minutes she was fast asleep.

Nicolette sat across from them, her discontent turning to hurt as her husband put the child to sleep. "That's all it took," she thought. "I missed my appointment, and that's all it took. A simple technique, and I didn't know to do it."

As she got up and walked toward the bedchamber it occurred to her that Nathan knew how to mother their children better than she did. The thought only made her feel worse, like she was a dismal failure as a mother.

But her anger at him went even deeper. Not only did he make her feel incompetent as a mother, lately, she felt he disapproved of her, disapproved of who she really was. Before they were married, he seemed to appreciate her more. She'd gotten involved with him in the first place because he told her he admired her mind, admired the fact that she was an independent thinker. When she lost friends because she accepted his courtship, he said he respected her for making choices based on what was right, instead of what other people said or thought. But since the birth of their children, all that had changed. He didn't want a wife who was an independent thinker anymore. He wanted a traditional wife, a wife who would be single-minded in her devotion to their children and home, whether it suited her or not. What she wanted didn't matter anymore, and it infuriated her. She loved him, loved the style of life he gave her, and she loved their children. But it simply wasn't enough. She needed more, something of her own. She only wished she knew what to do about it.

Chapter 12

Nathan strolled into the First Class Smoking Room, his newspaper tucked under his arm. Except for the bartender and three stodgy old gents assembled in front of the marble fireplace, the place was empty. The men glanced over at him through a cloud of cigar smoke and went back to their discussion of Plymouth Harbour. A picture of the harbor hung over the mantel and Nathan heard one of the men claim his ancestors had entered America through that very waterway.

Nathan took a seat at one of the round tables scattered about the room and opened his newspaper. After several minutes the bartender came over, pad in hand, and stood next to his table. He didn't say a word, just stood there, expressionless.

"I'll have a cognac," Nathan said, and the bartender scribbled it down and left.

Nathan went back to his newspaper and stared blindly at the print. He'd come to the Smoking Room to escape the tension bristling in their stateroom. Nicolette was in a sour mood and sorely trying his patience. He was fed up with her gloominess and sniping and thought it best to make himself scarce for a while. He shook his head, thinking about the situation. He thought she should have been pleased that he'd gotten the baby to sleep for her, but instead, she wasn't speaking to him. She should have been happy about it. She should be happy period! After all, she was on the *Titanic*. Before they left, it was all she talked about. But now that she was actually here, she was moody and argumentative. It was almost as if she was looking for something to be angry with him about. There seemed to be no satisfying the woman.

The bartender brought his drink and sat it on the table in front of him. Again, he said nothing, just stood there.

Nathan reached in his pocket, took out some money and laid it on the table. The bartender scooped it up without saying a word and left.

Nathan took a sip of his Cognac, his mind turning again to his wife: *Perhaps it's the strain of travel, or the pregnancy. I've heard some women get very moody when they're pregnant. But it's kind of strange. She wasn't this way with Trista and Cecile.*

Just then, a friendly voice broke into Nathan musings. "Excuse me. Mind if I borrow some of your newspaper?" A courtly gentlemen with friendly gray eyes smiled down at him.

"Not at all." Nathan opened the newspaper and handed him part of it.

"Gerard Hale," the man said, and offered his hand. "If I'm going to borrow from you, I should at least introduce myself."

Nathan shook his hand. "Please to make your acquaintance. I'm Nathan Legarde. Where are you bound for, Gerard?"

Hale pulled a chair out from the table and sat across from him. "New York. I was born there, but all my family is in England now. I'm going back on sort of a mission."

"Is that so?" Nathan was curious. "Religious?"

"No." Gerard laughed. "Romantic. I'm in pursuit of the girl of my dreams."

"I see. Well, I hope you find her," Nathan said. He liked the man's openness and he seemed easy to talk to.

"Oh, I have," Gerard replied. "In fact, she's on the ship. I'm hoping to convince her to marry me."

"Is that so?" Nathan smiled, genuinely hoping he would get his wish. But right now, he didn't want to talk about marriage, so he tactfully changed the subject.

"What do you think of the magnificent *Titanic*, Mr. Hale?"

"It's like nothing I've ever seen." Wonder filled his eyes. "Why, you can't even tell she's moving. I've sailed the Atlantic several times, and I've never felt safer. And just look at the grandeur of this room." He made an expansive gesture with his hand. "The architecture is breathtaking."

"It is something to behold," Nathan agreed, taking in the mahogany paneled walls and mother of pearl inlaid work; the painted glass windows that depicted mythological figures, ancient ships and pastoral landscapes. "One couldn't ask for more opulent accommodations. It's the people I have a problem with."

"Really? What kind of problem?"

Gerard sounded genuinely interested and appeared to be the kind of man Nathan could level with, so he replied, "Well, for starters, the woman in the stateroom next to ours tried to have us moved our first night on board. I think her name is Agatha Boyle...or something like that. We had a very unpleasant confrontation."

"Oh, the incomparable Agatha strikes again," Gerard shook his head knowingly.

"You know her?" Nathan exclaimed.

"Let's just say I've made her acquaintance. Unfortunately, she's my intended's aunt. And when I say unfortunately, I mean it. Very unpleasant woman, thinks she's holier than Christ himself. I'm not surprised you had trouble with her."

"Sounds to me like she'd get along famously with the men in the inquiry office," Nathan quipped.

Gerard looked puzzled. "Inquiry office?"

"Yes. They could use a good dose of humanity up there if you ask me." He told him about how he was treated when he went up there to send his telegram.

Gerard suggested he tell Captain Smith about the incident. "I know E.J. He's a fair man and very particular about how his passengers are treated."

"I thought about it," Nathan confessed, "but I figured it would just make matters worse."

"No, no," Gerard insisted, "report it. They should have listened to your side of the story too."

Nathan thought about it for a minute. *Perhaps he's right. Perhaps the Captain will be more open-minded. And I am due an apology. I certainly won't get it if I don't report it.*

"You've convinced me," Nathan said and downed the last of his brandy. "I'm going to talk to the Captain." He and Gerard made plans to meet the next day, they shook hands and Nathan left.

He started for his stateroom, then changed his mind. He decided to look Captain Smith up while he was out and get the incident off his mind. He climbed the metal stairs up to the sun-drenched boat deck, then walked to the bridge near the center of the ship, in front of the inquiry office.

Looking around, he realized the bridge wasn't what he expected it to be, especially for such a luxurious vessel. It was rather plain, equipped with no more than the usual equipment. Officers manned the docking telegraph, the binnacle, and whistle controllers while others went about checking gauges and pressures, calling out readings and confirmations. It was abuzz with activity and reminded him of a well-orchestrated ballet.

Through a glass window behind the bridge, Nathan spied the Captain talking to a

Quartermaster in the Wheel House. He headed toward the Wheel House and from out of nowhere, an officer stepped into his path. "What are you doing in here?" he said. "Passengers aren't allowed in 'ere exceptin' the Captain invites 'em."

"Oh, here we go again," Nathan groaned inwardly. But mercifully, the Captain stepped out of the Wheel House and waved toward them saying, "At ease, Officer Hendricks."

The officer walked away as the Captain approached and Nathan was impressed with his stern, confident persona. He had to be at least sixty, but fit, with intelligent blue eyes and a neatly trimmed white beard and moustache.

Reaching him, the Captain said, "You'll have to excuse us, Mr.?…"

"Legarde," Nathan said.

"Oh, so you're the infamous Monsieur Legarde," the Captain said. "Your reputation precedes you. The boys over in the inquiry office said you caused quite a stir over there."

"That's not true, sir," Nathan replied, respectfully. "I didn't start anything. Someone else did."

"Well-"

Just then another Officer walked over and handed Captain Smith a piece of paper and announced, "The latest compass readings, sir." Captain Smith glanced at it, then back at Nathan.

"Someone by the name of Horace Clinch started the whole thing," Nathan continued. "But when I tried to tell that to the wireless officer, he wouldn't listen."

Captain Smith dismissed the Officer and said to Nathan, "That's not what the boys over there told me. Now, as you can see, Mr. Legarde, we're very busy up here. So make your point. Exactly what do you expect me to do with your complaint?"

"First, I want you to listen to my side of the story. And then I want those officers reprimanded. I'm a paying passenger on this ship and I have a right to the same respect as anyone else."

"Afraid I can't help you on either score" the Captain answered abruptly.

"What?" Nathan was incredulous.

"That's right. As I said, we're very busy. See me when we dock in New York and I'll be glad to hear you out. As for the men in the wireless office, they don't work for us. They're employees of the Marconi Wireless Company so you'll need to talk to them about it."

Crushed, Nathan grumbled, "I see."

The Captain got a call from an officer at one of the ship's telegraphs. Backing away he said, "A word of friendly advice, Mr. Legarde. Try and stay out of trouble." He touched the brim of his cap and left.

Nathan felt like a fool. He'd come all the way up to the boat deck to be told to stay out of trouble. What the hell was he supposed to do? Act like he didn't exist? Hide in his stateroom? Had he known the *Titanic* would be like this, he'd have taken another ocean liner. Nothing had gone right since he boarded the ship. He wondered what kind of nonsense he'd have to deal with next.

That night, Nathan's dream smelled like kerosene. He was ten years old again and back in New Orleans, standing on the back doorstep of his mother's new customer's house. In his hands was a wicker basket full of clean white shirts. His mother stood beside him and knocked on the door. An elderly Negro butler with salt and pepper hair opened it. He looked at them, saw the basket of laundry and glanced over his shoulder. Turning back to them he whispered, "Ya'll come back Monday."

"I can't," Nathan's mother said, "I'll be working."

A man's voice called from inside the house, "Who's out there, Slappy?"

"The washer woman, Sir," the butler called back.

There were footsteps, then a red-faced man carrying a bottle of whiskey appeared in the doorway. A yellow haired boy peeked out at them from behind the man.

"Git my shirts," the man ordered the butler. He quickly grabbed the stack of neatly folded shirts Nathan's mother handed him and rushed off.

Wavering on his feet, but holding tight to his whiskey bottle, the red faced man reached in his pocket and pulled out ten cents. Palm open he thrust it at Nathan's mother saying, "Here gal."

But his mother wouldn't take it. She told him he promised to pay her fifteen cents.

The man got angry and said she was calling him a liar. She tried to explain that she wasn't, and that he must have forgotten, but the man just got madder. His red face puffed up and he looked to Nathan like a raging bull.

He shouted, "You're callin' me a liar, nigger," and slapped his mother across the mouth. She stumbled back, blood oozing from her lip.

Nathan felt his temper ignite and he dropped the basket he was holding. "You old drunken cracker," he hollered and crashed his fist into the man's face.

Then everything got confused. His mother started yelling, "Oh, no, son, you can't do that, you can't do that." The drunk swung at Nathan, missed, and careened face down on the steps. The little yellow-haired boy started screaming: "Slappy! Slappy! Come quick. They're beatin' up Pa. Hurry, Slappy."

On all fours, the drunk tried clumsily to get to his feet. "You ain't gittin' away with this, nigger," he said, his speech slurred. "You can believe that. You ain't gittin' away with this."

Nathan's mother apologized. "I'm sorry, Sir. My son didn't know what he was doing." She grabbed Nathan's hand and started to back away saying, "I'm sorry, I'm so sorry."

The butler reappeared and saw the man on his knees. His face a mask of fear he started screaming at them too, "Y'all better git outta heah, quick, if you know what's good for ya. Go on. Git. Git."

Nathan and his mother started running. Running and running in slow motion, but getting nowhere. He could hear his heart pounding in his ears, hear the sound of his breathing as he sucked oxygen from the air. Next to him, his mother was mouthing words he couldn't hear. But he knew what she was saying: "You've done it now, Nathan. You're in a heap of trouble now."

For some reason, he felt an incredible urge to look back. He was afraid to, but he couldn't stop himself. Still running, he glanced over his shoulder and saw a yellow wall of flames. Everything behind them was on fire. Flames leaped, crackled, and sparked, coming after them, getting closer and closer, until…

Nathan jerked awake. The smell of kerosene was still in his nostrils, his heart racing. He sat up and stared into the silent darkness. Nicolette stirred beside him and he remembered where he was: *On the Titanic. On the Titanic, in the middle of the ocean.*

The realization calmed him. He lay back down and in a few moments he was sleeping peacefully.

Chapter 13

It was all Helen could do to maintain her civility. She was having afternoon tea with her Aunt Agatha and cousin, Eliza, in their stateroom and was sick of their self-righteous probing into her personal affairs.

But she couldn't leave yet. She'd asked them to watch Dodie for her this evening and had yet to get a commitment. So, she was at their mercy.

"You know," her cousin, Eliza said, "a woman your age can't be choosy. There just aren't many prospects in your age group." She poured Helen another cup of tea.

Helen said nothing. She took the cobalt blue and gold demitasse cup and saucer from her cousin's hand, thinking, *You have some nerve. With your looks, you should be the last to talk about someone else's prospects.*

"Well, if you ask me," her aunt Agatha chimed in, "you'd be wise to marry Gerard Hale. The sooner the better, too. Remember, a man doesn't buy the cow when he can get the milk for free."

Helen gasped. "What's that supposed to mean?"

"Oh, just that we heard you were out all night with him the evening of Anabelle's wedding. Past day break I heard."

"Who told you that?" Helen gasped again, anger rising inside her.

"That's not important." Her aunt Agatha gave her one of her holier-than-thou looks. "What's important is whether it's true or not."

Helen felt like screaming at both of them, but she was not about to dignify her statement with a reply. What business was it of theirs anyway? She was a grown woman, not some under-aged debutante in need of their moral guidance.

But she had a good idea who the source of the gossip was: her spoiled, selfish sister-in-law, Eleanor. She'd gotten madder than a salted snail at her for leaving Dodie with them that evening. In fact, she'd felt so put upon that she barely spoke a word to either of them for the rest of their stay in England.

"I really must be going," Helen said, standing. "I have some mending and pressing to get done. So, can I count on you to watch Dodie this evening?"

Agatha and Eliza exchanged annoyed glances making it clear to her that neither of them wanted to be bothered. An awkward silence hung in the air.

Finally, Agatha crossed her bony arms and huffed, "I can't watch her. I'm playing Double Canfield with some friends in the Reception Room after dinner."

Helen turned to Eliza. "Please. All I'm asking for is one evening. Just one evening."

Another agonizing silence hung in the air.

"Oh, all right," Eliza replied abruptly. "But don't bring that mutt, Houlie, with you. He barks too much and he's always nipping at people. I can't stand him."

Relieved, she thanked Eliza, grabbed Dodie's hand and headed for the door. Over her shoulder she called, "I'll have her here at six-thirty."

When they got back to their Stateroom, Helen paused at the Queen Anne table in the Parlor where she'd put the rose Gerard had given her earlier in the day in a slim crystal vase. Smiling, she leaned over and inhaled the flower's sweet bouquet. Across the room, Dodie plopped down in an armchair with a magazine.

Helen went into their bedroom to get out her clothes for the evening. She recalled Gerard telling her once that powder blue was her best color because it complimented her sky blue eyes and milky skin. So she rummaged through everything - the armoire, her trunks, her suitcases - in search of something blue. Less than satisfied, she settled on a layered chiffon evening dress spattered with soft blue watercolor blossoms. The bodice plunged daringly and strings of cut crystals dangled from the ruched shoulders. She hung the dress at the front of the armoire and decided that her tiered crystal necklace would go perfect with it.

Crossing the room to lay out her jewelry, she caught a glimpse of Dodie through the open doorway. She was kneeling on the floor, chewing on something. In front of her was a pile of rose petals. Realizing what she'd done, Helen felt a volcanic rage overtake her. Somewhere deep in her conscience, a tiny voice told her it was really a small thing. But to her, it was so much more - symbolic of the last twenty years of her life. "Dodie!" She screamed and ran into the Parlor. "How could you? You stupid, gluttanous pig!" She slapped her across the face.

Shock registered on Dodie's face, then she started to cry. It was the first time Helen had hit her.

Helen fell to her knees and the floodgates opened, releasing years of pent-up bitterness and pain. "You've ruined everything my whole life," she cried, "and I'm sick of it. Sick of taking care of you. Sick of *looking* at you." She collapsed into a torrent of sobs, giving herself over to the sorrow she felt inside. "I can't take it anymore. I just can't take anymore."

For years she'd kept her pain hidden, under control as an act of defiance. Her feelings were the only thing she believed she had any real control over. But now she realized, she hadn't been feeling anything at all. She'd gotten so accustomed to bottling up her emotions it had become a habit.

But seeing Gerard again had done something to her. It was almost as if she'd been freed from a great block of ice and could really *feel* her emotions for the first time in twenty years. But now that she was feeling her emotions, she didn't know how to handle them. They were so intense she was afraid of losing control completely

Helen cried until there were no more tears inside her. Then she took the lace handkerchief from her waistband, dried her eyes, and picked the rose petals up from the floor. Standing, she said to Dodie, "I'm sorry. I shouldn't have hit you. I don't know what got into me."

Dodie was still whimpering and spit some of the chewed up rose petals into her hand. Some of it clung to the side of her mouth and chin. "I just wanted to taste it," she said, "that's all. I just wanted to taste it. Oh, I wish Houlie was here."

"I know. But you heard Eliza," Helen said. "We'll go to the kennel and get him tomorrow."

Dodie stood up and rubbed her eyes. "I wanna take a nap," she said, then went into the bedchamber and lay down.

Helen went into the lavatory. She soaked a towel in some cold water and lay down on the bed adjacent to Dodie's. She covered her eyes with the towel and thought about Gerard. She had to give him an answer. But if she agreed to marry him, it had to be on her terms, just him and her, without Dodie around to spoil everything with her needing, whining, and eating. The question was, how?

Her mind wandered for a while, then she remembered an article she'd read several years ago in the New York Times. It was about a woman in England who'd gotten rid of three husbands by putting rat poison in their food.

Maybe I could…No…I could never do such a thing. She pushed the thought away. But a moment later, it came back. *Maybe… But I'd never be able to find enough in Rochester. They want a signature for it everywhere you can get it. But if I could…*

She took the wet towel off her eyes. Staring over at Dodie who was fast asleep she thought, *I lost the best years of my life because of you. It's time I had some happiness before it's too late.*

Helen was ready for her date with Gerard. All she had left to do was get Dodie ready and take her to Eliza. But when she woke her up, she had a big, blotchy bruise on her face.

Alarmed, Helen groaned, "Oh, no. What am I going to do?" She held Dodie's chin up in her hand and inspected the bruise more closely. *I can't take her over there like this. They'll have everyone on the ship talking about it.*

Near panic, she ran and got a washcloth and wiped Dodie's face. Then she applied a thick covering of rouge to camouflage the bruise and dusted her face with powder. When she finished, she held Dodie's face up again and inspected her handiwork. "There. You look as good as new."

Dodie smiled up at her, "I'm a big girl now, aren't I?

"Yes, you're a big girl. Now get your sweater and come on."

They left and walked the short distance to her aunt and cousin's stateroom.

As soon as they walked in the door, Dodie ran to Eliza and announced proudly, "Look, I'm a big girl. I have on makeup, just like Helen."

Helen groaned inwardly, *Oh, no, , what am I going to say if they start asking questions.*

But she needn't have worried. Her Aunt Agatha was nowhere in sight and Eliza barely looked up from the book she was reading. She shoved a box of bon bons at Dodie, told her to sit on the sofa, and rudely went back to her book, completely ignoring Helen. Feeling awkward, Helen said goodbye and went back to her stateroom.

Gerard called for her promptly at eight. Leaving for the evening, she held his arm, imagining what it would be like to be his wife. They walked through the maze of beige corridors, down the ornate, grand staircase and on to the luxurious A la Carte restaurant. The large, French walnut paneled room gleamed with gilded details. Exquisitely comfortable arm chairs surrounded the elegantly dressed round tables. A tuxedoed maitre de escorted them to their table and helped Helen with her chair.

When they were seated, Gerard ordered for both of them, a main course of poached salmon with mousseline sauce and cucumbers, and a bottle of Cliquot 1900.

Throughout the meal, he gazed adoringly at her. Somehow, she managed to keep the conversation light and directed it away from herself. They talked about his sons, his granddaughter, Emma, The Queen of England, anything she could think of to delay the inevitable questions.

Finally, over a dessert of Waldorf pudding and coffee, Gerard said, "All these years I haven't been able to figure out why you broke off our engagement. I can't begin to tell you how devastated I was when you sent my ring back and refused to see me anymore. It caught me completely by surprise. I really believed you loved me." He reached over and took her hand. "Call me a hopeless romantic, but when I look at you, I still believe it's true. So help me understand what I did wrong."

"You didn't do anything wrong," she replied, "I did. No, I take that back. I tried to do the right thing, but it was the wrong thing. Only I didn't know it at the time."

Gerard's brow creased quizzically. "I still don't understand."

Summoning the courage to finally tell him what happened she said, "It was my step-mother, Beulah."

Her mind went back to that awful day in 1890, a cold and windy Friday, during Thanksgiving break. She was home from Vassar College where she was a freshman and Gerard was home from Adelphi University. He was a senior studying architecture. They'd been engaged for six months and were planning a June wedding.

That morning she and Gerard had gone house hunting and found a wonderful little cottage in Fairport. It was almost noon when they got finished and Gerard had to go back to work. So he dropped her off at the Ryerson mansion in Rochester, gave her a quick kiss and said, "I'll see you Saturday."

With romance in her heart, she watched him ride away in his carriage until it was out of sight. Then she opened the door and stepped into the foyer thinking, "In just six months, I'll be Mrs. Gerard Wilson Hale." She took off her hat, and threw it and her powder blue mantelet on the Hepplewhite stand next to the door. Humming *Let Me Call You Sweetheart* she twirled gaily around the foyer. Someone in back of her cleared their throat and she stopped in her tracks. She turned around to find Clive, their somber Welsh butler standing there.

"I'm sorry for frightening you, Miss," he said, "but Mrs. Ryerson asked me to have you come to Miss Dodie's room straight-away when you returned."

"Really? What does she want?" Helen was more than a little curious.

"I don't know, Miss."

"Thank you, Clive." She dismissed him with a nod. *Strange*... she thought, the heels of her brown, size five boots clicking on the marble floor, *Beulah has barely spoken to me since I came home. Except, to* complain about how much the wedding is costing. But Clive said Dodie's room. Hmmm…, I wonder if she's sick again…she's thrown up three times this week. If only Dodie would stop stuffing herself…"

She lifted her skirts and quickly climbed the stairs. When she reached Dodie's room she knocked softly before entering. Normally, she would have walked right in, but she knew not to do that with Beulah on the other side. Her step-mother was a stickler for proper etiquette, and Helen didn't want to suffer through one of her "lessons" today.

"Come in," Beulah's gruff voice commanded, "and close the door behind you."

Helen did as she was told. "Clive said you wanted to see me, Mother?" she said, the word 'mother' tasting bitter in her mouth. She hated calling her 'mother,' but Beulah demanded it. She'd started that right after their father died.

Helen walked warily across the room to where sixteen year old Dodie was sitting cross-legged in the middle of the bed. She was rocking gently, sucking contentedly on the corner of the quilt bunched up in her lap. Helen tousled her mousy brown hair, and sat down next to her. Dodie stopped sucking for a moment and beamed up at her.

Beulah got up from the overstuffed chair she was sitting in. She crossed her big, flabby arms over her heavy bosom and snapped, "It's about time you got back. It's not proper for a young lady your age to be trouncing about town all day with a man, unchaperoned." Her stern, heavy jowled features contrasted starkly with the cheery lightness of Dodie's room, the walls papered with delicate pink roses on white trellises, the pure white bedstead and furnishings.

"We went house hunting, Mother." Helen replied defensively. "The owners were there at both places, so we weren't exactly alone. And we found a beautiful little cottage in Fairport."

"Humph,…that's too bad," Beulah huffed, stepping in front of her, "because I've changed my mind. You're not going to marry Gerard Hale. You're going to give him back his ring and you won't be seeing him again."

Shocked, Helen exclaimed, "What on earth are you talking about? Of course we're getting married. We've been planning the wedding for months."

"I said you're *not* getting married," Beulah shouted. "You have another, more important obligation."

"Obligation? What obligation?" Helen asked, confused. "I don't-"

Beulah cut her off. "Your sister is in a motherly way and it's all your fault. Therefore, you have an obligation to her." Beulah's fixed her with a hate-filled glare.

Helen couldn't believe what she was hearing. She looked from her step-mother to Dodie. "In a…a motherly way? That's impossible.

How could…she…she's just a…a…" It was too incredible to fathom.

"She's pregnant," Beulah shouted again, "and you're responsible. If it hadn't been for you and your whorish ways, she wouldn't be in this mess. Look at her! Does she look like someone who should be having a baby?"

Helen struggled to take it all in. How could it be? Dodie was just a child. Certainly, her body was mature, even more womanly than most girls her age. But she was a child in her mind. Anyone could see that.

Oblivious to the import of what they were talking about, Dodie stopped sucking on the quilt and said to Helen, "What's pregnant, Helen? Huh? Mother and Doctor Barnes said I have it. Do you have it? Huh?"

"Doctor Barnes?" Helen said, looking at Beulah.

"That's right, Doctor Barnes confirmed it this morning while you were out doing God knows what with that Hale fellow."

"We went house shopping. We've done nothing wrong," Helen said, defensively.

Beulah pointed an accusing finger in her face. "You've done plenty wrong. It was you and that Gerard Hale that brought the culprit into this house. We were able to piece that much together. Dodie said you left her alone in the parlor with that Richard Cunningham fellow, and he made love to her while you and Gerard were in the garden. Probably doing the same thing, is my guess. But as luck would have it, your poor sister here is the one who gets caught."

"Oh, my God," Helen exclaimed, remembering, the Fourth of July, the first and last time she'd seen Gerard's friend, Richard Cunningham. He was a classmate of Gerard's from Adelphi. They'd arranged a blind date between him and her friend, Lucy Darcy. They were all supposed to go to Central Park for a picnic, but Lucy fell ill the night before. So they asked Beulah if Dodie could come with them, as a treat, since she rarely got out of the house. After much cajoling, Beulah relented. And Richard had been a real sport about it. In fact, he seemed really fond of Dodie. He told her jokes and competed with her to see who could make the funniest face.

When they got back from the park that evening, Beulah was still out visiting friends. And since the servants were off for the holiday. So Richard volunteered to sit with Dodie while she and Gerard went out to the garden for a while. They were only gone for maybe an hour. When she and Gerard came back inside, Richard was sitting in the drawing room alone. He said Dodie was tired and had gone to her room. At the time, she'd thought nothing of it. She would never have dreamed that Richard had done anything to Dodie.

"This is incredible," Helen murmured. "I had no idea."

"Well you should have. You should have known better than to leave your defenseless sister alone with a man. What were you thinking?" She threw up her hands. "No, don't tell me. I know exactly what you were thinking. All you wanted was to be alone with that penniless gigolo. You saw an opportunity to throw caution to the wind and you took it."

Helen jumped to her feet. "That's not true. We were gone just a short while. If anyone's responsible, it's Richard. I didn't cause him to -"

"Yes, you did cause it. By abdicating your responsibility." Beulah strode back and forth in front of her. "That makes you every bit as guilty as he. More so, because you know how vulnerable your sister is, how easily she can be manipulated. Yet you left her with that...that sex fiend."

"That's not the way it was." A lump rose in Helen's throat. "That's not the way it was at all."

Abruptly, Beulah stopped and faced her. She pointed her finger at Helen's nose. "Are you telling me that I don't know what I'm talking about? Because if you are, I'd advise you to remember that I don't take that sort of thing lightly. And I won't take any backtalk from you either - a mewling little tart that doesn't know the difference between a gentleman and a con man."

Anger flashed in her step-mother's eyes and Helen instinctively drew back from her, her hand going to the scar on the left side of her face. The scar felt like a question mark on her left cheek bone, physical evidence of what happened the last time she was foolish enough to challenge her stepmother.

Beulah's venomous glare made Helen drop her eyes to the floor, a response borne of years of emotional and physical intimidation.

A satisfied smirk curled Beulah's wide, thin lips. "That's more like it. It's about time you learned some respect...and some responsibility."

She started to pace again with the assurance of a great cat who'd fatally wounded its prey and was savoring the smell of blood before feasting on its flesh. "You wouldn't be responsible before, so I'm going to make sure you're responsible in the future."

"What...what are you talking about?" Helen asked meekly, dread creeping over her. She knew the steely blue glint in Beulah's eyes could mean only one thing: trouble. Big trouble.

"You're going to Boston with Dodie until she has the....well, until this whole thing blows over. My sister, Agatha, is friendly with some Catholic nuns up there who'll look after you both until... Well, they'll place it in a good home. Agatha will arrange for you and Dodie to stay in one of the convents."

Helen's insides turned to water. "But...but, Mother, I can't go. Classes resume next week, and-"

"Shut up!" Beulah shrieked. "You listen to me, Missy. You're not going back to Vassar and there isn't going to be a wedding. You are going to do exactly as I say. And you're going to stay up there until the scandal you brought on this family passes."

"No, please!" Helen cried. "I love, Gerard. I can't just walk out on him. If you won't let us get married we'll...we'll..."

"Elope?" Sarcasm lifted Beulah's thick eyebrows. "Try it. I'll have you back here before you can reach the state line. And that gigolo of yours will have himself a handy criminal record for kidnapping. You forgot, my brother's second in command at Pinkerton's. I know how to deal with Mr. Hale."

Helen gasped, "You wouldn't. Gerard is a good, decent person. He doesn't deserve this, and neither do I. I love him, Mother. Can't you understand that? Please don't do this."

Heartbroken, she sobbed, thinking to herself, *How can you be so cruel. Why are you taking this out on us...on me?*

Beulah walked over and grabbed Helen's left hand. "Give me this," she demanded, tugging at the ring on Helen's finger.

"No, please. Please let me keep it." Helen balled her hand into a fist, to keep Beulah from getting the ring off. But it was no use. She pried at Helen's fingers, her hard fingernails digging into her soft skin. Then somehow, Beulah got turned around. While still prying at Helen's hand, she sat on her chest, her two hundred and sixty pounds crushing her like a mountain, squeezing the breath from her.

Helen couldn't move. Against her will, her hand opened and Beulah snatched the ring off her finger. Triumphant, she stood up, put the ring in her pocket and proclaimed, "I'll see that Mr. Hale gets this back."

"Please...let me give it to him," Helen begged, sitting up on the bed. "It's the least I can do. If I tell him about Dodie, maybe..." *Maybe he'll wait for me...until Dodie has the baby, then...*

"No!" Beulah screeched. "You're not going to breathe a word about this to anyone. Don't you understand the severity of this? Our family...our reputation is at stake. If this gets out, we could be ostracized, expunged from the Social Register."

"Mother, please," Helen begged. "You don't know Gerard. He would never -"

"I said, No! I'm not taking any chances. When Gerard Hale gets this ring back, he's going to know it's over. For good."

Helen sank back on the bed, her dreams shattered. She couldn't imagine not seeing him again. Since the day they'd met, Gerard had given her life new meaning, new purpose. Without him there was nothing to live for... no love...no future...only nothingness.

Beulah stood over her and said, "Let me tell you what your choices are. You can go to Boston as I've arranged and forget about Gerard Hale, then come back here and take proper care of Dodie, as any self-respecting sister would, or you can watch me turn his future to ashes. If you try to cross me in any way, Missy, that penniless gigolo of yours will pay dearly."

Inside, Helen screamed, *No...no...I won't let you do this...I can't let you do this...,"* But she dared not speak it. Years of maltreatment at her step-mother's hands had taken their toll, reinforced by her viciousness and knowledge of her powerful, corrupt connections. In fact, Beulah's escapades were legendary in New York. She'd had a well-known actress deported to Austria, simply because she didn't like her. She had a former friend removed from the Social Register for entertaining the 'wrong sort of people.' And on more than one occasion, she'd made people simply disappear without a trace because they'd offended her. More than once Helen had overheard the hushed sentiment of the New York elite: "You have to be insanely cunning, or simply insane to cross Beulah Ryerson." Helen believed beyond a shadow of doubt that her step-mother would make good on her threat if she dared to cross her. All she could do was nod her head obediently and reply, "I understand, Mother."

Beulah walked to the door, stopped and looked disdainfully at Helen, "Oh, in case you get any stupid ideas, I want you to remember something. I control the purse strings around here. You can't buy a crust of day old bread without my permission. And I'm seeing to it that the trust fund Harland left you remains untouched until I'm good and ready for you to have it." With that she walked out and closed the door.

Helen threw herself on Dodie's bed and wept. She was supposed to be starting a new life soon with the man she loved. Just this morning their future together had looked so bright. She'd anticipated getting away from the Ryerson mansion with such joy. She thought she'd finally be getting away from Beulah and her evilness. But instead, she was trapped, forced to do as her stepmother demanded, her future snatched away from her in a few life changing minutes.

Lying on Dodie's bed, she felt her pudgy hand on her back. She patted Helen as if she was one of her dollies. "Don't cry, Helen," she soothed. "Don't cry."

Her first instinct was to push Dodie away. If it hadn't been for her, this wouldn't be happening. She and Gerard would get married and she would never have to see her or Beulah again.

But she knew Dodie didn't understand what was happening. Richard Cunningham had used her in the worst sort of way. And now, Beulah was using Dodie too, to hurt her and spitefully destroy her chance for happiness.

Yet deep down, she did feel a smidgen of guilt. Had she not left Dodie alone with Richard, a near stranger, none of this would have happened. Oh, how she wished she had used better judgment, wished that she could go back and change what happened that day.

But wishing was futile. Early the next morning, Beulah took her and Dodie to the Rochester railway depot to catch the train to Boston. When they arrived in Boston, they stayed with Beulah's sister, Agatha, for a few days and then went on to Saint Margaret's convent to wait out Dodie's pregnancy.

They were there three weeks when Helen received a letter from Beulah. Sister Natalie gave it to her at lunch one day and told her they were under strict instructions to intercept any mail that didn't come from Mrs. Ryerson. Helen opened the envelope and found a brief note inquiring after Dodie's health along with a newspaper clipping. Helen unfolded the clipping and read the headline, 'Man Struck By Train.' The article stated twenty-two year old Richard Cunningham of Poughkeepsie, New York was mysteriously killed when struck by a train in Buffalo. No one knew why or how Cunningham wound up on the train tracks.

But Helen knew. She knew only too well. A cold shiver ran through her body and her hands shook as she read the rest of the article. That night, and every night thereafter, she prayed that Gerard would not meet the same fate as his friend.

When she and Dodie returned to Rochester six months later, everything had changed. Beulah had replaced the entire household staff. Clive, the butler was gone. There was a new cook, a new groundskeeper, and a personal servant for Beulah, all of them loyal to her. And she was forced to do the work of a servant with her primary duty the care of her sister, Dodie.

She couldn't make a move without Beulah knowing it. Not that she would have tried anything with Gerard's life hanging in the balance. Still, every once in a while, her step-mother reminded her of Cunningham's 'untimely accident,' just to reinforce her power over her.

Until the day she died, Helen lived with the ever present fear that the man she loved could be Beulah's next target.

"So you see…, Helen said to Gerard, "Beulah forced me to break our engagement. She blackmailed me into staying put. I know I should have tried to contact you, I shouldn't have given up so easily. But I was scared to death of her, scared she'd have you murdered. It nearly drove me mad because-" she choked on the lump in her throat. "You see, I never really knew if she hadn't done it anyway. I didn't know if you were alive, or if she'd had you maimed in some way. That's why it was such a shock when I saw you at the church." She searched his face for a reaction, worried that he'd lost all respect for her now that he knew how weak and spineless she'd been.

Gerard shook his head and said softly, "All those years I thought you'd stopped loving me, and all the while you were sacrificing yourself, for me. There can't be any greater love than that. Oh, Helen, I promise you, if you'll marry me, I'll spend the rest of my life trying to make it up to you. I'll devote every day of my life to your happiness."

"Then you...you don't blame me? For not doing something, for not fighting her?" She fought to hold back the tears.

"How could I blame you? You did the only thing you could. I remember your step-mother well. A hard woman if ever there was one. I doubt I could have matched wits with her. And you were always so guileless and kind. It would be exceedingly unfair of me to expect you to have outmaneuvered her." Looking thoughtful, he twirled the champagne in his glass. "When you, or rather Beulah, sent my ring back, there was a note with it that said you'd changed your mind and couldn't go through with the marriage. The note had your initials on it, but I knew in my gut something wasn't right about it. So I came by your house every day for a week. Every time I was told you didn't want to see me. The last time I came there, your stepmother answered the door. I'll never forget it. She gave me a look that could have melted steel and told me that if I showed up there one more time, she'd have me arrested for disturbing the peace. That's when I started writing to you."

"Letters I never got," Helen said sadly. It was yet another vestige of Beulah's wickedness that she'd learned about since her death. The first came right after she died, when Beulah's lawyer informed Helen that all the Ryerson wealth and assets had been left to Dodie. Helen was named executor with a lifetime leasehold to the estate on the condition that she take care of Dodie for the rest of her life. Only upon Dodie's death would she become sole and complete heir to the Ryerson fortune.

Gerard reached across the table and took her hand. "If your feelings didn't change, tell me what it means, dearest," he said softly, "I need to know. I need to hear it from you."

"It means I still love you. I never stopped loving you," she answered over the lump in her throat.

"Then let's put the past behind us and go on with our lives. Together. Say you'll marry me, Helen, please." His eyes were full of longing. "I'm lonely, and I want to spend what's left of my life truly in love with the woman that shares my bed."

That was what Helen wanted more than anything. Though the question of what to do about Dodie still hung over her head, she found herself saying, "Yes, I'll marry you."

They lingered over the last of the champagne and quietly made plans for their future. They'd announce their engagement when they got to New York and would have a very private ceremony with only a few close friends and immediate family.

After dinner, she and Gerard took a walking tour of the ship, strolled the promenade hand in hand oblivious to anyone but each other. On the boat deck they stood at the rail, gazed out at the celestial display of yellow moon and silver stars reflecting on an endless canvas of black, rippling water as they stole kisses like young lovers.

At ten thirty, Helen reminded Gerard that she'd promised Eliza she'd be back by eleven o'clock. As luck would have it they encountered some of the ship's musicians giving an impromptu concert on the deck and Gerard insisted they stop for a few minutes. Against her protests he asked them for a special request and when they started playing *Let Me Call You Sweetheart*, he pulled her into his arms and waltzed her around the deck, singing in her ear. She was almost giddy with happiness and momentarily cast her inhibitions aside as she floated in his arms. For once, she didn't care who was watching or what they might say. She was finally where she belonged.

When the dance ended, Gerard walked with her to Agatha and Eliza's stateroom. They agreed to meet for breakfast the next morning and he kissed her goodnight outside their door. Watching him walk away she actually felt lucky for the first time in her life. Fate had given them a second chance.

She knocked on the door and a few seconds later Eliza snatched it open. Her face was slathered with cold cream and she had a pink evening bonnet on her head. "You're late," she snapped, placing a hand on her bony hip, "and you should have fed Dodie before bringing her over here. She ate all my bon bons and all of Mother's shortbread cookies."

"I'm sorry," Helen apologized. "I did feed her. We had a late lunch." She walked into the parlor and found Dodie sprawled on the sofa, asleep.

"Is that Helen?" her aunt Agatha called hurrying into the room. She had cold cream on too and a white silk scarf tied around her head. "You're going to have to pay me for those cookies," she croaked. "They were special made for me in London. Paid a pretty penny for them too."

Again Helen apologized. She reached in her purse and took out a dollar, more than enough to pay for the cookies, the bon bons and Eliza's time with Dodie. She handed the money to Agatha who all but snatched it from her hand.

What nerve, Helen thought as she went to the sofa and shook Dodie. *You'd think they were destitute.*

Finally she got Dodie awake. Avoiding eye contact with the two women, she thanked them for their trouble, and left.

Oh, how she resented their stinginess, resented having to beg them to help her with

Dodie, their own flesh and blood. She would have liked nothing better than to tell them how she *really* felt about them, but she knew she couldn't. They were the only ones on the ship she could ask for help, and she might need them to help with her again before they got back to New York.

Yet, what she learned later that evening almost made

her change her mind. She was getting Dodie ready for bed when she said, "Helen, where's my baby?"

The question blindsided her. "What? What baby?"

"*My baby*," Dodie replied. "Eliza said I have a baby."

Oh, that evil, meddling fool. Helen felt like screaming. *What could she have been thinking?* There was no reason in the world for her to bring that up to Dodie.

"Yes, you have a baby." Helen answered. Diverting her attention away from the real issue she added, "You have lots of babies, remember? You have Miss Eleanor, Lady Doolittle, Miss Beatrice. They're all waiting for you at home."

Delighted, Dodie clapped her hands. "I like Lady Doolittle best. She has hair like mine." She wrapped a clump of her mousy brown hair around her finger.

Helen thought the trouble had passed. She handed Dodie her pajamas and went into the bathroom to get a washcloth to remove her makeup.

When she came back into the bedchamber, Dodie shocked her again. "Helen, what's a whore?"

Helen gasped. "Dodie! That's an awful word. Where did you hear that?"

"Aunt Agatha said it." Dodie scratched under her arm. "She said you're a whore."

Helen exploded. "Why that lying, mean, evil bi…witch! How dare she call me that." Her blood was boiling. "If she was here right now, I swear, I'd box her ears. Malice runs in that family's blood like oxygen." She rubbed the makeup off of Dodie's face just a little too roughly.

She knew without a doubt why the Boyle's were maligning her. They were just like Beulah. They couldn't stand the idea of her being with Gerard. The last thing they wanted was for her to have the happiness and contentment Beulah spent the best part of her life preventing. She made up her mind that one of these days she was going to tell those two miserable shrews exactly what she thought of them. And by God, when she did, she would show them that Hell hath no fury like a woman wronged.

Chapter 14

Leaning against the rail of the *Titanic*'s boat deck Jimmy Ray Tuttle kept his eye on the entrance to the inquiry office. He flicked his cigarette overboard as he waited for his target to exit so he and Earl Lee could trail him. Once he knew where their man was staying, he could proceed to the next stage of his plan.

"Damn. What's takin' so long? He should have been out of there by now," he remarked impatiently as he pushed up the sleeve of his jacket and checked his watch. He'd been waiting fifteen minutes already.

"Aw, calm down, Jimmy Ray," his friend, Earl Lee replied. "He's got to come outta there sooner or later. No sense gittin' all worked up over nothin'."

Earl Lee's comment struck a nerve. "Don't you tell me to calm down. This might be nothin' to you, but it sure as hell is somethin' to me." He hated the high-pitched sound of his own voice, but he couldn't help it. It got that way when he was mad or excited.

"I didn't mean it that way." Earl Lee apologized. "But I still don't understand how you can be so sure it's him."

Jimmy Ray smacked the rail with his hand. "Well now, if that don't beat all. You heard the conversation this morning just like I did. How many *Negro* engineers do you think are runnin' around on this ship? Ten? Twenty? Hell, I bet there ain't a single Negro engineer in the entire state of Louisiana. That's him alright. I know it is."

He was eight years old the last time he'd laid eyes on Nathan Legarde. But he recognized him as soon as he walked into the inquiry office this morning, just like he knew he would. He'd lived with the memory of his face most of his life: those brown, almond shaped eyes, and smooth bronze skin. He had grown into a handsome man too, nothing less than what he'd expected. And according to his cousin in France, Legarde had an extraordinary confidence about him for a Negro. The man they'd seen in the inquiry office this morning certainly fit *that* description. He'd shown more pluck than any darky he'd ever seen.

He glanced over at Earl Lee whose back was against the rail and saw a look of concern reflecting on his face.

"You better not be goin' yella' on me," Jimmy Ray warned. "I didn't bring you all the way over here for you to chicken out before we even git the son-of-a-bitch."

"Don't go 'sinuatin' I'm yella,' 'Cause you know damn well I ain't," Earl Lee huffed. "I just don't want us goin' after the wrong man."

"Why the hell would you worry about somethin' like that? A coon's a coon. Just take my word for it, it's him. I know what I'm talkin' about."

He hoped that would be the last of Earl Lee's questions, though he didn't relish wasting his time going after the wrong coon either. Only this *particular* coon would satisfy him and they had only two more days to get the job done.

Maybe I should send Earl Lee to peek in there and see what's going on, he thought. But before he could open his mouth, two strange little old ladies walked up to them. They were all gussied up in matching red Chinese dresses with black shawls trimmed in gold covering their shoulders. A heavy layer of white powder covered their wrinkled faces and their thin white hair was pulled up on top of their heads in tight knots pierced with sticks. He'd never seen anything so queer in his life.

"Excuse me, gentlemen," one of the old ladies said in a shaky voice, "we were wondering if you'd be so kind as to help us with our postcards. Sister here, well, she doesn't see very well, and," (she paused, then continued in a confidential tone), "well, I'm afraid my handwriting isn't as nice as it used to be."

Earl Lee tipped his hat at the old crows. "Always willin' to oblige a lady."

It irritated the hell out of Jimmy Ray. He felt like smacking Earl Lee. He was supposed to be helping him track down Legarde, not playing Good Samaritan to a couple of loony old biddies.

"What in Sam Hill are you doin'?" he whispered through clinched teeth as Earl Lee took a postcard and pen from one of the old ladies' hands.

"I'll make it quick. I promise," he answered, then smiled down at the old lady and led her to a nearby bench. Jimmy Ray overheard the old gal say she was Millie Hennypecker and her sister was Tillie, with the same last name.

Damn it!, Jimmy Ray shouted inwardly, shooting a murderous glance at Earl Lee's back. *I should have known better than to count on this idiot.*

In his best Southern gentleman tone he said to the tiny woman standing in front of him, "Miss Tillie, perhaps you and your sister could git some help in the Mail Room, or perhaps one of the fine ladies that frequent the Writing Rooms could assist you. I hear there's several such rooms on the ship." Unlike Earl Lee, being a Good Samaritan just wasn't a part of his nature.

"Oh, we went to the First Class Reading Room already," the old lady replied. "It was deader than a tomb in there. That's why sister and I came out here. To catch some fresh air and mingle. I'm glad we found you nice gentlemen. The ship is so big it's hard to find people who want to socialize." She nodded at her sister, "Of course, I have my sister, but I do enjoy new faces once in a while." The old lady rattled on.

Jimmy Ray glanced over at Earl Lee who was still writing as Millie Hennypecker dictated to him. "Ma'am, we have an engagement," Jimmy Ray said, his patience running low. Just then, from the corner of his eye, he saw Legarde at the top of the stairs leading to the deck below. He'd come out onto the deck and made it to the stairs right under his nose!

"Earl Lee, it's him," he called, and pushed the old lady aside. He sprinted across the deck toward the stairs. Behind him he heard Earl Lee apologize to the old lady, then his rapid steps resounding on the wooden deck behind him.

When he reached the top of the stairs, Legarde had already ascended. He ran down the stairs to D deck, stopped, and looked all around for him. He saw a couple of English gentlemen wearing serious expressions and bowler hats amid an assemblage of round tables and deck chairs. They were discussing the coal strike and one of them remarked that the *Titanic* had scavenged coal from other vessels to get enough for its voyage. In the opposite direction, a group of women were discussing someone by the name of J.J. Astor, who was supposed to be onboard with his child bride who was 'in a family way.' Further away he saw a middle aged father watching his young son spin a wooden top on the shiny deck floor. Several couples, one of them with a pram, stopped to watch too. But there was no evidence of Legarde anywhere.

"Where'd he go?" Earl Lee asked, coming up behind him.

"I don't know." Jimmy Ray was dumbfounded. "It's like the son-of-a-bitch disappeared into thin air."

Overhearing his profanity, one of the gentlemen in the bowler hats shot Jimmy Ray a disapproving glance. *Aw, go to hell,* he thought, frowning at him, and walked away.

"I'm sorry," Earl Lee said following him. "I didn't see him come out."

Jimmy Ray snapped at him, "You're sorry, is right. If you hadn't been pussyfootin' around with that old biddy, we would've had him."

"I said I'm sorry," Earl Lee repeated, defensively. "I thought you were keeping an eye out for him."

Jimmy Ray ignored him and completely dismissed the fact that he'd gotten distracted too. Suddenly he got an idea, stopped and snapped his fingers. "I've got it. With a bit of luck, we can still find out where Legarde's cabin is." He slapped Earl Lee on the back. "Let's go." On their way up to C deck Jimmy Ray explained in a confidential tone, "The Purser has a list of everybody on this ship. He probably keeps a record of cabin assignments too. Anyway, if we can get our hands on that list, we won't need to go searchin' for him. We git the list, then all we have to do is find a way to lure him to our room. Once that happens,..." he smacked his fist in the palm of his hand, enjoying the pain of the impact, "his black ass is all mine."

"Wow, I didn't know you knew that kind of stuff." Earl Lee was clearly impressed.

"Yeah, well there's a lot I know that you don't. A lotta stuff I learned from my Pa." They went into the inquiry office again, walked past several lines of well-dressed passengers waiting to send Marconigrams, or conduct other business. They ambled nonchalantly among the other passengers searching for the Chief Purser's headquarters. But there wasn't a sign anywhere indicating the Chief Purser's post. So they went to the only office in the suite that didn't have a line. Above its window was a sign that said, 'Currency Exchange.'

"Excuse me," Jimmy Ray spoke to the spectacled man on the other side of the window. "I need to speak to the Chief Purser." The name 'Philpot' was on the badge pinned to the man's lapel.

"I can help you," the man pushed aside the coins he was wrapping.

"Are you the Chief Purser?" Jimmy Ray asked.

"No, but I can still help you," Philpot insisted. "What do you need?"

"I need to speak to the Chief Purser," Jimmy Ray insisted. "And only the Chief Purser."

"Well, if you need some money converted…"

"No. I don't need no money converted. Didn't you hear what I said? I want to speak with the Chief Purser. That's it. No one else."

Philpot glanced at the clock on the wall. "Well, Purser McSweeney is on inspection right now with the Captain. He should be back in his office in about an hour."

"Where's his office?"

"Starboard of the first class forward entrance."

Still irritated, Jimmy Ray mumbled, "Why the hell don't none of the crew on this ship speak normal English?

"Excuse me?" Philpot said.

"Just explain to me where it is."

Philpot pointed toward the exit. "Just go out the door and make a right. Keep going until you come to a corridor. It's the first office on the left, next to the Engineer's office."

Jimmy Ray walked away without thanking Philpot for his courtesy. They followed his directions, and sure as shootin', they found the door marked 'Chief Purser,' right next to the one marked 'Engineer.' Jimmy Ray knocked several times to make sure no one was inside, then told Earl Lee to keep watch at the end of the corridor.

When Earl Lee signaled the coast was clear, Jimmy Ray knelt on the floor in front of the door, reached in his pocket for his pocketknife and started to pick the lock. He'd learned the skill from some older boys when he was fourteen. They used to break into stores together and steal cash and other valuables. Grateful now for that knowledge, he inserted the knife in the keyhole and kept working it and turning the knob until he felt the internal spring mechanism give. Then he stood up, opened the door a crack, and whispered to Earl Lee that he was going in.

The Chief Purser's office was small and simple. A black, nail-trimmed chair sat behind his carved wooden desk in the middle of the room. The desk was strewn with papers, envelopes, a couple of rubber stamps, and rubber bands. A wooden, oval framed photograph of a large, round faced man in a white uniform sat near the right corner of the desk. Jimmy Ray assumed it was the Chief Purser. In the picture with him was a boy of about four or five in short pants and a white shirt and a young woman in a mannish suit and tie, wearing a hat with a veil that covered her face.

He was inspecting the stuff on the desk when suddenly he heard, "Kwawk! Kwawk!"

Startled, he jumped. His eyes darted around the room and he spotted a bird cage sitting atop a tall plant stand in a corner of the office. Inside was a parrot with brilliant sapphire, yellow, red and green feathers and beady, black eyes.

"Kwawk! *Titanic. Titanic.* Greatest ship that ever was," the bird squawked. "Greatest ship that ever was." He moved from side to side on the perch hanging inside the cage, squawking loudly, his beady eyes seemingly fixed on Jimmy Ray.

He tried to ignore the noisy varmint and continued to riffle through the papers on McSweeney's desk: a stack of bar receipts, Marconi

Wireless receipts, a letter with salutation to H.W., and a ticket stub from the Hippodrome Theatre. He picked up a Marconigram from the Empress of Britain that said: 'Purser, McSweeney. *Titanic,*' Congratulations and good luck, Whitman.' Underneath the Marconigram was a set of keys tagged: 'Linen Locker #1, C-Deck.' But there was no passenger list, and no list of room assignments.

Jimmy Ray's frustration mounted as he continued to search the desk. All the while the parrot's squawking and fluttering got louder and louder, stretching his nerves to the limit. It felt like the bird was sounding an alarm, trying to tell the whole world he was once again up to no good. Unable to take the bird's squawking any longer, he flung the papers he had in his hand onto the desk and dashed over to the cage. He snatched the door open and reached inside. The bird fluttered wildly, its feathers flying as he evaded his grasp, squawking even louder. Then the bastard pecked him on the back of his hand, drawing blood.

"Ow!" He jerked his hand out of the cage, and cursed. "You stupid son-of-a-bitch."

He sucked the sweet blood from his wound, hatred for the bird boiling over. Bent on revenge, he plunged his hand back inside the cage, nearly knocking it off the stand. He flailed his hand, getting pecked and scratched, but finally got his hand around the bird's throat. It thrashed wildly, flapping its wings, swinging in his hand, vainly trying to free itself from his grip.

Jimmy Ray grabbed a pencil from the Purser's desk. He plunged it into one of the bird's eyes and it jerked wildly. Then he plunged the pencil in the bird's other eye. Its body spasmed violently in his hand and it gave him a masterful feeling, a feeling of absolute power. Finally, he speared the bird in the chest and chucked it in the wastebasket beside the desk. "There. That'll teach you to go tattlin' on Jimmy Ray Tuttle," he remarked pulling a handkerchief from his pocket. He wiped sweat from his forehead, then wrapped the handkerchief around his bloody hand.

He went back to his task and tried to open the right hand desk drawer, but it was locked. He yanked at the wide middle drawer expecting it to be locked too, but surprisingly, it wasn't.

"Hallelujah!" He'd hit pay dirt. A large white envelope with the word 'Passengers' written across it lay under a crucifix in the drawer. He ignored the religious symbol, grabbed the envelope, stuffed it inside his jacket and rushed to the door. He peeked out to make sure the corridor was clear, then left.

Ten minutes later, he and Earl Lee were back in their quarters on E deck. He tore the envelope open and took out the Passenger list. Only, it wasn't the Passenger list! He'd stolen a stack of plain white writing paper with the White Star logo at the top of each sheet.

"Goddammit to hell!" he shouted, a white hot rage overtaking him. He threw the papers across the room, cursing and swearing. He kicked the sitting room settee and tore one of it's fine tasseled throw pillows to shreds. Finally exhausted, he slumped down on the settee. "After all that, and I'm not a bit closer to gittin' my hands on that nigger than when I got on this ship." He hung his head, completely disappointed. "Now I've got to start all over agin.'"

Earl Lee went to the secretary, opened a fresh bottle of Bourbon, and poured them both a drink. He handed one to Jimmy Ray saying, "Yeah, but how do we start over when we still don't know where his room is."

"Ain't no need in rubbin' it in," Jimmy Ray barked.

"I wasn't rubbin' it in. You said yourself we needed to find out where his room is first, then -"

"Shut up, dammit. I know what I said. And we *will* find him. It's just going to take a little more time. If my instincts are right, we'll come across him agin.' He's one of them darkies that likes to git noticed. Why else do you think he'd marry a white woman? So everybody will notice his black ass when they walk by. So everybody will think he's somebody. Mark my word, he'll be out and about. A little bad luck might've slowed me down, but it ain't over. Not until I see that darky take his last breath."

Chapter 15

It was Friday, their third day aboard the *Titanic* and Helen was on her way to meet Gerard for breakfast in the dining room. Dodie, her constant burden, was with her. Approaching the newfangled automatic lift that would take them up to B deck, they came upon a gaggle of woman waiting in front of it. They were making a huge fuss over a pleasantly stout woman whose arm was in a plaster cast.

Standing on the outer fringe of the noisy assemblage Helen overheard one of them say, "I heard you fell all the way to the bottom of the grand stair case."

The woman in the cast chuckled, "Nothing flies faster than a rumor around here, except a lie. I slipped on a teacake on the stairs going down to our room. Darn near brought poor Henry B. down with me."

Helen looked at the woman in the cast more closely. She recognized her face from the newspapers. She was none other than Irene Wallach Harris, wife and assistant to Henry B. Harris, the famous New York playwright. She called herself Renee.

"Oh, you poor dear," a matronly woman said soothingly to Mrs. Harris, "You must have been frightened out of your wits."

"To tell you the truth, it happened so fast, I didn't have time to get frightened," Mrs. Harris replied. "It hurt like the dickens though when I went down on my arm. But I didn't realize it was broken until I woke up this morning all black and blue, and aching to beat the band. So Henry B. took me down to the hospital."

The cackling surged anew. "Oh, you poor thing."

"You should be taking it easy!"

"Where's Henry now? You shouldn't be out by yourself." "There's something unsettling about this ship."

"Yes, a queer accident like that proves it's not as safe as they say it is. Are you still in pain, Renee?"

Mrs. Harris waved her hand, dismissing the brouhaha. "I can deal with the pain. Doctor Frauenthal wanted to give me a tincture of morphine, but I told him, no way. That stuff's deadly. I've heard of people accidently overdosing with it. Too much will stop your heart, you know."

Helen's mind latched onto Mrs. Harris' words. *Too much will stop your heart... Too much will stop your heart...* The words echoed inside her head, drowning out the women's chatter. When the lift arrived, she and Dodie piled in behind them. The lift jolted to a stop on B deck and the group disembarked. The words were still ringing in Helen's head: *Too much will stop your heart... Too much...*

Throughout breakfast, she struggled to keep her mind focused. She and Gerard settled on a June thirteenth wedding date. They agreed on a trip to the south of France for their honeymoon and she had to talk Gerard out of wiring his son's with the news of their engagement. He could hardly contain his excitement but Helen felt it would be better to give them the news face-to-face after they'd had the chance to at least meet her. Yet all the while, the words ...*Too much will stop your heart...*, kept playing in her head like a scratched phonograph. Gerard ate a hearty breakfast: stewed prunes, grilled ham, shirred eggs, jacket potatoes, sultana scones, and black currant conserve, but Helen had no appetite. She was absently pushing a piece of ham around on her plate when Gerard remarked, "Dearest, is something wrong? Dodie's eaten three scones already and you've barely touched a thing."

"No, uh, everything's fine. I was just thinking about all I have to do before the wedding. It's all rather daunting." She forced a reassuring smile.

After breakfast Gerard suggested they take a stroll on the promenade saying, "The exercise will do us all good."

But Helen begged off. "I'd love to, but I can't. I have arrangements at the Turkish bath and then I'm going to the hair salon."

"Oh." Gerard looked disappointed, but he didn't pressure her. Instead he said, "Well, how about dinner this evening? I can stop by for you girls, say around six o'clock."

"That's perfect." Helen smiled and pecked him on the cheek. She grabbed Dodie's hand and rushed back to their stateroom.

As soon as she entered the door, she gave Dodie some paper and crayons to occupy her and searched their stateroom for the little White Star handbook she'd been given upon boarding. It had the location and descriptions of all the services and amenities on the ship. She needed it to look up the location of the infirmary. She searched the Parlor but couldn't find it. Then, she went into their bedchamber, and there it was, lying on the floor next to Dodie's bed. Helen picked it up and saw that Dodie had scribbled the inside front cover and first page with red crayon. But thankfully, the rest of the handbook was readable.

She flipped through the pages until she came to the section that covered medical services. It said the ship had two hospitals, one for the Crew and Steerage passengers forward on C deck, and another for First and Second class passengers starboard on D deck near the galley. There was also a surgeon and assistant surgeon on board, along with a small staff including a matron, hospital steward and a Nurse/Stewardess available exclusively for First Class passengers.

Helen shoved the booklet into her handbag, went into the Parlor, got Dodie, and raced out again.

Fifteen minutes later, she and Dodie were seated in a curtained examination room in the hospital on D deck. Dr. John Edward Simpson, the ship's assistant surgeon was asking her some questions.

"And how long have you been getting these headaches, Miss Ryerson?" He twirled the end of his handlebar moustache with his left hand. In his right hand he held a pen, poised to note her answer on a chart.

"Most of my life," she answered feeling convicted under the doctor's dark, intense eyes. She reminded herself that she was only half lying. She did get headaches, occasionally.

"Have you seen your family doctor about them?"

"Yes, he usually gives me laudanum. But I didn't think to bring it with me."

"I see," he replied, scribbling something on his chart and Helen wondered if he could tell she was lying.

Suddenly, footsteps came from outside the curtain, and then it snapped open. An older, white-haired man with a bushy moustache, gold buttoned uniform, and fatherly presence spoke to Dr. Simpson, his tone urgent.

"Doctor, I need you in surgery on C deck immediately. They're bringing up one of the stokers. Third degree burns."

"Right away, Dr. O'Loughlin." Dr. Simpson stood up as the other doctor rushed away.

"I'm sorry, Miss. Ryerson. I'm sure you understand. Serious injuries take precedence. But if you'll take a seat in the corridor Nurse Marsden will help you when she returns. Or you can come back in a couple of hours."

He motioned for her and Dodie to follow him. On their way out, Helen caught sight of something she hadn't seen coming in: a glass-paned door on the left side of the Infirmary with a sign on it that said, "*dispensary.*" Through the glass she spied rows of shelves stocked with porcelain containers and glass-stoppered bottles. No one was inside, at least not that she could see.

There has got to be something in there that would work…, morphine, laudanum, something, she thought. The very idea sent adrenaline to her nerves. She and Dodie sat in some chairs against the wall in the corridor and Helen herself to be still until Dr. Simpson was out of sight. She opened her handbag, took out her ever present lace handkerchief, and blotted the fine net of moisture covering her face.

Wiping sweat from her palms she said to Dodie, "I want you to listen to me very carefully. I want you to stay right here and don't move. But if you see someone coming, I want you to come inside and get me right away. Understand?"

Dodie nodded her head, "Okay." Then she reached into her dress pocket and took out a half-eaten scone she'd pilfered from breakfast and bit into it.

Warily, Helen walked back inside the little hospital. She stood just inside the door a few seconds and scanned the room, listening intently. She heard nothing but the beating of her own heart.

On tiptoe, she sneaked to the dispensary, opened the door and she stepped inside, amazed that the door wasn't locked.

"Hello," she called several times, expecting someone to appear from behind the narrow, gated counter. But no one did.

The room felt cold and sterile, its stark white walls illuminated by electric lights hanging from the ceiling. She saw copies of *"The Ship Captain's Medical Guide,"* and *"First Aid to the Injured,"* lying on the counter next to a set of scales and weights and two glass measures. To her left was an entire wall of shelves neatly arranged with surgical instruments and supplies from bandages and plaster of Paris to a large assortment of forceps. Across the room to her right was yet another door. On it was a sign that said, *"Authorized Personnel Only,"* underscored by a black skull and crossbones. The sight of it gave her the willies.

Helen drew her eyes away and scanned the porcelain containers and bottles on the shelves behind the counter. Most of them were clear, but others were green. They all had red and white labels with their contents in English and Latin.

She pushed open the little gate and went behind the counter her heart thudding like a team of racing Clydesdales. She looked up and read the labels under her breath: *Dover's Powder...,*

Aspirin..., Nitre of Saltpeter..., Epsom Salts..., Blue Pill...,Paregoric...,Sulphur...,Tincture of Morphine..., *Tincture of Morphine!*

She was about to reach for it when a female voice boomed from behind her. "What are you doing in here?! This area is off-limits to passengers."

Startled, Helen jumped and turned around. A hard faced woman dressed in a white uniform was glaring at her. She assumed she was Nurse Marsden. "I, uh, I was looking for you. For a headache..., Dr. Simpson said..."

"I know he didn't tell you to look for me in here." She eyed Helen suspiciously. "What's your name anyway? I'm reporting this to Dr. Simpson."

Panic-stricken, Helen bolted through the gate and ran past the nurse, nearly knocking her down. She dashed through the infirmary and glanced behind her. Thank heavens, she wasn't coming after her.

Helen found Dodie in the corridor where she'd left her. She grabbed her hand and ran until they were both out of breath. When they reached their stateroom Helen threw her purse on the sofa and screamed at Dodie. "Why didn't you warn me?! I told you to come and get me if you saw someone coming. Why couldn't you at least do that much?" She panted, catching her breath.

"I don't know. I forgot," Dodie answered in her child-like voice. She picked up a copy of *Vanity*

Fair from the parlor table, opened it and sat on the settee.

"I don't know. I forgot," Helen mimicked angrily. *I'll be glad when I can forget you. You just don't know how glad I'll be,* she thought. And this time, she didn't feel an ounce of guilt.

Chapter 16

The effervescent Molly Brown made her way along the glass enclosed First Class promenade waving and chatting here and there with people she knew. But when she reached Nicolette, she harrumphed, stuck her nose in the air and walked right past her. Several onlookers gave them both curious glances.

Nicolette felt her cheeks redden, thinking, *I can't blame her. She doesn't understand.* Watching her walk away, Nicolette made up her mind that she had to talk to her. She couldn't let her go on thinking she was in the habit of standing people up.

Trista was standing next to her and raised her little hands, "Mama, play patty cake with me."

Nicolette complied and clapped hands with her as Trista chanted a French rhyme in a sing songy voice.

But her mind wasn't on the game. Her gaze kept drifting to Molly Brown who was having an animated conversation with two strange looking old ladies several feet away. They were dressed in rawhide fringed skirts and vests and wearing cowgirl boots. Huge silver and turquoise brooches adorned their vests. One of the women had a lariat slung over her shoulder, and the other had an empty gun holster slung low on her plump hips. She'd seen the two white-haired old ladies on the ship before and each time she saw them, they looked more bizarre than the last. But their presentation didn't seem to affect their popularity. Everyone seemed to adore them and took their strangeness in stride. Though she hadn't met them personally, she admired them for their boldness and unconventionality.

One of the old ladies tugged at the other's arm signaling to Nicolette that their conversation with Mrs. Brown was ending. It was Nicolette's chance to make a move.

"Ma cherie," she said to Trista. "Mama has to speak to someone. I want you to stay here with Sabine and Cecile." She nodded toward the au pair who was sitting next to them reading a book, one foot poised on the brake of the baby's pram. "I'll only be just a minute."

"Oh non, Mama." Trista started to pout, sticking out her bottom lip, "I want to go with you."

Nicolette leaned down and scooped her up. "I'm only going right over there." She pointed in the direction of Molly Brown. "You'll be able to see me every minute and I'll be back in a twinkling. If you're good and don't make a fuss, we'll have vanilla ice cream later. Okay?"

"Okay." Trista smiled and looked over at a group of children playing nearby. Nicolette sat her down next to Sabine and quickly strode away.

She reached Molly Brown just as the three women were parting and grabbed her arm "Please, wait."

Molly Brown turned and looked down at her blue silk clad arm encircled by Nicolette's determined grip. Her deep blue eyes snapped, "Now you listen here, Madame Legarde," she snatched her arm away, "I don't take kindly to being manhandled, and I won't put up with being woman handled. So if you know what's good for you, you'll unhand me this minute."

"Oh, I'm sorry," Nicolette released her arm. "I didn't mean to…, it's just that I…, I wanted to explain…to apologize."

"And rightly you should." Molly huffed. "I'm listening."

"Well, I,…I didn't show up yesterday because my baby was crying. I thought she was sick…but she wasn't…I wanted to keep the appointment, really I did, but I couldn't. She wouldn't stop crying, so I couldn't leave."

From the look on Molly's face, Nicolette imagined she must sound like a babbling idiot. Molly harrumphed again and crossed her arms in front of her. "Well, I suppose your nurse maid over there was indisposed yesterday."

"No, no, she wasn't. I could have left the baby with her, but I was afraid she was really sick. So I couldn't leave. Please try to understand. You wouldn't expect me to leave a sick child would you?"

Molly didn't answer her question. Instead she replied, "Well, I guess it would've been too much to ask for you to send a steward around to let us know why you couldn't make it. Lady Gordon was miffed. She wasted over an hour waiting for you. And personally, I don't like being made a fool of in front of my friends."

"I'm truly sorry," Nicolette apologized again. "You probably think I'm the rudest, most dim witted woman you ever met, and I don't blame you. But I was so upset with the baby crying and missing our appointment, I didn't even think about it. Believe me I was heartbroken at missing the chance to meet Madame."

"Hmmph." She gave Nicolette a hard look, like she was still unconvinced, so Nicolette tried again to get through to her.

"Please, Margaret, I mean Molly. Try to understand. My husband was out at the time. If he'd come back and found me gone, the baby bawling, and the au pair alone with the girls, he'd have accused me of neglecting the children. Half the time, I feel like a terrible mother anyway. And sure enough, when he came in the baby was still crying. He took her and a few minutes later she was fast asleep, when nothing I did would quiet her. But by then, it was too late. Please believe me, I was devastated, just devastated."

Molly's skeptical demeanor softened and Nicolette sensed that something she'd said resonated with her. "I have a daughter too," she replied. "Yes sir, a real daddy's girl, always was. I used to have the notion we'd get closer when she got older. Well, she's all grown up now and I'm still second fiddle in her book, probably always will be."

Molly's eyes were misty and she reached out and squeezed Nicolette's hand forging an invisible bond of understanding between them. After a brief moment, she blotted around her eyes with her fingers and gushed, "Oh, don't mind me. I'm too sentimental for my own good. You're still young. Things could turn out different for you and your girls." She took a deep breath, pulled herself up to her full five foot three inches, and announced as if nothing had happened, "Well, Nicolette, looks like I'm going to have to convince Lady Gordon to sacrifice another hour of her time."

Nicolette caught her breath. "Oh, my, do you mean it? Do you think she would still see me?" She was almost afraid to believe she was getting a second chance.

Molly laughed. "Oh, I'll probably have to smooth her Highness's feathers some more, maybe do a little arm twisting. But you leave it to me." She gave Nicolette a sly wink. "I'll get her to come around. Meet us in the Café Parisienne, at two o'clock this afternoon."

"Oh, thank you," Nicolette said. "I'll be there. Early." She rushed away, checking her watch as she went. She had less than an hour to get the children back to their stateroom, get them situated, and get herself over to the Café Parisienne.

When she got back to their stateroom, she found a note from Nathan on the parlor table.

Below the White Star logo was written: "Went to the Smoking Room. Be back soon. Avec amour, Nathan."

One less problem to worry about, she thought, and dropped the note back on the table. She helped put the children down for their naps and ran into their bedchamber to freshen up. She looked in the vanity mirror, re-applied her lipstick, smoothed her coiffure and sprayed her pulse points with Houbigant's *Roses* perfume. Finally, she took her latest sketch book down from the top of the wardrobe and dashed from the room.

True to her word, she reached the Café Parisienne five minutes early. It was mid-afternoon so only a few patrons were in the enchanting sunlit café. She sat at a table and waited for Molly Brown and Madame Lucile to arrive, taking in the white trellised walls that reminded her of their veranda back home. She ordered a cup of one of the exotic teas the Café was famous for, and waited. A half later she was still waiting. She wondered if she'd been spitefully duped.

Disappointed, she got ready to leave. She was reaching in her purse for a tip for the waiter when she heard Molly Brown's cheerful voice a ways off.

"Well, if it isn't Major Butt and Colonel Gracie," Molly chirped at two older, important looking men sitting at one of the tables. "Sipping tea no less. Don't let this get out boys. Your reputations could be compromised."

The two men laughed, greeted her and a moment later Molly breezed over to her table. "Sorry, I'm late," she said to Nicolette as she sat in the wicker chair across the table from her. "Lady Gordon sends her regrets. Poor gal has a splitting headache."

"I see." Nicolette said, unsure of whether to believe her or not. "If she doesn't want to meet me, I understand. You don't have to protect my feelings."

"Hog wash! I'm leveling with you," Molly said, "You'll get to meet her. I just can't say for sure when. Hopefully, her headache will be gone by tomorrow."

The waiter returned and Molly ordered a cup of strong black coffee. Nicolette ordered another cup of tea and they spent over an hour talking and laughing. Nicolette learned they had something in common that very few of the *Titanic*'s First Class passengers could lay claim to: they'd both grown up in poverty. Nicolette, a tattered waif in a humble tailor's shop on the outskirts of Paris, and Margaret, a shoeless country girl in Hannibal, Missouri.

Later, as they said adieu at the bottom of the Grand staircase, Nicolette realized their time together had done her a world of good. She felt revitalized, more energetic than anytime since boarding the ship.

With a lilt in her step she made her way back to their stateroom. Approaching the door, she heard Cecile's cries and rushed through the door to find Nathan changing the baby's nappy while Trista sat on the floor eating a chocolate bar.

He looked up at her and yelled over the baby's cries, "Where have you been?"

"Out, at the Café Parisien."

"Great! That's just great! I give you help so you don't have to exhaust yourself caring for our family, and what do you do? Abscond your responsibility to go cavorting around with some English rag maker." He picked the baby up and handed her to Sabine.

Nicolette yelled back, "that's not true, she…"

Before she could finish her sentence, Nathan was in front of her. "Don't lie to me," he shouted, and snatched her sketch book from her hand. "That's exactly what you were doing. Running around with this nonsense while your baby is here crying her head off." He ripped several pages from her sketch book and threw it across the room.

Nicolette couldn't have been more shocked, or hurt, had he hit her. He knew how much her sketches meant to her, how she'd poured herself into them. Even if he didn't approve of them, he didn't have to destroy them.

For a long moment, they stood there glaring at each other, locked in an angry standoff. Finally, Nicolette stooped down, picked up her sketch book and gathered the torn pages from the floor. Breaking the silence she stood up and waved the battered sketchbook at her husband, "Until you apologize for this, don't bother speaking to me. I have nothing to say to you. Nothing!"

She stomped away and he followed her.

"Wait," he called, but she didn't want to hear a word he had to say and slammed the door in his face.

Nicolette wasn't ready to talk to Nathan. She was still too hurt and angry at him for what he'd done to her sketchbook. So she locked herself in their bedchamber and ignored the apologies he tried to make to her from the other side of the door. Stewing with anger, she spent the afternoon trying to re-create the designs he'd so maliciously ruined.

Around five o'clock Sabine knocked on the door and told her it was time for the children to eat dinner. Nicolette laid her sketchbook down on the bed and walked through the parlor, pointedly ignoring Nathan who sitting on the sofa reading a book. She helped the au pair change the children's clothes, and comb their hair. Then she gave them both big kisses and took them in to their father.Your daughters are ready for dinner," she announced, sitting Cecile on his lap while Trista climbed up on the sofa next to him.

Nathan looked up at her, "Aren't you coming with us?"

"No, I don't care for the company," she answered spitefully. "Sabine can go and help you with the children."

"Nicolette, this is absurb. You have to-"

"Let's not upset the children," she said icily, cutting him off, then turned and marched into the bedchamber. A few minutes later she heard them leave.

For a while she sat cross-legged on the bed, her face cupped in her hands. She stared blankly at the open armoire across the room and watched her clothes sway on their hangers to the rhythm of the ship's engine.

It's got to be this trip...this ship, she thought. *Nathan is changing, he's so angry and tense all the time, and I'm beginning to feel it too.*

Every time they stepped outside their stateroom together they got raised eyebrows, or nasty comments from the crew and passengers. They'd never had to endure this level of bigotry and malice before.

Just this morning they were walking on the deck after breakfast and Nathan was pushing Cecile in her pram when a couple of men, clearly Americans from their accents, came up to them. One of them tapped Nathan on the shoulder, pushed several coins at him and said, "Boy, I need a shoeshine. Run and get your kit."

A dark cloud set on Nathan's face and she could tell he was fuming, but he managed to keep his composure and walked away. Afterwards, however, he was sullen and silent. When they got back to their stateroom he didn't say anything to her, or even look at her for the longest time. Instead, he hid his hurt and shame by isolating himself behind his newspaper.

And then there was the run-in he'd had with the wireless operators yesterday and the Captain simply dismissing him. She sensed he was still smarting about that too.

But none of that is my fault, she thought angrily. *He doesn't have the right to take it out on me. Ripping my sketchbook was mean and vicious.* And though she hated to admit it, it scared her. She'd never seen him so angry before. It made her wonder if she'd misjudged him, if next he would be hitting her. He'd always sworn he'd never do such a thing, that he wasn't that kind of man. But now she wasn't so sure. She'd learned as a small child that some men would do anything to control their wives and she wondered if that was how he was becoming.

The unsettling question swirled in her head, leading her mind to a cold Saturday night in 1897. She was four years old at the time and lived in the little town of Villejuef with her natural parents, Gaston and Lynette Malveau.

At first, that Saturday night seemed like any other in the Malveau house. Her father had had too much wine and her mother moved nervously about the small kitchen. She sat on a tiny stool next to the cook stove with her favorite doll on her lap, hoping there wouldn't be blood like last time.

Her father scowled at her, "Nicolette, put that blasted doll away and get over here and eat." He wavered back and forth next to his chair at the head of the rough-hewn kitchen table.

"Oui Papa," she leaped from the stool, lay her doll down, and scampered across the room to the table. Using her scrawny little arms, elbows and every bit of her strength, she hoisted herself up into one of the big chairs. Sitting up straight, she was just tall enough to reach her plate and feed herself.

A white, cracked bowl of boiled cabbage was steaming in the center of the table. Next to it was the loaf of fresh bread her mother had slaved over most of the day. The only thing missing was the roasted chicken.

She was so hungry, the sight and smell of the food made her stomach grumble. She could hardly wait to eat. The meager piece of cheese and stale bread her mother had given her that morning had long since been digested.

"Lynette! Dammit de Dieu!" Her father banged his fist on the table, bellowing and slurring his speech. "What's taking so long? A man could perish waiting on you."

Across the room, her mother was taking the chicken out of the oven. *Mama, please hurry,* she begged silently, *You know what happens when Papa gets angry.*

Her mother rushed to the table with the hot chicken on an old, chipped serving platter. "I'm sorry it took so long, Gaston. I ran out of wood this afternoon," she feigned a smile. "I had to split some logs before I could finish cooking. Nicolette and I nearly froze out there." She sat the platter of chicken in front of him then took a seat at the table, across from Nicolette.

Without a word, her father dug into the chicken. He heaped most of it on his plate, leaving a wing and drumstick for her and her mother.

Nicolette watched her mother bow her head and silently say grace. *Oh, Mama,* she thought nervously, *Why do you have to do that? You know Papa hates it.* Her father always said praying was just a bunch of useless mumbling, that it didn't do a damned thing. Nicolette almost sighed with relief when her mother finished. She sat quietly as her mother reached over and spooned some cabbage onto her plate.

Suddenly her father stopped sawing the chicken in front of him. Cursing, he raised the carving knife high above his head and slammed the blade deep into the wooden tabletop making everything on the table bounce and rattle.

"How the hell do you expect me to eat this slop?" he yelled, and shoved his plate at her Mama. "It's bloody inside."

"I…I'm sorry, Gaston…," her Mama stammered. "Let…let me put it back in the oven for you. I guess it didn't cook long enough. I told you, I ran out of-"

Her father jumped up from his chair and struck her Mama hard across the face. She snapped back and she and the chair crashed to the floor.

Nicolette scrunched down in her chair. She lowered her head, hiding her fright and the water pooling in her eyes lest she attract her father's attention.

"I'm sick and tired of your apologies," her Papa yelled. Big blue veins popped out in his neck, his face was red, contorted with rage. He took two steps, leaned over her Mama sprawled on the floor, and grabbed her by the bosom of her dress. He yanked her petite frame from the floor and stood her on her feet, shouting, "When I come home after working all week, I want a decent cooked meal, not apologies, damned you. You've been feeding me nothing but garbage since I married you."

He slapped her again and Nicolette flinched at the awful, cracking sound. Terrified, she looked away as he slapped her over and over, in the face, on her head, all the while cursing, calling her stupid, worthless, yelling that he was going to kill her.

Against her will, Nicolette's tear-filled eyes were drawn to the terror unfolding in front of her as her father's slaps became thudding punches to her mother's upper body and arms. Her Mama cried, and begged, "Please Gaston. Please stop. You're hurting me. Please, stop. Please…"

Nicolette's heart raced in her chest. She'd seen her Papa beat her Mama before, and every time it got worse. A few months ago, he hit her with a splintered piece of kindling and punctured her leg. Blood spewed like a geyser from the wound, spraying everything in sight. She believed it was the sight of so much blood that time that finally made him stop beating her.

Nicolette cried softly, cowering in her chair, too afraid to move. Then, for some strange reason, her mother's tortured eyes locked with hers while she was still being beaten. "Run, Nicolette," she screamed, "Get out of here! Run! Run!"

That seemed to make her Papa even angrier. He yelled, "I'm going to kill the both of you worthless bitches!" He knocked her Mama to the floor again and screamed, "You hear me Lynette? You hear me?"

For an instant, Nicolette was paralyzed, afraid to obey, yet too afraid not to. *What if he sees me? He'll kill me too…I know he will…*

Her Papa straddled her Mama on the floor, clasped his big hands around her next and choked her, growling like a mad man. Her mother's face turned red, then blue, as she squirmed and thrashed, trying in vain to pry his hands from around her neck.

Sure that he was killing her, Nicolette slid from her chair and ran across the room as fast as her little legs would carry her to the stack of firewood in the corner next to the kitchen stove. She quickly squeezed her little body behind the logs, then peeked out to see if he had finished killing her Mama.

She saw him get up, and for the longest time he just stood there swaying back and forth, staring down at her Mama's motionless body. Her wavy, strawberry blond hair was fanned about her battered face, her arms and legs splayed awkwardly.

The entire house was eerily quiet. Nicolette cowered behind the wood pile too scared to move. *Oh, non, she's dead. He killed her. He killed her.* She just knew her mother was dead. Afraid her Papa would hear her crying, she covered her mouth and got snot on her hands.

An ember popped inside the cook stove, cracking the silence. Her Papa grunted then called her name sending a shock wave through her. "Nicolette! Answer me you little red haired rat! Nicolette! Where are you, girl? Nicolette!"

She was terrified. Afraid of what he'd do if she didn't answer him, yet too petrified to open her mouth. Her heart thundered as she imagined him finding her, picking her up by the throat, and choking her until she was dead like Mama.

Her father stumbled about the kitchen like a lead foot giant, then she heard him walk out of the room. She summoned the courage to peek out from behind the logs and saw her Mama still lying on the floor, motionless. She wanted so badly to run to her, but her father came stumbling back into the kitchen carrying a jug of wine. He went over and nudged her Mama's thigh with the toe of his boot. Still, she didn't move. He grunted nonchalantly, turned his wine jug up and took a long swig. Then he stumbled over to the table and plopped down in his chair, He poured another glass of wine, gulped it down, and laid his head on the table.

Nicolette waited, silently waited, for him to go to sleep and it seemed to take forever. She heard a dog bark outside in the distance and saw her Papa raise his head and look around. A little later, some logs shifted inside the stove and she heard him grunt.

Finally, he started to snore and she eased out from behind the logs. She tiptoed over to where her Mama lay on the floor and knelt beside her. Grief wrenched her heart and she gently touched her Mama's cheek. To her amazement, her Mama moaned. Slowly, she opened her eyes and moved her head.

"Oh, Mama, I thought you were dead." Nicolette sobbed uncontrollably. "He hurt you so bad. He hurt you so."

Grimacing, her Mama sat up and pressed her fingertips to her temples. Only she didn't look like her pretty Mama any more. Her face was swollen, her skin an ugly mixture of red, green and blue. Her mouth was split in the crease on one side and was still bleeding. Her left eye was purple, puffy, and nearly closed, and her right eye was blood shot with a blue-black ring around it. She looked over at Nicolette's Papa snoring at the kitchen table, then back at Nicolette.

"Ma cheri, be a good girl and help Mama up," she said quietly.

Nicolette grabbed her mother's hand, pulled hard and helped her to her feet. She pressed her fingers to her swollen lips, warning Nicolette to be quiet, then motioned for her to follow her. They tiptoed into the family bedroom where Nicolette slept in a small cot across from her parent's bed. Her Mama went over to her dresser and looked at her face in the mirror. Crying softly, she shook her head murmuring, "No more, Gaston. I can't take any more." She went to the closet next to Nicolette's cot, opened the door and took out their coats. She put hers on then helped Nicolette with hers.

"Where are we going, Mama?" Nicolette asked, as her mother tied a white cotton scarf on her head. She shooshed her then took Nicolette's hand. Again on tiptoe, she led her from the bedroom, through the kitchen and out the kitchen door.

Once outside, Nicolette asked her Mama again where they were going. "Away from Villejuef," she answered. "Someplace where we won't have to be afraid."

It was so cold, and Nicolette was *so* hungry. But she didn't complain. She held fast to her Mama's hand, trusting that she'd find food and warmth for them soon. They walked the silent streets all night, until Nicolette's little feet were numb from the cold. The sun was rising when they came to a quaint little shop with a giant pair of wooden scissors hanging above the door. She had no idea where they were.

Her Mama knocked on the door for the longest time before a stooped old man in a nightshirt, baggy trousers and no shoes cracked the door a peg. "Who's there?" he asked.

"C'est Lynette, Monsieur Bonschear… Lynette Malveau."

"Lynette?" the old man opened the door wider. For a few seconds he didn't seem to know who she was, then suddenly he recognized her beneath the grotesque mask of bruised flesh. "Lynette! Oh mon Dieu!" he exclaimed. "Entrez… entrez. What happened?"

An old woman with long white braids stepped from behind the old man and practically dragged them into the room.

Her Mama started to cry as the old woman chastised her husband. "Honore, it's obvious what's happened to her. She's been assaulted." She put her arm around her Mama's shoulder, comforting her.

The man found them some chairs and Nicolette's Mama collapsed into one. Crying, she told them her husband had been beating her since their wedding night. "I try so hard to be a good wife," she sobbed, "but nothing I do is good enough. He goes into a rage over the slightest thing. He almost killed me this time. And he keeps threatening to kill

Nicolette. He's so jealous of her. I'm afraid if I go back, he'll kill us both."

When her Mama finally stopped crying, she said, "Olivie, I must speak with you and Honore alone, please."

The grown ups went into the kitchen leaving Nicolette alone in the little room. She looked around, taking in boxes of various shapes and sizes stacked here and there, spilling over with fabrics, laces and yarn. Jars of buckles, buttons and notions she couldn't identify sat on several shelves. To one side of the room, two sewing machines stood head-to-head, their cabinets touching. A fine sheen of dust covered everything in the room, but it was warm and had a safe, comforting feel to it, like nothing bad could ever happen there.

Nicolette's feet finally got warm. She was nodding off when Honore came back into the room with a big bowl of porridge. "Come, eat something," he said, and sat the steaming bowl at the end of a long, smooth, worktable. He pushed the clutter on it to one side and helped Nicolette bring her chair over. After she was settled, he shook his head muttering, "pauve ti bete." He smiled at her, then went back into the other room with Mama and Madame Bonschear.

Porridge was Nicolette's favorite breakfast and she ate with gusto. By the time the adults re-appeared she had finished it and was nodding off again.

"Nicolette, take off your coat," her Mama said. She came over and helped her out of it. Handing it to Madame Bonscher she added, "I have to go out ma cheri, and I want you to stay here with the Bonschears."

"Why can't I go with you?" Nicolette asked.

"Because it's cold and I want you to stay here and keep warm. The Bonschears will take good care of you while I'm gone." She leaned down, kissed her on the cheek and gave her a very long hug. "Now…," she held Nicolette at arms length and looked at her, a tear rolling from her bloodshot eye, "you be a good girl and mind the Bonschears, okay? And remember, Mama loves you always, no matter what."

"I will," Nicolette replied, trying not to cry.

At the door, her Mama said goodbye to the Bonschears and looked lovingly at Nicolette. Her swollen bottom lip quivered and a fat tear rolled down her bruised face. She wiped it away and walked out the door.

Nicolette wanted so much to be a good girl for her Mama. She told herself that her Mama would be back, that she had to come back. She had to take care of her. Unable to hold back the tears, she burst into sobs and ran to the window. "Mama come back," she cried, "Please don't leave me. Please come back. Come back."

But her Mama couldn't hear her. She didn't turn around. And she didn't come back. She never came back.

Noise coming from the Sitting Room brought Nicolette back to the present. Nathan and the children were back and Trista bounded into the bedchamber followed by Cecile who dawdled behind her.

"Look Mama, look what Papa gave us," Trista turned her head so Nicolette could see the white carnation tucked beneath the blue ribbon in her hair. "Isn't it pretty?" she climbed up onto the bed with her.

"Oui. C'est belle!" She kissed her on the forehead and reached down and picked up Cecile. She had a carnation in her fine black hair too, held firmly by a small barrette. Nicolette hugged them both and said, "I missed my girls."

"I saw the Renard's at dinner," Nathan announced

coming into the room. "They told me to tell you hello."

Nicolette ignored him. She picked up one of the children's books from the foot of the bed and started to read it to them. It wasn't long before they were both asleep. Nathan came in, picked them up carried them into the room they shared with Sabine.

When he came back he closed the door and said, "Nicolette, "I'm sorry. I know I shouldn't have ripped your sketchbook. I was wrong and I apologize."

After a moment, she answered, "I accept your apology, but I'm still not over what you did, and I'm not up to talking yet, so let's just leave it at that, all right?"

He started to say something, evidently thought better of it, and left the room.

She wanted to forgive him, *really* forgive him, but she couldn't. Something had changed. For the first time she realized just how much he needed to control her, and she hadn't come to terms with it yet. She still loved him, after all, he was the father of her children. And he was a loving father, a good provider, and an otherwise good husband. But he'd destroyed something precious between them: the absolute assurance that no matter what happened, no matter how angry they got with each other, she would always be safe with him. She wasn't sure she could live with him without that assurance.

Yet, it was the very worst time for her to find out her husband wasn't really the kind of man she thought he was, especially with two small children and one on the way.

So what *could* she do? Try to live with it and hope things wouldn't get worse? Try to make him change? She doubted that would work. Or, she could strike out on her own and hope she'd find a way to take care of her children. None of the possibilities appealed to her. But she *was* sure of a few things. She would not let him abuse her the way her father had abused her mother, and she would never give up her children, no matter how inept she felt. If she had to leave Nathan, she'd find a way to take care of them.

Chapter 17

"Well I'll be." Jimmy Ray stopped on the deck outside the First Class Smoking room and looked through the window. It was night, around ten o'clock and the room was lit as brightly as a Christmas tree. He saw Nathan Legarde seated at a table, talking with a distinguished looking white man. "That Nigger's got more nerve than a zebras got stripes," he said to Earl Lee. "You know what this means don't you?"

"What?"

"It means he's roomin' somewhere in First Class, while we're in Second Class. He wouldn't be allowed to sit in there if he wasn't. Burns me the hell up. What right does he have being in a higher class than us?"

"I guess he must've bought First Class tickets," Earl Lee replied, fanning Jimmy Ray's ire.

"The hell you say! You just don't git it do ya? Niggers ain't supposed to have better'n whites folks under no circumstances. It ain't right. Violates the natural order God intended."

Duly chastised, Earl Lee replied, "You're right. I wasn't thinkin' straight. So, what do we do now?"

"Wait. If he heads for the inside exit we go in and follow him, find out exactly where his room is. If he comes out here," he pointed towards a dark spot on the deck between the Smoking

Room windows and the First Class entrance, "we hide over there and nab him when he walks by."

"Aw shit!" Earl Lee complained. "Why can't we wait for him inside? It's freezing out here."

"'Cause I don't want him seein' us, stupid." Jimmy Ray cupped his own hands and blew on them to warm them up.

"I told you to stop callin' me stupid, Jimmy Ray," Earl Lee grumbled, his feelings hurt.

They heard footsteps approaching and turned to see a smartly uniformed officer coming in their direction. When he reached them, the officer touched the brim of his cap and stopped. "Good evening gentlemen. Looks a lot warmer in there." He nodded toward the smoking room window. "Why don't you gents come inside?"

"Then we'd miss the show," Jimmy Ray exclaimed, pretending excitement. "Been hearin' folks say the Big Dipper's gonna be in the sky tonight and we're hankerin' to see it."

"I guess I've been working too hard," the officer looked up at the starry night sky. "I didn't hear a thing about it." He touched the brim of his cap again, "Well, gentlemen, enjoy your stargazing." He opened the door to the Smoking room and stepped inside.

Jimmy Ray and Earl Lee shivered in the frosty night air another twenty minutes. The thought of finally taking his revenge on Legarde kept his mind off his feet that were slowly going numb in his boots. He imagined plunging a knife deep into his heart, could almost feel the pleasure of putting a gun to his head and pulling the trigger. Then he'd throw his black ass overboard.

Through the window he saw Legarde get up and walk toward the door leading to the deck. Realizing he was finally going to get his chance, he felt like sending up a rebel yell.

He poked Earl Lee in the side. "All right now, he's makin' a move. Remember what I told you."

"I remember. I just want to get this shit over with. I'm darned near froze."

Hot damn, we got ya' now, Jimmy Ray, thought as he and Earl Lee sprinted for cover in a dark patch on the deck.

From then on, everything happened at breakneck speed. Legarde, walked briskly past the smoking room windows into the shadowy darkness. Within seconds he was directly in front of them. Jimmy Ray grabbed the gun from his pocket, lunged, and hit him on the side of the head with it. Legarde fell to the deck in a heap. At the same time they heard someone yell: "Hey! What's going on there?! Hey!"

Jimmy Ray looked up and saw the nigger lover Legarde had been talking to in the smoking room. He was running toward them, yelling.

"Dammit," Jimmy Ray mumbled through clinched teeth, a mixture of frustration and anxiety coursing through him. Realizing his well laid plan was being foiled, he said to Earl Lee, "Come on, we gotta git outta here."

But Earl Lee hesitated. He was looking down at Legarde lying on the deck. "You mean after all-"

"Come on, God dammit!" Jimmy Ray growled. He grabbed his arm and pulled him away from Legarde' body. They ran toward the bow of the ship staying in the shadows as much as they could. At the Second Class entrance they ducked inside, found the first set of stairs leading to the deck below and high tailed it back to their quarters.

Jimmy Ray slammed the door behind them and yelled, "Dammit! I had him in the palm of my hand and the bastard gits away. If it weren't for that nigger-lover interfering, I would've had him."

Earl Lee took off his overcoat and scarf, threw them on the sofa and darted into the lavatory. Jimmy Ray followed him, cussing and ranting. "But he ain't seen the last of Jimmy Ray Tuttle. Not by a long shot." He watched as Earl Lee ran warm water over his brick-like hands to warm them. "Legarde got lucky," he continued, "but sooner or later, I'm gonna catch him in the right place at the right time. You mark my word. His luck's gonna run out. And when it does, his ass belongs to me."

Chapter 18

When Nathan regained consciousness he was sitting on the floor of A deck. The loudest drum he'd ever heard was beating inside his skull. He reached up and felt a bump the size of a walnut on the right side of his head. "Ow!" He flinched, and jerked his hand away.

Gerard Hale was kneeling beside him. "What happened?" he asked as a small crowd gathered around them.

"I'm not sure. It looked like a couple of hoodlums, probably from steerage. I didn't see their faces. They ran when they saw me. Check your wallet. They could have been robbers."

Nathan felt inside his evening jacket and patted his wallet. "I have it," he said, and let Gerard help him to his feet. "Wow, I didn't see a thing." He wavered on his feet a little trying to get his bearings and heard a man in the crowd comment, "Must've had too much to drink, passed out on the deck..."

Nathan blinked, focusing his eyes in the semi-darkness and saw the two women from the stateroom next to theirs walking by. Over the pounding in his head he heard the older woman harrumph, "See, morally bankrupt. That's why those people have no business in First Class."

He wanted to scream at the old bat, tell her she was wrong, that it wasn't what she thought.

But what good would it do? It would only lead to another altercation that would in all likelihood end up making him look bad. And it certainly wouldn't help the pounding in his head.

"Perhaps you should see a doctor, get checked out," Gerard suggested. Nathan made a dismissive gesture with his hand. "No. I'm all right. I'll be fine."

"If you say so, but I'm seeing you to your quarters just the same." He stuck out his arm and cleared a wedge in the crowd for him and Nathan to pass.

Going from A deck down to B deck in the automatic lift Nathan commented, "How ridiculous, *me* of all people getting clobbered by a couple of second rate pickpockets. They couldn't have been first-rate, or they'd have gone after someone like J.J. Astor, or one of the Wideners. The *real* money on this ship." He laughed, causing the pounding in his head to shoot up a decibel.

Yet, the attack did make him uneasy. Silently, he wondered if they were merely pickpockets out for some fast cash, or if it was something else.

Gerard's voice broke into his thoughts as they got off the lift. "I've always thought of myself as an optimist. I like to think that everyone is basically decent, that the world is generally benevolent. But more and more these days, I find myself wondering if I'm simply naive."

When they reached his stateroom, Nathan hesitated at the door, caught in a two-fold quandary.

He wasn't sure if he should invite Gerard in. He seemed like a genuinely decent sort. After all, they'd just spent an enjoyable hour over drinks, talking about the recent miner's strike in Ireland, Nathan's plans for starting his own engineering firm when he returned to France, Gerard's upcoming marriage to the love of his life. But he was still unsure of their easy camaraderie, and he wasn't sure how he'd react when he met his wife.

And he wasn't sure how Nicolette would respond either. She'd barely spoken to him all evening and he didn't want Gerard to know they were having marital problems.

Not wanting to appear ungrateful for his help, Nathan decided to take the risk and invited him in for a drink. When they stepped inside, all was quiet. He found Nicolette sitting on the sofa darning one of the children's socks. He introduced her to Gerard who didn't seem at all concerned that she was white.

As she shook Gerard's hand, Nathan covertly beseeched her with his eyes to be gracious. But he needn't have worried. She smiled warmly at Gerard and chatted cordially with him while Nathan poured them a couple of brandies. He was relieved and proud of how she rose to the occasion in spite of their earlier argument. In fact, she comported herself with such dignity and poise, it reminded him of why he fell in love with her; it was her eloquence and refinement that he found so appealing, characteristics she embodied in spite of her background. They were also qualities that reminded him of his mother, though he would never confess that to her.

Gerard took one of the brandies Nathan offered him saying, "I can't stay long. I just wanted to make sure Nathan got in all right. He took a really nasty blow to the head."

"A blow?" Nicolette looked over at Nathan. "What happened?"

Nathan explained that he'd gotten clobbered outside the First Class smoking room and assured her he was fine, adding, "I've got a whopping headache though."

"I'll make you something for it." She excused herself and went into the lavatory.

Gerard sat his drink on the table next to his chair and stood. "Well, my good man, it's late. I must be getting along."

Nathan walked him to the door. He thanked him again for his concern, and stepped back into the room just as Nicolette came in with a towel in her hand and he could tell by the set of her shoulders that her attitude had changed completely. Without a word she handed him a packet of headache powder and went to the ice bucket sitting on a cart on the opposite side of the room. She filled the towel with ice, folded it neatly, and walked over to him. "Here," she said, and shoved it at him. Then she left and went into their bedchamber. A moment later, she returned with a pillow and blanket and threw them on the sofa. "I'm sorry you got hurt," she said, "and I wouldn't let on in front of Monsieur Hale, but I'm still very upset with you. So you'll be sleeping out here tonight."

"Out here?!" Nathan said. "I thought we settled this. You accepted my apology, remember?"

"Yes, I accepted your apology, but it's not settled. And right now, I'm not sure it can be. So for now, you can sleep on the sofa. Or on the floor. It's up to you."

She left him standing in the middle of the Parlor with a banging head and a too small sofa to sleep on.

Chapter 19

It was Saturday morning, the fourth day of their voyage and Nathan decided to report to the Captain that he'd been assaulted the night before. After an awkwardly silent breakfast with Nicolette and the children he went up to the Bridge and was told by one of the officers that he might find Captain Smith in the map room. When he got there, the map room was teeming with activity. He found Captain Smith, told him what happened to him the night before and was waiting for a response. But every time he started to speak, he got interrupted. Frustrated, Nathan tried to wait patiently as the Captain spoke to yet another one of his crew.

Though he'd played the whole thing down last night with Nicolette, the incident had stayed on his mind. He wondered if he had simply been in the wrong place at the wrong time or if someone on board had been so enraged by seeing a Negro with a white wife that they physically attacked him. He and Nicolette had certainly been subjected to enough dirty looks and nasty comments that, to his mind, it wasn't unimaginable. On the other hand, he could have been reading too much into it.

Regardless, whoever it was could be dangerous and it was his duty to report it. If he hadn't been singled out, other passengers could be at risk.

Nathan shifted his weight from one foot to the other as Captain Smith said to one of his officers, "…Three hundred and eighty six miles. We might get that speed prize after all, Officer Murdoch." Then he saluted, dismissing the officer, and turned back to Nathan.

"Now, about this so called incident," Captain Smith said. "I was informed about it first thing this morning. You see, my crew keeps on top of things around here. According to the report I got, you passed out on the deck. Drunk."

"What?! That's an absolute lie." Nathan was outraged. "Sure, I had a drink, but I was far from drunk. It happened exactly as I told you. Someone…, I don't know who it was, hit me on the head in the dark. I have the lump on my head to prove it." He reached up and touched the tender spot on his head, emphasizing his point.

The Captain chuckled, his blue eyes twinkling mischievously. "I don't doubt you have a lump on your head. That's what happens sometimes when you try to walk after over imbibing."

"But I wasn't drunk. And I have a witness that will vouch for me. Gerard Hale, he said he knows you. He'll tell you the same thing I did."

"Fine man, Hale," the Captain remarked, "good businessman too. Even so, what would you have me do? I can't go knocking on doors interrogating people. Besides, we haven't had any other reports of attacks, not even a petty pick pocket."

"Perhaps it's just a matter of time, Captain. It wouldn't hurt to have more surveillance of the decks at night. It could be a deterrent."

"Now, now, Mr. Legarde...," the Captain's tone was patronizing, "there's no need for such measures. The passengers on this ship are perfectly safe. And I'd appreciate it if you'd keep mum about your little mishap. White Star has a sterling reputation and I want to keep it that way."

Nathan was dumbfounded. *Is that all you care about?* he thought, *your damned reputation? The smooth running of your ship?*

It was crystal clear to him now that Captain Smith saw his complaints as trivial and his presence as an inconvenience. Twice he'd tried to get him to do the right thing, and both times he'd refused.

Disgusted, Nathan was about to leave when an entourage of important-looking men came into the map room flanked by two crisply attired officers. Nathan recognized one of the men as Nathanial Bell, the chief engineer. Gerard Hale had introduced them last night. The other man was the ship's Purser. At the center of the group was a short man in a blue serge suit and stiff white collar. His dark hair was slicked back and he was animated, laughing and talking, in obvious command of the assemblage.

"Ah, Mr. Ismay, gentlemen," Captain Smith said, turning his back on Nathan, surreptitiously dismissing him.

Ismay. The name rang a bell. Nathan remembered hearing somewhere - perhaps he'd read it - that Ismay was the White Star Line's managing director. He had a lot of clout and it was very evident in the way the other men fawned over him. *But that doesn't mean he's not fair minded,* Nathan thought. *Perhaps if I speak to him, he'd convince the Captain to step up the watch on the decks. Certainly something should be done.*

As soon as Captain Smith finished shaking Ismay's hand, Nathan stepped forward. "Excuse me, Mr. Ismay, but I'd like a short word with you, sir," Nathan said, interrupting the jocular, back slapping banter among the group. Everyone, including Captain Smith went silent. They stared at him as if he'd committed a major social blunder.

Ismay fished in his waistband pocket, took out a monocle on a gold chain and held it up. He looked through it, inspecting Nathan as if he were a giant insect. "You called my name," Ismay said curtly, "I don't recall making your acquaintance."

Nathan sensed immediately that he'd made a big mistake in giving Ismay the benefit of the doubt. But he'd opened his mouth, so he had to finish what he'd started.

"No sir, we haven't met…," Nathan replied, "…but it's important that I speak with you. I was attacked last night. Knocked unconscious and…"

"What did you say your name was?" Ismay said, interrupting him.

"Legarde. Nathan Badeau Legarde."

"One name's quite enough," Ismay quipped, eliciting tense laughter from his entourage. "Listen, Legarde, I'm a very important and busy man. I have an historic goal set for this voyage and I don't have time for nonsense. So I suggest you take your concern to the proper authorities."

"That's the problem," Nathan countered, "I've tried."

"Well, try again," Ismay snapped and turned his back on him.

Instinctively, Nathan stepped forward, hoping he would reconsider. "But Mr. Ismay…"

Ismay jerked around to face him, his face flushed with contempt. He snapped his fingers and the officer standing to his left reached for his gun.

"Hey! I wouldn't do that if I were you," Nathan shouted, eyeing the officer warily. "If you draw that gun on me, you'd damned sure better be ready to use it."

The officer kept his hand on the gun and his eyes on Nathan.

Nathan was afraid to move, but determined not to let it show.

Finally, Captain Smith stepped forward. "Gentlemen, Bruce," he said in a peacemaking tone, "Legarde here got hit on the head last night. He's overwrought, probably not thinking clearly. Why don't we all just simmer down and conduct ourselves with proper decorum."

Everyone in the group seemed happy to let it go, with the exception of Ismay, whose contemptuous glare at Nathan signaled he was still fuming.

Nathan took a slow step back thinking the worst had passed when suddenly Ismay snapped his fingers again. "Throw the bum out," he commanded the officers and they both lunged at Nathan and grabbed his arms.

From somewhere deep inside him rose a strength he didn't know he had. The power of Sampson coursed through him as the injustices heaped upon him from the moment he'd boarded the ship flashed through his mind. He shrugged the officers off and sent them sprawling to the floor at Ismay's feet. Stunned, they both lay there, looking up at him in amazement.

With a fierce stare he issued the officers a warning: "If you come at me again, you'd better come ready to do battle because I *won't* be taken down without a fight."

Slowly, he backed out of the open map room door. Walking away down the corridor he heard Captain Smith remark, "Oh, let it go, Bruce. We don't want the press getting wind of this. Let's turn our minds to something more productive, like that blue ribbon speed record."

Chapter 20

Helen had barely slept all night. She couldn't get what happened yesterday at the ship's Infirmary out of her head. Now she paced the floor of her stateroom while Dodie sat on the sofa scribbling in a coloring book. "I have to go back," she thought, "it's the only way I can get enough Morphine, and I don't have much time. We'll be docking in New York on Saturday." But she was afraid of getting caught again. She could be branded a thief and her reputation ruined. *And poor Gerard, oh what would he think of me? He would be mortified.*

There was a rap on the door and Helen jumped. She could feel her hands trembling as she went to answer it, afraid the ship's authorities had tracked her down. She leaned against the door and called, "Who is it?"

"It's me, Agatha," came the reply.

Relieved, she let out a heavy sigh. Her hands still trembling, she opened the door. Agatha breezed in and Eliza followed her. They both ignored Dodie, and Agatha immediately started talking.

"You've got to sign this petition," she handed Helen a piece of paper with a few signatures on it. "I made it up last night. I want that Negro next door to us moved immediately. It's scandal enough having a white woman openly mixing with one of them, flaunting it in front of everybody. But it turns out, he's also inebriate."

"Inebriate?" That didn't sound right. It didn't coincide with what Gerard had told her about Mr. Legarde.. He'd praised him, said he was very clean-cut, intelligent and educated. He'd told her the Legardes were fine people, very dignified and upstanding.

"He was passed out on the deck last night…," Agatha huffed, indignantly, "…immoral through and through. It's our responsibility to speak out against such behavior." Eliza stood rooted next to her mother, apparently every bit as offended as she was.

Looking at them, it occurred to Helen that they really believed they were the only true moral authority in existence. Yet, she knew they were lying. Gerard had stopped in briefly last night after he left the Legarde's Stateroom. He'd told her Mr. Legarde had been attacked and knocked unconscious, perhaps by a couple of thieves.

"I heard something quite different." Helen said. "Gerard told me -"

"And that's another thing," Agatha cut her off, pointing her finger in the air for emphasis. "He ought to be more careful. How does he think it looks, him taking up with a Negro?"

Helen felt her blood rush to her head and she just couldn't hold her peace any longer. "Who do you think you are judging Gerard? You… you…hypocrite!" she yelled. "With all your talk about morality. Where was your morality when your sister called off our wedding, and kept me all those years as her slave? Where was your sense of morality then? When she blamed me for what happened to Dodie? You knew darned well what she was doing. You even helped her, supported her in her wickedness, and didn't lift a finger, or utter a word in my defense. And here you are, talking to me about morality. Well here's what I think of your perverted sense of morality." She marched over to the fireplace and threw the petition onto the black embers of a nearly spent log. The paper started to smoke then burst into flames.

"Mother...," Eliza looked frightened, "...I think she's gone mad."

"Indeed," Agatha concurred. "No decent person in their right mind would take the side of a Negro against their own flesh and blood."

Helen whirled around and stepped toward them. "Don't you dare talk about me like I'm not here," she shouted, "You bigoted, spiteful old crows, always looking down your noses at people, pointing your fingers. I can see right through you. You're after the Legardes because they've got the guts to love each other in spite of hateful people like you, people who need to look down on someone else to feel superior. It's the only way the two of you can feel good about yourselves. As for flesh and blood," she pointed at Dodie, *"she's* your flesh and blood. Thank heavens, I'm not."

"Well," Agatha huffed, drawing her skinny body into a stiff vertical line. "Beulah always said you weren't the innocent, angel you pretended to be.

Now I see what she meant. You're vile and vicious, and we don't have to put up with your despicable accusations." She turned to her daughter, "Let's go, Eliza." The two of them strode swiftly for the door. Agatha yanked it open and walked out, but Eliza paused for one last swipe at Helen. "You've burned your bridges with us," she huffed, "Don't think you can come around and pawn Dodie off on us anymore. We're through with the both of you." She walked out and slammed the door behind her.

Helen stood in the middle of the room and covered her face with her hands. *Oh, God, what's come over me,* she thought. *Perhaps I really am mad. What if I do need their help again? Sooner or later, I've got to get back to the dispensary."* Already she regretted the things she'd said.

She went into the lavatory, adjusted the taps, and splashed some water on her face. *Think logically, Helen, think logically,* she urged herself. *You'll find help. Soon it'll all be over.*

Chapter 21

Jimmy Ray stopped in his tracks. "Git a load o' that." He pointed at a group of youngsters surrounding a boy of about seven or eight. The boy was spinning a wooden top on the deck, and the children, all younger than him, watched intently.

"Them kids?" Earl Lee said, indifferent.

"Yeah, look at the little girl in the blue coat…the one with the blue ribbon in her hair. That's Legarde's kid."

"How do you know that?" Earl Lee's face was a mask of skepticism.

"'Cause she's a half-breed. Looks just like the little mulatto bastards runnin' around New Orleans…same skin color, same hair." He turned and looked in the opposite direction. "See those two women over there. One of them's Legarde's wife, that half-breed's Momma."

"How can you be so sure, Jimmy Ray?" Earl Lee looked from the child to the women.

Earl Lee's doubting was getting on Jimmy Ray's nerves, so he lashed out, "'Cause I said so, dammit! I know what I'm talkin' about. Besides, my cousin, Anton, over in Paris told me all about Legarde. Said he had two little girls and his wife had strawberry blonde hair. That number with her hand on the pram sure looks like a strawberry blonde to me."

"Pretty too," Earl Lee commented. "Nice figure."

"Maybe. But she can't be quality, not married to a nigger."

Just then Jimmy Ray caught the faint cords of a carnival tune. He looked past the two women and saw an organ grinder with a monkey on his shoulder in the distance. Next to them was a balloon peddler with a multi-colored bouquet of balloons floating way above his head. The sight gave Jimmy Ray a new idea.

"See that fella' with the balloons," he pointed to the fat man holding the balloons. "I want you to go down there and buy me one." He reached in his pocket and took out some change. "I got an idea, guaranteed to bring that darky to me in no time flat."

"What do you need a -" Understanding flashed in Earl Lee's eyes. "Oh, no, Jimmy Ray, I ain't up for hurtin' no kids. I don't care what they are. You didn't say nothin' about messin' with no kids."

"We're not goin' to hurt her, just borrow her. That's all. I swear. Nothin' else." Jimmy Ray dropped several pennies in his hand.

Earl Lee hesitated a few seconds then said, "All right. "But you better keep your word."

"Just hurry up."

Jimmy Ray stood in the alcove at the deck entrance and tried to act normal while keeping an eye on the group of children and the two women chatting nearby. The one he believed was

Legarde's wife turned sideways and looked over at the children. He caught a full view of her and an acid mixture of jealousy and disgust bubbled inside him. *Why would a woman like that want a Nigger?* he wondered. *Why would any white woman, even a Frenchy, lay with one of them? It's a slap in the face of every white man on earth.* Consoling himself he thought, *Aw, she's probably just white trash. Maybe even one of them French whores. Probably just got tired of whorin.'*

It seemed to take forever for Earl Lee to get the damned balloon. Finally, he came back and handed him a bright red balloon on a long string. Jimmy Ray looked over and saw that the children were still engrossed in the boy with the spinning top, oooing and squealing with delight as the top twirled and wobbled on the hardwood deck.

Stepping from the cover of the alcove, Jimmy Ray glanced about to make sure no one was observing. "Pssst! Pssst! Hey, little girl," he called in a low voice trying to get the attention of the girl in the blue coat. A girl with blonde, poker straight hair turned and looked at him questioningly. He shook his head, *no,* and the child turned away.

He called again. "Pssst! Hey, little girl. Pssst! Pssst!"

This time, the Legarde child turned around and he whispered, "Hey, look what I've got. You want it? You want a balloon?" He leaned back into the alcove, making sure the women couldn't see him, and held out the balloon.

The cute little girl smiled at him. She pressed a small finger to her pink lips as if considering his offer, then ran over to him. He bent down with the string of the balloon in his right hand ready to grab her as soon as she got close enough.

Then the unforeseen happened. He heard footsteps and glanced around to find an elderly couple coming up the stairs. Quick as a flash, the child yanked the string from his hand. He whirled around and reached for the child, but all he got was the blue satin ribbon from her hair. The little devil scampered like a jackrabbit to her mother shouting something in French he couldn't understand.

"Aw shit! he motioned for Earl Lee to follow him before the child could reach her mother. He turned, pushed the octogenarians out of his way and ducked down the stairs, mad as hell.

Chapter 22

Nathan wandered aimlessly on the shelter deck, trying to let the effects of the adrenaline rush on his body wear off before returning to his stateroom. In his present state, he knew that wouldn't be a good idea. It wouldn't take much right now for him to say or do the wrong thing. He'd apologized to his wife twice already and she still wasn't speaking to him and frankly, he was fed up with her nonsense. She was blowing everything completely out of proportion and the mean-spirited people he was running into on the ship wasn't making her behavior any easier to take.

He leaned against the deck rail and looked out at the endless blue sea. He stared at the gentle white capped waves glinting in the morning sun, cresting and breaking as far as the eye could see. He shook his head, still thinking about his wife. "She is so stubborn," he thought, and almost instantly, "and so are you," echoed inside his head. The realization that they were so much alike in spite of their differences, almost made him smile. As much as he hated to admit it, deep down he knew it was his own stubborn pride that was contributing to his troubles. It was his pride that made it impossible to accept the idea of his wife working. It was the reason he couldn't let it go when Captain Smith dismissed him, why he refused to take it when Ismay treated him like dirt. Had he just walked away and waited to report the attack to the White Star Line when he got to New York, things wouldn't have turned so ugly.

A gust of wind swept the deck and Nathan considered going to the smoking room for a glass of Cognac to take the chill off. But he changed his mind. It was too early in the day. He'd already been labeled a drunkard and buying the first drink of the day would only reinforce that belief in people's minds.

He looked up at the *Titanic*'s towering smoke stacks, its majestic white masts billowing in the wind. A few people were walking around on the upper decks, but for some reason, he felt a profound separateness from them, as if he, and they, were entirely different species in the great sea of humanity. An intense loneliness washed over him and pushing it away, he decided to pay his new friend, Gerard Hale, a visit.

When he reached Gerard's quarters he knocked on the door several times and waited, but no one answered. Summoning a passing hall steward he asked if he knew the cabin's occupant.

"Mr. Ale?" the gangly youth replied with a cockney accent. "Yes sir, he's gone up to the gymnasium, said he was going to try out that new rowing machine today."

"Thank you," Nathan reached in his pocket and fished out a couple of coins and handed them to him. He left and walked to the automatic lift under the Grand staircase and took it up to A deck, as far as it would go. He got off, took the stairs up to the Boat Deck and found the gymnasium adjacent to the staircase. He stepped inside and looked around the large gymnasium. The first thing he saw was a couple of fellows in striped bathing suits using the rowing machines. Then he saw a really fat man using one of the electric camels; the machine labored and groaned under his weight.

Nathan heard voices coming from the back of the gymnasium. He looked over and saw Gerard Hale playing some kind of floor game with another man. He walked toward them, his heels echoing on the hardwood floor.

Gerard looked up and saw him. "Legarde! Come, join us." He raised his hand and beckoned him over.

"Bonjour, gentlemen," Nathan said when he reached them.

"Good to see you," Gerard said and slapped him on the back. Then he introduced him to his young companion.

"Nathan, this is Victor Penasco, world traveler and Madrid's worst quoits player. Victor, meet Nathan Legarde. He's a construction engineer. You might have heard about him. He's the chap the newspapers were making such a fuss about last year, the one who designed the headgear for the French Metro workers.

Penasco changed the quoit he was holding from his right hand to his left and shook Nathan's hand. "My pleasure, Senore Legarde." He gave him a warm, welcoming smile.

Nathan couldn't help but notice the large, expensive emerald ring he was wearing on the ring finger of his left hand. He couldn't miss the man's suave sophistication either. In fact, everything about him bespoke class and privilege, from his casually worn, starched white shirt to his brown suede oxfords. And he was handsome by anyone's standards: a princely face with hazel eyes and wavy brown hair.

Gerard made the final quoit toss of their game, handily losing to Victor, then asked Nathan to join them for a three-way challenge. Competitive by nature, Nathan accepted.

As they played, Nathan told them about the confrontation he'd had earlier in the map room.

When he finished, Gerard said, "I'm disappointed in E.J. I always thought of him as a fair minded man. But Ismay...," he paused and shook his head, "...a puffed up, pompous bigot if I ever saw one. Thinks the rest of the world is his personal spittoon."

"I'm glad I heard about this attack," Victor interjected. "From now on, no one in our party goes out on the decks after dark."

They went back to their quoits and Nathan lost the first game to Victor by five points and they started a second game. As they played, he found out quite a bit about Victor Penasco. He was the son of a famous author and on a two year honeymoon with his bride, Maria Josefa, whom he affectionately called Pepita. He also learned that he had become friends with Gerard when Gerard's company designed some buildings for the Premier of Spain, his wife's uncle.

By the third game, Nathan had gotten the hang of quoits and was scoring higher than both of his opponents. They were in the middle of the game when the two unsavory characters Nathan had seen in the inquiry office came into the gymnasium. They walked toward them and Nathan could feel the tension in his body return as they stationed themselves a few feet away and watched them play. At first, they didn't say anything, just stood there watching, whispering back and forth to each other.

The game was winding down and Nathan and his companions were starting the last round of tosses when the thin, blond man wearing the Stetson stepped forward. Speaking to Nathan he drawled, "You got a pretty good arm. Looks like you're gonna win this thing."

"I do okay," Nathan replied curtly. He turned his attention to Gerard, watched him make his toss and miss the hob.

"Ever done any boxin'?" the blond man asked.

"Not much," Nathan replied. "Fencing is my forte."

"Well, I'll be. Did you hear that, Earl Lee?" the blond man laughed, "... that's one of them big words I never heard before. Oh, I almost forgot my manners. I'm Jimmy Ray Tuttle. This here is my friend, Earl Lee Earl Lee."

Nathan wouldn't offer his hand. He nodded and replied, "Mr. Tuttle…, Mr. Earl Lee."

Victor wouldn't shake their hands either. "Gentlemen," he said, acknowledging their presence and Gerard simply said, "Hello."

It was Nathan's final toss. He was glad for an excuse to ignore the two men. He hoped they'd get the message and leave. But they stood fast and continued to watch them.

Nathan held the quoit up in his hand, lined the hob up in his sight, drew back and tossed. The quoit sailed through the air and ringed the hob.

"Good show," Gerard exclaimed. Victor congratulated him too and suggested they go to the smoking room for some refreshment. They were picking up the game pieces when Jimmy Ray called to Nathan, "Listen, how about a real game. Somethin' that takes some guts. Not this high falutin foreign stuff, but a good old American type game."

"Like what?" Nathan stooped down and picked up a quoit.

"Well, my friend Earl Lee here would like to challenge you to a boxin' match."

"A boxing match?! You have to be kidding," Nathan exclaimed.

"Nope. Figured we might stir up a little excitement around here. We've about had our fill of fancy teas and sight seeing."

For a brief moment, Nathan wondered why they didn't offer the challenge to one of his companions. He looked at Gerard and Victor thinking, *Well, Gerard is a bit over the hill for such things, but Victor isn't.* So he asked, "Why me?"

"Because me and Earl Lee think you can offer some competition." Jimmy Ray gestured toward Gerard and Victor. "No disrespect to your friends, but you're a fine, strappin' young fella'. Got a fighter's build too. You'd be more of a challenge."

Gerard and Victor looked at Nathan and warned him with their eyes not to get involved. Heeding their message, he said, "I'm not interested."

"Well, I'll be damned." The Earl Lee fellow slapped his friend on the back. "He's not interested. Now ain't that somethin'? Looks to me like the boy's yella.' But that ain't no real surprise." They both laughed and Gerard and Victor exchanged embarrassed glances.

Nathan could feel his nerves recharging. "No, I'm not afraid to fight you," he shot back defensively, "I'm just not in the habit of fighting imbeciles."

"The hell you say," Earl Lee barked, taking a step toward him. "You better watch your mouth boy, or I'll kick your ass right here."

Jimmy Ray grabbed Earl Lee's arm and pulled him back, speaking to him soothingly. "Now, Earl Lee, don't go gettin' all riled up over some coward. He probably heard how you knocked that nig…, er, that colored boxer, Jack Johnson on his ass. Figures you'll do the same to him. He's chicken, plain and simple. You can see that."

"Yeah, chicken," Earl Lee laughed. "Just like them cluckers back home. You can pluck 'em, spit on 'em, kick 'em in the ass, and all they do is squawk." He flapped his arms imitating a chicken. "Squawk, squawk, squawk, squawk, squawk, squawk."

Nathan was humiliated to the core. He was about to tell them to go to hell when Gerard stepped in. "Why don't you gentlemen just leave," he said sternly.

"Sure." Jimmy Ray took a cigar from the inside breast pocket of his jacket, ran it between his thin wet lips and quipped, "It's obvious your friend doesn't have any guts."

Nathan was so mad it took every ounce of his self control not to grab one of them. He bent down and picked up another quoit. When he stood up, he was struck by the look on Victor Penasco's face, a mixture of pity and embarrassment. In a hushed tone he remarked to Nathan, "In my country, a man is honor bound to defend his machismo. Anything less is a disgrace, for him and for his entire family."

The words cut straight to Nathan's ego. He was a man, equal to any man on the ship, and he'd be damned if he was going to let Victor Penasco or anyone else think he wasn't. He was fed up with being a target for every bigot and racist on board to take pot shots at. He'd had it up to here with haughty looks and insults. There'd been so many, he'd lost count. They could say what they wanted to about him, but one thing was for sure, no one was going to call him a coward, including this riff raff.

"What are your terms?" Nathan directed his question at Jimmy Ray, who seemed to be the spokesperson for both of them.

"Three, three minute rounds." He nodded at Gerard. "If you'd like, your friend can be the timekeeper. What do ya' say?"

"Don't do it," Gerard whispered in Nathan's ear, "I don't like the looks of these two. They've got trouble written all over them."

"Yes, well, I know what they're up to," Nathan whispered back. He hadn't forgotten how they egged that old codger, Clinch, on in the inquiry office. *They want a good laugh, want to make sport of me, try to belittle me, well, we'll see who gets the last laugh.*

He scrutinized Earl Lee, his would-be opponent, looking him up and down. He was at least forty pounds heavier than he was, had at least a four inch reach advantage, and apparently had some professional boxing experience. That is, if they were telling the truth about him fighting Jack Johnson. But the blubber circling his mid-section signaled he was out of shape, probably hadn't fought in a while. Plus, he didn't look very bright.

"Where do you propose to have the match?" Nathan asked.

"Right here, ten o'clock tonight," Jimmy Ray said. "I'll make all the arrangements. All you have to do is show up and watch out for Earl Lee's haymakers."

Nathan looked at his companions. Gerard's expression said, "Don't do it," but Victor's said, "You must."

He'd never boxed professionally before but Nathan had always been athletic. He'd gone a few rounds with classmates at the University, done some wrestling, and had four years of fencing lessons. He'd read books on pugilism, but that was a far cry from the experience of this guy. Silently, he weighed the odds of him winning against the probability of losing and made a decision. He'd rather carry the weight of being beaten physically than the shame of being seen as a coward.

"I accept your challenge, Mr. Tuttle," Nathan said, then gamely boasted to Earl Lee, "It's going to be a pleasure to knock your block off."

Earl Lee gave him a big, square-toothed grin. "We'll see about that."

Jimmy Ray tipped his grey Stetson, "Legarde, gentlemen…," he said, backing away, "We'll see you all back here tonight, ten o'clock."

Chapter 23

When Nathan got back to his Stateroom early that evening, Nicolette was sitting on the sofa thumbing through a copy of *Vanity Fair*. He hadn't seen the magazine before so he guessed she'd been out and picked it up somewhere on the ship. Little Trista was sitting next to her pretending to read one of her picture books.

"Good afternoon, ladies," he said in a light tone, testing the waters.

"Bonjour, Papa." Beaming, Trista looked up at him and showed him her picture book. "I read myself."

"Ah, tres bien," he patted her head approvingly then took off his jacket and laid it on the back of one of the wing chairs. "Perhaps you can read it to me sometime."

"Okay," she said and went back to her book.

Sitting in the chair across from his wife, Nathan asked, "Where's Cecile?"

Her answer was curt. "In with Sabine. Asleep." She gave him an icy look and went back to her magazine, freezing him out.

For a few moments, he sat there thinking of how he was going to break it to her about the boxing match knowing how she deplored violence. He was certain she wouldn't approve, but what worried him even more was that she might not care at all. That would hurt him more than her being upset with him. As it was, the gulf between them seemed almost unbridgeable. It seemed like nothing he did or said could break through her defenses.

"I have something to tell you," he said quietly.

"Oui" She didn't bother to look at him.

"I'm taking part in a boxing match tonight, in the gymnasium, ten o'clock."

Nicolette jerked her head up. She looked at him as if he'd suddenly started speaking Swahili. "You're doing what?!"

"Boxing…, you know…, the sport…, three rounds, that's it."

"Don't patronize me, Nathan. I know what it is." She threw her magazine on the end table. "You know how I feel about fighting. Why would you get involved in such a thing?"

"Well, a couple of fellows stopped by the gymnasium and challenged me to a few rounds. So, I took them up on it." He wouldn't dare tell her he was goaded into it. She'd *really* be upset with him then.

"What fellows? Do you know them?"

"Well, no, not really. They're the morons I saw at the inquiry office, the ones I told you were doing all the laughing."

"And you're going to fight them?" she said, incredulity reflecting on her face. "Did it ever occur to you that *they* might have attacked you last night?"

"I doubt that," he replied. "They're just a couple of smart aleck southerners. They want the chance to make me look bad, not rob me."

"And you're going to give it to them."

He thought he heard a smidgen of concern in her voice and tried to reassure her. "It's only three rounds. I'll be fine."

"You could still get seriously hurt. You're an engineer, not a fighter."

He didn't know why, except that he must've temporarily lost his senses, because he blurted out sarcastically, "Oh, you sound like you actually care." Immediately he wished he could call the words back. But the damage was done.

Nicolette sprang up from the sofa her green eyes flashing. "No, I don't care. If you want to get yourself beat up by a couple of ruffians, that's your business. I should know by now there's nothing I could say that would change your mind. After all, you're the only one around here who has any sense. You're the only one who's capable of making good decisions."

"Oh, don't start on that again," Nathan said, tiredly. He knew exactly where she was going next.

"Why shouldn't I? It involves my life too. And you act as if I don't even have a say in it."

"I never said that."

"You might as well have. Especially when you become totally irrational at the mere idea of me meeting Madame Lucile. Well, I've made up my mind. If I get another chance to meet her, I'm going to take it, whether you like it or not." She started for their bedchamber, stopped abruptly and whirled around. "Oh, if you get hurt tonight, don't expect me to patch you up. My days of servitude are over!" She stomped out of the room and slammed the door behind her.

A few seconds later the bedchamber door opened and a blanket and pillow came sailing into the parlor. He went over and picked them up off the floor, put them in the chair and sat down next to Trista on the sofa. She put her picture book down and crawled into his lap. Looking up at him she said, "Papa, you said not to fight. Why are you fighting?"

Smiling he thought to himself, *Three years old and already she's catching my contradictions. What am I going to do when she's sixteen?* She was such a beautiful child, smart, inquisitive, and headstrong, just like her mother. He was proud of her, proud of both of his daughters, and his wife. He just wished Nicolette was a little more conventional and a lot more reasonable.

Unsure of how to explain it to her, he said, "Because."

"Because why?" she asked, her head cocked to one side. The look on her face was proof that she believed he knew everything.

"Because…, well, I guess because some people think that people like me shouldn't have any rights, or pride, or self-respect."

She seemed engrossed in his words, listening as if she really *did* understand what he was saying.

"Well…," he continued, "…these people think they're the only ones who should be able to go certain places, do certain things, or have certain things."

"Why?" she asked, her voice full of innocence.

"I honestly don't know, sweetheart. I guess they're just blind."

"What's blind, Papa?" she asked, then let out a big, sleepy yawn.

"I'll tell you another time, when you're not so sleepy." He picked her up, carried her into the adjoining room and put her to bed. Snuggling the cover up to her chin it occurred to him that in spite of the injustices he'd faced, and in spite of the problems he and Nicolette had, he was the luckiest man in the world.

Chapter 24

"Oh no, Mr. Tuttle, I can't do that." Elmer Weikman, the ship's barber and overseer of the gymnasium looked at the proffered ten dollar bill in Jimmy Ray's hand. "I could lose my job for letting you have a boxing match in here. You'll need authorization." He scanned the room to see if anyone was watching them.

Though truth wasn't Jimmy Ray's strong suit, he tried to appear genuine. "Look, it's not that big a deal and I don't want to have to go through a bunch of red tape. You know how a bunch of bureaucrats are. They have to hem and haw and chew the fat 'fore anything gits done. We ain't got time for that. Hell, we'd be in New York before they made a decision. And we'll keep it real hush hush. What do ya say?" He looked over at Earl Lee, who shook his head, confirming his statement.

"I don't know," Weikman scratched the part at the center of his round head. "That's a pretty big risk. I'll be the first one they come looking for if it gets out there's a fight going on in here. I can't afford to lose my job you know."

"You're not going to lose your job," Jimmy Ray assured him. "There'll only be a few people here to watch. The big brass won't know a thing about it. Besides, if by some great accident they did found out, we'd take full responsibility, say we went ahead and did it ourselves, that you had nothin' to do with it."

"Well," Weikman went from scratching his head to scratching the back of his neck.

Like a bloodhound sniffing the fresh trail of a rabbit, Jimmy Ray sensed he was close. Just a little more pressure and he'd have the space for the fight tonight.

"Look, Mr. Weikman, you don't have to lift a finger. All you have to do is show us around, tell us where we can lay hands on a few chairs, some chalk, and turn a shut eye. That's it. We'll do the rest."

"What do you mean a 'shut' eye?" Weikman looked suspicious.

"Like I explained. Just give us what we need and act like you don't know nothin.'"

Weikman took a white handkerchief from his pocket and mopped his brow, "Oh boy, oh boy, oh boy."

Jimmy Ray took the next step. He took out his billfold, drew out a twenty dollar bill, and grabbed Weikman's hand. Closing his fingers around the bill he said, "That's double my original offer. I'd say that's pretty good pay for doin' nothin.'" He gave him a conspiratorial wink.

For a few seconds Weikman stared at the money in his hand. "Then he looked up a Jimmy Ray and said, "All right, but I'm going out on a limb for you gentlemen, so don't make me regret it."

Weikman took them on a tour of the gymnasium. He took them to the left rear section of the large room where there was a bench press and weights, a speed bag, punching bag, medicine ball and a couple pairs of boxing gloves hanging on a coat rack. Jimmy Ray surmised that with a little rearranging the area would be ideal for a boxing ring.

To their right was the locker room. When they stepped inside they were greeted by the smell of fresh paint, a large expanse of gray concrete floor and a line of wooden benches perpendicular to six rows of shiny black metal lockers. Weikman pointed to the back of the locker room. "There are several lavatories behind the lockers, where you can freshen up."

"We've seen enough," Jimmy Ray said. "Just show us where we can get some chalk and a few chairs."

Weikman took them to the gymnasium storage room where they found several stacks of folding wooden chairs and a couple of benches. After rummaging through a variety of balls, game pieces and supplies he found a box of chalk and handed it to Jimmy Ray.

"Meet us back here at nine o'clock tonight," Jimmy Ray said, taking the chalk. Then he pointed toward the left rear section of the gymnasium. "We'll need a little time to get things set up over there. Once we're in, just leave the door unlocked and go on back to your barberin', or whatever it is you do at night."

The three of them walked across the gymnasium floor their heels making a racket on the polished hardwood. At the door, Weikman looked about anxiously. "Nine o'clock, gentlemen," he whispered, and scurried away.

Jimmy Ray and Earl Lee left too, and went down to the First Class smoking room on A deck. Very casually, they went from table to table and passed the news around that there was going to be a boxing match in the gymnasium at ten o'clock, and Earl Lee was going to teach that fancy Negro in First Class a lesson or two. They told everyone it was an exclusive, private boxing match and shouldn't be made common knowledge. Next, they went to the Second Class smoking room on B deck and spread the news again. Finally, they went back to their room.

"You'd better get your supper early tonight," Jimmy Ray said to Earl Lee as they walked in the door. "Eat light, and lay off the booze. We don't want to give that coon any advantages."

"All right," Earl Lee answered and went into their sleeping room. A few seconds later he raced back into the Sitting Area with one of his Marvel comics in his hand. As if the world was coming to an end he exclaimed, "Lordy, Jimmy Ray, we forgot somethin', plum forgot!"

"What the hell are you talkin' about?" Jimmy Ray snapped.

"The bell. We ain't got no bell." Earl Lee gestured emphatically. "How're we going to keep time? How am I supposed know when three minutes is up?"

"Aw damn. You git upset about the stupidest things," Jimmy Ray scoffed. "If it was real important, you wouldn't have even thought about it."

"This *is* important." Earl Lee started to sulk.

"All right, all right," Jimmy Ray held up a pint bottle of Jim Beam to see how much he had left in it. "We'll find you a God damned bell."

He gulped down the last of the liquor in the bottle. As the alcohol burned its way to his stomach, he mentally added another chore to the list of things they had to get done before the fight.

After dinner, Nicolette and Sabine took the children to the First Class lounge for a Children's Concert, so Nathan decided to take a short nap before the fight. He'd been dozing, straddling the edge of sleep when he opened his eyes and saw three men, one short, their heads covered in white hoods. One of them, a rather tall man had a rifle in his hand. The other was carrying a flaming torch that smelled like kerosene. A very short man stood between them.

"All right, nigger, you're comin' with us." The man holding the rifle pointed it at Nathan.

Nathan recognized the man's voice. He was the man who'd slapped his mother, the man he'd punched. His mother was there too. She was standing next to him, screaming, "Please don't take my son. He's just a boy. Please don't take him," and Nathan realized he was ten years old again.

"Shut up…," the man with the gun ordered his mother, "…or we'll string your ass up with him."

"Oh no, no," his Mama sobbed.

The man holding the torch grabbed Nathan's arm and he started to cry. He was scared, shaking, but he couldn't bring himself to beg the men to let him go. He hated them too much; hated them because they were cowards, because they didn't have the guts to show their faces; because they sneaked around in the dark to do their dirty work against people who were helpless. They were despicable, not nearly as decent as him and his Mama. Yet, they had the power of life and death over them. They could kill them and never be punished for it.

Nathan struggled against the man's grasp but couldn't get free. Then he saw that the man's hairy forearm was exposed. Desperate, he bit down hard on the man's arm, grinding his teeth into his flesh.

"Ow!" the man screamed, struggling to get free of Nathan's teeth without dropping the torch he was holding.

"Let him loose," the man with the rifle yelled and cocked his gun.

Nathan let go. The man with the torch slapped him so hard a bolt of lightening crackled through his head and he crashed to the floor behind the table.

"Please, sir," his Mama cried, "I'll pay you. I'll work for you. Anything you want, but don't take my son. He's my only child. Please."

The man with the rifle growled at her, "Didn't I tell you to shut up? I ought to blow your brains out just for the hell of it."

Nathan was frightened, trembling all over. As the man holding the torch jerked him to his feet, he caught sight of the kerosene lamp on the table. Instinctively, he grabbed it and hurled it at the man holding the rifle. But it fell short and struck the short man standing next to him in the head.

"Whoosh!" An inferno of yellow flames engulfed the man and he started to run around in a flaming circle, screaming and flailing his arms, "Ahhhhhh! Ahhhhhh! Ahhhhhh!"

"Son-of-a-bitch!" the man with the rifle yelled as the short man ran out the open kitchen door. The man with the torch ran after him.

"This ain't over," the man with the rifle warned and headed for the door. "This ain't over by a long shot."

Then Nathan was running from a yellow wall of flame as the man's words echoed in his head: *this ain't over…, this ain't over…, this ain't over…*

Chapter 25

At eight thirty Saturday evening, Jimmy Ray and Earl Lee placed the last row of chairs around the square perimeter of a twelve by twelve chalk-drawn boxing ring.

"We still don't have a bell," Earl Lee complained as they headed for the locker room. "We can't have a fight with no bell."

"Will you just shut up about the damned bell," Jimmy Ray snapped. "I told you. We'll make do somehow, even if I have to follow the time on my watch and holler when it's up." He was sick of being harangued about it. He had other things on his mind. Like making sure he beat the shit out of Legarde. Earl Lee had whipped some pretty fierce opponents in his day, but he hadn't been in the ring in three years. The last time he fought he wound up with a detached retina and his manager put him out to pasture. Even so, Jimmy Ray was pretty sure he could beat Legarde. And with a little help from him, he couldn't lose.

He heard the gymnasium door open, looked over and saw a group of gentlemen walk in. One of the men shouted over the wide expanse of the gymnasium, "Is this where the fight's going to be?"

"Sure is," he called back, waving them over. "You gentlemen come on in and take a seat. I've got to git my champion here ready." He slapped Earl Lee's shoulder.

The men took seats and Jimmy Ray and Earl Lee went into the locker room. While Earl Lee was changing into his boxing trunks, he went to the showers and found some towels. When he came back Earl Lee was bouncing around on his toes, shadow boxing.

"Why don't you do some stretches and save yourself for the fight," Jimmy Ray suggested. "You might need that energy later." He reached into one of the lockers and took out a brown paper sack.

Earl Lee continued to swing his fists, bobbing his head as if an opponent was in front of him. "Aw, I can beat Legarde with one hand tied behind my back, and the other in a plaster cast," he joked between breaths.

"I know you can. But we don't want to be foolish. See, I know a few things about this darky you don't."

In fact, he knew a lot about Legarde because his Pa had washed his face with his accomplishments most of his life. And what his Pa didn't tell him, he learned from his cousin, Anton, in France.

"Like what do you know?" Earl Lee asked.

"Well, for one thing, he's won some awards for fencin', and I hear he's done some amateur wrestlin'."

"Yeah, well my record's ten and five. I bet he can't say that." Earl Lee sliced the air with an uppercut.

"That's true," Jimmy Ray replied, noticing noise coming from outside the locker room. He went to the door and peeked out.

"Sweet Jesus in the manger. Look at that." He motioned for Earl Lee.

Earl Lee came over, peeked out at the crowd and let out a long, low whistle. "Goddamn! Would you look at that. Hell, we shoulda' charged admission. We'd have made a killin.'"

They had set out fifty chairs and all of them, plus two benches, were full. Men and women stood around in bunches, waiting, all dressed up like they were going to the opera or some fancy dress ball. They were all gussied up in expensive gowns, sparkly jewels, silk top hats and tails. There were far more people than Jimmy Ray had reckoned on.

Awestruck, he closed the door and checked his watch. It was already nine thirty. He'd have to rush to take care of a little matter of fight insurance before Legarde got there. Taking a brown bottle from the paper sack he said to Earl Lee, "Look, I want you to have a little edge. This'll guarantee us a win."

"Aw, I don't need that stuff," Earl Lee said, looking hurt, "this guy ain't even competition for me."

"Maybe not, but I don't want to take no chances." "We're not takin' no chances." He held up his fists.

"All I need is these right here."

"Maybe so," Jimmy Ray argued, "but it don't hurt none to have insurance. My Pa always said, 'when ya git a nigger down, the best way to keep him there is to stomp him.'" He shook the bottle. "This here is just a little ass-kickin' insurance." They both laughed and Earl Lee went to get a pair of gloves.

Jimmy Ray was still chuckling when the locker room door opened and Weikman rushed in. Panic covered his face and he was sweating profusely. "You've got to get these people out of here," he said to Jimmy Ray. "You can hear them clear down the corridor. The Captain or some of the officers are bound to find out about what's going on in here. You promised you'd keep it quiet, that there would only be a few people."

"Oh, no you don't," Jimmy Ray growled. He grabbed Weikman by the collar and walked him backwards between a row of lockers. "We have a deal, and you're going to keep it."

"No, no." Weikman's eyes bulged with fear. "I-I can't keep it. I'll lose my job."

"I got people out there waitin' to see that Nigger get his ass whipped," Jimmy Ray shouted, "and I'm not about to call it off now." He stood over Weikman scowling down at him. "I don't give a shit about your job" he growled, and punched him in the gut. Weikman doubled over, clutching his stomach. To guarantee he wouldn't be a further problem, he took a step back and kicked him in the groin with his steel-toed boot.

Weikman screeched and crumpled to the floor, his face contorted with pain. As he groaned helplessly at his feet, Jimmy Ray nonchalantly said to Earl Lee, "Bring me that rope out of your bag."

Earl Lee did as he was told. A few seconds later Earl Lee showed up returned with his jump rope and handed it to Jimmy Ray saying, "Shit, Jimmy Ray, Legarde will be here any minute. What if he walks in? How the hell would we explain this?"

"We won't have to explain nothin' if we hurry up." Jimmy Ray took a used white handkerchief out of his pocket, balled it up and forced it into Weikman's mouth. He took the rope from Earl Lee's hand, cut it in half with his pocket knife, and instructed him to grab Weikman's hands and hold them together. As they tied Weikman's hands and feet Earl Lee asked, "Why'd you have to hit him anyhow?"

Jimmy Ray shook his head as if he pitied the big man, "Don't you understand nothin?' The piece of horse shit got spooked and wanted to cancel the fight. But he made a bargain, and by God, he's gonna keep it. Grab his shoulders and follow me."

They picked Weikman up and carried him to the last locker in the last row in the locker room and shoved him inside. Jimmy Ray was about to close the door when he noticed a whistle on a blue lanyard hanging around Weikman's neck. He lifted the lanyard up over his head, held the whistle in front of Earl Lee, and said, "Here's your damned bell."

"That's a whistle," Earl Lee frowned.

"Nope. Tonight it's a bell."

Jimmy Ray slammed the locker door then took a combination lock from his pocket and locked it.

They left laughing, ready for the fight.

Chapter 26

The crowd booed as Nathan made his way through the gymnasium with Gerard Hale at his side. He recognized some of the faces in the crowd from his forays around the ship. He saw that trouble maker, Molly Brown standing next to a petite redhead he guessed was the famous Madame Lucile that Nicolette was pining to meet. A distinguished gentleman held the redhead's hand and he assumed he was her husband. Major Archibald Butt, Jacques Futrelle and Colonel John Jacob Astor was there too. Gerard had introduced him to them in the smoking room Friday night. And, there was J. Bruce Ismay, surrounded by a bunch of cigar smoking men in various stages of inebriation.

"Now we'll see just how ferocious the chap really is," Ismay said loudly as Nathan and Gerard neared his group. "I'll bet you a hundred to one they'll have to carry him out of here." Ismay's friends guffawed as if he'd told a great joke.

Nathan stopped right in front of Ismay and looked him in the eye. "If you want to bet on a loser, that's your business. But I'm the winner of this fight. It just hasn't been announced yet."

"See gentlemen," Ismay made a contemptuous gesture with his hand, "I told you he was an arrogant son-of-a-gun. But we'll see him taken down a peg or two tonight." As an aside he remarked to Gerard, "How did you get mixed up with that piece of garbage?"

"I won't favor that remark with an answer, Bruce," Gerard replied, "but I will say this: Legarde is more of a gentleman than half the men on this ship."

As they walked away from Ismay and his cronies, Nathan made up his mind that he *had* to win, precisely because they all expected him to lose. Never in his life had he conformed to people's expectations of him; not academically, professionally, or socially, and he wasn't about to start now. He'd beaten the odds all his life, and tonight he'd have to beat them again.

When they reached the locker room, Victor Pensaco was there waiting for them with a blonde, athletic-looking man.

The young man shoved a pair of boxing gloves in Nathan's hands. "I'm Quigg Baxter," he said, introducing himself. "I'm going to be refereeing the fight. Victor is going to keep the time; round endings will be signaled by a whistle." Victor blew the whistle producing a high-pitched, screeching noise. "Okay," Nathan said and excused himself to get changed.

Ten minutes later he was sitting on a stool in a corner of a chalk-drawn square, his heavy weight opponent glaring at him from the opposite corner. For some reason, he recalled the time his mother read the story of David and Goliath to him when he was a little boy. He imagined David must have felt a lot like he did right then. But he didn't have much time to ponder it because Quigg Baxter stepped into the makeshift ring and summoned him and Earl Lee for instructions.

"I know we're making due here," Baxter said, "but that's no excuse for not having a good, clean fight. There'll be no standing eight count, no hitting below the belt, and you'll break when I tell you to. Okay, gentlemen, touch gloves and go to your corners."

Nathan touched his gloves to Earl Lee's and went back to his corner as ordered. As he sat on his stool, Gerard cautioned him, "Stay away from him as much as you can, Nathan. Don't let him have his way. Just tire him out."

"Okay," Nathan nodded.

Victor blew the whistle signaling the start of the first round. Nathan stood and Earl Lee ran from his corner and met him before he could reach the middle of the ring. He peppered him with punches. Fast and furious, he felt the blows to his body, the sting of leather on his face. He raised his arms to protect his face and hunched down shielding his body as best he could. For the first half of the round he was so busy ducking and backpedaling to avoid Earl Lee' sledgehammer blows, he couldn't get off a single shot.

Then gradually, Earl Lee's rapid fire punches slowed to a steady rhythm and he was able to get in a few punches. He threw an uppercut that snapped Earl Lee's head back, drawing a collective, "Whoa…," from the crowd. It bolstered his confidence and for the rest of the round he matched Earl Lee almost blow for blow.

Victor blew the whistle signaling the end of round one and the crowd booed as Nathan walked back to his corner.

I can win this, he thought, sitting on his stool. *If that's his best, I really do have a chance.*

Gerard sponged Nathan's face and asked him if he wanted some water. "No, not yet," he replied, as Victor leaned down to speak to him.

"You have a natural talent, my friend," Victor said, "I am impressed."

The seconds flew by and the whistle sounded for the second round. This time, Earl Lee didn't run out to meet him. They met in the middle of the ring and Nathan confidently threw the first volley of punches. Earl Lee answered with a flurry of his own, connecting several times with Nathan's forehead and cheeks. He shook the punches off, rubbed sweat from his face and took a defensive stance.

Then his eyes began to sting. He blinked furiously and rubbed them with his forearm, but the stinging progressed to a searing burn. He stumbled blindly around the ring and Earl Lee pounded him with renewed ferocity, sending shock waves through his body. The crowd went wild with excitement and started to chant: "Put him down, put him down, put him down…"

Nathan backed away from the blurred figure of Earl Lee that pummeled his body and chased him like an angry ghost bent on taking his life. A couple of times he backed into spectators at the edge of the makeshift ring. Each time someone pushed him back at his opponent. Finally, he got close enough to Earl Lee to wrap his arms around him. He held on until the referee forced him to let go. Earl Lee battered his body relentlessly until Nathan grabbed him again and tied him up. Mercifully, Victor blew the whistle and he found his way back to his stool.

He was losing. Badly.

"There's something on his gloves," Nathan told Gerard and Victor. "I can hardly see."

"I can smell it," Victor said, sniffing the air.

"Don't go back out there," Gerard said. "We can call it off right now."

Victor shook his head in agreement.

"No." Nathan said as Gerard wiped his eyes and face with a wet towel. "They'll think I quit because I was losing."

Victor disagreed. "No, senore. We know you are brave. Your opponent is dishonorable. You have nothing else to prove."

"Yes, I do." Nathan squeezed his eyes shut trying to rid them of the contaminant making them tear. "They think I'm a whiner and a pushover. If I quit, that's the opinion they'll keep of me."

"To hell with their opinion," Gerard cried. "It would be suicide to go back out there in this condition."

Victor looked at his watch then handed Nathan the dry towel he had flung over his shoulder. "You have fifteen seconds to change your mind.

Nathan wiped sweat from his face and neck. Squinting and blinking, he gave the towel to Gerard and said, "I'll be all right. I can almost keep my eyes open."

Victor blew the whistle and Nathan stood up for the final round. Again, Earl Lee came to meet him with a whirlwind of punches. He was putting everything he had into them clearly aiming for a knockout.

Nathan's eyes were still watering a little, but he could see Earl Lee now and was able to protect his body and deflect most of his punches. He ducked, weaved and forced Earl Lee to chase him around the ring. He dodged a haymaker aimed for his face and felt the wind whistle past his ear. The power of the missed punch threw Earl Lee off balance and he almost fell, eliciting a few strained laughs and hushed murmurs from the crowd. In the brief few seconds it took him to regain his balance, Nathan caught a glimpse of his friend, Jimmy Ray, over in his corner. His face was flaming crimson and maniacally contorted. He was screaming something

Nathan couldn't hear above the non-stop cheering and cursing around the ring.

Nathan threw several combinations that connected with Earl Lee's jaw and abdomen, but the blows barely fazed the big man. He kept coming after him. He threw several more wild punches then crashed his glove into Nathan's left cheek bone. It snapped his head back and Nathan stumbled backwards, nearly losing his balance. Again the crowd howled with excitement.

Regaining his composure, Nathan mentally assessed the fight. They were in the middle of the last round and so far, he'd made a poor showing. He was going to lose if he didn't come up with something, and quick.

He could tell Earl Lee was tired; his punches were losing their sting and his arms were drooping. Seeing an opening, he plastered Earl Lee' face with a torrent of punches. But they still had little effect.

Then, Nathan recalled something that happened to him when he was sixteen. He'd been sparring with an upper classman in the school gymnasium when the guy struck him in the kidneys. He fell to the floor in pain so excruciating he could hardly breathe. For ten minutes he was paralyzed with agony, unable to move. The memory gave him an idea.

He took several blows to the body as he got himself into position. Putting all his strength into it, he swung and landed a thundering blow to the big man's left kidney.

Earl Lee dropped to the floor like a dead buffalo. For an instant, the crowd was silent. Stunned. Quigg Baxter ran into the ring. But instead of counting Earl Lee out, he kept asking him if he was okay. Sugg's reply was an ugly grimace and series of moans.

Suddenly, the crowd went berserk. Everyone rushed into the makeshift ring, pushing, shoving, and cursing. Somehow, in the crush of bodies, Nathan made eye contact with Gerard who was still standing next to Victor in their corner. Above the crowd, Gerard pointed to the locker room. Nathan dropped to his knees and pushed his way through the thicket of bodies and ran to the locker room as fast as he could.

It wasn't long before the blood thirsty mob noticed he had slipped away and marched to the locker room.

Through the door, he heard the mob screaming: "He cheated!" "That's illegal tactics!" "He hit him below the belt!" "We can't let him get away with this!"

Gerard and Victor were already in the locker room. The three of them put their backs to the door to keep the crazed posse out. The crowd banged, cursed and pushed on the door.

Nathan, Gerard, and Victor held the door as best they could, but they were outnumbered and quickly losing ground.

Nathan spotted a couple of steel framed chairs at the end of the benches and told Gerard to go and get one.

Nearly out of breath, Gerard replied, "How will you hold it? If I leave, they're sure to break through."

"Just go! Nathan hollered. "Hurry!"

Gerard sprinted to get the chair while he and Victor continued to strain against the mob with every ounce of their strength. Yet, the door was opening more and more with each push from the opposite side. It was almost ajar enough for a body to squeeze through when Gerard got back with the chair.

Nathan and Victor made a Herculean push against the door as Gerard tipped the chair back and secured the upper back edge beneath the door knob. Nathan made sure it was going to hold, then slowly, he and Victor moved away from the door.

"I don't think they're any windows in here," Nathan said, breathing hard. He looked around the locker room as Gerard and Victor mopped their faces with clean white handkerchiefs. "I don't think there are any other doors either."

Outside, the crowd continued to bang on the door, shouting epithets.

Gerard went to see if there was another way out and came back shaking his head. "Well, gentlemen, I guess we'll just have to wait them out." He sat on one of the benches.

Looking bone weary and worried, Victor plopped down next to Gerard. "I can't stay in here," he lamented, "I told Pepita I'd be gone no more than an hour. Never would I have guessed I'd be locked up in a locker room on my honeymoon." He made a failed attempt to smile.

Nathan sat down too. He felt terrible, responsible for everything. "Listen, I'm sorry for getting you involved in this mess," he looked from Gerard to Victor. "I had no idea it would turn out like this. Had I known I would never have-"

"Ssssh...," Victor raised a finger to his lips, interrupting him. "Did you hear that?"

They all cocked their heads, listening intently. Nathan noticed the noisy crowd quieting down. Someone was calling for order. The three of them ran to the door.

"I want every one of you out of here immediately," a stern voice on the other side of the door shouted, "...or I'll have you all arrested for disturbing the peace."

"It's E.J." Gerard exclaimed.

Victor made the sign of the cross. He clasped his hands together, kissed them, and glanced heavenward.

Captain Smith's voice called from outside the door, "Open up in there. Now! Do you hear me? Open this door!"

Nathan took the chair from behind the door and opened it. Captain Smith walked in with a couple of officers. "Legarde!" He looked at Nathan with disgust. "I should have known you'd be mixed up in this."

Before Nathan could utter a word, Gerard and Victor started talking at the same time.

"Pipe down, pipe down," Captain Smith ordered, "...you'll get your chance to explain."

He turned to Gerard. "I hear there was a boxing match and a bunch of illegal gambling going on out there. What do you know about it?"

"Not a thing about any gambling," Gerard replied. "But yes, my friend Nathan here went a few rounds with that Earl Lee fellow."

Victor interjected anxiously, "I just want to get to my Pepita. She must be beside herself with worry. Please Captain, might I be excused. I'll come to your office in the morning if you want. But really, I must leave."

"Go ahead," Captain Smith replied. "These two can tell me what I need to know."

Victor said goodnight and rushed out of the locker room.

Captain Smith turned back to Gerard and Nathan who took turns telling him what had happened. When they were done, the Captain said to Gerard, "I know you to be an upstanding citizen, Gerard. White Star has never had a problem with you before, so I'm going to let you off this time with a warning. If you get involved in anymore shenanigans, I'll have to take action against you. Understand?"

"Sure, E.J.," Gerard said with a knowing smile.

The Captain turned to Nathan. "Legarde, I've had it up to here with you." He raised his hand above his head. "Every time I turn around you're causing some kind of trouble."

Nathan opened his mouth to defend himself, but the Captain stopped him. "Not a word, Legarde. Let me finish. From what I gather, a lot of people lost a lot of money betting on this fight tonight. Being a Christian and opposed to such sins, I say they got what they deserved. But this fight, and the subsequent riot in here caused a lot of damage, and I hold you personally responsible for it. Therefore, you'll be receiving a bill for damages, payable in thirty days. Is that clear?"

"Yes," Nathan said, realizing Gerard had been right about the Captain after all. He *was* a fair man. Had he wanted to press charges against him, he could have.

"For the last time, Legarde, stay out of trouble," the Captain said sternly. He shook hands with Gerard, said goodnight, and headed for the door. Suddenly, Captain Smith turned around and asked, "Where's Weikman?

Nathan and Gerard exchanged puzzled glances. They both shrugged and said in unison, "Who's Weikman?"

Chapter 27

Quigg Baxter helped Jimmy Ray carry Earl Lee back to their quarters. After laying him on the sofa in the Sitting Room, Jimmy Ray showed Baxter to the door. As soon as the door closed behind him, Jimmy Ray lit into Earl Lee. "How in the hell does a so called professional lose a fight to a rank amateur? You were supposed to humiliate Legarde, show him for the inferior piece of trash he is. Instead, you go and make me look like a damned fool in front of all those high falutin' aristocrats. Half of them think their shit don't stink anyway. Now they'll be looking down on us the same as they do that nigger. Maybe more, 'cause *you* cost them money. I heard that fella' Ismay bet a thousand dollars on you, and lost it to some Colonel by the name of Astor. A bunch of them folks are hoppin' mad. And you know what? I don't blame 'em. Not one bit."

"I'm sorry," Earl Lee moaned.

Jimmy Ray threw up his hands, pacing the floor. He could see Earl Lee was still hurting, but he had no sympathy for him. "I'm sorry, I'm sorry," he mimicked him. "Yeah, you're sorry all right. I rig the damned fight for you, put it in the palm of your hand, and you still manage to lose it. There ain't no excuse for that. None! How the hell you let Legarde sucker punch you like that, I'll never understand. I should'a never brought your good for nothin' ass with me. You botch up everything I ask you to do."

"It wasn't a sucker punch," Earl Lee groaned. "He hit me in my kidneys. You'd have gone down too if he'd hit you like that."

"Yeah, well I ain't the one with all the professional fightin' experience. You wasn't supposed to git beat. You was supposed to know how to handle yourself. Instead, you disappoint the hell out of me and every white man on this ship."

"I told you I'm sorry," Earl Lee whined.

"Aw, shut up. I don't want to hear no more of your 'I'm sorrys.'" He felt like strangling him.

He went and poured himself a glass of Jim Beam and plopped down in one of the wing chairs across from the sofa thinking, *Time's wastin.' I've got to stop foolin' around and get rid of Legarde. One more day and we'll be in New York, and I still have the same problem: how to get to him with no one around."*

He stood up to get himself another drink and out of the blue he remembered the announcement he'd seen earlier in the day at the bottom of the Grand Staircase. Suddenly, he got an idea. "That's it! That's it! He snapped his fingers and whooped, "That'll draw Legarde like a blow fly to horse shit."

Chapter 28

It was Sunday noon and the girls were napping. Nicolette tucked her sketchbook under her arm and headed for the door. Ignoring Nathan she said to the Sabine, "I'm going out. I'll be back shortly."

Nathan's voice came from behind the newspaper he was reading. "Where are you going?"

She looked back to find him peering over the top of the newspaper at her. Summoning courage she replied, "I'm having tea with Molly Brown and Madame Lucile."

Nathan laid his newspaper on the coffee table next to his chair, "You insist on doing this even after I've told you how I feel about it."

"That's right. I told you that yesterday evening. Evidently, you didn't take me seriously."

"I thought that given ample time to think it over more carefully you'd see reason. Meeting with this woman is sheer folly."

"Folly! Reason? You should be the last one to talk to me about folly and reason, especially after last night. You get yourself into a brawl, get chased by a bunch of drunks, and come back here with your face bleeding. Oh, yes, that's the epitome of reason." She glared at him, wishing now that she hadn't gone back on her word and patched him up last night. But she couldn't help it, the blood on his face stirred her feelings for him. The wound proved to be minor, but he'd evidently misconstrued her ministering as evidence that she was going to continue to let him dominate her.

"What happened last night has nothing to do with this," Nathan argued.

She waved her hand dismissively, "If you say so," and turned to leave.

She'd taken only a few steps when Nathan called out, "I am still your husband, and I'm telling you not to go. If you defy me, then as far as I'm concerned, you are walking out on our marriage. Do I make myself clear?"

He'd taken a stand. The expression on his face dared her to walk out the door.

She stood there glaring back at him. In the core of her being she knew this was her moment of truth. All the discussions, pleading and arguments they'd had had led to this moment. Either she obeyed and continued to be a good, unfulfilled wife, or disobeyed and risked losing her marriage and financial security. A lump rose in her throat as questions crowded her mind. *Do I have the right to destroy our family for what I want? And what about the children? Will they grow up to hate me for separating them from their precious Papa? Do I really have what it takes to raise them alone?*

To protect her resolve, she closed her mind to the questions and replied, "I'm leaving," and ran out the door. An invisible hand squeezed her heart as she quickened her steps, afraid that if she stopped now, she would lose her chance to choose what she wanted for her life forever.

She ran to the automatic lift, took it up to A deck and hurried down the corridor to A20. She reached for the brass knocker on the door and rapped it several times.

A few second later, a swarthy complexioned young woman with chestnut hair opened the door. "Do come in." Her smile was welcoming. "Lady Gordon and Mrs. Brown are expecting you."

Nicolette followed her through an exquisite Louis Quatorze styled foyer into an even more elaborate parlor. Fresh white carnations and yellow roses dotted the room in porcelain, cobalt blue vases with the gold White Star emblem etched on them. Madame Lucile and Molly Brown stood as she came into the room.

"Well, you made it," Molly Brown walked over to her and put her arm around her shoulder. "Meet my good friend, Lady Gordon, couturier extraordinaire." She waved toward Madame Lucile who extended a delicate hand, dwarfed by a large diamond sparkling on her ring finger. "How do you do?" she said, smiling.

"I'm well, thank you," Nicolette said, shaking her hand. She was surprised to find that the woman standing in front of her bore little resemblance to the imposing pictures of her she'd seen in *Harper's* and *Vanity Fair*. In person, she was actually quite petite, with flaming red hair and a splash of freckles covering her nose. She was stylishly attired in a deep green silk kimono lounging ensemble.

"I am a bit nervous," Nicolette confessed. "I still can't quite believe I'm here, meeting you. I've followed your work for years."

"Thank you for the compliment. Do sit down." Madame nodded toward a comfortable looking arm chair that complimented the room's gold tapestry sofa. At the center of the grouping was a coffee table set with three glasses of Champagne and a platter of chocolate covered strawberries.

Nicolette sat down. Molly Brown gave her a wink and said, "Well, ladies, my work here is done. Sorry I can't stay, but I have an appointment at the hair salon. Colonel Gracie is taking me to the Ball tonight. So if you'll excuse me…"

They all said their goodbyes and Madame Lucile's servant saw her out.

"Well now," Madame Lucile turned her attention to Nicolette, "Molly has simply raved about you. She thinks you're quite talented." She nodded at the sketch book on Nicolette's lap. "May I?"

"Please do." Nicolette handed it to her.

As Madame Lucile flipped through the sketchbook, Nicolette tried to read her expressions. At one point, she paused and cocked her head to one side as if a different angle would bring what she was viewing into sharper focus. Next, she turned the page and narrowed her eyes as if trying to figure something out. Then she held the sketchbook at arms length, nodded her head and murmured, "yes."

Finally, Madame closed the sketchbook and handed it back to Nicolette. "I dare say Molly was right. You do have a good eye for fashion. But how are your practical skills? Can you make patterns for these drawings? Do you sew?"

Nicolette laughed. "I can do all that and more. I grew up with it. My step-parents are tailors. They taught me to sew, how to dye fabric, make lace, everything, with the exception of drawing. I learned that on my own."

"I see." Madame Lucile touched her chin pensively. "I'm going to be opening a fashion house in Paris this summer or early Fall. I could use someone with your skill. Will you be returning to France?"

"Yes," Nicolette answered, excited. "My husband has business in New Orleans, but we should be back by the first week of August."

Immediately, Lady Gordon's expression changed. "Oh, Molly didn't tell me you were married. You're very talented, indeed, but I have a policy of never hiring married women. Not that I have anything against matrimony. It's purely a business decision."

In an instant, Nicolette's excitement turned to disappointment. "What difference does it make?" she asked, "It doesn't change what I can do."

Madame gave her an understanding smile. "Of course not. But experience has taught me that married women are not as reliable as their unmarried sisters. They miss so much more time from work and it seems as soon as I get them trained, they quit. I have several salons in different parts of the world, so I have to travel a great deal. Therefore, it's imperative that I have dependable people."

"I am dependable," Nicolette insisted, "when I commit to something, I live up to my commitment."

"I know you mean that...," Madame countered, "...but let me ask you something. Do you have children?"

"Yes."

"And if your child was sick, which would come first, your job or your child?"

"Of course, my child would come first. But, luckily, I have an au pair to help with their care."

"Well, then, if that's the case, I'd think working wouldn't be a necessity for you." Madame eyed her curiously.

"Well, uh, it isn't, I don't think," Nicolette stammered, convinced that she sounded utterly foolish, as though she was unsure of herself. And the truth was, she *was* unsure. Her life was in limbo. She had no idea what was going to become of her, how all the details of a divorce might play out, or what starting a new life as a single woman would entail. But she couldn't very well tell Madame Lucile that she was on the verge of divorce.

"Tell me," Madame persisted, "how does your husband feel about you working? Most men want their wives to stay at home. Would your husband agree to it?"

There was no doubt about it, Madame was a shrewd woman. She knew exactly what to ask to get to the heart of the matter.

Nicolette felt a wave of embarrassment flood her face as she answered, "Not exactly."

In a tone that implied the discussion was over, Madame remarked, "Then surely you understand why I don't hire married women."

"Oui," Nicolette answered softly and dropped her eyes to the sketchbook on her lap.

"I'm sorry. I can see you're upset," Madame said compassionately. "You have a strong temperament, a quality I possess myself, though I daresay it's one that's often an impediment for our sex."

"What do you mean?" Nicolette wondered if she thought her flighty, or prone to bouts of emotion and whimsy?

Madame took a sip from her Champagne glass and sat it back on the table. "Please don't think ill of me for saying this, but it is the best advice I can give you. If your husband is a good provider, try to be happy with that. Forget about working. Use your talent to beautify yourself and your home. I can tell you from experience, it's far easier to subdue ambition and let a man take care of you, than it is to make a living in the big, bad world out there."

The comment caught her by surprise, especially since Madame was known the world over for her entrepreneurial spirit and innovative ideas.

"Well, that's not exactly what I expected to hear," Nicolette replied.

"I'm sure it isn't. But you've heard the old adage about necessity being the mother of invention. Well, it fits me to a T. In spite of all the accolades, I merely did what I had to do to make a living after my first marriage ended. I grew the business as a sort of insurance. Men can be fickle sometimes," she let out a deep sigh, "and Fate creates a new widow every day."

"Well, it was still nice meeting you," Nicolette said, standing. They shook hands and Madame saw her to the door.

Walking down the corridor Nicolette thought, *okay, so that avenue is closed. I've put everything on the line, so I can't back down now. I'll just have to find another way.*

But the trouble was, she had no idea what that way would be.

Chapter 29

After church services, Helen and Gerard played pinochle with the Hennypeckers in the First Class lounge. They'd all had lunch together and decided to digest it over a game of cards. The two old ladies considered themselves world class pinochle players, and would have been formidable opponents indeed, had they possessed adequate sight and hearing. Out of respect for their age, and a desire to let them maintain their illusions, Helen and Gerard let them win.

One of the Hennypeckers looked over the top of her hand and asked, "Are you lovebirds going to the Ball tonight?

"A Ball? Helen replied, "Sunday night seems rather odd for such a thing. Are you sure it wasn't last night?"

"No, it's tonight," Gerard spoke up. "Eight o'clock. I saw an announcement earlier near the foot of the Grand staircase. It starts at eight o'clock. I'd intended to ask you later to accompany me. But since the subject's been broached, I guess this is it. Would you do me the honor? I can think of nothing more delightful than waltzing the night away with my best girl." He flashed her an endearing smile.

"I'd like to, but I don't have anyone to watch Dodie."

"Check with the steward on your corridor," the other Hennypecker suggested, peering over the top of her hand. "I'm sure they'd be able to help you find someone to stay with her. Ours helped us find escorts for the evening. I'm going with Washington Roebling, the racer, and sister is going with his friend, Stephen Blackwell. They're a little young, but who cares. We'd rather have them young and strong than old and flabby."

Helen chuckled, "I'll see what I can do."

The round ended and Gerard cut the cards for another game. Just as he started to deal them, they heard, "Brrrrrrrrr!" as Dodie casually broke wind.

Helen tried to pretend she didn't hear it, but the stink bomb quickly enveloped them.

"Damn it, sister!" one of the Hennypeckers exclaimed. "Have you been drinking milk again? You know how gasey it makes you."

"I haven't had milk in months," her sister snapped. She fanned the air with her hand. "Phewww, that's awful. Smells like someone let a skunk loose in here."

Helen looked at Dodie who didn't change expressions. A few seconds later, she let loose again. "Brrrrrrrrrrrr!"

"Dodie! Stop it this minute," Helen shrieked.

Standing, one of the Hennypeckers said, "You'll have to excuse me. I need some fresh air. Come along, sister."

The two old ladies walked away and Helen looked down at the table, her cheeks burning.

Sensing her feelings, Gerard reached out and squeezed her hand. "Don't take it so seriously. It was just a little accident, not the end of the world. Perhaps we'd better get her back to your cabin, though, so you can check her."

"Sure," she answered quietly, her mind raging. *Just another little accident, in a lifetime full of accidents. And I'm the lucky dolt who gets to clean up after all of them.*

Gerard walked her and Dodie back to their stateroom. As soon as he left, she helped Dodie freshen up then turned her mind to finding someone to sit with her while she went to the Ball. She checked the corridor several times to see if she could nab a passing stewardess. Finally, she was able to stop a woman by the name of Mrs. Snape. "I need someone to sit with my sister this evening," she explained. "Would you be available?"

"I'm sorry, Miss," the plump little woman replied, "I've already committed the evening to another couple." She started to walk away, but Helen stopped her.

"Perhaps, you could recommend another stewardess."

"Everyone I know is already committed for the evening. Seems everyone's going to the Ball."

Helen sighed, "Oh, well, just my luck to find out about it too late." Disappointed, she turned and started to walk back to her Stateroom.

"Wait a minute," Mrs. Snape, called after her and Helen turned around. "I can't promise anything, but I'll check with some of the deck stewards. Perhaps one of them might be available."

Helen thanked her and went back to her Stateroom.

At seven o'clock she was dressed for the Ball just in case Mrs. Snape was able to find someone. So far, she hadn't heard a word, so she monitored the corridor until she found an assistant steward passing by. She asked if he'd seen Mrs. Snape, but he said he'd never heard of her.

Frustrated, she went back to her stateroom. She considered apologizing to her Aunt Agatha and cousin Eliza, but realized it wouldn't help. Even if they accepted her apology, she doubted either of them would miss the Ball to watch Dodie for her. She checked the time every few minutes watching the minutes tick by. At seven thirty she resigned herself to not going. If she had to have Dodie come with them, she'd rather not go at all. She'd have to make up some excuse to give Gerard for changing her mind.

Dodie was sitting on the sofa with one of her picture books and Helen slumped into a chair across from her to wait for Gerard. She picked up her copy of *Lady Audley's Secret* from the end table and removed the lace handkerchief she'd used to mark the page where she stopped reading the night before. She'd just started reading when she heard a knock at the door. She glanced at her watch. It was seven thirty so she braced herself to face Gerard's disappointment.

But when she opened the door, a very pretty young woman with big, grey-blue eyes and auburn hair was standing there. "Are you Miss Ryerson?" she asked, with an Irish accent.

"Yes. Can I help you?"

"I'm Violet Jessop. Mrs. Snape told me you need assistance."

"Do come in," Helen gushed. "I thought she'd forgotten all about me. Yes, I need someone to stay with my sister for the evening." She gestured toward Dodie. "Might you be able to sit with her?"

"Yes ma'am, that's why I'm here." She followed Helen into the room. Miss Jessop smiled at Dodie and said, "Hello," but Dodie ignored her.

Helen disregarded Dodie's coolness, thinking she'd warm up to Ms. Jessop in a little while. She was usually very open to people.

Helen took the stewardess into their bedchamber and showed her where Dodie's night clothes were. Coming back into the Parlor she remarked, "She's usually asleep by ten, but if she's not sleepy, let her stay up."

Suddenly, Dodie made a loud screech. She slammed her book on the floor, jumped up and ran past them into the bedchamber.

Helen apologized to Miss Jessop, wondering what had gotten into Dodie. "She's normally not like this," she said. "Make yourself comfortable while I speak to her."

When she went into the bedchamber, Dodie was sitting cross-legged on the bed with her lip poked out, pouting.

"What's wrong?" Helen asked closing the door behind her. "Why are you behaving so rudely toward Miss Jessop?"

"'Cause." Dodie folded her arms and rocked back and forth.

"Because of what?"

"'Cause I don't want to stay with her. I want to go with you."

"Well you can't go with me this time. You can go with me tomorrow."

"But I want to go now." Dodie rocked even harder, tears welling in her eyes.

Oh for heaven's sake! Why does she have to start this now? Helen thought. *Just when I think I'm going to have a little time for myself, she throws a tantrum.*

Helen was stern with her. "Look, you are not going to have your way this time. If you want to stay in here and act like a baby the rest of the night, that's fine by me. But you can't go, and that's that." She started for the door.

Determined to have her way, Dodie jumped up from the bed, ran after Helen and grabbed her arm, screaming, "No, I want to go. Let me go with you! Let me go!"

Angry that she was once again making the simplest thing difficult, Helen spun around, and drew back her hand, ready to strike. But she caught herself.

Dodie saw her raised hand and cowered. She slid to the floor, crying.

Seized by an emotional mixture of shame and despair, Helen knelt on the floor next to her. Through her own tears she murmured, "Okay, Dodie, I won't go either. I'll tell Miss. Jessop I don't need her."

Dodie wiped her face with her sleeve. She looked up at her and said, "Can we go get Houlie? I want to play with him. Can we get him? Huh?"

Suddenly it dawned on Helen. She was being hoodwinked. Dodie didn't really want to go with her. She wanted her dog. She'd asked Helen several times during the day if they could get him and she'd put her off, told her they'd get him tomorrow.

Helen looked down at her thinking, *Well, I'll be. She's as manipulative as Beulah was. Only I would never have guessed it.*

"I'll go get Houlie for you on one condition," she said, not letting on that she knew what she was up to, "that you'll agree to stay with Miss Jessop while Gerard and I go out this evening. Is that a deal?"

Dodie stood up and clasped her hands together. "Deal."

Helen checked her watch again. She had less than twenty minutes to get up to the kennels and get back before Gerard arrived.

Coming out of the bedchamber, Helen said to Miss Jessop, "My sister won't give you any trouble. She just wants her dog. I hope that won't be an imposition."

"Oh, no, I love animals," Miss Jessop replied.

"Good, I just have to run up to the kennel and get him. If my escort, Mr. Hale, arrives before I get back, tell him I'll only be a few minutes."

Helen raced up to the kennel. When she got there, she unlocked Houlie's wire cage amid a cacophony of barking, chirping and miscellaneous animal noises. She hooked the leash onto his collar and took him out thinking, *I'm so tired of this. All my life I've been nothing but a slave, passed down from one mistress to the next. But not for much longer. Soon, I'll be free. Free to live the life I want, with the person I want to live it with.*"

Chapter 30

Nicolette had just returned from Sunday dinner with the children and au pair. She left the girls in the Parlor with Nathan who was giving them pony rides, and went into their bedchamber. She walked over to the closet and searched through her evening gowns. She'd seen a poster at the entrance of the restaurant about a Ball this evening and decided she was going. Alone! It would be the first time she'd gone to such an event unescorted, but she was determined to try it out for size since it looked like she might be a divorcee soon.

She and Nathan were still at a stalemate. They spoke to each other only if it involved the children or was necessary. She'd expected him to be hopping mad when she got back from Madame Lucile's this morning, even imagined he'd have a personally written divorce decree waiting for her. But he kept working on the musical walking stick he was repairing and completely ignored her. Shortly after, he left and she didn't see him again until she and Sabine got back from dinner with the children.

She'd considered telling him what happened in her meeting with Madame Lucile but decided against it. It would only have started an argument anyway. Besides, her meeting with Madame Lucile hadn't changed anything. She was still determined to have a career of her own, to be a designer. She knew her husband was never going to give her his blessings, so there was no point in continuing to talk about it. She'd made up her mind anyway. When they got back to France, she was going to do whatever she had to do to make her ambitions a reality.

She reached in the closet and grabbed a hanger holding a floral embroidered, seafoam green gown with a matching chiffon overblouse, both trimmed with tiny pearls and beads. She held it up in front of her and walked over to the bureau. She was inspecting the ensemble in the mirror, trying to figure out which pieces of jewelry would best compliment it when Nathan walked in.

He paused giving her a stern look. "And just where do you think you're going?" he asked in an authoritarian tone.

"Oh, are you talking to me?" she replied sarcastically.

He folded his arms in front of him. "Yes. I'm talking to you. I asked you where you're going."

"Out. To the Ball to be exact." She stuck her chin in the air, walked past him to the bed and laid the gown on it.

"Unaccompanied?"

"Yes. Unaccompanied. Since it appears I'm soon to be single woman, I thought I should get used to going out alone."

"Do you have any idea what you're doing, Nicolette?" He was looking at her as if she was being completely unreasonable. "First, you defy me and go traipsing off to see that rag maker, and now you plan on going to a social event unaccompanied. How do you think that looks?"

She could tell he was fuming, but she didn't care. She shot back, "That's all you care about. Appearances. How you're going to look in other people's eyes. Well, I don't care how it looks. Or what anyone thinks. If that's what mattered to me, I wouldn't have married you." She walked over and snatched open the nightstand drawer, took out her jewelry case and dropped it on the top of the nightstand with a bang.

"Fine. That's just fine." He threw up his hands. "Well you are not single yet, and you're still my wife." He started unbuttoning his shirt and taking off his shoes at the same time, using his right foot to remove his left shoe.

Nicolette took her pearl choker from the jewel case. "You gave me an ultimatum, remember?"

"I remember." He walked over to his side of the closet and took out his tuxedo. "Since we got on this ship I've been ridiculed, spit at and almost killed," he said angrily. "I've been disrespected by just about everyone I've come across. But I'll be damned if I'm going to sit by and let my wife disrespect me too."

He threw the tuxedo on the bed and glared at her. For a long moment they stood there, locked in a hopeless, invisible embrace of bittersweet love and cloying resentment.

Nicolette broke the trance. "Suit yourself." They dressed in silence.

An hour later they stood at the entrance to the *Titanic*'s massive Ballroom waiting to be seated, counterfeit smiles firmly in place.

Nicolette peeked inside the Ballroom. She imagined the Palace at Versaille couldn't have been more majestic. Three enormous gold and crystal chandeliers sparkled above the room. Matching sconces echoed their splendor on the walls. Graceful green and white calla lilies in tall crystal vases sat on round linen covered tables that made a semi-circle around a gleaming hardwood dance floor. The sweet strains of *In The Shadows* floated from the bandstand at the head of the room.

Finally, an elegantly attired maitre d' walked up to them and bowed gracefully. "Good evening, madam, can I escort you to your party?" He completely ignored Nathan standing next to her and she noticed his jaw tighten.

Taking Nicolette's arm, Nathan said, "This is my wife. "We're a party of two."

The maitre d' flashed him a contemptuous look and replied, "I see. Follow me." He quickly led them to the worst table in the vast Ballroom, the one closest to the bandstand. He made a peremptory flourish toward a chair at the table and strode away.

Nathan muttered something about rudeness under his breath and helped her with her chair. She purposely made no comment on the man's behavior. She wasn't in the mood to hear more of Nathan's complaints anyway. He acted like he was the only one being treated badly. She wasn't immune to the insults or deaf to the whispers any more than he was. It all made her long for the familiarity of home, for the refinement and manners of her countrymen.

She was listening to the band, pointedly ignoring Nathan when an elegant young couple walked over to their table.

"Nathan, mi amigo," the young man shouted over the music from the band. They shook hands and Victor Penasco introduced them to his bride, Pepita. Shouting over the music, Senore Penasco said, "Come, join us at our table. Gerard and his fiancé are sitting with us. We will all have a wonderful evening together."

After a little coaxing, Nathan agreed and Nicolette was glad he did. The Penasco's table offered a panoramic view of the Ballroom and the friendliest people they'd met the entire voyage. Gerard Hale introduced them to his fiancée, Miss Ryerson and they all settled around the table for an evening of fun. It wasn't long before Nicolette noticed that both of the other couples were holding hands. They were so clearly in love it filled her with sadness. Not so long ago, she and Nathan had been like that. *What happened to us?* she mused as the band started playing *The Merry Widow Waltz*. In her heart she knew she still loved her husband, but in her head she knew love wasn't enough anymore.

As the evening commenced, the Ballroom quickly filled to capacity and it wasn't long before the men were huddled on one side of the table discussing politics while the women convened on the other discussing Nicolette's favorite subject - fashion. Helen asked her to stop in New York to visit her before they returned to France and Pepita told her about the magnificent fashion houses she'd frequented in London and Madrid.

Nicolette overheard Victor Penasco say something about a dual and jerked her head in the direction of the men, exclaiming, "A dual?"

"Yes, Senora," he smiled. "I assure you, it is completely civilized. Are you familiar with the Tango?"

"Yes." she replied. She and Nathan had learned the dance before they were married from friends who had picked it up in Argentina. "But it's been a couple of years since-"

"Oh, do give it a try," Pepita chortled, getting up from her chair. "It will be fun." She stuck her hip out, placed a hand on it, threw her head back and gracefully held her other hand over her head. "Let's show these bluebloods some *real* dancing."

Nicolette peered over at Nathan. "I'm up for the challenge if you are," he said, smiling at her as if nothing was amiss between them. She couldn't help but think, *Of course, if it's competitive, you're all for it.* But she kept her thoughts to herself.

She didn't want to ruin the fun for everyone else so she said, "Okay, I'll try it. I just hope I can remember the steps."

Victor went over to the band and she saw him whisper something in the band leader's ear. He discreetly slipped something in his pocket and breezed back to the table. The band finished playing *The Merry Widow Waltz* and a few seconds later she heard the first romantic strains of Albeniz's *Tango*.

"Mi amour?" Victor said to his wife and led her away from the table as the last few dancers cleared the floor.

Nathan gave her a seductive smile and reached for her hand. She followed him to the middle of the dance floor and he spun her out as if she was some great prize he was presenting to the world. As she stepped into the rhythm of the music he put his arm around her waist, looked lovingly into her eyes and encouraged her with his body to lead him in the dance. They were so close, she could smell the bergamot in his hair. It took her back to the days of their courtship when she'd work all week in the shop with Mama and Papa Bonschear, her heart filled with longing for him, anticipating the weekend. They'd go to one of the nightclubs downtown and dance the Tango, enticing each other with their eyes, with the provocative movements of their bodies until the passion between them was fanned to a fever pitch.

Now, she found herself unwittingly succumbing to the exhilarating rhythm, the intoxicating sensuality of Nathan's body. He anticipated her every move, complimented each step so effortlessly it was as if he could read her soul.

It made her realize why she'd been keeping him at a distance. It was the magnetism between them. It was so strong it clouded her thinking, so hypnotic it could reduce her to putty in his hands. He twined his leg around hers and gazed into her eyes with such passion she could actually feel his love for her.

She drew her eyes away from his. Without missing a beat, he placed his finger under her chin forcing her to look at him and said, "Nicolette, we have to save our marriage. Everyone has problems. We simply have to make up our minds to work ours out."

"Hummph! Let me guess," she answered following the rhythm of the dance, "your solution is for me to be an obedient wife and behave as you want me to. Well, if that's working it out, I want no part of it. I know who I am and what I have to do to be happy. Since you can't accept that, there's nothing to work out."

"So you're giving up on us, without a fight," he said as they strode across the floor, cheek to cheek.

"I'm tired of fighting," she sighed. "That's all we've been doing for I don't know how long. When we get back to France, I'll give you your divorce. In fact, I completely agree with it. I think it best we go our separate ways."

For the next few seconds, Nathan said nothing. Then just as the music was winding down he pulled her to him, kissed her full on the mouth and whispered, "I still love you, Nicolette. We'll work this out, somehow."

A collective gasp went through the Ballroom. The dance ended and was followed by a spattering of applause as they left the dance floor.

When they arrived back at their table, Victor remarked to Nathan, "You Tango very well my friend. We couldn't have had more admirable competition."

"That's because I have the perfect partner." Nathan cast an admiring glance at Nicolette, then added, "But you and Senora Penasco are perfect as well. So why don't we call it a draw?"

Victor slapped him on the back, laughing. "A true gentleman. I like your style, Legarde."

Sick of the hypocrisy and the false smile she'd been wearing all evening, Nicolette decided to go to the powder room. Helen and Pepita offered to go with her and the three of them left the men to their masculine conversation.

They'd gone about thirty feet when Helen Ryerson was stopped by the two women who occupied the stateroom next to theirs. They both flashed her a denigrating look. She noticed that Helen suddenly looked uncomfortable and suggested that she and Pepita catch up with her later. They walked away but hadn't gone very far before Pepita came upon a friend of hers. Pepita introduced her to Charlotte Drake Cardeza, and after standing there for a few minutes and listening to them chat, Nicolette excused herself and continued on to the powder room.

She wound her way through tables, past the bandstand, through a set of double doors and into a noisy, dimly lit corridor. It took her five minutes to get through the crush of bodies to the powder room. Inside, she had to wait another five minutes before she could use the facilities.

Afterwards, she was standing at the sink washing her hands when she heard the strangest sound -like a large chair being scraped against the floor. She felt the ship vibrate beneath her feet. The lights flickered, once, twice, then came back on.

"What was that?" a woman called from one of the stalls behind her as a chorus of "Whoa," came though the walls from the outside corridor.

"I don't know, but I don't like it," a gray haired woman at the sink next to hers remarked.

A third women fluffing her hair at a large gilded mirror across the room poo pooed them all: "Oh, really, ladies, let's not make much ado about nothing. Everyone knows how unrealiable these fancy electric lights can be. I'm sure that's all it is."

Nicolette didn't comment, but thought to herself, *electric lights wouldn't make a sound like that...they wouldn't make the ship shake like that either.* It made her uneasy so she quickly dried her hands and left.

In the corridor, she inched along with the crush of people. She'd gone about ten feet when she felt something sharp poke her in the back.

Instinctively, she reached around to touch the spot, but someone pushed her hand away.

"Keep lookin' ahead," a voice warned, "and keep your mouth shut, or I'll gut you like a spring trout right here." She wanted to turn, to see who it was, but the voice was so menacing she was afraid to. Around her, people were talking and laughing, absorbed in themselves. No one was paying attention to her, or noticed that she was being threatened. An icy hand of fear gripped her throat and she realized she was completely vulnerable in this sea of people. Terror paralyzed her legs.

From somewhere in the crowd, a man with a blue-black ring circling his left eye stepped in front of her. Instinctively, she knew he was the man Nathan had had the fight with. He dangled a blue satin ribbon in front of her and leaned forward as if speaking to her in confidence. "If you want to see your little girl again, you'll do as he says," he whispered.

Oh my God, that's Trista's ribbon! Nicolette looked about frantically, hoping someone would notice them. But no one did. She felt the point of the knife in her back again and the man behind her whispered low and moist in her ear, "Turn around real slow and keep walkin.' Do what I say and you won't git hurt."

Nicolette's heart thudded against her chest. She forced her feet to move, and slowly made her way through the crowd. *Oh, Trista, my poor baby. Please God, let her be all right.*

Chapter 31

As soon as they got Legarde's wife back to their cabin, Jimmy Ray shouted at her, "I told you to shut up," and slapped her across the face. Already, he was sick of her. She'd been a pain in the ass ever since they found her. He'd had to threaten her every step of the way to keep her quiet and moving. She kept asking why they'd taken her little girl, wanted them to reassure her that the child was all right. She made such a fuss he finally had to cut her a little, just deep enough to draw blood, to show her he meant business. That made her simmer down a little. But she was still sniffling and he was afraid someone would notice and get suspicious. He pushed her into the bedroom and slammed the door in Earl Lee's face, leaving him in the sitting room, then shoved her and sent her sprawling onto the bed.

Mrs. Legarde sat up on the bed, pleading, with tears in her eyes, "Please, let me see my baby, I have to-"

"Don't make me have to smack you agin,'" Jimmy Ray snarled, cutting her off. "I ain't got your young un, least ways not yet. I told you that to git you down here. Figured that was the easiest way to git to that Nigger husband of yours."

Her green eyes widened like she thought she'd heard him wrong. "My husband?"

"That's right, your husband. Son-of-a-bitch ruined my life. Now it's time for him to pay for it."

Sitting there on the bed with those strawberry blond tendrils framing her face, he couldn't help but notice how beautiful she was. *A fine piece of womanhood,* he thought, taking in the smooth alabaster skin, delicate facial features, full, shapely figure. *Yep, real fine. Something I'll never have. Least ways, not for love.*

All he'd ever have was what he'd always had: ugly bitches and ten cent whores. And here *she* was married to a Nigger. It only deepened his hurt, and his hatred for Legarde.

"How could my husband have ruined your life?" The question broke his reverie. "He had a ridiculous boxing match with your friend. He doesn't even know you."

In a split second Jimmy Ray exploded with anger, yanked his Stetson off his head and threw it on the bed beside her. With it came the blonde hair sewn to the hat's band, the hair that concealed the burn scarred skin on the right side of his face, extending from behind his cheek bone and down the side of his neck. He threw off his jacket and ripped off his shirt revealing a hideous, scar ravaged torso.

"Your Nigger husband did this to me, you stupid bitch!" He pointed his finger at his chest, emphasizing his words. "This! And by God, I'm gonna make him pay for it if it's the last thing I do."

Mrs. Legarde gasped and turned her head away.

"Oh, that's all right, Don't look," he said, pacing in front of her. "You ain't the first one to turn away. I just wanted you to see for yourself how he turned me into a monster. A Monster! Even turned my own Pa-" Suddenly a sob rose in his throat, catching him off guard. He tried to stifle it, but it broke through anyway.

Monster! Monster! He'd never said that word before today. And now it seemed to echo in his head. Since he was eight years old he'd been taunted with it by his peers, teased and labeled with it, even by adults. He'd learned to accept it. It was who he was, how he felt inside - an outcast, a freak, scarred beyond redemption. But somehow, he knew the word wouldn't have the same sting after today - because TODAY, he was going to be the tormenter. TODAY he would exact vengeance.

Earl Lee called from the other side of the door, "Hey, Jimmy Ray, what ya doin' in there? You promised me, remember? Come on."

Jimmy Ray choked off his tears. "All right," he called back. "Just give me a minute." He threw on his shirt, hurriedly fastened the few remaining buttons and put on his hat and jacket. He took a handkerchief from his pocket and blew his nose. Walking to the door, he said to Mrs. Legarde, "Me and Earl Lee's got a treat for ya."

He opened the door and Earl Lee rushed in with one of his Girlie magazines in his hand. "I'm ready," he announced, "Boy am I ready." He threw the magazine on the floor and rubbed his hands together.

"Wait!" Jimmy Ray stopped him. "Tie her up first. And gag her. When I git mine I don't want to have to hear no cryin'."

Mrs. Legarde looked at them, wild-eyed. "Please, don't, please. I'm pregnant. Please."

It was news to Jimmy Ray. He thought Anton had told him everything. Either he didn't know it, or the fat slob forgot to tell him. "But hell, it don't matter," he thought dismissing her pleas, "she'll still do."

Earl Lee gave him a questioning look and he gave his permission with a wave of his hand, turning a deaf ear to Mrs. Legarde's pleas. He walked over and sat on Earl Lee's bed and watched as he made her take off her stockings and give them to him. He cut one of the stockings in half with his pocketknife, tied her hands to the bed with one half and tied the other half around her mouth. Pushing up her dress he told her, "Now just be still and you won't git hurt. I'll take it real easy."

Mrs. Legarde struggled vainly as Earl Lee lowered his body on top of her. As the rape unfolded before him Jimmy Ray unzipped his trousers and stroked his genitals. He waited for the excitement to build, for the familiar tension in his member. But nothing happened. He closed his eyes and tried to will himself hard. Still, nothing happened.

Earl Lee grunted and groaned. A couple of minutes later he stood up and zipped his fly exclaiming, "Ooooeeee, that was good. She's all yours."

Earl Lee left the room and Jimmy Ray walked over to the bed. He dropped his trousers and lowered his body on top of his prey. He rubbed his body against hers, roughly caressing her face and breasts. Yet nothing happened. He tried harder and harder, but his manhood wouldn't respond. The harder he tried, the softer he seemed to get.

Frustrated, he murmured in her ear, "You're less than a whore. Got a Nigger's seed in ya.' But you still probably think you're too good for me."

He grabbed her face in his hands and squeezed so hard he could feel her molars. He wanted to destroy her pretty face, mutilate her body. It was all he could do to keep himself from grabbing her neck and choking the life out of her.

"Damn you to hell," he yelled and jumped up. He yanked up his trousers and was tucking his shirt in when Earl Lee came back in the room and stopped abruptly, concern etched on his face. "Listen! he said, cocking his head, "the ship's stopped. Something's wrong, I know it. I told you when the lights blinked something was- "

"What are you whining about now?" Jimmy Ray said, buckling his belt.

"We've stopped. Come here, I'll prove it."

More curious than concerned, he followed Earl Lee into the lavatory. "Now how the hell are you gonna to prove the ship's stopped in here?" he chided.

"Here," Earl Lee put his hand on the side of the claw-footed bathtub. "Before I could feel the engine's vibration when I touched the bathtub. Now I can't."

Jimmy Ray put his hand on the cool porcelain and looked up at Earl Lee. This time the big ox was right. He'd felt the vibration before too. Now he didn't. But he dismissed it.

"So we stopped for a minute. That don't mean nothin.' We coulda' stopped for any number of reasons."

"Yeah, like what?"

"How the hell should I know. I ain't the captain."

"No, but it seems awful strange to me."

"Look, don't start worryin' about somethin' that ain't our job to worry about. We've got business to take care of, like gittin' Legarde down here."

Earl Lee followed him out of the lavatory. Walking through the bedroom, he looked over at Nicolette and remarked, "Maybe we ought to untie her, let her get herself cleaned up."

"Aw, now ain't you real thoughtful," Jimmy Ray scoffed. "That bitch is stayin' right where she is." He went to the secretary in the sitting room, picked up a brass fountain pen and a White Star writing tablet. Beneath the blue logo he wrote:

I have your wife. Come to E261 ALONE! Fifteen minutes or she dies.

He ripped the sheet from the tablet and went back into the bedroom. Legarde's wife was curled up in a ball on the bed, whimpering, her back to him. Her dress was torn where he'd cut her and he went over and touched the paper to the wound. She flinched, but he still got enough blood on it to make sure Legarde would take the note serious. He took the gag from around her mouth and demanded, "What's your room number?"

"Why? What are you going to do?" she asked.

He slapped her again. "I ask the questions around here, not you, understand? Now what's your room number?"

"B21." Blood oozed from the corner of her mouth.

He went back to the secretary, put the note in an envelope and sealed it. On the outside he wrote, 'Nathan Legarde.'

Earl Lee was sitting in an arm chair with his head in a *Yellow Kids* comic book. Jimmy Ray walked over, snatched it out of his hand and gave him the envelope. "Take this to Legarde's cabin, number B21, and you make sure he doesn't see you. Matter of fact, don't let anybody see you. Think you can handle that without messin' it up?"

"Yeah, but you don't have to go snatchin' things from me."

"Aw, quit your bellyachin' and git movin.'"
He pointed toward the bedroom. "Blondie in there
says Legarde'll be looking for her. I want to make
sure he looks in the right place."

Earl Lee grabbed his jacket off the back
of a chair and left. Jimmy Ray went back to the
secretary, opened the top right hand drawer and
took out a pistol. He carried it into the bedroom
and took a seat in the chair near the bed. "I got
a real treat lined up for that nigger husband of
yours," he announced as he snapped open the
pistol's chamber and checked to make sure it was
still loaded. "But before I kill him I'm gonna give
him a taste of what he put me through. But you
needn't worry none. I'll make yours quick. I ain't
got nothin' against you, except marryin' a nigger."

He clicked the gun's chamber shut. In his
mind's eye he imagined putting the gun to Legarde's
head and pulling the trigger. *BANG!*

Chapter 32

When Helen and Pepita came back from the powder room without Nicolette, Nathan thought nothing of it. He assumed she was off somewhere talking to her new friend, Molly Brown, or had come across her idol, the great Madame Lucile. But forty minutes later, she still hadn't returned. He checked his watch and saw that it was a couple of minutes to midnight. Concerned, he excused himself from his friends and took a stroll around the Ballroom. He didn't see her anywhere and decided to check the corridor. She wasn't there either. When he got back to their table the orchestra was playing the *Destiny* waltz. He shouted over the music to Helen and Pepita, "Do you know where Nicolette is? She should have been back by now."

Both of the women shook their heads. "I haven't seen her since we left," Miss Ryerson said, looking from him to Pepita.

"Perhaps she went back to look in on your children," Pepita suggested, then added, "but of course, she would have told you."

"Of course," Nathan replied. "Still, I think I'll have another look around." Pepita and Helen volunteered to check the powder room while the men made a complete search of the Ballroom. Fifteen minutes later they convened at their table. No one had seen Nicolette.

"Well, perhaps she did go to check on the children," Nathan said, embarrassed and worried. "I don't know where else she would have gone at this hour of the night. I think I'll say good evening and make sure she's turned in."

"I think we should be leaving too," Helen said to Gerard. "Sometimes Dodie fights going to sleep, especially when Houlie's around for her to play with."

"Whatever you say, my dear," Gerard helped her from her chair.

They all said goodnight to the Penascos and Nathan left the Ballroom with Gerard and Miss Ryerson. Ascending the stairs of the Grand Staircase, Gerard remarked to Nathan, "I can see you're concerned about your wife. I would be too." He looked lovingly at Helen and added, "Look, let me see Helen to her room and I'll drop by your quarters afterwards to make sure everything is all right."

"That won't be necessary," Nathan replied.

Gerard made an arresting gesture with his hand. "Nonsense, that's what friends are for."

"All right," Nathan said and rushed away. He navigated the maze of off-white corridors until he reached their stateroom. He rushed inside and found Sabine in the parlor, nodding with a book open on her lap.

"Is Nicolette here?" he looked toward their bedchamber, hoping she was in there.

"Non Monsieur. I thought she was with you."

"Yes, she was. But she left, I think. Anyway, I can't find her. She wasn't in the Ballroom so I thought she might have come back here to check on the children."

"Non, Monsieur, she hasn't been back. The children are asleep." Sabine looked worried and Nathan didn't know what to think. *Where could she be?*

"Monsieur Legarde, Sabine said tentatively, "I know it's none of my business, but I've noticed that you and Madame have been quarreling a lot lately, and I'm afraid it's starting to upset the children, especially Cecile. She's crankier than ever and I can't help but wonder if she's not somehow aware of the trouble between you and Madame."

Nathan didn't like what he was hearing one bit. But he had to concede that it could be true. It was even more reason for him and Nicolette to solve the problem that was tearing them apart. But right now, he had to *find* her. Only the ship was so large, he didn't know where to start. He was thinking of going back to the Ballroom when an announcement came over the ship's intercom: *All passengers on deck with lifebelts on. All passengers on deck with lifebelts on…*

Sabine stood up, the worry on her face deepening. "What's going on, Monsieur?"

"I don't know."

Just then, they heard talking coming from outside their door. Curious, Nathan went over and opened it. What he saw only increased his foreboding. People were milling about in various stages of dress, some wearing lifebelts, some carrying lifebelts. Everyone was talking, complaining and questioning all at once, moving in a confused fashion, clearly not sure of which direction to go. He caught snatches of conversation from the building cacophony: *Why are they bothering us in the middle of the night?"...,*

I heard we hit an iceberg. That's what made the lights blink awhile ago...,

No, one of our stewards told me it's a routine drill. Nothing to worry about...,

Well, iceberg or no iceberg, I'm glad this ship's unsinkable!

To Hell with it, I'm going back to bed.

Down the corridor, a steward was knocking on doors, rousing the occupants while another steward walked through the crowd calling above the noise, "All passengers go up to top deck. Now. Leave everything. It's only a precaution. You can return to your cabins later." He repeated it over and over as he tried to herd everyone in the direction of the stairs to the upper decks.

Sabine's voice came from behind him, "Oh, Monsieur, I'm scared." Her eyes were filled with dread.

Nathan didn't want to increase her fear but he had to tell her the truth. "I think we have reason for concern. Ships don't conduct drills in the middle of the night. Something's definitely wrong." Under his breath he murmured to himself, "Oh, my God, Nicolette, where are you?"

Sabine's face had blanched white with fright. "What are we going to do, Monsieur?" she asked in a shaky voice.

For a paralyzing moment, Nathan felt overwhelmed. He was in a terrible bind. He had to get the children and Sabine up to the boat deck and make sure they were safe. But he had to find Nicolette, too. If the ship floundered, he had to be sure his family was in a lifeboat, and that included his wife. *Of all the crazy, irresponsible stunts for her to pull, she had to pick this night to do it.*

"We have to wake the children, get them up on deck," he said to Sabine just as he saw Gerard Hale emerge from the crowd in the corridor. "Hurry, I'll be in to help you in a moment."

Sabine hesitated. "But what about Madame Nicolette? She won't know where we are."

"I'll take care of that. You take care of the children. Now hurry."

When Gerard finally reached him he exclaimed, "I've got news. We should talk inside."

As soon as Nathan closed the door, Gerard blurted out, "We've hit an iceberg. I just saw E.J. He, Andrews and some of his engineers are headed down to assess the damage right now. Andrews claims there's no real danger because of the ship's watertight compartments. But I think they're downplaying the danger to prevent a panic." He looked past Nathan into the parlor. "Is your Mrs. here?"

"No. And I'm really worried. Wherever she is, I'm sure she heard the announcement. If something wasn't wrong, I know she'd have returned by now."

Gerard nodded his agreement and said, "Listen, I'm on my way to make sure Helen and Dodie go topside. Afterwards, I'll check the Ballroom again."

Nathan thanked him.

"Think nothing of it," Gerard slapped him on he back and they shook hands. "You'd do the same for me. I'll see you in a little while."

Nathan closed the door, rushed to get their lifebelts from the top of the wardrobe in their bedchamber, and sprinted into the adjoining room. Sabine was sitting on the bed with the children. She had them all bundled up in their coats and hats. The baby was still sleeping, but Trista was wide awake.

"What's this, Papa?" she asked as he strapped her lifebelt on.

"A newfangled toy for little girls," he lied.

"Oh." She smiled up at him.

A few seconds later he picked her up and stood her on the floor. "Where's Mama?" she asked.

He and Sabine exchanged a pregnant glance. How could he tell her the truth? That he didn't know where her Mama was? He replied in a lighthearted tone, hiding his worry, "Mama will be along soon."

Sabine finished buckling her lifebelt and picked up the sleeping baby while Nathan picked up Trista. "Let's go, he said, deciding to take them up to the Boat deck, then look for Nicolette.

They were rushing toward the door when Sabine exclaimed, "Look!" She pointed to a white envelope on the floor and Nathan picked it up. His name was on it, but he didn't recognize the handwriting. He ripped it open and saw blood smeared on the paper. The sight sent a jolt of fear through him.

Quickly, he read the note: *"I have your wife. Come to E261. ALONE! Fifteen minutes or she dies."* For a brief moment, he was frozen with shock.

Sabine read his expression and shrieked, "What is it? What's wrong?"

"Nothing." He stuffed the envelope in his pocket. He didn't want to alarm her further or get Trista upset. "It's just something I have to take care of. That's all."

But now he knew the awful truth: Nicolette hadn't left of her own accord. Someone had taken her and she could be in grave danger. Judging from the blood stained paper, whoever it was may have already hurt her.

So he had to choose - take his children to safety, or find his wife. And he had only fifteen minutes to do it.

"We have to hurry," he said and scooped Trista up. He ran down the corridor with her past several men wearing lifebelts. They were casually walking away from the stairs that led to the upper deck. Sabine ran behind him with the baby in her arms. When they reached the bottom of the stairs leading to the upper decks, he said to Sabine, his voice cracking, "I'm going to have to trust you to get the girls up to the boat deck. I can't go with you. I have to find Nicolette."

Sabine adjusted the baby on her shoulder. "All right Monsieur, but how long are you going to be?"

"I don't know. But I'll be back as quickly as I can. When you get to the boat deck, go to the starboard side and wait for us there, okay. The starboard side."

She nodded, "Oui, Monsieur." He kissed the children and watched as she took Trista's hand and started up the stairs.

He tore himself away and ran in the opposite direction. As he sped past their stateroom, a voice yelled inside his head: *Stop! Where the Hell are you going with nothing to protect yourself? You don't know what you're rushing into.*

He spun around and ran back to their stateroom and into their bedchamber. He got down on the floor, reached under the bed and pulled out the carpetbag, Toussaint, his father's lawyer, had given him. He dropped it on the bed, opened it and took out the wooden case inside that held the matching knife and pistol his father had left him.

He slipped the pistol into the side of his boot and anchored the knife to the back of his belt. All the while he had the oddest feeling, like somehow his father was watching him, guiding him. He remembered that day in Toussaint's office when he'd given him the carpetbag. He recalled that even then it felt like his father had left the weapons for a reason, to protect him from something. *But how could he know Nicolette would be kidnapped?* He snapped the carpetbag shut, threw it under the bed and raced out again.

A few minutes later he knocked on the door of cabin E261. No one answered. So he knocked again and again. Still no answer. He wondered if someone was playing a malicious prank, and tried the door knob. It opened and he stepped inside. "Hello?" he called, but all he heard was silence. Cautiously, he scanned the room and took a few steps forward. That's when he saw Nicolette. She was lying on a bed in the next room. Her thighs were exposed and she was bound and gagged. She saw him, struggled against her restraints and made a muffled cry, terror in her eyes.

"Nicolette!" He took a step in her direction.

Then something that felt like a ton of steel crashed into his skull and sent him spiraling, down, down, down, deep into darkness.

Chapter 33

Jimmy Ray dragged Nathan's body into the bedroom. He and Earl Lee sat him in a straight backed chair, and used his wife's stockings to tie his wrists behind his back and bind his feet. Certain he couldn't get loose Jimmy Ray poured a glass of water from the pitcher on the nightstand. He wanted Legarde awake so he could fully appreciate Hell before he sent him there. He threw the water in his face and Legarde came to with a gasping start.

"Welcome to Second Class, Monsieur Legarde," he laughed.

Legarde tried to get up from the chair, but quickly realized he couldn't. He looked over at his wife still lying on the bed then back at Jimmy Ray standing over him. "What have you done to my wife? What's this about?"

From the loveseat across the room, Earl Lee called over the top of his *Yellow Kids* comic book. "Oh, we had a real good time with your wife. Had some of that French delight. Didn't we Jimmy Ray?"

"Sure did. But if you ask me, French delight's a might overrated."

Legarde jerked against his restraint again. "You rotten son-of-a-bi-"

Jimmy Ray cracked him across the face with the back of his hand, "Don't make me lose my temper Legarde. I don't won't to kill you just yet. You've got some sufferin' to do first."

"What are you talking about?" Legarde repeated. "Is this about the boxing match? This makes no sense."

"Oh, the boxin' was just for fun," Jimmy Ray chuckled. "Just wanted to see you git your ass kicked. I was pretty disappointed though when you got that lucky punch in on Earl Lee."

Earl Lee hollered from across the room, "Yeah, well this time he ain't gettin' in *any* punches." He laughed and went back to his comic book.

"My wife didn't have anything to do with that," Legarde said, glancing over at Nicolette. "Please, let her go. Our children need her."

"To hell with your half breed mulattos. She ain't goin' nowhere. Besides, I want her to watch you die. Her reward for marryin' a nigger."

"Please. We've done nothing to you," Legarde begged. "Why do you want to kill us? I don't even know you."

I don't even know you. I don't even know you, echoed in Jimmy Ray's head, stoking his anger to a simmering rage. "Oh, you know me, Legarde," he said, taking a cigar from his inside jacket pocket. He bit off the end and lit it, took several quick puffs and remarked, "Matter of fact, you left a lastin' impression on me. Guess I just have to jog your memory." He took a quick step forward and aimed the cigar at Legarde's right eye. Legarde jerked his head back and the cigar seared the flesh of his cheekbone. He screamed and jerked as Jimmy Ray ground the cigar into his skin.

When he drew the cigar away, Legarde begged, " Please, what do you want from me? I don't know what you want from me."

Jimmy Ray stuck the cigar back in his mouth, took a puff and replied, "Right now, all I want you to do is remember me." He paced back and forth in front of him, feeling invincible. "You see, I never forgot you. I know everything about you. Like you goin' to that fancy University in Paris, the-"(he paused, and snapped his fingers), "yeah, the Ecole Polytechnique. You got a couple medals too, one for track and field and another for academic excellence. You lived with your Pa on Rue Montessuey until he died a few months back. He paused again. "And, oh yeah, accordin' to my cousin, you got your name in a bunch of newspapers for some kind of invention." He blew a couple of smoke rings. "See, I know all about you. Even know the day you married Frenchy over there."

"How do you know all this about me?" Legarde asked.

"The name Andre Mendes ring a bell with you?"

Legarde looked surprised, "Andre? Robert Toussaint's assistant?"

"Yep, my Pa's nephew. He let me know you were goin' to be on this fancy rig. Real smart fella, a real good squealer too."

"Okay, so Mendes knows who I am. That still doesn't make me know you. The first time I saw you was on this ship."

"Liar!" Jimmy Ray grabbed Legarde by the hair and ground his cigar into the side of his neck. "How's that feel Legarde?" he asked as Legarde screamed. "Fire don't jog your memory? Fire don't mean nothing' to ya? Huh?"

When he finally let Legarde go, he called to Earl Lee, "soften him up. I need a drink." He went into the sitting room, poured himself a glass of Jim Beam, and reclined in a chair for several minutes. Twirling the glass in his hand, he savored the taste of the liquor and the thud of punches coming from the next room. A few minutes later he went back in and said to Legarde, "memory workin' any better?"

Legarde didn't answer so he walked over and tilted his chin up with his finger.

Legarde peered up at him, his left eye swollen and blood shot. "If I remembered you, I'd tell you. So, if you're going to kill me, just do it."

"Oh, so you *want* to die," Jimmy Ray mocked. "Funny. Thanks to you, I know just how that feels." He strode across the room, took his suitcase off the rack next to the loveseat and took out a picture framed in burl wood. A handsome, blonde-haired boy smiled from the picture. He took it over and showed it to Legarde. "Remember him?"

Legarde looked at the picture and slowly a mixture of recognition and surprise crept into his face. "You? You were... He looked up at Jimmy Ray. "I had no idea. All this time, I thought it was three men who came to our house that night. But you...you were the short one in the middle."

"Yep, that was me." He threw the picture onto the bed next to Nicolette. "Pa figured bringing me along for a hangin' would help make a man outta' me, show me how to keep Niggers in their place. But thanks to you, this is what I got instead." He took off his hat and showed Legarde his burn-scarred skin. "I've had to live with this since that day."

"Look, your Pa and his friend were going to kill me" Legarde said, "I did the only thing I could think to do. I didn't set out to hurt you."

"Yeah, well you know what hurt me even more than this?" He pulled his hair back and pointed at his ravaged flesh, "Ever since that night my Pa has washed my face with you. Old Marcel would brag to him about what you were doin' over there in France, how you were always at the top of your class, and Pa would tell me I couldn't hold a candle to you, said I wasn't half as good as you. Imagine that, me, his own son, not half as good as a nigger."

"My father knew your Pa?" Legarde's tone was incredulous.

"Sure did. Matter of fact, him and Pa were business partners, owned Delta Ferryboats together."

"That's impossible," Legarde exclaimed, "My father would never do business with someone who'd tried to kill me."

"Oh, but he did," Jimmy Ray chided. "But don't git too worked up over it. He didn't know nothin.' After Pa found out Marcel was your Pappy, him and your Ma made a deal. Pa promised not to give her no more trouble long as she kept her mouth shut about what happened that night. So it worked out right nice for everybody. Except me. I was the one wound up payin.'"

"I don't understand," Legarde looked confused. "The man who struck my mother was named LeBlanc."

"That's right," Jimmy Ray replied proudly. "Cholly LeBlanc, about the richest man in Orleans Parish, Louisiana."

"Your Pa, he was out to commit murder that night and put you in danger. For God's sake man, can't you see that? Can't you see what happened? We were children! We *both* got hurt. You got burned and I had to leave everything I knew and stow away in a casket for nine days. Do you have any idea what that did to me? Any idea how that scars a child's mind?"

"I don't give a damn," Jimmy Ray shouted. "What you went through was temporary. What you did to me is permanent."

"Please, listen to me," Legarde pleaded, "Your Pa is responsible for you getting burned. If he hadn't brought you there that night, it never would have happened. If he'd cared about you, he wouldn't have involved you in his dirty work. Look, he wouldn't even give you his name. Doesn't that tell you something?"

Legarde's words cut deep and he lashed out at him in emotional pain and anger. "Shut up!" he yelled and crashed his fist into his face. "I won't have you badmouthin' my Pa. I know what you're up to, tryin' to turn me against my Pa, twistin' the truth so I'll change my mind about killin' you. Well it ain't gonna work. You was the one who threw that lantern. That makes you responsible." He called to Earl Lee, "Untie Frenchy over there."

Earl Lee put his comic book down and did as ordered.

"Come here," Jimmy Ray beckoned to Nicolette with his finger.

She stepped forward and he told Earl Lee to give her his pocketknife.

Earl Lee looked at him as if he'd lost his mind.

"Give it to her dammit. If she tries anything other than what I tell her, she'll die before he does."

Tears rolled down her face as she took the knife from Earl Lee's hand.

Speaking to her, Jimmy Ray pointed to her husband. "I want you to cut off one of his fingers, a little souvenir for my Pa. Make it a pinky, I don't want him to bleed to death before I can kill him."

She shook her head, "no," her cries muffled by the gag around her mouth.

Jimmy Ray grabbed her by the neck and squeezed. "Do as I say, you worthless piece of trash."

"Do it, Nicolette. It's alright," Legarde said.

Jimmy Ray released her and watched as she took her husbands left pinky in her hand and started to cut.

Legarde screamed once and she collapsed to the floor in a dead faint.

"Son-of-a-bitch!" Jimmy Ray smacked his fist in his hand. "Git her out of my way before I stomp the shit out of her."

Earl Lee rushed over, picked her limp body up off the floor and carried her back to the bed.

Jimmy Ray picked the knife up off the floor, grabbed Legarde's bloody pinky and severed it through the middle joint in one quick slice. Legarde screamed once and went silent, his head dropping to his chest.

Wait till Pa sees this, Jimmy Ray thought, looking at the bloody pinky in his hand. *He's gonna respect me. He's gonna have to respect me.* He took a handkerchief from his pocket and wrapped the pinky in it.

Chapter 34

Helen checked her watch. It was twelve forty-five A.M. She'd just closed the door behind Miss Jessop when she heard a knock. She thought that perhaps the young lady had forgotten something. So, when she opened it she was surprised to find her Aunt Agatha and cousin, Eliza, standing there in their mink coats. Eliza had her hands in a big, mink muff and Aunt Agatha was holding two lifebelts.

"You are going up to the boat deck, aren't you?" Aunt Agatha asked, "Or are you indisposed?" She craned her neck and looked past Helen, apparently to see if Gerard was there.

"No," Helen answered. "I spoke to one of the hall stewards a half hour ago. He said they're having a lifeboat drill. Dodie's asleep and I'm not waking her for that." In the corridor behind the two women, groups of excited people passed, laughing and talking, as if the nighttime drill was another decadent feature of the illustrious *Titanic*. Eliza merely stood there with her mouth clamped shut, tapping her foot.

"Well, suit yourself," her Aunt Agatha chirped, "I just thought I'd ask, though I don't know why, after the shoddy way you've treated us. But far be it from me to hold a grudge." She nudged Eliza and huffed, "Let's go."

Oh, good riddance, Helen thought. She closed the door behind them and went to look in on Dodie. She was still asleep, snoring softly with her protector, Houlie, lying next to her bed. The dog opened sleep heavy eyes, yawned expansively then settled back down to his snoozing.

She went into the parlor, picked up a book from the coffee table and sat on the sofa. Opening it, she got an idea. *With everyone involved in the drill, now might be a good time to get into the infirmary. I heard they're open all night and Dodie will never even know I was gone.*

She picked up her white velvet evening bag and lace trimmed handkerchief from the coffee table and quietly sneaked out. In the corridor, she passed a few people rushing in the opposite direction, but she was in a too much of a hurry to pay any attention to them.

When she finally reached the automatic lift a round-faced attendant stepped in front of her. "I'm sorry, Mam, the lift is closed for the night, Captain's orders."

"Why? I thought it ran all night," she said.

"Normally, yes, but I was told to shut it down." He shrugged, "That's all I can tell you."

"Oh, for heaven's sakes," she grumbled, walked to the Grand Staircase and took the stairs. When she reached D deck and entered the corridor, she got the queerest sensation, like she was off center. She entered the corridor leading to the infirmary and still felt a little off balance. She recalled the four, or was it five? glasses of champagne she'd had at the Ball, and smiled to herself thinking, *I believe you're tipsy, Helen.*

As she made her way down the corridor she couldn't help but notice the silence. No one was around. No attendants, no passengers. Many of the doors she passed were open, as if the occupants had left in a hurry. She stepped on something, looked down and saw a child's doll lying on the floor. A few feet ahead, someone had left a suitcase in the middle of the corridor, its contents spilling out of it. A woman's black cotton shawl lay on the floor just inside one of the open doors.

Sensing that the entire corridor had been evacuated, she stopped, and listened, wondering if she was mistaken, if perhaps there were people behind some of the doors, sleeping. The eerie silence hung in the air like an invisible fog. It gave her a ghostly, creepy feeling.

Hurry, she told herself, pushing the feeling aside, *they'll all be back directly.*

When she reached the infirmary, she peeked through the glass pane in the door and found she wasn't alone after all. Dr. O'Loughlin was inside. He was holding two lifebelts and talking to the nurse who'd caught her in the dispensary a couple of days before. The sight of the woman made her nervous all over again. She saw Dr. O'Loughlin hand the nurse one of the lifebelts and she headed for the door. Helen turned around and ran. She heard the door open and close behind her and slowed down, trying to act normal. At the next intersecting corridor she made a right turn, and furtively glanced over her shoulder, her heart racing. The Nurse walked past the corridor, and thankfully, she was looking straight ahead and didn't see her.

Whew! Helen opened her purse, took out a handkerchief and wiped the moisture from her hands. She turned and headed back to her stateroom, but when she reached the end of the corridor, she ran headlong into a couple of uniformed officers.

"Whoa," one of them grabbed her to keep her from falling, "What are you doing down here? We cleared this area thirty minutes ago."

"Oh, I -I," she stammered, trying to think of what to say.

"You should be up on the boat deck," the other officer said, "We might have to abandon ship."

"Abandon ship?" Helen said, suddenly concerned. "We're supposed to be having a lifeboat drill. That's what I was told."

"It's not a drill anymore," the officer with J.P. Moody on his lapel pin said. "We hit an iceberg. Don't know how much damage was done, but you'd best come along."

Behind them, Helen saw Dr. O'Loughlin appear at the end of the corridor. One of the officers turned around and the doctor pleaded guilty. "I know…, I know…, I'm not supposed to be down here. But there's a poor woman in steerage with an awful abscess. She's in terrible pain." He held up a small brown bottle, and strode away.

Officer Moody shook his head and commented to his fellow officer, "Foolish if you ask me, risking his hide for some riff raff's rotten tooth." They both turned back to Helen and Officer Moody asked her, "Where's your lifebelt?"

"In my room."

"Then you'd better get it," the other officer said, "You might need it."

"Uh, yes, well I was just going to get it." She walked away toward a room that had its door ajar, pretended it was hers. She stepped inside the doorway and smiled sweetly at the officers saying, "Oh, you needn't wait. It'll just take me a second to find it. I'll be right up."

The officers exchanged looks of exasperation and left. She waited just inside the door, her heart thundering, then peeked out to make sure they were gone. They were, so she ran back to the infirmary. Thankfully, this time she didn't see anyone inside. She turned the door knob, half expecting it to be locked, but incredibly, it wasn't.

I must hurry, she thought, rushing through the sterile white infirmary to the dispensary. *If the ship's really in trouble, Oh...* She pushed the worrisome thought away."

She stepped inside the dispensary and closed the door behind her. In her haste, she didn't notice the looseness of the white porcelain door knob in her hand. She pulled the door shut behind her, heard a soft click and went straight to her task. She opened the gate, walked behind the counter and quickly scanned the shelf where she'd seen the Tincture of Morphine the last time she was there. She read the labels under her breath: *Blue pill…, Paragoric…, Sulphur…oh, here it is, Tincture of Morphine.* She stood on her toes and reach for it.

Suddenly, the whole room tilted to the left. She grabbed the bottle of morphine just as all the bottles slid from the shelf. They crashed to the floor around her feet, scattering pills, powders and liquids among the glass. At the same time, she heard a tremendous, booming crash on the right side of the room. It came from behind the door marked with the skull and crossbones and "Authorized Personnel Only" sign. The sound was like nothing she'd ever heard, like a million steel drums being dropped from the sky, banging and rolling into each other. The walls shook and she felt the noise vibrate in her chest. Finally, the rumbling subsided. Then she heard something else: the muffled sound of people coming from below, in the far distance. They seemed to be running, shouting, and screaming.

At that moment, she knew the awful truth. The ship was sinking. *Sinking! Oh, dear God.* She grabbed onto the counter with one hand, steadying herself. *I have to get up to the boat deck,* she thought stuffing the bottle of morphine in her purse.

Fighting against the crazy tilt of the room, she made her way from behind the counter. Approaching the door, she looked through its glass pane and saw that everything in the infirmary, including the beds from the left side of the room were crushed against the wall on the right side of the room.

Oh, God, don't panic. Don't panic, she told herself as she reached for the door and turned the knob. It was loose, and turned and turned in her hand. *Oh dear. Something's wrong. It's not catching.* Her fear escalated. She shook the door knob violently, hoping something would happen, but nothing did. It wouldn't catch. She banged on the door's windowpane and shouted, "Help, please…, is anybody out there? Help me, please. Help!" Over and over, she banged on the windowpane hoping it would break, but it wouldn't. She continued to shout for help, but no one answered.

Her fists hurt from banging and she was getting tired and sweaty. Her throat felt raw, she had a metallic taste in her mouth and started to cough.

Frantic, she looked around for something to break the door's windowpane with. That's when she noticed a strange, silvery liquid oozing from under the door of the room marked "Authorized Personnel Only." Tiny beads broke off at the periphery of the pool of liquid and rolled in all directions across the floor. She had no idea what it was.

A crutch had fallen from its anchor on the wall and lay about a foot from the spreading liquid. *If I can just get to it,* she thought, *I can break the glass.*

She tried to take a step but her body felt like it weighed a thousand pounds. Her heart was racing wildly. She felt hot all over and was sweating profusely. Again she tried to move, but her legs felt like short, concrete pillars. Nausea rose from her stomach, and gagging, she dropped to her knees in an inch of water.

It was the first time she'd noticed the water.

Oh, God, I'm so sick, she thought, coughing and heaving. *I've got to get out of here. Gerard...*, *he'll be looking for me. I have to get to him... I must...*

She struggled to get her breath, tried to stand, but couldn't. All her strength was gone. She fell to the floor, wheezing and shivering.

The water rose slowly around her as she lay helpless on the floor. Foam bubbled from between her lips. A violent seizure overtook her and her limbs jerked and thrashed in the water.

A few minutes later it was over. Her handbag lay beside her, the morphine still in it, as water covered her silent, dead body.

Chapter 35

Nathan heard knocking coming from the Sitting Room.

Jimmy Ray spoke to his friend in a low voice and told him to get rid of whoever it was. Earl Lee went to answer the door and Nathan could hear him talking to someone as Jimmy Ray walked over to the nightstand beside the bed and opened the drawer.

While Jimmy Ray had his eyes off of him, Nathan tried to free his hands. He strained against the binding around his wrists and it gave a little, but not enough to free his hands.

When Jimmy Ray turned back around he had a pistol in his hands. He walked over to the bed where Nicolette was lying and said to Nathan in an ominous tone, "You try anything stupid, and I'll blow her brains out." He yanked the pillow from under her head, put it over her face and pressed the nozzle of the gun into it.

Nathan felt the muscles of his jaws tighten. He'd never felt so powerless in his life. Nicolette had nothing to do with this. Yet these hoodlums wouldn't let her go, and he couldn't do anything about it. God, he'd never be able to forgive himself for what they'd done to her already.

He looked over at his wife and noticed she wasn't struggling beneath the pillow. He saw her leg move and could sense somehow that she was managing to breathe. At least for now.

A few seconds later, Earl Lee came back in. Concern was etched on his beefy face. "That was one of the hall stewards. He said the ship's hit an iceberg and we should get our lifebelts and come up on deck. He don't know how bad it is, but he said it could be a problem. He seemed awful worried to me." He went over to the bed and got down on all fours. He pulled two lifebelts from underneath it, and stood up with them in his hands.

Jimmy Ray took the gun from the pillow and put it in his pocket. He threw the pillow against the wall and yanked the lifebelts out of Earl Lee's hand. He threw them on the floor hollering, "Stop actin' like a scaredy cat sissy, Earl Lee. So what if we hit an iceberg. It couldn't do no real damage to a ship this size. I know what I'm talkin' about. My Pa's in the shippin' business, remember? Besides...," he walked over and stood in front of Nathan, "...I ain't finished with this coon yet."

He smiled down at Nathan, a cold, murderous smile that left no doubt in his mind that he intended to kill him.

"Please, listen to him," Nathan pleaded. "They were getting the women and children on deck when I came down here. That means trouble. This ship is in real danger. Depending on the size of that iceberg and where it hit, there could be serious damage. Please, listen to me."

"Shut up, Goddamit," Jimmy Ray yelled, "before I lose my patience and kill you before I'm ready. Fancy, educated nigger, with your degrees and book learnin'. Well that don't mean shit to me, not anymore. 'Cause right now, you ain't the one callin' the shots. I am."

"Maybe...maybe he's right, Jimmy Ray," Earl Lee stammered. "They said this ship was unsinkable, but they coulda' been wrong. Or, maybe they just said that so people would believe it was better. But it ain't."

"Aw, hell, Earl Lee, just shut up and stop trying to figure things out," Jimmy Ray snapped. "I've told you a thousand times, you ain't good at it. So just sit down and let me handle this."

The big man shuffled across the room and slumped down on a settee with a sullen look on his face.

Desperation egging him on, Nathan decided to try another tact. "Listen," he said to Jimmy Ray, hoping he was as greedy as he was malicious, "I have money. Lots of it. It's in our stateroom. I'll give it to you. All of it, if you'll let my wife go. Please. Our children need her."

"Now ain't that a hoot." Jimmy Ray laughed. "Did you hear that, Earl Lee? Did you hear that? We got ourselves a rich coon." He laughed and gradually Earl Lee started laughing too. They guffawed for a couple of minutes, then Jimmy Ray said, "Hell, boy, I know you got money. Matter of fact, me and my Pa's takin' every cent of it, right along with that plantation old Marcel left you in New Orleans, *and* his share of Delta Ferryboats." He stood there and smiled at Nathan as if he wanted to let it sink in before adding, "oh, and once your ass is fish bait, I don't 'spect we'll have much trouble takin' over that fancy chatelet of yours in Paris too."

He started laughing again and in a matter of seconds he and Earl Lee were slapping their thighs and howling like two rabid hyenas.

While they were occupied with their amusement, Nathan got an epiphany. *The knife! Why didn't I think of it before? If I can just get to it…If I can…* Keeping his eyes on Jimmy Ray and Earl Lee, he carefully lifted the tail of his tuxedo jacket. Straining until he felt like his shoulders were going to pop out of their sockets, he connected with the hard, smooth handle of the knife. Slowly, he pushed up on the knife's guard and lifted it from its hard leather sheath until he felt the deadly, sharp steel of the blade.

"Oooeeee, he's one funny nigger," Jimmy Ray remarked, winding down from his laughter. He took out his handkerchief and wiped tears of mirth from his eyes.

Suddenly, the ship's intercom crackled to life: *All passengers on deck with lifebelts on. All passengers on deck with lifebelts on.*

It was the second time they'd heard the call and it seemed to bring Nicolette out of her trance. Struggling against her restraints she beseeched Jimmy Ray, "Please, let us go. Our children are in danger. Don't you understand?"

"Shut up," Jimmy Ray glared over at her, "Ain't neither of you goin' nowhere."

Nicolette started to sob, "My babies…, my poor babies…" "Maybe we ought to at least check and see what's goin' on out there," Earl Lee suggested.

"All right, all right," Jimmy Ray answered impatiently, "it's time I wrapped this shit up anyway. Soon as I git his signature on them papers we'll finish them off, and head on up."

Curious, Nathan asked, "What papers?"

"Oh, just a couple of Sales Agreements. You're goin' to sign Belle Lafourche over to me, and sign your share of Delta Ferryboats over to my Pa's company, Louisiana Steamers." He said to Earl Lee, "Keep an eye on 'em," and went into the sitting room.

Earl Lee picked up the Girlie magazine lying next to him on the settee and started to leaf through it.

While Jimmy Ray was busy in the sitting room, and Earl Lee engrossed in his Girlie magazine, Nathan maneuvered his wrists over the blade of the knife. He sawed at the nylon binding his wrists and gradually, he felt it loosen. Then the knife blade slipped and sliced the side of his hand.

He choked back a scream, repositioned the knife and continued to move his hands up and down against the blade. *Just a little more…just a little more,* he repeated in his mind, his heart racing.

Finally, he was able to slip his hands out. Quickly, he grabbed the knife and leaned down to cut the binding around his ankles. That's when Earl Lee caught him.

"Hey! What do you think you're doin'?" He jumped to his feet."

Nathan's survival instincts kicked in. In a flash, he threw the knife and it landed in the big man's heart. As he fell to the floor, Nathan glanced through the open doorway into the sitting room. He saw Jimmy Ray drop a handful of papers that seemed to float to the floor in slow motion. As they landed, he saw water spreading across the floor.

Jimmy Ray rushed into the room. He ran to Earl Lee, turned him over and cradled his head in his lap. "You killed him," he cried, looking over at Nathan. "My best friend. The only friend I ever had, and you killed him. You killed him! You lousy, filthy nigger!" He dropped Earl Lee's body and stood up, reaching for his gun.

Nathan's hand was already on the handle of the gun stuck in the side of his boot. He whipped it out and fired, gunshot ringing in his ears.

Jimmy Ray froze. Blood trickled from a dime-sized hole between his eyes and he fell face down on top of his friend.

Chapter 36

Nathan and Nicolette raced through a maze of corridors and finally found the steel ladder leading up to the Boat deck. Climbing the ladder, they shivered in the frosty night air.

In a way, Nathan was grateful for the cold. It numbed the pain of his cuts and bruises, helped keep the stump of his finger from bleeding. But it couldn't blunt the pain of knowledge. When they stepped onto the deck, he saw that the bow of the ship was slowly sinking and recalled the code of the sea: 'Women and children first.' For him, that meant certain-

Nicolette's frantic voice broke through his thoughts. "I don't see them, Nathan. You said they'd be up here." She looked around anxiously.

This is exactly where they should be, he thought. But he couldn't tell her that. It would only upset her more to know they weren't where they should have been. "Don't worry, we'll find them," he reassured her, hiding his own concern. "They're up here somewhere."

Together, they scoured the deck, searched through large groups and small clumps of people. At each loading platform they passed, the crew was uncovering lifeboats, readying the davits, but there was no sense of urgency about it at all. Indeed, it seemed they were oblivious to the sinking of the bow. They went about their tasks mechanically, as if they *were* conducting a drill, and once it was over, everything would go on as before. As he and Nicolette made their way astern, he was struck by the calmness of the passengers. No one seemed unduly alarmed and he wondered if their apathy was from shock, or denial of what was happening.

Yet in the distance, a flare went up turning everything daytime bright. That's when they saw Trista dart out from behind a group of people walking toward them. "Papa, Mama," she cried, and ran as fast as her chubby little legs would carry her. Sabine chased after her with Cecile in her arms, calling out for her to wait.

Nathan felt a surge of relief. The sight of his children made his heart ache, especially knowing - Again, he pushed the thought away.

Nicolette scooped Trista up in her arms, laughing and crying at the same time, covering her with kisses. A few seconds later, they were all united, hugging and clinging to each other.

An officer holding a lantern called out across the deck, "This one's ready folks. We need some brave souls to take her down. It's safe. I assure you it's safe." Only a few people stepped forward.

"Look how tiny it is," Nicolette remarked as they came closer to the loading area. "Is there any wonder no one wants to get in it? Why, a miniature wave would capsize it."

"Tiny or not, you and the girls are going to have to get into one," Nathan said. "Right now, one of those dinghies is a whole lot safer than this floating behemoth."

"No, Nathan, I can't," she cried.

"You can, and you will. It may be the only chance you and the girls have. You have to. For me." He swallowed hard on the emotion rising in his throat.

"We're not going anywhere without you," she said stubbornly. "If you get in, we'll go. That's the only way I'll feel safe."

"Nicolette, you know I can't do that." He stared at her in the moonlight. "Not as long as there are women and children on this ship. And from what I've seen, I doubt there are enough lifeboats for half of them."

"But Nathan…"

"No buts, you have to go."

Suddenly, he remembered the carpetbag in their stateroom, remembered what this trip was about in the first place: his inheritance. He couldn't just forget about it. Nicolette was going to need it for the children.

"Nathan? What is it? What's wrong?" she asked, apparently sensing his thoughts had drifted elsewhere.

"Nothing's wrong," he tried to lie, then everything spilled out in a rush, a feeling of urgency overtaking him. "What I mean is, it's not going to stay wrong. Not if I can help it. But you'll have to help me."

"Help you? What are you talking about?"

"Wait for me," he said, backing away from her, "right here until I get back. I'm going to our room, to get my carpetbag. If I'm not back in twenty minutes, you and the girls get in a lifeboat. Understand? Get into a lifeboat." He whirled around and sprinted for the stairs.

Nicolette called after him. "No! Nathan, don't! It's too dangerous. Please, don't go down there."

But he ignored her and bounded down the stairs. When he reached the end of the stairs on B deck, he stepped down into bone-chilling cold water almost to his knees. He trudged through corridor after corridor until he reached the one leading to their stateroom. When he finally reached it, he slogged his way through the parlor and into the bedchamber.

"Oh, shit," he exclaimed, remembering he'd thrown the carpetbag under the bed. He looked at the bed and noticed for the first time just how low it was to the floor. The water was already up to the mattress and rising fast. He took a deep breath, dropped to his knees beneath the sea green water and snaked his body underneath the bed. He saw the carpetbag right away at the head of the bed, over in the far right corner. He pushed himself over to it with his arms and pulled at it. But it wouldn't budge. Somehow it had gotten wedged in the corner between the bedpost and the wall. He yanked and pulled, but it still wouldn't move. He could tell he didn't have his normal strength and guessed it was due to all the blood he'd lost. But right now he had an even greater concern. Air! He couldn't hold his breath much longer. Frantic, he backed out from under the bed and shot to the surface of the water.

Whooooh! He gulped the air, his heart racing. The water was up to his waist now, and rising faster and faster. In another twenty minutes, it would be up to the ceiling. He glanced at his watch. He only had ten minutes before Nicolette and the girls would be gone.

He dove under again. Again he tugged at the carpetbag with what meager strength he was able to muster. Again it wouldn't budge. His need for oxygen quickly became so intense he had to scrambled from beneath the bed and shoot to the surface again as fast as he could. Heaving for air he tried to think of another way to get the carpetbag unstuck. He pulled on the heavy wooden bedpost at the head of the bed, but it felt like it was bolted to the floor.

He looked around for something that could give him some leverage. He thought about his walking sticks in the wardrobe, but dismissed the idea. They were made of wood and would break too easily. Then he thought of the fireplace tools in the Parlor. He dove into the water that was littered with his family's belongings: Trista's picture book, one of Nicolette's white lace gloves, Cecile's slipper, and swam into the Parlor. He stood up, waded over to the fireplace, and this time had a stroke of good luck. The fireplace poker was exactly where he'd seen it last. He grabbed it and swam back into the bedchamber.

He filled his lungs with air, shimmied under the bed and to the immovable carpetbag. He pushed and pushed and was finally able to wedge the poker between the carpetbag and the bedpost. That's when he realized what the problem was: the case inside the carpetbag. It was the object keeping the carpetbag stuck. He pulled the poker out, stuck it underneath the carpetbag and used it like a jack, lifting up on it. Slowly, it started to move. But again, his air was almost gone. In one last tremendous effort he heaved the poker up and the carpetbag dislodged. He grabbed it and scrambled for the surface, almost certain his air would run out before he could reach it.

Panic driving him he broke through the surface of the water with a huge splash. For almost a minute, he stood there heaving for breath. Holding the handle of the carpetbag with his left hand, he reached in his trouser pocket and took out his watch.

He was already late. In spite of what he'd told Nicolette, he hoped that she hadn't left. Desperate, he swam out into the corridor praying, *Please God, just one more time. Let me see my girls, just one more time.*

By the time Nathan reached mid-ship the icy water had taken away his pain. His face didn't hurt anymore and the throbbing of his left hand had stopped. He was numb all over. He waded toward a group of people gathered at the bottom of the stairs leading up to the boat deck and could tell by their faces that things had changed dramatically in the short time he'd been gone. They were standing in knee deep water, some of them dressed warmly in overcoats and furs, while others shivered miserably in bathrobes and flannel pajamas. Some of the women were crying, clinging to their children and husbands. The faces of the men reflected a range of emotion from stark fear to hopeless resignation.

Nathan joined the assembly and noticed two men who'd regarded him with pompous indignation at the Ball earlier in the evening. They saw him too, but were so completely absorbed in their own plight they didn't seem to notice his bruises or the blood all over him.

Finally, it was Nathan's turn. Climbing, the stairs he looked up and saw a brilliant black velvet sky splattered with sparkling, diamond-like stars. He was struck by the sheer beauty of it. *How ironic,* he thought, *that such majesty should exist on this night, in this place, at this time.* But there was no time for philosophy now. He had to find Nicolette and the children.

He stepped onto the boat deck and looked around, shivering in his heavy, water soaked clothes.

Light spilled from the windows of the offices and buildings on the deck casting a patchwork pattern of light that illuminated a mounting chaos. Everywhere he looked, people were running, screaming, crying, calling out the names of loved ones and friends. The crew rushed about, frantically barking orders and replies, cursing and scolding passengers, doing their best to do their jobs and simultaneously control the panic around them.

Nathan steeled his mind. He couldn't let himself think about what was happening around him, any more than he could think about what lay ahead. He had to ignore the stern that was rising before his eyes, ignore the distress flares that intermittently lit up the night sky. The only thing that mattered now was his family. If they were still on the ship, he had to find them.

In the distance, he saw a lifeboat being lowered. He sprinted toward it and ran straight into an officer.

"Stop right there…," the officer commanded, halting him with a hand to his chest. "You're not jumping the rail, not while I'm here."

"I don't want to jump the rail," Nathan said. "I just want to see if my wife and children are in that lifeboat."

The officer was unsympathetic. "I helped load that boat," he said. "There are no Negroes in it."

"My wife is French," Nathan said. "Please, all I want to do is say goodbye and give this to her."

He took the carpetbag from under his arm and showed it to him.

"Yes, and my wife is Chinese," the officer quipped.

Nathan looked past him at the crew lowering the lifeboat. "Please officer," he begged, and took a couple of anxious steps forward.

The officer drew his revolver and aimed it at him. "Take another step and you'll force me to use this. I can tell from the looks of you, you're up to no good."

Nathan froze. Slowly, he reversed his steps.

"Okay, officer. You win. But perhaps you can take this and ask if Nicolette Legarde is in the lifeboat and throw it down to her. That's all I ask." He held out the carpetbag.

The officer put his revolver back in its holster saying, "I don't have time for making deliveries."

Nathan considered waiting until the he left, but by then it, could be too late. So, he pretended to walk away, then whirled around and charged him, ramming him in the gut with the carpetbag. As soon as he hit the deck, he punched hit him in the face, knocking him out cold. He grabbed the carpetbag, ran to the rail and called for his wife. "Nicolette! Nicolette!"

The people in the lifeboat looked up at him, but no one called back. Someone in the lifeboat was holding up a lantern and it basked the occupants in a dull yellow light. To his surprise, he saw as many men as women in the lifeboat. But he didn't see any children, or anyone that looked like Nicolette.

His hope sank and he turned from the rail thinking his family had probably left already. But then he knew there was a slim chance they were still on the boat deck. Holding onto a sliver of hope he decided to keep searching. Unsure of where to look, he headed aft to where the next lifeboat was being loaded. He was about thirty feet away when he heard the unmistakable voice of Horace Potter Clinch, the old tycoon he'd had words with in the inquiry office. He was demanding to be put in a Lifeboat.

"I've got a company to run," Clinch shouted at the crewmen doing the loading. "Where are your priorities? My life's a damned sight more important than some of this riff raff you've been letting on. Besides, I'm handicapped. That should count for something. Put me in that boat right now, or I'll report you to the Captain."

"I'm sorry sir, we have our orders," one of the crewman told him.

The argument continued as Nathan neared the lifeboat. Then, he saw Dodie Ryerson walk out from a knot of people waiting to be boarded. She had her dog, Houlie, in her arms and was dressed only in a nightgown. She wandered from person to person asking in a lost sounding voice: "Have you seen my sister? Have you seen Helen? Huh? Have you seen my sister?" Everyone ignored her or shook their heads, no.

"Good Lord, what is she doing out here in this madness by herself?" Nathan thought. "She and Helen must have gotten separated." He was completely unprepared for what happened next.

In the light of a flare, he saw Clinch take a pistol from under the blanket covering his knees. He waved it at the crewmen, "I'm done reasoning with you thick-headed, Irish potato mashers," he growled. "Put me in that boat now or I'll…" Just then Dodie walked in between Clinch and the crewmen.

Nathan hollered, "Dodie!" and sprinted to get her out of the way. But it was too late. Her dog, Houlie, barked and leaped at Clinch. The gun fired and Dodie was hit in the chest. She fell backwards onto the deck just as Nathan reached her. Everyone looked on in shock.

Spurred by a mixture of instinct and anger, Nathan wrested the gun away from the old codger. He threw it overboard and told him, "I ought to throw you over with it."

The two crewmen standing nearby looked at each other and one of them remarked, "That's a ripping idea." They went over, pushed Clinch's manservant aside, and picked the old man up in his wheelchair. Clinch cursed and threatened as they hoisted him up and dumped him and his wheelchair overboard.

Nathan knelt beside Dodie. She was still breathing. Looking up at him she said, "Have you seen Helen?" Then she took her last breath. Nathan felt so sorry for her, sorry for the terror-stricken people scrambling around him, desperate to avoid their fate.

Determined not to give in to despair, he closed Dodie's eyes and carried her body to the side of the ship. He laid her down and murmured, "God keep your soul." He prayed that God was watching over his family as he ran along the port side of the ship toward the stern. He passed two davits devoid of their lifeboats and saw Victor and Pepita Penasco crossing the deck to where another lifeboat was being launched.

He ran up to them and asked, breathlessly, "Have you seen Nicolette and my children?"

"My friend, what happened to you?" Victor asked, not answering his question. In the semi-darkness, he could see Victor's concerned reaction to the burns and bruises on his face.

"I can't explain now," Nathan replied breathlessly, "I have to find my family. Have you seen them?"

Pepita pointed toward the stern. "A couple of minutes ago. They were waiting for a lifeboat, but the crew was having trouble getting it down."

Nathan thanked them and continued on his way. He weaved in and out of crowds of people. Then he saw several crewmen trying to lower a lifeboat with the Welin davits. They were having a terrible time trying to maneuver the thing, and several male passengers stepped forward to help. That's when he saw his family standing among a group of women and children. "Nicolette!" he called, and she looked up and saw him. She ran to meet him with the baby in her arms and Sabine and Trista followed her.

"Oh, grace a Dieu," she cried when he reached her. "You're all right. I was so worried."

He enveloped her and the children in his arms and kissed them. "Thank God, you didn't leave." He kissed the baby, then kissed Nicolette again. When Trista and Sabine reached them, he kissed them too. "I almost gave up," he said, catching his breath. "Especially when you weren't...why did you leave?"

"The lifeboat left. They told me that if I wanted to catch another one, I had to come over here."

"Oh, I'm just so glad I found you."

"Papa...Papa." Trista yanked on his wet coat. "Sabine says we're going for a...aventure."

"Adventure," he corrected, and picked her up. "And I want you to be brave on your adventure, okay, and listen to your Mama and Sabine. Will you do that for Papa?"

She nodded her head, "yes," then touched the cigar burn on his face. "You have a hurt."

"It's nothing," he lied, "it'll go away." He swallowed the emotion in his throat and handed her over to Sabine, saying, "Now you be a good girl like I told you."

Behind them, the crew had finally gotten the lifeboat down and was starting to load it.

He saw Madame Lucile and her secretary being helped into the boat. Then her husband, Cosmo Gordon, stepped forward and was stopped by an ßofficer.

"Let him in," Madame called from the lifeboat. "You don't expect us women to row do you?"

"You'll row if you want to save your skins," an officer called back. Then, as an afterthought, he added, "Oh, what the hell, come on." He gestured for Gordon to get in the lifeboat and he promptly did.

He heard Emma Bucknell, the Philadelphia socialite call up to Captain Smith who was standing nearby with a basket in his hand. "I had a bad feeling about this voyage from the start, E.J. I told Molly Brown about it in Cherbourge. When will I ever learn to listen to my own mind?" She took the basket the Captain handed down to her.

"Now, Emma," Captain Smith chided while personally helping her maid into the lifeboat, "I'm counting on you to keep these folks spirits up. So no more talk of trepidation and gloom." Boarding behind Mrs. Bucknell was the Countess of Rothes and several other women Nathan remembered seeing during their voyage.

Captain Smith looked over at Nathan and his brood and hollered to one of the officers loading the boat: "We need some means of getting the little ones into the boat. They can't be carried on, it's too dangerous."

"I know where I can get some canvas sacks," the officer replied.

"Get them," the Captain ordered. "We don't have a minute to waste." The officer rushed away.

The lifeboat was half full with more than enough people to fill it waiting to get in.

"You've got to get in while there's still room," Nathan said to Nicolette and Sabine. "I'll make sure the children are lowered down to you.

"Yes, sir," Sabine replied. Nathan reached out and gently grabbed her hand. "Merci, Sabine for taking care of the children. Madame Legarde and the girls are going to need you more than ever now. I'm counting on you in my absence."

"I'll do my best, Monsieur," she replied and turned away, crying.

"I'm not going without you, Nathan," Nicolette said. "I can't. I just can't." She burst into tears. Then Trista grabbed his leg, crying pitifully, "Papa's coming with us, Mama. Papa's coming with us."

It was the most bitter torment of Nathan's life. He wanted to scream, curse, run, ANYTHING! but lose his wife and children. But he knew he had no choice in the matter. Fate had already chosen his end. But he wouldn't die in vain, not if his family was saved.

He held Nicolette at arms length. "Listen to me. You have to get in the lifeboat. It's your only chance. This ship won't stay afloat much longer."

Nicolette was wild-eyed with grief, the animosity that had plagued them the entire trip forgotten. "No, I won't leave you. I won't, leave you here."

He shook her by the shoulders. "You have to. For the children's sake and for me. You have to go to New Orleans and claim my inheritance. That's what this trip was all about, remember? That's why those goons wanted me dead. Otherwise, everything we've been through would be for nothing."

"But I wouldn't know what to do. I-"

"You'll figure it out. You're smart, and strong and talented. You can do anything you set your mind to. That's why I've always loved you so. For your passion. For the way you fight for what you believe in."

"But I thought you didn't…"

"I know…I know what you thought. And you were right. I was selfish and unfair. I had no right to try to take away your dream, to try to make you something you weren't. It's crazy, but I realize now I was trying protect you from something that hadn't even happened, from something that had nothing to do with you." He paused, searching for the right words. "It's just that I…, I saw you becoming more independent, more like my mother. And it scared me. I guess I thought that being too ambitous would make you vulnerable, a target. I really didn't realize until now that deep down I blamed my mother for what happened that day with Tuttle's father.

I guess I believed that it wouldn't have happened if she hadn't been a working woman. But Tuttle made me realize how wrong I was. My mother's ambition didn't cause his father to abuse her any more than I caused Tuttle's behavior. They were responsible for the things they did."

"Oh, Nathan, I wish you'd told me," Nicolette replied, lovingly touching the burns on his face. "We wasted so much time arguing, and now...," she choked on a sob.

He pulled her close and whispered in her ear, "Oh, Nicolette, je t'aime..., je t'aime."

"Je t'aime aussi," she replied and their lips met in a soul wrenching kiss. When he released her, he picked up Trista and held his family in his arms one last time. Tears streamed down his face as he inhaled the sweet scent of Nicolette's perfume, caressed the tender faces of his daughters.

Ahead, he saw Officer Lightoller run over to the Lifeboat carrying several canvas bags. "We can get the children loaded now," he heard him tell Captain Smith.

The Captain gestured toward the group of people waiting to get into the lifeboat. "Mother's with little ones had better step up now," he commanded. "The drop on this side is going to be a bit treacherous, so be careful. But we still have to move smart. She's going down pretty fast."

Nathan released his family. He quickly took off the St. Jude's medal he'd worn since he was a boy and put it around Nicolette's neck. "It protected me once. When you get to New Orleans, give it to my mother. Tell her I love her and I'm sorry I couldn't return it to her myself."

"I will." Her lip quivered as if she might burst into tears again.

Nathan took Cecile from her, then picked up the carpetbag. "Here, you're going to need this," he said, handing it to Nicolette. "There's cash in there, the deed to Belle Lafourche and ownership papers to my share in Delta Ferryboats. They'll dry out." He gave her a reassuring wink.

"Oh, Nathan, what will I do without you?" Nicolette cried, looking painfully beautiful in the semi-darkness. It was all he could do to keep from breaking down himself.

"Shhhh. You'll raise our children." He patted her stomach. "All three of them. And you'll be the best couturier Paris has ever seen. And I'll be the proudest husband that ever lived." Abruptly, he tore himself away from his wife, afraid the lifeboat would fill up before he could get his family in it. Carrying both children in his arms, he walked Nicolette and Sabine over to where the Lifeboat was being loaded. A couple of crewman helped Sabine and Nicolette get in. Then they helped him put his girls in the canvas bags. One at a time, they lowered Trista, then Cecile over the side of the ship to Nicolette and Sabine waiting in the lifeboat.

As he looked down at his family, the painful knowledge that he would never see them again hit him full force. Overwhelmed with emotion, he grabbed onto the side of the ship to steady himself. Next to him, just at the edge of his awareness, he overheard Officer Lightoller urging an elderly woman named Mrs. Strauss to get into the lifeboat. But she refused and nothing Lightoller or the woman's soft-spoken husband said could change her mind.

The sound of rapid footsteps broke into Nathan's consciousness. He looked up to see the Penascos and their maid running toward them. "Wait! Wait! Please! Let my wife in! Please," Victor Penasco called. As soon as they reached the loading area, Officer Lightoller said, "It's full. No more room."

"Oh, please, Officer," Victor started to plead. "You must let my wife in."

Before Lightoller could respond, Mrs. Strauss stepped forward. "She can take my place. I told you, I'm staying with my husband."

"Momma, please, go with the other ladies," Mr. Strauss interjected.

"No, where you go, I go," she insisted and put her arm through his.

Pepita Penasco didn't want to leave her husband either and was finally hauled into the lifeboat screaming for her husband to be allowed in with her. Officer Lightoller wouldn't allow it. But he did let the Penasco's maid in, though he claimed there were too many bodies in the lifeboat already.

Finally, the lifeboat was launched. Nathan stood at the rail next to Victor and watched with helpless anxiety as it was clumsily lowered, one side down, then the other, nearly spilling his family and the other occupants into the ocean. Intermittent screams floated up to them increasing their angst. By the time it reached the ocean's surface, Victor Penasco was nearly insane with grief. He sobbed, calling Pepita's name over and over. Then he climbed up on the rail to throw himself overboard, but Nathan grabbed him, and he and Captain Smith wrestled him to the deck. He collapsed into a mass of misery, moaning that he'd lost his bride, lost everything.

His tormented cries seemed to echo the hurt burning in Nathan's chest. He understood what he was feeling because he felt it too. It was sheer agony knowing what lay ahead, knowing that he'd lost the most precious thing in his life: his family.

After several minutes he tried to offer Victor some comfort and touched his shoulder. But he was inconsolable and waved him away.

So Nathan returned to the rail and searched the lifeboats in the water until he found the one he believed his family was in. He waved and focused on it until it was just a speck in the vast black ocean.

Turning around, he said to Victor, "Come on, let's go to the smoking room." He reached out and helped him to his feet. Then Victor just stood there transfixed. His eyes were glazed and he looked at

Nathan like he'd never seen him before. Without a word, he wandered away into the mass of terror-stricken humanity scurrying toward the stern of the ship.

Officer Lightoller noticed them and said to Nathan as Victor shuffled away, "Just as well. He's probably better off than we are."

Captain Smith walked over to the rail of the ship. He had a megaphone in his hand, raised it and shouted to the boats in the water: "This is Captain Smith. Please return for additional passengers. We need your help. Please return to the ship for additional passengers."

For a moment, Nathan stood at the rail in the semi-darkness and watched the lifeboats dotting the calm, dark ocean. Other passengers, full of fear and hope pressed against the rail too, waiting for the lifeboats to return. But they didn't. Slowly, they disappeared into the darkness.

Tired and freezing cold, Nathan turned from the rail. He looked aft and saw that the ship's stern had risen remarkably and was jutting above the water at a frightening angle. From somewhere nearby he heard music. The band was playing *Nearer My God To Thee.*

He set out for the First Class smoking room. Trudging along, his feet felt like awkward clumps of ice in his boots.

A distress rocket exploded above the ship shooting stars hundreds of feet into the sky, then cascading in a brilliant show of light. In the brightness, he saw some men climbing up the ship's cranes, several of them holding on for dear life.

He saw another lifeboat being launched and heard shouts and screams coming from the water. When he glanced over the side of the ship, he saw that it was being lowered directly on top of another lifeboat sitting in the water. The crew finally figured out what the commotion was about and halted their load a few feet above the lifeboat below.

Then, Nathan's eyes fell on a pitiful scene. A shabbily dressed woman, obviously from steerage tugged at the arm of an officer. A scruffy bunch of children stood nearby.

"How can all the Lifeboats be gone?" the woman cried. "What about my children? Please, can't you find something?"

"I told you, there's nothing I can do," the officer replied, snatching away from her. He left her standing there and muttered as he walked away, "Hope the little buggers can swim."

The family walked away joining the great exodus of people scrambling like crabs for the stern. Some of them were soaking wet and Nathan guessed they were probably steerage passengers who'd fought their way up to the boat deck. Everywhere he looked, the nightmare was escalating. People were wailing and screaming with terror. The sound was gut-wrenching, too vivid and horrible for human ears.

Suddenly, a deafening roar overpowered the cries of the passengers. He saw steam shooting from the fore and aft exhaust ports on the ship's smokestacks and knew that water had filled the ship's furnaces.

The roaring subsided as he neared the gymnasium. In the light pouring from the windows he saw a man waving a Bible, trying to stop the people running in front of him. "Believe on the name of the Lord Jesus,' he cried out, "and you will be saved. It's not too late. Accept him now people. Accept him now."

Instinctively, Nathan's hand went to his neck and he realized he'd never really thought much about God and religion before, or even about the St. Jude's medal that he'd always worn. His mother had read the Bible to him as a child but he'd been too busy since then planning for his future, working for the future, yes, even living for the future to think much about God or religion. He'd always believed that one day when he had time to stop and really enjoy his life he'd delve into religion again. But now there would be no future, and no more time. He heard the voice again: "Believe on the name of the Lord. You must accept him. It's not too late."

It occurred to Nathan that he didn't have the power to escape his Fate, but he did have the power to control what happened afterwards. So he set out in the direction of the man with the Bible. As he twined his way through the panic-stricken crowd he smiled to himself recalling how

Nicolette had always said he needed to control everything, that he was enamored with power. Perhaps she was right. He certainly needed power now. The highest power.

When he reached the man, he said simply, "I want to be saved, you know, for afterwards."

The man smiled and shook his hand. "I'm Pastor Harper. All you have to do is repeat after me."

"Okay," Nathan replied, "I'm ready."

Pastor Harper put his hand on his shoulder and they both bowed their heads.

"Heavenly Father, I come to you in prayer asking for forgiveness of my sins. I confess with my mouth and believe in my heart …"

Nathan repeated the words of the Sinner's Prayer after Pastor Harper. When they said Amen, he was surprised at how much calmer he felt. In his head, he knew nothing had changed. The ship was still sinking, faster by the minute. Everyone around him was going to die. *He* was going to die. Yet, somehow, everything had changed. He felt in control again, because he knew where he was going.

He thanked Pastor Harper. They wished each other good luck and Nathan went on to the First Class Smoking Room. When he got there he stepped inside and took a seat at a table in the middle of the room. Immediately, he noticed he wasn't getting any of the haughty looks he'd gotten every other time he'd been in there. Quite the contrary. For the very first time since boarding the ship, he could see and feel real acceptance. Major Butt raised his brandy glass toward him and J.J. Astor cast a salutatory nod in his direction. Coal magnate, Lucien Smith gave him a nervous smile and even Quigg Baxter waved at him from the bar.

He couldn't help but think, *how ironic, they all seem to realize now that race really doesn't matter. We're all the same, all equally helpless. Their wealth and prestige can't save them any more than the money in my pocket can save me.*

He looked up and saw Gerard Hale come through the Smoking Room door. His hair was disheveled, his evening jacket ripped and he looked frantically about the room. Nathan raised his hand and he rushed over to him. Nearly out of breath he asked, "Have you seen Helen and Dodie?" I went to their Stateroom but they weren't there. Do you know if they got in a lifeboat?" Panic showed on his face.

"I saw Dodie, but Helen wasn't with her." Nathan replied. "Unfortunately, Dodie was -"

Gerard cut him off, his panic rising. "I have to find Helen. I've asked everyone I could. No one saw her get in a lifeboat. She has to be on the ship somewhere. I have to find her." He started to rush away and Nathan grabbed his arm. "Gerard, don't go back out there. You'll never find her in that madness. It's chaos."

"I have to find her." He pulled away from him and ran across the room. He opened the door and stepped out into the horror unfolding on the deck.

Suddenly, there was a great roar followed by a tremendous rolling sound, then - Boom! Boom! Boom! The room vibrated and shook like they were in the middle of a great earthquake. The mirror and glasses on the shelves behind the bar shattered. The lights flickered. Paintings fell from the walls and everyone in the room started to scream. And scream. The room tilted and Nathan's chair slid from under him. He careened across the room along with everything and everyone in it. As he was sliding, he saw a giant wave roll over the deck outside. It smashed into the room, its fury engulfing everything.

Nathan grabbed the edge of a table and held on until his grip was wrested away by the force of the water. The icy cold water. It cut into his body like a million tiny razor blades slicing his flesh. Holding his breath, he swam for the surface. But the more he swam, the deeper the water became. He continued to swim and struggle, but got nowhere. Still he held his breath and swam... until...until... He couldn't hold out any longer. He had to **Breathe!**

His head felt like it was going to explode. An unbearable pressure crushed his sternum, his spine, squeezed his chest in a vise grip, holding him there, squeezing...squeezing...squeezing... Then gradually, it released him. The pain subsided and disappeared. He looked down and wasn't in the water anymore. He was floating high above it. He could see through the water, see the unsinkable *Titanic* drifting down, down, down to the ocean floor. He looked up into the endless, star-studded sky and utter peace enveloped him. He was one with the sky, one with the infinite all around him. He had made it home.

Chapter 37

Nicolette huddled with the children and Sabine in the lifeboat about a quarter of a mile away from the sinking *Titanic*. A monstrous cacophony of screams, rumbling, and crashing reached her ears as the great ship made a headstand in the water. Incredibly, the lights were still on in the part of the ship jutting up from the water. Everyone in the lifeboat watched in stunned silence as the ship made an almost perpendicular dive, extinguishing the lights from its portholes and windows, one by one, as it sank beneath the dark, glassy ocean. As she watched the ship disappear, Nicolette got the queerest sensation, like her heart had dropped to her stomach, but her stomach wasn't there.

A large wave rolled toward them from where the Titanic went down and gently pushed them out to sea along with cakes of ice.

The queer feeling remained and Nicolette felt like she was in an awful nightmare. Everything seemed so unreal. She told herself she was dreaming, that she'd wake up in her own bed, warm and safe with Nathan beside her. Yet, even as she thought it she knew it wasn't true. The screams of the people still struggling and dying in the freezing water were too undeniably real.

"We have to go back. My husband's out there," she heard someone say. "We might be able to save him. Please, we must go back."

A woman named Mrs. Pears held up a lantern and Nicolette noticed that everyone was looking at her. That's when she realized that it was *her* own voice she'd heard.

Mrs. Pears agreed with her. "Yes, we should go back. We can make some room."

They were promptly overruled by Officer Lowe, who'd put himself in charge of the lifeboat. "We'll do no such thing." He stood up. "We've got our hands full just keeping this vessel afloat. We shouldn't go asking for more trouble."

"You, insensitive brut," Nicolette cried, "My husband was on that ship. Most every woman in this boat has someone who was left on that…that gilded deathtrap. Someone who could be saved if we reach them in time. I don't care what you say, we're going back."

She called to the Countess of Rothes who'd taken charge of the rowing. "Turn the boat around, Countess."

"And I say stay on course," Officer Lowe commanded angrily. "I'm the authority on this boat. You take orders from me. Is that clear? No one else."

Nicolette was outraged. She'd endured enough abuse in the last few hours to last a lifetime and she wasn't going to take any more.

"Your authority ended when the *Titanic* went down," she replied, "There are people still alive out there and we're going to help."

In one swift motion, Officer Lowe snatched a revolver from under his coat. He raised it, shot into the air and bellowed, "I'm the officer on this boat, ladies. You'll take orders-"

Something inside of Nicolette snapped. She lunged at him and knocked him backwards. The revolver flew from his hand and hit the water with a splash, just before he did.

Mrs. Bucknell, who was sitting beside her cried, "Oh dear, this is getting out of hand. We should help, of course, but we can't allow ourselves to act like barbarians."

"Barbarians?!" Nicolette's emotions careened out of control. "Barbarians?! I'll show you barbarian." She went to the side of the boat where Officer Lowe was trying to pull himself back in and kicked his hands. "That's barbarian! That's barbarian" she kept kicking until Mrs. Bucknell pulled her away.

She collapsed in the woman's arms, a paroxysm of grief shaking her body. "My husband's out there, dying, and I can't help him," she sobbed. "I can't help him." She sat back down and cried until there were no more tears.

Meanwhile, Mrs. Bucknell and another woman helped Officer Lowe back into the boat. He sat shivering in silence as the Countess of Rothes and the other women at the oars turned the lifeboat around to search for survivors.

It was a mournful quest. For the longest time, the only sounds were the knocking of the oars, chunks of ice bumping up against the lifeboat, the lapping of the ocean. They passed a young woman, probably about Nicolette's age, dressed only in her nightdress, face up in the water with an infant clutched to her breast. A man she could have sworn was Gerard Hale floated past them; he was holding onto a chair. A boy of about eight or nine she'd seen playing with his Bulldog on the Promenade of the *Titanic* was floating in the water with the dog next to him. Bodies were strewn everywhere, most of them with their lifebelts on.

Heartsick, Nicolette searched the water for her husband as the lifeboat skirted around the carnage. From the forward most oar, the Countess of Rothes called, "Hello? Hello? Is anyone out there? Hello?" But no one replied. Gradually, Nicolette's hopes faded.

She huddled in the lifeboat with her children and Sabine, thinking that she shouldn't have insisted on coming back when she heard a moan coming from the water.

She cocked her head listeninig, then said to Mrs. Bucknell, "Did you hear that?"

"Hear what?"

"A moan." She heard it again. "Someone moaning."

"Yes," Mrs. Bucknell pointed to a door with a man strapped to it, floating in the water almost parallel to them. "I think it's coming from over there."

The man moaned again, but he didn't move. He was as stiff as the door he was lying on as the sea splashed over him.

He's alive," Nicolelette said, overjoyed that they'd actually found a survivor. She could tell from the way the man was dressed that it wasn't Nathan, but at least their effort hadn't been for naught.

The women at the oars maneuvered the Lifeboat until it was inches from the door. Mrs. Pears raised the lantern so they could see the man a little better.

"I think he's Japanese," Mrs. Bucknell remarked.

"Help him in," Nicolette said to Officer Lowe, who was shivering in his wet uniform beneath a shawl one of the women had loaned him.

"Ah, what's the use? He's probably dead," Lowe scoffed. "If he isn't, there's others more worth saving than a Jap."

Cold as she was, Nicolette felt a surge of heat course through her. "Don't you have even a shred of decency? If it was you on that door, you'd want someone to save your hide, and I doubt you'd care if they were Japanese."

The officer stood up, complaining, "A bunch of shrewish women." He crawled out onto the door, hauled the little man into the Lifeboat and sat him on one of the benches.

The poor fellow was nearly frozen through. Mrs. Pears, Mrs. Bucknell and a couple other women took charge of him. They rubbed his feet, chest and back with their hands and he quickly came to life. He said something in his native tongue they couldn't understand and stood up. He waved his arms and stamped his feet. Chattering in Japanese he shook all of their hands as if trying to thank them for saving him. Then he tapped the shoulder of one of the women at the tiller conveying that he wanted to take her place. She gave him her oar, and row he did. Watching his enthusiasm for the task, Officer Lowe remarked, "By Jove! I'm ashamed of what I said about the little blighter. I'd save the likes o'him six times over if I got the chance."

They rowed on and in the next hour they found three more people alive in the water, all men. The women did their best to warm and revive them. But in spite of their efforts, one of their rescued died and his body was let over the side of the lifeboat.

None of them knew their location, so, aborting their rescue mission they all agreed to head in the direction they believed the bow of the *Titanic* was pointing when it sank.

Another hour passed and the only sounds were the steady knocking of the oars in their locks, the splash of the water as the oars parted the ocean. Gradually, a faint, soft glow appeared in the sky on the starboard side of the boat. Unsure of the time, they thought it was day breaking, but their hopes were soon dashed. The glow got brighter and brighter for a time, died away then came back. It lasted another few minutes then died away again.

"Hmmph, damned Northern Lights," Officer Lowe grunted and returned to his miserable silence.

Both of Nicolette's girls were fast asleep, worn out from all the excitement. Sabine sat next to her with Trista on her lap. Nicolette was holding Cecile. She shifted her weight on her lap and stretched her legs. That's when she realized she couldn't feel her feet. They were completely numb from the cold. She recalled hearing about people who'd been so badly frostbitten they had to have their legs amputated and her mind filled with worry. *What if no one finds us? We could be out here for days...Maybe no one knows we're out here...Oh, God, what if I have to have my legs amputated?*

But gradually, dawn began to break, a beautiful, quiet glimmer in the east that slowly spread its soft golden glow behind the sky-line. Stealthily, it stole over the sea radiating an almost holy light that illuminated several tall icebergs and large chunks of ice that sparkled around them, beautiful and iridescent. Not far away they saw other lifeboats making their way around the floating ice.

They heard a faint boom like canon fire in the distance, and Nicolette and the others looked around, straining to see where it had came from. But they saw nothing, until a half hour later when a red light, and then a green light, was spied coming over the horizon. Realizing it was a ship speeding to their rescue, a joyous cheer went up in their Lifeboat and spread to the lifeboats nearby.

"Oh, grace a Dieu," Nicolette murmured. "We're going to be saved. We're going to be saved."

It was five thirty in the morning when Nicolette and her family boarded the *Carpathia*. Her feet had to be treated for frostbite and she spent her first couple of hours on board with them immersed in a basin of warm water. Reviving her circulation was painful and the aspirin she was given did nothing to ease it. Through it all she couldn't help but think of how terribly her Nathan must have suffered.

Misery surrounded her everywhere on the *Carpathia*. Grieving parents searched in vain for lost children. Death abandoned children wandered around pathetically, crying and looking for their parents. Everywhere, she saw fellow *Titanic* passengers staring blankly, in shock. Others were on crutches or in casts from broken bones. And like herself, some had their feet wrapped in rags to keep them warm after being treated for frostbite. She was amazed at the valiant efforts of the *Carpathia's* crew, at their determination to meet the needs of the *Titanic's* survivors in spite of inadequate provisions. Even the *Carpathia's* passengers pitched in. They helped the crew dispense aid, shared their quarters and personal effects with the *Titanic's* survivors, and offered comfort to the bereaved.

With Sabine's help, Nicolette managed the best she could. But the children were a handful. She knew they were too young to understand what had happened, but she suspected that somehow they sensed something had happened to their beloved Papa. Cecile was crankier than ever. She cried and fretted constantly when she was awake and Trista kept asking her, "Where is Papa? Isn't Papa coming? Why isn't Papa here?" Not sure of what to say, she finally told her her Papa had gone to stay with God. But it didn't satisfy her for long. She came back with the same questions, again and again, until Nicolette was completely bewildered.

News of the *Titanic's* sinking had reached New York before they arrived and the whole city turned out to help. A group of socialites led by Mrs. William K. Vanderbilt, Jr. chartered a fleet of limousines to take survivors to local hotels. Thus on Tuesday morning, Nicolette and her family were whisked away to the Lafayette Menhoff Hotel.

Two days later, Molly Brown stopped by to see how she and the children were faring. They sat in a secluded nook of the Hotel lobby, chatting, and Nicolette recounted the ordeal she and Nathan had gone through before the Titanic sank. She told her Nathan had insisted that she go on to New Orleans and collect his inheritance.

"Sounds to me like your man was planning for his family's future right up to the end," Molly Brown remarked.

Nicolette agreed. "I don't expect it'll be too difficult to claim the plantation his father left him, but I'm almost tempted to forget about his part of the shipping business."

"Just give it away?" Molly screeched. "That's the most ridiculous thing I've heard you say since I've known you. Why on earth would you want to give away something that's rightfully yours?"

Nicolette stood up from her chair and started to pace, "I know you're right, it's what I should do, but..."

Molly's brow creased, "But what?"

"But, I guess I'm afraid. You see, that Tuttle fellow didn't want my husband dead merely for revenge. There's more to it than that. He and his stepfather didn't want Nathan to inherit his part of the shipping business my father-in-law left him. There's no telling what he'd do if I showed up in Nathan's place. Besides, I don't know anything about American law, and the papers are all but destroyed." She wrung her hands, guilt and fear gnawing at her.

"Hmmm," Molly placed her hand on her chin. She was pensive for a long moment, as Nicolette paced the floor. Then she waved her hand at her and said, "For heaven's sake, sit down. You're going to wear a hole in the carpet. The Hotel charges for property damage, you know."

But Nicolette noticed a twinkle in Molly's eyes. "What is it, Molly? What are you thinking?" she asked, sitting in the chair across from her.

"I think I can help," she answered. "You'll have to get over your fright, and be a darned good actress. But if you're willing to take the chance…"

Denoument

A timid looking man wearing a bib cap opened the door and Nicolette assumed he was a clerk. "I'm here to see Mr. LeBlanc," she said, looking past him into the cozy little entrance hall. She saw a plaque that read, *C. LeBlanc, Director,* on one of the doors off the hall.

The clerk smiled revealing yellow buckteeth. "Yes ma'am, come on in." She and her companions followed him into the hall and sat down to wait on a small black bench and matching chair against the wall. The clerk went to LeBlanc's door and knocked. She heard a gruff voice ask, "What is it?"

"Someone's here to see you, sir" the clerk answered quietly.

An exasperated baritone voice drifted into the hall, "Aw hell, how am I supposed to git anything done around here. Send 'em in."

A few seconds later, the clerk came back. "You can go in," he announced, then disappeared into another office off the hall.

Nicolette walked across the hall and stepped into LeBlanc's office. As soon as he saw her his ruddy face broke into a smile. "Well now, what can I do for you pretty lady?" he said, standing up from the chair behind his desk.

He waved at the chair in front of his desk, indicating she should sit. She walked over, sat down and tried to speak, but the words got caught in her throat. "I...I...," she was so nervous she almost wished she hadn't come. She'd been preparing for this moment for weeks, but now that she was face to face with him, she didn't know where to start. She clutched her handbag. "I'm Nicolette Legarde. My father-in-law was Marcel Legarde, your former business partner."

LeBlanc's skinny body stiffened and his eyes suddenly reflected wariness.

"Weeell...,is that right?" He flashed a fake smile. "Old Marcel was a fine man. We miss him somethin' awful around these parts. We're sorely grieved at his passin.'

I'll bet you are, Nicolette thought, flashing him a false smile of her own. "I'm in New Orleans to settle my late father-in-law's estate," she said. "Part of that estate is my husband's share in Delta Ferryboats. You probably already know that my husband, Nathan Legarde is also deceased. He died in the sinking of the Titanic, *not* at the hands of your step-son."

"My step-son? I don't know what you're talkin' about?" he said, feigning innocence.

Nicolette took a deep breath and replied, "Yes you do. You sent him to kill my husband, to keep him from claiming what Marcel left him. Your stepson tortured my husband and he and his friend, they-" She couldn't bring herself to say it. "But you're responsible, for what he did to both of us."

LeBlanc scowled. "Now you just hold on right there. I don't know what you're talkin' about and I don't have to listen-"

"Oh, you're going to listen, Monsieur LeBlanc," she said, her temper flaring. "You poisoned your stepson's mind against my husband, made him believe Nathan was responsible for him getting burned, when all along, *you* were responsible. You took him to Nathan's mother's house that night. But you twisted the whole thing, twisted your step-son's mind, filled him with self-loathing and hatred for my husband. You're a sick man, Monsieur LeBlanc, sick in your soul. But you didn't get away with your evil manipulation this time."

"Now you look here, Missy," LeBlanc stood up from his chair, his face red. "You can't come into my place of business and talk to me-"

"I'll say whatever I please," she shot back at him. "I own sixty percent of it."

"Like hell you do," he glared at her, his eyes smoldering with anger.

Nicolette opened her handbag, took out a copy of Marcel's Last Will and a copy of the new Bill of Sale for Delta Ferryboats she'd had drawn up in New York. She stood up, handed them to LeBlanc and sat back down saying, "I have copies."

He quickly scanned the documents, dropped them on his desk and scoffed, "This don't mean shit. When Marcel died, his share went to me, by default."

"That's not true, and you know it. Read the Will. Marcel's property, including his percentage of Delta Ferryboats went to his heirs. My husband was Marcel's only heir."

"Your husband was Marcel's bastard," Le Blanc spat. "He never had any rights to anything."

Nicolette banged her fist on his desk. "He had every right. Marcel named him his heir in his Will. That's all the proof I need. Now that my husband's gone, I, as his widow, have a legal right to his property."

"The hell you say," LeBlanc's eyes widened. "Let me put you straight right now, Frenchy. Ain't no nigger lovin' white trash gonna be a partner in my business. Not long as I'm alive."

Nicolette hoped her fear didn't show as she looked him straight in the eye and countered, "We have at least one thing in common, Monsieur LeBlanc. I don't want to be in business with you any more than you want to be in business with me. In fact, I'd trust a starving rattlesnake more than I'd trust you. So I'm willing to compromise." She opened her handbag again and took out a copy of the Sales Agreement for Delta Ferryboats she'd had drawn up in New York. "You can buy me out." She handed it to LeBlanc.

A minute passed as LeBlanc read the document. Behind his desk, the clock on the wall ticked off the seconds. Finally he grunted, "Hmmph. Ten thousand dollars, eh?" He looked up at her through narrow, blood-shot eyes that really *did* remind her of a snake. He stroked his chin as if mulling over her proposition.

Then, to her surprise, he said, "All right, Madame Legarde, I'll take you up on your proposition. You see, in spite of our differences, I'm a gentleman, and I'll always honor a fair deal. Matter of fact, I can give you the money today, show you I'm an honorable businessman. I don't like a bunch of distrust and accusations, so the sooner we dispense with this the better." He stepped from behind his desk. "If you'll excuse me," he added, and walked across the room to where a large portrait of Thomas Jefferson hung on the wall.

Nicolette was relieved that things were going as smoothly as they were. Still, she could hardly wait to get it over with and get out of his office. She sensed something predatory about him that she found unnerving.

LeBlanc removed the portrait from the far wall and sat it on the floor, revealing a safe. He opened it and Nicolette leaned sideways in her chair, straining to see what was inside. She managed to spy several stacks of currency.

LeBlanc reached inside the safe. When he turned around, instead of having cash in his hand, he was holding a pistol. "I changed my mind," he said, aiming it at her. "I'm not payin' you one red cent. I made Delta Ferryboats profitable. I did all the work while Marcel was off travelin', selling his goods in Europe. The little time he was in New Orleans he spent down at his plantation, or galavantin' all over town with a bunch of darkies. All Marcel did was supply the seed money. Hell, I run this company for nigh over thirty years and I'll be damned if I'm gonna pay you or anybody else for what's already mine." He took a few steps toward her. "Git up," he ordered, "we're goin' for a little walk. And leave your stuff right there 'cause you ain't comin' back, so you won't be needin' it." He nodded toward a door to his right and Nicolette assumed it led to the rear of the building.

She stood up and walked across the room. LeBlanc poked the nozzle of the gun in her back and she continued to walk. She was two feet from the door when she heard a gun cock.

"Drop the gun, Cholley," a voice called from across the room.

Nicolette and LeBlanc turned simultaneously. The parish Constable was facing them, his gun drawn on LeBlanc. Standing next to him was Benjamin Goldstein, the New York lawyer her friend Molly Brown had referred her to.

LeBlanc dropped the gun and the Constable went over, picked it up and handed it to Goldstein.

"Now, I'm gonna give you a chance to give Madame Legarde what you owe her," the Constable said. "And don't try anything, Cholley. I'll be aiming right at your head."

LeBlanc walked back to the safe and took out several stacks of bills. He brought them over to his desk and counted out ten thousand dollars in one hundred dollar bills.

Nicolette put the money in her handbag as the Constable said to LeBlanc, "Well, Cholley, I hate to tell you this, but you're under arrest for suspicion of murder, attempted murder and larceny." He slapped a pair of handcuffs on him and escorted him out of his office.

Later that evening, Nicolette and Benjamin Goldstein were the guests of honor at Belle Lafourche. Nathan's mother, Annie Badeau hosted a lavish dinner for them. She was a gracious hostess and made them all feel exceedingly welcome in her home and at her table.

After they'd feasted on the best cuisine in New Orleans, they all sat around the dinner table talking for hours. Nicolette and Goldstein took turns telling Annie about their mutual friend, Molly Brown. Goldstein told her that Molly had described the ordeal Nicolette and Nathan had suffered on the *Titanic* at the hands of LeBlanc's son. She'd convinced him that he had to come to New Orleans with her to make sure she received Nathan's inheritance. But it hadn't taken much convincing really. His heart had been touched by the *Titanic* tragedy and helping Nicolette was his humble way of making a contribution to the *Titanic's* survivors.

Before they left New York, Goldstein had a colleague of his in New Orleans investigate LeBlanc. The colleague found that LeBlanc had a long history of swindling people, and a few of his business partners had been mysteriously murdered. In every instance, LeBlanc was a suspect, but there was never enough proof to make a case against him. They also learned that LeBlanc had threatened his murdered partner's families if they tried to take ownership of the business holdings left by their loved ones.

Fortunately, Goldstein had had the foresight to ask the Constable to accompany them to LeBlanc's office. Because the Constable personally heard LeBlanc threaten Nicolette, they were able to get him to re-open the old cases. They'd even found a few people who were willing to testify against him. So, with a little luck, LeBlanc would spend the rest of his life behind bars.

Around nine o'clock, Goldstein bid them a good night and went up to bed. Nicolette and her mother-in-law lingered at the table talking and sipping tea splashed with Bourbon. "I'm curious about something," Nicolette said to her mother-in-law. "That Tuttle fellow told us you made a deal with LeBlanc not to tell Marcel that he'd tried to kill Nathan. Why did you keep it? Why didn't you tell Marcel what he did?"

Annie sighed, "What good would it have done? It would only have led to more violence. Marcel would have killed that man for sure. Then Marcel would have had to deal with the law and I would have had blood on my hands. Besides, by then Nathan was safe in France. So I saw no sense in stirring up a bunch of trouble." A faraway look came into her eyes and she added, "Isn't it something how good can come out of some of the worst situations."

"What do you mean?" Nicolette asked.

"Well, like my Nathan. I know he had a good life because of what happened that night. He got a chance to go to college, to be somebody. And he married you, had two beautiful little girls. He had people in his life who loved him. I'd say that's something *real* good."

A lump rose in Nicolette's throat. She remembered the St. Jude's medal hanging around her neck, took it off and handed it to her mother-in-law. "Nathan asked me to give you this, to tell you that he loved you and he wished he could have given it to you himself."

"Just like my Nathan," Mrs. Badeau smiled, her eyes filling with tears.

Nicolette was crying too. She reached out and took her mother-in-law's hand. "Thank you. Thank you for saving him and sending him to me. I'll always be grateful for that, for the time we had together."

They sat there holding hands, each remembering the man they knew as husband and son.

THE END

Made in the USA